The Whale H

Volume 3 - Holding the Barrier

by David Row

Published by David Row at Createspace

Copyright 2013 by David Row

Other titles and further information on David Row's books (including the previous books in this series) can be found at

http://astrodragon.co.uk/Books/TheWhaleHasWings.htm

The earlier books can be purchased from Amazon at the various local stores
Vol1 - The Whale Has Wings, Rebirth
Vol 2 - The Whale Has Wings, From Taranto to Singapore

Acknowledgements

I would like to thank Kevin Reagh for providing the cover art.
And thanks to Adrian Cengia and Clive Loebenstein-Peckham for their invaluable help in preparing the book for publication.

Table of Contents

Maps

Introduction

What has gone before...

This is the third book in the Whale Has Wings series. While I hope you have read the previous two, the books do stand alone. However if you have not you will probably be slightly confused as to how history arrived here, so this is a summary to set the scene for the next act.

In 1932, the British Royal Navy finally reached the end of its patience with the RAF's penurial control of the Fleet Air Arm. They demanded its return, and after a short political campaign managed this. They were then in a position to make the changes and implement the plans they had been working on for some years. This meant new carrier planes more suited for the job they had foreseen. With more planes available, they reverted to the large-capacity carrier designs that started with the Ark Royal.

Through the 1930s the Fleet Air Arm continued to build steadily in strength. Although funds were short before 1937, the force was more capable than in our history. By the start of the war in 1939, there were a handful of light carriers available as well as the slightly earlier completion of large fleet carriers. This enabled a heavy night attack on the German port of Wilhelmshaven on the night of the 31st December 1939, which caused considerable damage to the German Fleet.

While the greater air power available to the Royal Navy was advantageous in the Norway campaign, it was insufficient to force the German Army back, and although the fighting was somewhat more successful, the Allies were forces to withdraw after France was invaded.

There was nothing the Fleet Air Arm could do to help the land fighting in France. However the stronger air arm available, led to somewhat different results of operations against the French after the fall of France.

Seeing a chance to pick over the spoils of the defeated Allies, Italy entered the war and the Royal Navy dusted off their plans for an attack on the Italian fleet. This took place at Taranto, and this time the carrier force was the three carriers originally planned. The Italian fleet did not fare well.

The successful Taranto strike did have an unexpected side effect. Paralysed by the shock, the Italian Navy demanded a delay in the Italian attack on Greece. While this did proceed, it was some weeks later than in our history. This meant that the attack against the Italian Army had a little more time to develop before being halted. With this extra time, and with more help from the French, the British advanced further into Italian North Africa. With the front line troops further forward, they decided to reinforce Greece with fresh troops rather than the tired veterans. However, this put the British in a far better defensive position when the German Africa Korps and the Italians counterattacked, and after a short campaign, the Allies had full control of North Africa.

This success wasn't enough to help Greece, which fell to a joint German and Italian force. The presence of fighters from British carriers helped the withdrawal, and with these and more troops brought out of Greece, Crete was held. With the Allies in no position to effectively attack in 1941, Hitler went ahead with Operation Barbarossa, the attack on Russia, meant to break the Soviet Union by Christmas. The Allies could do little to help except to provide an increasing stream of arms and supplies to the beleaguered Russians. The occupation in North Africa had one beneficial effect for the British. Without the need to constantly resupply and add to the forces there, it was possible to start the long-planned reinforcement of Malaya and Burma slightly earlier, and send some better officers east. This was seen as desperately needed, as with the fall of France and the fighting in Europe the Japanese Empire was casting covetous eyes on the resources of Southeast Asia and the Dutch East Indies.

Before the British defensive build-up could be completed, the Japanese Navy struck a terrible blow to the Americans, sinking most of their Pacific Battle Fleet at Pearl Harbor. The British land forces moved to their defensive positions while the Far Eastern Fleet, thankfully reinforced due to less need in the Mediterranean, prepared to take action against the Japanese invasion force.

This story is what happens next.

* * *

Chapter 1 - The Invasion of Malaya

Attack on Kota Bharu, Malaya.

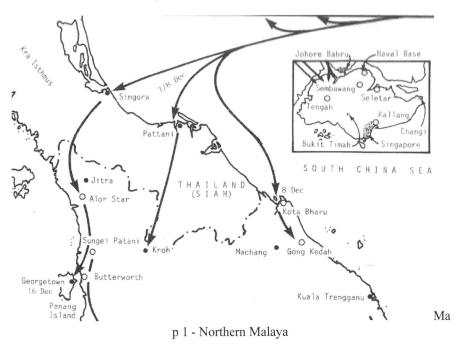

p 1 - Northern Malaya

During the night of the 7th, the Japanese convoy heading for the Malay Peninsula had split up. Most of the ships headed west of northwest towards Siam, but a group of three large transports were heading south down the coast. This is noted with interest by the Singapore command; the SeaLance planes were keeping the Japanese under observation by radar, and due to the poor weather the planes themselves had been undetected by the Japanese. While there had been a number of technical issues, the ships didn't seem to realise they were being tracked, and no large course changes had been made which could have caused them to be lost. The splitting up of the fleet posed a problem; Park decided to keep tracking the southern force by radar (this was the only one that looked like it could directly attack Malaya), while a Hudson was sent out to try and keep the northern force under observation.

Unfortunately the poor weather - heavy cloud and intense rain - meant the Hudson could not find the northern group, and two Catalinas sent from Singapore had no better luck. One of the Catalinas failed to return. At the time, this was thought to be due to the bad weather but in fact this aircraft was the first Imperial casualty in the Pacific war, having been shot down by Japanese fighters escorting the convoy. The submarine patrol line had better luck. After dark, a signal was received that the northern group was indeed heading for Siam.

6

Because no invasion of the country or request for help from the Empire had been made by Siam, Operation Matador could not be put into action, as had been expected by both Park and Alexander. Instead, the troops and airfield at Koto Bharu were warned that an enemy landing 'may take place within the next 12-36 hours'. Non-essential personnel were evacuated from the forward air base and its satellite fields, and some of the reconnaissance planes flown south. The planes remaining were readied for immediate action. The forces in Malaya had already been put on alert when the convoys were spotted, and the state of readiness was increased. No hostile actions were to be permitted unless the Japanese actually attacked. While it was realised that this meant waiting and giving the invader the advantage, it was politically impossible to risk starting a war over what might, after all, just be a feint or an action not aimed at the Empire.

Just before midnight off Koto Bharu a heavy blanket of cloud set in, reaching almost 50 miles out to sea and coming down very low, giving the invasion transports excellent cover. The group consisted of three large transport ships, four destroyers and the cruiser HMIJS Chokai. Unfortunately, these clouds did nothing to hide them from the southernmost submarine in the British patrol line (HMS Urge), who had been waiting off the coast in case all or part of the convoy was indeed headed there. As the transports anchored, and started to lower their boats (some coming to grief in the heavy swell), her captain decided that this fell well within his remit to attack, and at 0130 he put three torpedoes into the biggest of the ships, the Ayatosan Maru, which immediately started to list heavily. In 10 minutes, she had rolled over and sunk with heavy loss of life. As expected, the escorting destroyers made an attack on where they thought the submarine was, but this was ineffective and she crept away to make her action report. The attack did not stop the Japanese troops unloading, indeed if anything the sight of the ship burning and listing gave them an extra incentive to get into the boats.

The sound of the torpedo explosions and the burning ship had been noticed by the Indian troops defending the beach. Already on alert, they fully manned their defences (the beach was covered by pillboxes, barbed wire and mines). At around 0230, heavy fire from the escorting Japanese warships landed on them. This was observed with satisfaction by HMS Urge, who used the concentration of the destroyers on the beach to put two torpedoes into the destroyer Isonami, which started to sink by the head immediately, bow broken off by one of the torpedoes. This time the counterattack was more accurate, and it took the submarine some hours to get clear, meaning she was unable to put in any more attacks that night.

While this had been happening, the airfield commander had been alerted and, on the assumption that this was a landing by the reported ships, an air strike was being assembled. His orders, while pointing out that no offensive action should be taken as long as the Japanese stayed outside territorial waters, left any response to his discretion if they moved inside them. The first planes to take off were a flight of nine torpedo-armed Beaufighters (based at the Gong Kedah satellite field), with two flare-carrying Hudsons to illuminate the targets. The airfield was very close to the coast, and it only took minutes before they reached the transports. Ironically, the burning ship which had for a time beautifully illuminated the area had sunk too quickly to be of use to them, and the Hudsons were forced to make a number of passes dropping flares. AA fire was heavy, and the second Hudson was hit and had to abort its run; it was close enough to be able to recover to the airfield despite its damage.

The Beaufighters went into their attack runs despite the limited illumination and the AA fire. One plane was hit and plunged into the sea, but the other eight dropped their torpedoes at the two anchored transports. Three torpedoes hit one of the ships (the other luckily being shielded by its compatriot) and it immediately began to sink, rolling over in only some 15 minutes.

While the air attacks were going in, the first of the Japanese landing craft were approaching the beach. The Indian troops defending it were well dug in behind barbed wire and pillboxes. Already on alert, the pyrotechnics out to sea had been watched by them with interest as they prepared, and while the limited bombardment by the Japanese had been unwelcome, it had done little to upset their preparations. The first thing they noticed was a couple of large craft (these were the lead Japanese assault craft) nosing in to shore. Considering it highly unlikely that this was a friendly tourist visit, they opened fire with machine guns and mortars, sinking one of the craft and leaving men swimming in the water. Despite this setback, and an increasing number of craft damaged (and in some cases sunk) by the defenders, the Japanese pressed on with their landing (perhaps encouraged by the fact that due to the attacks on the ships they had little hope of escape in any case), and a number of craft managed to unload their troops, although often in confused circumstances.

Reports of the actions and the attack on the ships had already been reported to Command in Singapore even before the submarine had managed to elude her attackers and make her report. It was obvious that if the Japanese were already attacking Malaya then it was too late to implement Matador. Indeed, any chance of actually using that plan had always been considered unlikely by Alexander and Park, and so the order was given for the alternative plan, Operation Krohcol, to proceed. Alexander had always felt that this was the plan that would actually be implemented, and had prepared the forces required accordingly. At Singapore, the fleet was ordered to sail before dawn; while no immediate night attack had been made (as had been feared), a daytime attack was considered a possibility, and in any case it was obvious that it might be possible to intercept some of the Japanese invasion force or their cover. What was unknown at the moment was how heavy any covering force was (due mainly to the bad weather, it had still not been spotted), and also what level of air support the invasion would have. Somerville had no intention of recklessly risking his ships for little gain, although he was happy to employ them in a calculated risk if the benefits warranted it. At the moment the only naval vessels reported was the small group accompanying the Koto Bharu invasion force, and he expected to be able to handle that with his submarines and RAF support unless the weather closed in dramatically. It seemed highly unlikely that this was the only IJN force in the area, and he wanted his force available to attack any larger force that presented itself.

An RAF Beaufighter squadron (torpedoes) and a Cormorant dive bomber squadron were put on alert for a dawn strike at the Koto Bharu invasion force and its escort.

They would take off in a few hours. It was also intended to strike at the rest of the invasion fleet, which it was presumed was now attacking Siam; a reconnaissance was planned for dawn, followed by a torpedo strike once the ships had been located. Somerville's second line of submarines was currently oriented east-west to block off the lower part of the peninsula from an attack force. At the moment this would stay in place, however the northernmost two boats of the north-south line were ordered to be ready to attack the main part of the troop convoy once it had been located.

Meanwhile the aircraft at Koto Bharu were still taking very aggressive action against the landing force. There were eight Hudsons available, and these took off loaded with bombs to attack the remaining troop transport, which was also under fire from shore batteries. The Japanese AA fire was both heavy and accurate, one Hudson being shot down and three badly damaged, but they managed to hit the remaining transport ship with at least a dozen small bombs. It may also have been hit by the shore batteries, but in the confusion, this was impossible to determine. The ship was left on fire and slowly withdrawing from the landing zone, leaving her offloaded troops to take care of themselves.

The landing itself was a bloody affair. The landing craft themselves had been engaged by the defender's heavy weapons, causing a number of the boats to be sunk. The Japanese then had to make their way through the minefields and barbed wire, all the time under machine gun fire. Despite all this, many of them got as far as the Indian unit's trenches, where the battle came down to hand to hand fighting, the Japanese desperate to get ashore. The situation was only resolved in favour of the defence by the intervention of two Matilda tanks - due to the outlying but important geographical position of the airfield, it had been provided with a detachment of four tanks for its defence. Invulnerable to anything the Japanese could do, these acted as mobile machine gun positions to roll up the Japanese, and in the case of those men who did not retreat, rolling over them. By 0700, the landing had been defeated, although it took almost another day to mop up the final elements, the Japanese infantry preferring to die fighting rather than to surrender.

While the situation on the beaches near Koto Bharu had been contained by the early morning, the situation seen by the commanders at Singapore was far less comforting. During the night the action at Pearl Harbor had been reported, and had not gone down well. The naval contingent in particular was torn between sympathy for the American losses and amazement that they could have let themselves get caught in this way. The troops marked for Operation Khrocol, already alerted, were ordered to advance as soon as Singapore had confirmation that Siam had been attacked.

The Japanese also made a much larger impression on the staff when at 0320 a number of unknown aircraft were spotted by radar heading for Singapore. These were 17 G3M Nells (a total of 65 had been sent out, but this group was the only one to find the island given the bad weather). While the air defences of Singapore had been put on alert, only three night fighters were currently ready - these were sent up at 0345 to intercept the planes. The radar control was still unpractised at vectoring fighters into a close enough range that they could use their own radar to intercept the bombers, and as a result only four of them were shot down. The fighter pilots were surprised at how readily the Japanese bombers burst into flames compared to the bombers the Luftwaffe had been using over Britain. Also due to inexperience, and despite the drills, the civil defence and AA of Singapore did not perform well. While sirens were sounded at 0350, the response was poor, and for some reason the city was still not blacked out when the bombers arrived. The AA was ineffective, and no bombers were shot down. For their part, although some 50 people were killed, the bombers spread their attack between the naval base, the city, and two of the airfields, instead of concentrating on one target. As a result of this, no serious damage was done.

A reconnaissance flight had been sent off north just before dawn, to report on what it could find at the most likely landing places. It was anticipated that these would be close enough to French Indo China for the Japanese to have arranged some sort of fighter cover, so a Whirlwind was used rather than a Hudson. While it was hoped to get photographs, the plane was ordered to radio immediately if it found Siam being attacked, as that would allow Alexander to order his forces into the country. As soon as the ships had been detected, a strike would be sent off from Singapore, hopefully not only catching some of the ships but some of the troops as well.

At 0600, the first report was received from the Whirlwind - "Transport ships close inshore at Patani, looks like a landing is taking place". While Alexander had already been in contact with the British embassy in Siam to try and find out what was happening, he had obtained little useful information. But in any case, the presence of the transport ships was enough to release the waiting strike squadrons. He also authorised the columns to head off into Siam, in particular the one from Kroh headed for the 'Ledge'.

Reports were also coming in of confused fighting at various coastal areas in Eastern Siam, which were considered to be the rest of the invasion convoy. The landings most worrying were the ones at Patani and Singora, as they had usable airfields. Accordingly, the Cormorant squadron readied at Singapore was ordered to attack the ships lying off Patani. The longer-ranged Beaufighters would attack the landings at Singora.

Three transports had been assigned to land troops of the 42nd Infantry Regiment. In retrospect, attacking Patani was the wrong decision - the landing at Singora was much larger, although at long range for the Cormorants. By the time the attack arrived, the assault troops had been landed and the ships were unloading their supplies and transport. The arrival of 16 dive bombers was a very unwelcome surprise - while air support had been planned, there had not yet been time to bring the fighters forward onto captured airfields. While the Japanese AA from the transports was accurate, there were no planes to stop the bombers turning over into their near-vertical dives. The 1,000lb bombs shattered the transports, leaving two sinking and one burning and obviously out of control, along with much of the Japanese equipment. One Cormorant was damaged by AA fire, but managed to limp to Kota Bharu where it landed with some difficulty, the plane being a write-off.

Further to the north, fifteen torpedo-armed Beaufighters had found their targets, the shipping unloading troops of the Japanese 5th Division at Singora. Originally, the Japanese had hoped to fly fighters into the airfield there at dawn, but unexpected resistance had made this impossible. Instead, some of the Ki-27 Nate fighters due to base themselves at Singora were instead covering the landing. Twelve of the Japanese army planes were in the air.

Without the benefit of radar, the Beaufighters were not spotted until some of them had started to make their attack runs, and the first six planes managed to drop their torpedoes without interference, hitting two of the transport ships. The next flights were intercepted by the fighters, who despite their weak armament managed to shoot down two of the Beaufighters as they attacked - the torpedo planes were not expecting fighters so far from the Japanese bases in French Indo China, and were taken by surprise. The fighters also disrupted the attack, and disappointingly, only one more transport was sunk. Once their torpedoes were gone, the Beaufighters turned to engage the Japanese. This proved difficult at low level, as the Beaufighters, not the most manoeuvrable of aeroplanes, found that the light and agile Japanese planes very difficult to hit. This was balanced by the difficulty the Japanese had of doing serious damage of the Beaufighters with their two 7.7mm guns. A number of the Beaufighters simply escaped combat by flying away from them - the torpedo plane was noticeably faster than the Japanese fighter was when unloaded. The result was a further three Beaufighters shot down for the loss of seven Ki-27's - the RAF pilots found that the light Japanese planes came apart when hit by the Beaufighter's heavy armament. The Japanese fighters for their part had seemed surprised that torpedo planes would attempt to attack them. Although the landing was not stopped, considerable disruption was caused and part of the 5th Divisions transport and artillery destroyed as well as numbers of the support troops killed.

In retrospect, both formations were lucky to find their targets, as in general the weather east of Siam was poor, with heavy and frequent rain showers that blinded the crews and made it impossible to navigate with any accuracy. Aircraft were also sent from the airfield at Sungei Patani. At 0645, a force of Beaufighters had headed for Patani, but was unable to locate the invasion force amid torrential rainstorms.

Also with daylight came the first Japanese air attacks against the airfields in Malaya. At 0700, shortly after the Beaufighter force had disappeared into the northeast, the forward observers at Sungei Patani reported a small formation of planes heading towards them from the west. This was an unexpected direction for an attack, and only the four ready Sparrowhawks were scrambled. They were still clawing for altitude when a formation of five Ki-21's arrived at the airfield. The Ki-21 was fast for a bomber, and the Sparrowhawks were not in position to attack them before they attacked. Despite being close to the border, shortages had meant that the base only had eight 40mm Bofors for defence.

The bombers made their attack runs ignoring the AA fire, which only managed to damage one plane, although this did cause it to break off its attack run. The other four carried on to bomb the revetments holding the rest of the Beaufighter squadron and the other Sparrowhawks. A number of ground personnel were killed, one

Beaufighter being destroyed and two Sparrowhawks being damaged. Due to the rain soaked ground around the airfield, the aircraft could only be dispersed in a limited fashion. The concrete runway was also hit by two bombs, but would still be long enough to operate fighters, although loaded Beaufighters would be unable to take off until the damage was repaired.

The bombers were intercepted on their escape by the defending Sparrowhawks. Considerably faster than the Japanese bombers, they shot down three of them, the other two managing to escape and hide in cloud. Without radar control, once visual contact had been lost there was little hope of finding them.

The airfield at Koto Bharu was also to see a visit by the Japanese. It had been realised early on that the airfield was far too exposed and close to the border to be useful if the enemy established himself, but it had not been expected to face serious air attack so early on with the Japanese air force not yet established in Siam. Bomber raids from French Indo-China had been expected, but it was thought too far for fighter raids from those airfields. The airfield was keeping four fighters on patrol in case of bomber attacks, but like Sungei Patani, it depended on a visual observer, the radar net not covering the airfields this far north.

The original Japanese plans had included constant raids on Koto Bharu to suppress it, but while the transports were coming under attack most of the planes allocated had been reassigned to cover the ships until they had unloaded. However at mid-morning eight fighters were seen approaching the field. These were A6M Zeros from Soc Trang. This would be the first time British fighters had encountered the Zero, and being outnumbered they climbed to get a height advantage before attacking. This was to prove very useful. The Sparrowhawks dived on the Japanese planes as they approached the airfield, presumably intending to strafe as they were at quite a low altitude. Two of the Zeros were shot down in the initial surprise attack, both of the planes breaking up under the heavy fire of the Sparrowhawks four 20mm cannon. After this, the fight broke up into a melee as the Zeros turned to engage the fighters in a turning dogfight. This was to prove an unpleasant surprise for the British pilots, the agile Zero being able to outturn and outmanoeuvre them in a low speed fight. The Zero also had a heavy armament, and as a result was able to inflict serious damage on the heavier and more durable Sparrowhawks. Three of the four were shot down, although one pilot bailed out and another survived a crash landing (although injured) for the loss of only one more Zero. The fourth Sparrowhawk, outnumbered five to one, dived away, finding that the Zero could not stay with his escaping fighter.

Force Z had sailed at dawn under the command of Admiral Holland, even though the main covering force for the invasion had not yet been found. It was thought better to have them at sea than caught in Singapore harbour, which the Japanese had already shown they could attack. The force consisted of the fast battleship HMS King George V, the light carrier HMAS Melbourne, the cruisers HMAS Canberra, HMS Gloucester and HMS Bonaventure, six RN and two RAN destroyers. Its course of action would depend on locating the covering force and determining how powerful it was. If it was weaker or similar to Force Z, Holland's orders were to engage and destroy. If the covering force was too powerful, he was to damage and slow it (in conjunction with the RAF's land based planes if possible), causing the maximum damage for the minimum loss while Somerville's more powerful Eastern Fleet came up in support.

Orders had also been sent out before dawn to two of the T-class boats operating south of Formosa to move southward to try and sink Japanese shipping operating out of French Indo China. While positioning them there pre-war had been considered, it had been thought too provocative and could cause an incident the British didn't want. Now the Japanese had invaded, it was likely they would be trying to reinforce and resupply from there.

Also after dawn, a heavy reconnaissance patrol was sent out. Twelve Hudsons and twelve Blenhiems were to search well out to sea to try and discover where the Japanese covering force was hiding. The search was not helped by the bad weather, but just after noon one of the Blenhiems found a force reported as 'at least six ships, three probably cruisers' heading west. This was the Japanese 7th Cruiser squadron of four heavy cruisers and three destroyers, part of the naval escort for the invasion fleet. Force Z changed course north, keeping within range of fighter cover from the coast, as Singapore attempted to get more information about the Japanese ships. This was proving difficult, as the poor weather that was helping the Blenheim hide was also making it difficult to observe the Japanese.

It was not only the British who were responding to the attack on Pearl Harbor; the American command at Manila had also received news of the attack. General Brereton had put his pilots on alert at 4am local time, ready for a planned attack by his B-17's against the Japanese air bases on Formosa. However, this was postponed by General MacArthur and his staff, who insisted on a reconnaissance mission before a raid was sent off. Despite a cable from Washington directing him to execute the Rainbow 5 War Plan immediately, and a report from Admiral Hart's HQ that Japanese carrier planes were already attacking a seaplane tender, he continued to refuse Brereton permission to attack.

The Japanese were themselves unable to launch the dawn attack they had planned for the Philippines, but this was due to the weather rather than the Americans - thick fog made it impossible to take off. At 0715 (PI local time), the radar at Iba reported unidentified aircraft approaching. The available P-40 fighters and B-17's were scrambled, but this warning proved to be a false alarm. The B-17's were left circling, while MacArthur's Chief of Staff again refused Brereton permission to strike at Formosa.

At 0900, 32 Japanese bombers attacked the airfields of Baguio and Ruguegarao in northern Luzon. The fog had by now cleared in Formosa, and 192 planes of the Japanese Navy's 11th air fleet were on their way to the Philippine Islands. Despite the raid, yet again Brereton was refused permission to land his planes, load them with bombs and raid Formosa. It took another hour to inform him he could send another reconnaissance plane, and then if it located targets he could make an attack. This allowed him to land his B-17's and refuel and arm them.

Shortly after noon, the radar at Iba detected the incoming raid. However the mechanism for informing Clark field proved dysfunctional, and both the airfields fighters and bombers were caught on the ground. Although a few fighters managed to get off the ground, they proved ineffective. By the time that the bombers left, an hour later, there were only 17 B-17's left serviceable and 80% of the fighters had been destroyed.

The Japanese air force also attacked the US island of Guam from its bases in Saipan. The island had no AA guns, and the raid sank a number of the ships in the harbour as well as destroying the Marine barracks.

In Malaya, the orders to implement Operation Krohcol had led to the Australians of 9th Australian Div starting out at first light. The main thrust was a lorried assault, let by three tanks, for a feature known as the 'Ledge', which would give them a good defensive position to help hold the airfields on the west coast. It was a six-mile stretch of road cut through a steep hillside and bounded on the other side by a sheer drop into a river; demolishing the hillside on to the road would cause the Japanese invasion force considerable delay. The force left some five hours after the Japanese attack on Kota Bharu, and ran into some opposition from armed Thai constabulary. This caused a number of casualties in both sides as the Australians responded with some enthusiasm. The police tried to block the road for the lorried infantry with a number of felled rubber trees, but these were quickly pushed out of the way by the accompanying tanks. However this did slow them, and they did not reach the town of Betong, five miles inside Siam, until afternoon. This time they did not meet any opposition, and pressed on, reaching the Ledge just before dawn on the following day, where they covered the engineers setting the charges on the road.

The second column consisted of lorried infantry and an anti-tank section. This headed towards Songkhla to delay the enemy. It reached a position at Ban Sadao, some ten miles north of the frontier, at dusk, and dug in. The final column was in fact an armoured train, which set off into Thailand until it reached Khlong Ngae in Siam, where it destroyed the 200-foot bridge, and slowly returned south, the Australians destroying the railway and anything else they could reach as it did so.

The airfield at Kota Bharu had always been considered to be by Air Marshal Park to be extremely exposed if there was a Japanese landing on the East coast, and his experience with far-forward RAF bases in the Battle of Britain had made him decide to treat it as an expendable field. Indeed, if it had not been so well positioned to attack an invasion he would have turned it into a flak trap with dummy aircraft. As it was, the number of aircraft had been limited, as was the support for them. Many of the maintenance crews had been evacuated some days ago, along with all non-essential personnel, leaving only enough to patch up a lightly damaged plane sufficiently for it to fly south clear of immediate danger. The airfield (and its satellite fields) was not just set for destruction, but heavily booby-trapped as well. Park was specific that the Japanese would not get anything useful out of the base after he had been forced out of it.

At the start of the invasion, it had been home to three small squadrons - twelve Hudsons, twelve Beaufighters (intended for use as torpedo planes) and twelve Sparrowhawks. During the night and early morning, they had already lost one Beaufighter, three Sparrowhawks and a Hudson, and four more Hudsons had been damaged. Two of these had been patched up and sent south, the other were irreparable in any reasonable time and were positioned as decoys.

The original Japanese plan had been to keep mounting small raids on the airfield as soon as they had landed (having assumed that they would be able to operate fighters almost immediately), but delays meant they would not be in this position until tomorrow. As a result, it was decided to send a heavy raid of 24 Ki-21 bombers escorted by twelve Ki-43 'Oscar' fighters to close down the base temporarily. They did not want to do too much damage as the Japanese wanted to use the base themselves (while their intelligence had informed them that the British intended to destroy it, they were not aware of how comprehensive Park's instructions had been). The bombers were loaded with 100lb bombs, the intention being to destroy as many planes on the ground as possible without causing serious damage to the runways.

Realizing that the base would be attacked, the commander had four Sparrowhawks ready to take off and four of the long-endurance Beaufighters in the air covering the airfield when the raid was spotted. The ready planes were scrambled, but as soon as it was realized there would not be time to get any more planes in the air, the pilots were ordered to abandon them and take cover. The first to attack the raid were the Beaufighters. Orbiting at altitude, they were able to dive down onto the bombers, who were approaching quite low, presumably for accuracy of bombing. The heavy armament of the British planes resulted in five of the Ki-21 'Sallys' destroyed or plunging into the jungle. As they turned to come around again, they were intercepted by six of the protecting Oscars. The resulting fight showed that the Japanese fighters were, like the Zero, very manoeuvrable, but also very lightly armed - rather the opposite of the Beaufighter. However, the veteran Japanese pilots were more skilled than the defenders and the net result was two Oscars shot down for three Beaufighters. The combat also stopped the Beaufighters intercepting any more of the bombers.

The Sparrowhawks had to climb up to the attacking force, and in fact engaged it from slightly below. The remaining six Oscars turned to intercept them, but in a closing engagement the four cannon and durability of the British planes were a considerable advantage, the Oscars being unable to exploit their agility, and two Oscars were shot down for the loss of one Sparrowhawk damaged. The fighters then carried on into the bombers, shooting down three of them (one more Sparrowhawk being damaged by their defensive fire). This left, however, some sixteen bombers about to bomb the airbase. The Sparrowhawks were prevented from re-engaging the bombers by the fighter escort, who managed to lure one of the remaining planes into a dogfight, resulting in it being shot down by the Japanese pilot. The other Sparrowhawk pilot declined to get into a turning fight, and instead used his superior speed to get into a position for a straight attack, shooting down one more Oscar before he was forced to break off.

The remaining bombers unloaded onto the airfield and one of the satellite fields, the accuracy of the Japanese bombing being commendably precise. A considerable number of the airfield buildings were damaged or destroyed, and some aircraft destroyed - three Hudsons and two Beaufighters were left in flames as the bombers curved away to the north. The AA fire was mostly ineffective, only one bomber being shot down.

As a result of the raid the airfield was left with a number of craters, although the satellite field was still operational. However, the number of aircraft left operational had been reduced considerably. There had been six planes out on patrol over the sea at the time of the raid - three Hudsons and three torpedo-armed Beaufighters. Given the damage, the planes in the air were sent south, as was the remaining Hudson. This left the field with only six Sparrowhawks and three Beaufighters.

At the same time as the troops headed into Siam to delay the Japanese attack, a number of groups of SOE-trained men had also entered the country. Their tasks included aiding the regular troops when possible, destroying railway lines and preparing bridges for demolition for when the Japanese reached them, and to seize transport. In addition, they were to occupy the crossroads at Yala and the airfield at Phuket Island. Another group boarded an old coaster and sailed to the port of Tonkah, where three Italian ships had been hiding from the Royal Navy. Their job was to seize the port and destroy the ships, but on their approach the Italians scuttled the ships, although the force remained occupying the port.

Chapter 2 - Meeting the Assault

Dec 8th-9th

The British and Australian governments had already declared war against the Japanese Empire; today so would the American, Canadian and Free French, as well as a number of other countries. While the Japanese invasion had hardly been unexpected, until yesterday it had not been known exactly what pattern it would take; the destruction of much of the US Fleet at Pearl Harbor had certainly not been allowed for by the planners. The US Navy planning department was frantically trying to sort out which of the pre-war plans were still viable, which would have to be abandoned and which needed to be changed. In the meantime preliminary orders were sent to the US carriers in the Atlantic to head for port to refuel and replenish ready for deployment in the Pacific Ocean, as were the modern fast battleships (the older, slower battleships would stay where they were for the meantime). At Pearl Harbor they were still working on the damage from the attack, as well as trying to rescue men trapped in some of the sunken battleships.

The British had been less surprised, an assault on Malaya had always been the obvious focus of a Japanese attack on them. Fortunately, due to the lull in the Mediterranean, the forces in place had been reinforced and strengthened, and the preparations were a considerable improvement on what had been the case only a few months before. However, the plans were not complete, and additional troops and supplies were still on their way. It now depended on how well and how fast additional resources could be made available. One obvious area was a temporary stopping of the supplies to Russia; luckily, the Russian winter offensive seemed to be going quite well. The British were delivering some 100 Hurricanes and a similar number of tanks a month; the shipments currently in Persia were stopped, arrangements being made to ship the tanks to East India, and the Hurricanes to Ceylon, in the first instance. Pilots would have to be found for the fighters, and they would also go to Ceylon before being deployed operationally. Additional forces would have to come from the Mediterranean in the first instance, followed by more convoys from Britain. It was fortunate that, with a limited amount of risk, convoys could be sent through the Mediterranean, and Admiral Cunningham was informed to start preparations to escort them through the most dangerous part of their passage. Admiral Somerville was also told to arrange an escort for the convoy carrying the 18th British Division, expected to arrive at Singapore on the 20th December.

At sea off Malaya, the situation was starting to become more complex. While the initial invasion convoys had now unloaded (or been sunk by the British), a new convoy was heading for the coast. This was spotted by a Hudson at around 0900, and was escorted by seven 'cruisers and destroyers' as the report made out. This was Admiral Kurita's Escort Force. While Force Z was still too far south to intercept, the convoy was well within range of the RAF torpedo planes based at Gong Kedah. The twelve Beaufighters there were briefed for the attack as the Hudson returned south.

The weather was still poor and only one of the two groups of Beaufighters managed to find the convoy, which was escorted by two of the cruisers and four Zeros. In the poor conditions, the Beaufighters failed to spot the fighters, and elected to attack the cruiser Mikuma. The poor weather also helped conceal them from the fighters, who only realized the cruiser was under attack when they saw the splashes from her main armament lifting huge plumes of water into the air. As a result the first three torpedo planes were able to drop without any interference except the cruisers own AA, which the pilots later reported as 'reasonable', and all three dropped successfully at quite close range. The heavy cruiser managed to evade two of the torpedoes, but one of them hit her amidships. The large cruiser slowed as one of her machinery spaces filled with water, but was still under control and able to manoeuvre. The second flight was far less successful, as the diving Zeros shot one of them down before they realised they were there, and damaged another, which turned away trailing smoke from one of its engines. The third plane tried to press on with its attack, but the attention of the Zeros made this impossible, and it too was shot down.

Meanwhile the planes that had dropped turned to engage the fighters. One of the Zeros was shot down (the Japanese pilots seeming as surprised as their Army compatriots that torpedo planes would voluntarily engage them), and the rest of the fight turned into confusion. All three of the Beaufighters were damaged, but the Japanese planes seemed to have used up their 20mm ammunition in their first attacks, and their machine guns did not do sufficient damage to the sturdy Beaufighters to disable them. On their part, the Beaufighters found it almost impossible to get at the Zeros due to their manoeuvrability, although in the few instances that they did, one of the Japanese fighters was caught in the stream of cannon-fire and came apart in the air. The bombers finally retreated having only managed to cause moderate damage to the cruiser.

On the western coast, a reconnaissance mission of four Sparrowhawks from Alor Star (this was also considered an airfield at risk of being too close to a Japanese attack, like Kota Bharu) spotted a column of about a dozen light tanks heading south from the Japanese landings at Singora. They attacked the column with their 20mm cannon, noticing a Japanese soldier waving a flag at them (it was assumed he had miss-identified the planes as Japanese, something that was to occur fairly frequently on both sides with the single-engined fighters), and left five of them burning before returning to base.

The Japanese were obviously starting to push south from their landings, and later that morning a column, again headed by tanks, was seen to approach the Ledge. The Australian commander watched the approach with interest, noting that the Japanese did not seem to be paying as close attention to possible opposition as he would have, and once the column had reached an opportune point ordered the charges detonated to block the road. This also buried at least three tanks and quite a few men under the collapse, and the blocked road would take considerable time to clear (so much so in fact that the Japanese decided to bypass this route, as it could not be cleared in fast enough).

An attack was also made on the airfield at Victoria point, on the southern tip of Burma, which was in range of Singora. A force of Ki-27 Nate fighters strafed the airfield, causing little damage as the only 'aircraft' on the field being decoys. A further force of some 80 Sally bombers from French Indo-China was forced to turn back due to thick cloud. Their escorting fighters refuelled at Singora, then flew south to strafe Penang Island and Butterworth airfield.

Penang was only occupied by a number of biplane trainers, which the Japanese duly shot up. Butterworth was now occupied by a squadron of Sparrowhawks and a number of Blenheim bombers and the four planes on patrol dived on the attacking fighters as soon as they started their strafing runs (detection of planes was still causing problems in the poor weather). The ten Oscars were concentrating on the airfield and their attack destroyed two of the Sparrowhawks on the ground, as well as one of the Blenheims. The defending fighters seemed to take the Japanese by surprise, and shot down three in their first diving attack. The Oscars then broke off to try and get the Sparrowhawks into a turning fight. This succeeded with two of the planes, but the other two declined, and instead broke off to make another attack on the Oscars. The attackers shot down both the Sparrowhawks they had lured into a dogfight, one Oscar being damaged (it was later seen to crash as it tried to make it back to Siam), but the remaining Sparrowhawks shot down two more Oscars, although one was damaged and had to land at Butterworth.

Having been informed of the bombing of another convoy and its escort east of Siam, Admiral Holland intended to move Force Z north so he could intercept it. That afternoon a report was received from one of the T-class boats operating off French Indo China, to the effect that a large Japanese fleet, including two carriers and at least one battleship as well as a number of cruisers had been spotted. Given the location of Japanese bombers in Siam and French Indo China, this was too large a force for Force Z to engage with a reasonable chance of success, and Holland was ordered to turn south and wait for reinforcements. The spotted force was in fact the Distant Cover Force under Admiral Kondo, who had instructed his ships to concentrate on him after Force Z had been spotted and reported by a Japanese submarine.

The next Japanese attack was against the airfield at Kuantan. This airfield had been hurriedly improved over the last few months, as it was the northernmost east coast field involved in the radar net. As a result it was home to eight Hudsons used for naval reconnaissance as well as a Sparrowhawk squadron. A number of ancillary and training aircraft had been sent south out of the way to Singapore at first light. The Japanese did not seem to be aware that there were fighters based at the field, as at 1100 the radar detected nine G3M Nells approaching from the north. The field was keeping four Sparrowhawks in the air (the Japanese having already shown a distressing tendency to target the RAF's airfields), and four more were scrambled. The result was a catastrophe for the Japanese bombers, all nine being shot down with only two of the defending fighters slightly damaged.

As a result of the attacks in the northwest, it was decided to evacuate all non-essential aircraft from Butterworth; due to their proximity to the invasion, Kota

Bharu and Alor Star were designated emergency fields only, and preparations were made for demolition if the Japanese advanced south. The Japanese seemed to have been spending the day bringing their aircraft south onto the fields in Siam, as the only other major event was the interception of a flight of six Blenheims, escorted by four Sparrowhawks, out of Butterworth intending to attack the Japanese and to delay their anticipated move towards Jitra. The raid failed to find its targets in the poor weather, and was bounced by Japanese fighters as they returned to their base. Apparently, the fighters were escorts for a formation of Sally bombers, who attacked the airfield even as the returning planes were under attack by twelve Nate fighters. The escorting Sparrowhawks attempted to intercept the fighters, but the Japanese had surprise on their side, and shot down two in the initial engagement. The remaining two Sparrowhawks shot down one Nate before being mobbed and shot down. Four of the fighters had attacked the Blenhiems, who attempted to fight them off. Two Blenhiems were shot down, and one damaged, although they did shoot down one of the attackers. The Japanese bombers also damaged the airfield (although again they were only using light bombs, presumably hoping to preserve the runway for their own use), destroying a Sparrowhawk and a Blenheim on the ground, as well as three training Buffaloes which had not yet been evacuated. The only Japanese bomber casualty was one Sally shot down by the base AA defences

In the Philippines, the Americans were taking stock of their remaining planes. Fortunately for them, a planned strike from Formosa had to be cancelled due to the weather. Indeed the USAAF started to prepare their B-17's for a strike against the Formosan airfields, although with now only 17 planes this was not going to be decisive.

In Hong Kong, the Japanese had started their expected attack with a heavy aerial bombardment, intended to demoralise and weaken the defenders before the actual assault

There was also activity in the Dutch East Indies, as a force of Dutch submarines sortied north. They would base out of Singapore when they returned south, preparations having been made quietly over the last few months to stockpile sufficient supplies for them at the naval base. The Dutch forces in the islands were also on alert, but at the moment, there was no sign of any direct Japanese action against the islands.

In the USA, the President addressed congress, demanding a declaration of war against the Empire of Japan. This was passed by both houses with only one dissenting vote in the Senate. America was still shuddering under the news of the Pearl Harbor attack - although the chance of finding any Japanese ships east of the International Date Line was slim at best, cities like San Francisco and Los Angeles were under their first ever blackout. Prime Minister Churchill was rather more sanguine, as he looked forward to the aid of the USA in the war.

At sea, Admiral Somerville was ordering his submarines to close on the reported enemy positions and to keep track of the fleet assembling off French Indo China. He had already sent a list of additional forces he would like now the Japanese had already attacked to London. Meanwhile a heavy squadron including two battleships and two fleet carriers was heading south down the western side of Malaya, covered by Goshawk fighters operating out of Singapore and Kuala Lumpur. While he had no wish to engage the Japanese fleet under their own land-based air if he could avoid it, if they remained where they were he felt they had left themselves open to an attack while their air force was preoccupied in Malaya and the Philippines.

The Japanese command is pleased with the first few days of the war. Pearl Harbor was a major success, the USAAF in the Philippines has been neutralized, and the RAF has taken serious losses. The Japanese themselves had lost some 50 planes in Malaya to combat, plus about 25 more to operational use. They estimated the RAF had lost around 120 planes, and that they will soon have air superiority. In fact, the Japanese pilots are heavily overestimating the number of planes they have shot down. The RAF has in fact lost 47 planes in combat and bombing attacks, plus some 15 in operational incidents. While the RAF pilots are also overestimating, the more experienced Command is reducing the figures to what they feel is a more realistic figure, based on earlier estimates in the Battle of Britain. They were assuming Japanese losses to be around 65-70 planes, which gave them cause for cautious optimism.

Dec 9th-10th

In Britain, the first of the production Spitfire Mk8 is delivered to the RAF. It is hoped that this plane will even the odds over France, where the Luftwaffe's Fw190 has been taking a steadily increasing toll of the MkV Spitfire. This is planned to be the last Spitfire model with the Merlin engine, development now concentrating on the Griffon-engined version. The RAF has been growing increasingly curious as to how the Fw190 manages such performance, combat photographs indicating something unusual about the cowling arrangement. A suggestion of a Commando raid to capture one and fly it back is receiving serious attention. The Mk8 also carries additional fuel to give it a longer range, something seen as more important now that the RAF is contemplating more offensive operations over enemy territory.

In North America the first of the production models of the Mustang fighter (with the Merlin engine) have been accepted by a joint RAF/USAAF testing unit for final acceptance trials. This project was already a priority even before the Japanese attack, but as a result of this, the unit has been told to 'get the damn thing certified as fast as possible'.

Hitler accepts the fact that the current Blitzkrieg attack on Russia has failed, and that a new campaign will have to be launched in the spring. The Germans are currently being slowly pushed back by the Russian winter offensive, but are planning for their own offensive once the weather again permits movement.

In the Mediterranean the news from the Far East has been greeted with dismay, not just because of the attack, but what it will likely mean to the plans for assaulting Sicily in the spring. Joint talks are started with the French on the (possibly optimistic) assumption that the supply of landing craft will continue and that the armoured force at least will be brought up to the needed levels. Wavell and his staff are told to see what units can be earmarked for the Far East if the situation there deteriorates. While there is not a huge time saving in sending troops from the Middle East rather than Britain, the troops are already acclimatised to hot weather conditions. If such reinforcement becomes necessary, fresh units will be sent out from Britain as replacements. The RAF in the Middle East is ordered to prepare some of the spare pilots kept as replacements and reserves for travel to Ceylon to meet up with the planes being diverted there.

Having consolidated their landings in Siam, the Japanese army started a planned move south. This was hindered in the west by the delaying tactics and units put out by the defenders. Their job was to buy time for the British to stiffen their defences, particularly around Jitra which was seen as the key to the northwest part of Burma. In the east, Blamey was moving up elements of the 9th Australian division to reinforce the line between the 7th Australian in the west, and the 11th Indian Division (which was mainly spread down the eastern coast in case of landings). Reports had already reported the presence of Japanese tanks, so 2nd Armoured Brigade was used to reinforce the defence lines. It was known from exercises that the large-scale armoured manoeuvres of the desert would not work nearly so well in the jungle. The Brigade had been split - half remaining as a heavy armour force in case an opportunity for a counterattack emerged, the other 50-odd tanks used to stiffen the troops. While this was seen as somewhat of a return to outdated 'infantry-tank' tactics, in the jungle if the tanks were not close and ideally visible to the infantry they were of far less use. For their part, the tank crews were eager to see how good the Japanese tanks were - reports had indicated that they were on a level with the early Italian armour, which left the Brigade with few worries.

Park and his commanders (and a selected few senior pilots with earlier combat experience) were analyzing the initial performance against the Japanese. In general, they weren't too displeased, but there were a number of issues giving Park concern. The main one was the performance of the Japanese fighters, which was far better than had been anticipated. Preliminary reports from some of the squadrons indicated that the two most dangerous planes, the Oscar and Zero, were extremely manoeuvrable, even more so than the Italian planes some of them had experience fighting in the Mediterranean. If that was the case, then his pilots needed to avoid dogfighting and adopt other tactics. At least one senior pilot had noted that so-called boom and zoom worked well, and that allowed them to use their own advantages, tougher planes and a much heavier armament. There wasn't really sufficient data yet to decide on the best tactics, but it was pointed out by a couple of the squadron commanders that the pilots who got into dogfights tended to not have come back, while those who avoided them (or escaped out of them) had got back. Instructions to try these new tactics and to avoid a dogfight if at all possible would go out to the squadrons that evening, and they would be reviewed in some days to see if they worked. The experience of Park and some of his senior officers in such 'on the fly' evaluations and alterations during the Battle of Britain would be invaluable here.

Consideration was also given to the possibilities of supporting the Army, but in view of the heavy aircraft losses so far, Park had to reluctantly inform Blamey and Alexander that he did not think this feasible until he received reinforcements. At the moment, his main aim was to try and stop the Japanese getting command of the air. The good news was that they had recovered quite a few pilots, and that if they could get more aircraft they should have the pilots for them.

Late in the morning, the squadron from the Eastern Fleet under Admiral Somerville rendezvoused with Force Z west of Singapore. The fleet had added two more KGV-class battleships (Prince of Wales and Anson), the French battleship Richelieu, the two fleet carriers Implacable and Illustrious, plus four cruisers and another eight destroyers. It was Somerville's intention to be off the coast of Sarawak in two days. The fleet would be covered for the first day by Goshawks operating out of Singapore, as well as by its own fighters. Somerville had hoped to leapfrog some Goshawks forward to give extra fighter cover, but lack of suitable airfields had made this impractical.

In the jungle of northern Malaya, the Japanese had started to push south towards the airfield at Kota Bharu. This was the part of the line where it hadn't been possible to form too much in the way of a delaying defence. The Japanese infantry, led by tanks, was moving steadily in the direction of the airfield which seemed to be their target. The advance was held up a couple of times during the day by defensive ambushes by the Indians, but each time part of the Japanese force faded into the jungle, to appear again behind them. Both times this happened it caused panic to the still-inexperienced troops, and the Japanese breakthrough was only stopped when the lead tanks ran into a Matilda. The British tank, manned by a crew who had learnt their trade in Cyrenaica, proceeded to calmly put its 2-pdr rounds through four of the Japanese tanks, ignoring the shots aimed at them which merely bounced off the Matilda's armour. As two more Japanese tanks tried to pull back, they shot them up too, and then proceeded to machine gun the infantry until they had all gone to ground. This attack was credited with stopping a larger panic and breakdown among the Indians, but there was concern that more of this type of attacks might cause the units to break and allow an easy Japanese advance. To forestall this, Blamey ordered 18 Brigade of the 7th Australian division to back up the Indians in the northeast. Despite the holding of the Japanese advance close to the border, the airfield is simply too close now to be used safely, and Park orders the remaining planes and men to be evacuated and the airfield and its satellite strips to be demolished.

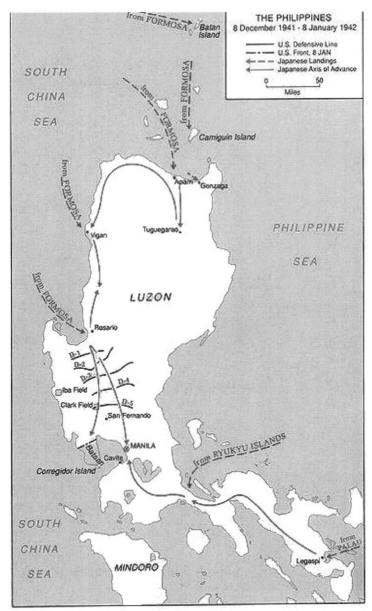

Map 2 - The Philippines

In the Philippines, the proposed B-17 attack on Formosa had to be cancelled when Japanese troops from General Homma's 14th Army began landing in northern Luzon. Six transports, covered by a cruiser and destroyers, landed 2,000 men at Vigan, while another force landed a similar number at Aparri. The airfields were the invaders first priority, and they immediately secured the airfields near the two towns. A force from Batan Island (a small island north of Luzon which had been taken some two days ago) landed on Camiguin Island to secure another airfield.

The invasion force had been spotted at dawn, and a number of rather uncoordinated attacks had been made by torpedo-armed PBY's and bombing B-17's. No serious damage was done to the invasion fleet, or to its covering warships. The Japanese air forces on Formosa were taking advantage of the better weather to strike hard at the Philippines. Both airfields and the naval base at Cavite were heavily bombed, and a number of planes destroyed on the ground as well as those shot down by the Zeros escorting the strikes. The most serious damage was to the naval base, where the bombing destroyed the Asiatic fleets stock of torpedoes and damaged two of the submarines at the base. That evening Admiral Hart evacuated two destroyers and his few minesweepers south, leaving the defence of the islands to his submarines.

At Wake Island, the Japanese air attacks had left the defenders with only eleven Wildcat fighters for defence, although a number of Japanese aircraft had been destroyed in return. An invasion force of four transports, escorted by two light cruisers and four destroyers, was on its way. The invasion force was detected at 0300, but while the defences were alerted it was decided not to attack until the Japanese were close inshore. By 0645, the Japanese warships were within 2500 yards of the battery at Peacock point, which opened fire, hitting the Japanese flagship Yubari twice. As the ship pulled back, they hit her twice more. The battery at Peale Island then landed a salvo directly on the destroyer Hayate, which exploded, breaking in two and sinking immediately. They then hit another destroyer and set one of the transport ships on fire. The second battery on the island hit two more destroyers, which made smoke and retreated behind its cover.

The Wildcats, each loaded with two bombs, were launched to attack the retreating force. Four of them attacked the destroyers, landing a hit on the Kisargi, which blew her up with her own depth charges. The other seven planes attacked the transports, hitting two of them and leaving them on fire, although none of them sank. The Japanese force retreated to its base at Kwajalein. Meanwhile at Pearl Harbor the seaplane tender Tangier was being loaded with ammunition and supplies as a relief expedition was made ready for the island.

In the eastern Mediterranean, the battleship HMS Barham is hit by two torpedoes from one of the U-boats operating in the Mediterranean. The old battleship is hit twice on the starboard side, and although the U-boat is attacked by her escort (and considered probably sunk), the Barham succumbs to the underwater damage, sinking an hour later.

Dec 11th.

The War widens as Germany and Italy declare war on the USA. In a gesture of reciprocity, Congress declares war on Germany and Italy. In other diplomatic initiatives, Nicaragua and Cuba declare war on Japan. The Japanese government shows no signs of concern over this.

In Malaya, the Japanese 5th division increases the intensity of its attack north of Kota Bharu, and finally makes contact with the outlying defences of the town of Jitra. While successful, the progress has been slower than anticipated. It has also resulted in more casualties, and General Yamashita is pressing hard to get more of his force into Siam. Sea transport is proving expensive, as the RAF torpedo bombers have not been suppressed as planned, and so he is trying to bring as much as possible in from French Indo China by the land route. This is much slower than by sea, but he hopes that his reinforcements will be on hand by the time he needs to support 5th Division. With the airfield at Kota Bharu now destroyed, the Indian troops are falling back southwards, while elements of the 9th Australian Division are moved up in support. Blamey intends to hold far enough to the north to support Jitra, in the hope the prepared defences there can hold out for some time. If this proves impossible, he will form a defence line further south. The training exercises held during the autumn have helped to identify feasible lines of defence and choke points, but the capability of the Japanese to infiltrate around strongpoints has been an unpleasant surprise.

At sea, the reinforced Force Z was heading east for the coast of Borneo, covered by its CAP and a flight of Goshawks out of Singapore. While Somerville thought it unlikely he would be attacked this far south, he was hoping to intercept and destroy any reconnaissance planes to keep his movements secret. He was also worried about the presence of Japanese submarines in the area. A Spearfish from HMS Implacable had caught one on the surface during the night with its ASV radar, and while the plane's bombs had caught the boat unaware and sunk it, he was sure that there were more of them in his path.

South of French Indo China, the Japanese naval force had now consolidated and had moved a little south and west. After hearing the pleas from General Yamashita to protect his troop convoys, it was intended to use the fleet to cover a series of convoys into Siam.

The first raid of the Bomber Command winter offensive took place tonight against Hamburg. The RAF had been perfecting its bombing techniques over the last six months while waiting for the bomber force, and in particular the Lancaster force, to reach a level sufficient to do serious damage to its targets. The program of raids is also intended to see how the attacks work in practice. Later in 1942 it is intended, if these work as hoped, to add the new high-altitude bomber the Supermarine-Vickers Coventry to the raids. The tactics are fairly straightforward. The target will be marked by a Pathfinder squadron using the new Mosquito. Two other squadrons of Mosquitoes will perform deception raids and also engage night fighters. The Pathfinders will be followed by the first part of the Lancaster force, which will use high explosive bombs to damage and degrade the cities defences while opening up buildings with blast damage. This will be followed by the Halifax force, using incendiaries and some smaller bombs to keep the city from fighting the fires until they are well established. Finally, the last part of the Lancaster force will again drop HE bombs to hinder the firefighting and cause more damage. In order to confuse the Luftwaffe defences further, Wellingtons and Coastal Command will carry out Gardening raids on the coast and in the river/canal network in northern Germany.

In the Mediterranean, Operation Remus is put into operation. This has been planned in advance, a contingency plan if the Japanese were to attack in the East. It consists of a steady program of bombing raids on Italy (particularly on any harbours), small Commando raids, mining, and a general low level but continuous program of annoyance to keep the Italians busy and off balance. While there is still hope the spring offensive may go as planned (if perhaps late), Remus is designed to keep pressure on Italy while not forcing the Allies to commit too many forces.

The weather again causes a lull in the air attacks in the Philippines. With more pilots than planes, only experienced pilots are to fly, and the fighters are now reserved for reconnaissance missions.

In Malaya, the Japanese stage a heavy raid on Penang Island, attacking ships in the harbour and the town itself and causing significant civilian casualties. From a military point of view, the attack achieved little. Most of the Japanese aircraft now established in Siam were engaged in aiding their troops to push south. This is a problem for the RAF; with fewer aircraft than the Japanese, they can either use them to attack the Japanese at sea or the army at land, but not both. For the moment, priority is given to the naval element, as the RAF units have not received much training in army support. Most of the operations in the north are now to be staged out of Taiping airfield, which is far enough to the north to allow raids while being the northernmost airfield inside the radar net. As in the Philippines, it is noted that the Japanese use a tactic of attacking an airfield in a number of small strikes, intended to catch planes after they have returned from a mission or from defence of the base, and destroy them on the ground. The results of the Luftwaffe raids on RAF airfields during the Battle of Britain had showed that it was very difficult to close an airfield down for long with bomb damage. The Japanese seem to be trying a different tactic which involves using small raids to keep the defenders busy, and catch aircraft on the ground when they inevitably have to refuel. The tactic has been quite effective on the exposed northern airfields, but the RAF command feels that it will be far less successful once the Japanese have to attack bases under the cover of the radar net, when it will be possible to concentrate the defending fighters against a small raid.

In a welcome boost to the defence force, 30 Beaufighters arrive from Australia. The versatile plane has suffered heavily in the past few days, and the new aircraft will allow the RAF to stage limited aggressive attacks again. While the pilots of the two squadrons are not sufficiently trained for Park's standards, there are experienced pilots available and these will be used in preference to the new pilots. There is also news that 50 Hurricanes have been removed from the Russian supply route in Iran and are being shipped east; they are expected in Ceylon in a few weeks, where they will be assembled and flown out to Singapore. Additional planes and equipment as well as replacement pilots are being loaded onto a convoy in Britain, but even going through the Mediterranean it will not arrive for some time.

Dec 12th

Force Z had now destroyed one Japanese reconnaissance plane, and fighters operating out of Singapore at least one more. The availability of radar is proving an increasing advantage to the Royal Navy, as unless they have been reported by a patrolling submarine, it seems they have got close to Borneo without being spotted. The same cannot be said for the Japanese fleet off Indo China, which has both been spotted by a Dutch submarine (which unfortunately was not in a position to make an attack), and by a Whirlwind sent specifically to photograph them. The fleet was now considered to consist of two battleships, two carriers, and a large number of cruisers. Although the Whirlwind had been spotted by a Japanese CAP, the pilot had simply flown away from them, the fighters quite unable to catch the 400+mph plane. Somerville and his air advisors are now debating whether to stage an attack at night or day on the Japanese once they are in range. With the knowledge that there are certainly Japanese submarines in the area, the thought is that a day strike would probably involve less submarine risk. Currently it is expected that the strike will be made far enough away that escorted land-based strikes will not be possible, although some of the air advisors are worried; a third Japanese carrier has still not been spotted, and either one is hiding somewhere or the Japanese planes have considerably more range than was thought.

Somerville has also been moving his submarine force; at present, except for intervention against some of the landings, the subs have been used in patrol lines. This is about to change; the four T-boats north of Indochina are moving a little south, and those in the south will be realigned on a line along the Indochina coast; assuming the strike on the Japanese fleet is successful, he hopes they will be well-positioned to take out any damaged ships. The U-class boats in the north are moving on the last-known position of the Japanese fleet; with luck they may get some action, if not they will remain to interdict the Indo China-Siam sea route, probably supported by the southern group. Once the Japanese fleet has been neutralized, Somerville thinks any more landings on the eastern coast of Malaya will be unlikely, and the submarines will do better in the northern waters.

In the Philippines, the Japanese land another 2,500 men of the 16th Division at Legazpi, again against minimal opposition. Mutterings are starting to be heard in Washington as to why the Philippines army seems to be unable to contain or even attack the invaders while the Imperial forces are fighting hard and, for the moment at least, successfully, in Malaya. The USAAF in the Philippines sends six B-17's to bomb Vigan, but the raid causes little damage. The Japanese air force is starting to operate from the airfields they have captured; there are now over 50 Ki-27 Nate fighters in northern Luzon, with more planes arriving steadily. The Japanese continue their tactics of sending planes continuously over the Allied fields as much as possible, and an increasing number of American aircraft are being destroyed on the ground.

In Malaya, the Japanese 5th Division takes Kota Bharu and pushes south as the defenders move back to hastily prepared defensive positions. The withdrawal is made more difficult by the way that the Japanese troops press their advance, and it requires a retreat of 20 miles before they can break contact and re-establish a defensive line. The Japanese air force is not happy with the state of the Kota Bharu airfield. The men who designed its demolition had been briefed by an officer selected by Park from one of his men who had designed the ones for 11 Groups advanced airfields in case of a German invasion, and the result is that not much is left intact. The main buildings and supplies have been burnt, and the runway itself broken by explosives. Still, it will be possible with work to use the old un-surfaced runways, and the Japanese ground crews and engineers start working on the problem.

News has been received that the US island of Guam has fallen to a Japanese invasion force. The island was always at risk, and while the invasion was hardly unexpected, the preparations to relieve Wake, which it seems possible to hold, are going ahead as fast as possible.

Dec 13th

Alexander receives news that 250 Valentine tanks, due for shipment to Russia over the next three months, will be redirected to him. The first are already waiting in Iran for shipping. The Australians have been training men to form their own armoured division in North Africa; the plan is for these to be diverted to Ceylon to meet with the tanks, and then be sent on to Malaya to give Blamey the means to mount an offensive once the Japanese advance has been held. The tanks are some of the older versions, with the 2-pdr gun rather than the 6-pdr, but this is felt not to be such an issue against the Japanese, as the 2-pdr has already shown to be perfectly capable of destroying the Japanese tanks. Alexander is promised that if the Japanese do deploy more capable armour, some of the new tanks now starting to equip 8th Army will be sent to him. An additional British infantry division will also arrive before the end of January, although he is warned they will probably need a short period of acclimatization, as they will be coming from the UK.

The first of the American 'Flying Tiger' squadrons, originally based in China, arrives in Burma. Preparations are under way to prepare a field to allow them to operate.

In Hong Kong, the continuing pressure of the Japanese attacks has forced the Imperial troops defending the colony to retreat from the mainland.

Japanese troops move on the airfield at Victoria point. It has long been realized that the airfield would be unusable in the event of a Japanese invasion of Thailand, and the Japanese only find a carefully demolished base, with the unwelcome addition of a considerable amount of lovingly designed booby-traps.

Indian troops prepare demolitions at the oil installations in Sarawak and Brunei in order to deny them to the Japanese in case of invasion. While the British would prefer to keep this resource, the defence of Malaya is vital at this point and they would rather destroy the installations than let them fall into the hands of the Japanese.

While Stalin is unhappy at the British decision to suspend supplies of armaments to him for some months, the British are adamant that their own need in the Far East takes priority. They point to the Russian winter offensive, slowly pushing the German Army back, as evidence that the Germans are temporarily less of an immediate threat.

Force Z is heading north on a course to intercept the Japanese fleet south of Indo-China. The Japanese are finally aware of Somerville's presence, as a patrolling Japanese submarine spotted them last night. However its report on the fleet does not include all the ships present - the captain reports two battleships (rather than four), and two carriers (instead of three), plus 'cruisers and destroyers'.

Somerville and his staff have finally decided on their attack option. Given the relative sizes of the fleets involved, Somerville feels he has sufficient force, if correctly applied, to shatter the Japanese fleet and, hopefully, buy additional time by making them much more cautious. He accepts that he may get attacked by land-based aircraft, but after the Navy's experiences in the Mediterranean theatre, he feels confident he can cope with this while he withdraws. The plan is a mix of a night and dawn raid. The fleet will close to, ideally, about 150 miles during the first part of the night, then launch a full-strength raid with his torpedo planes. The main targets are obviously the carriers. They will be recovered as a dawn strike by his dive bombers (this time with a fighter escort) makes sure the carriers cannot fly off aircraft, then will sink or disable as many of the cruisers as possible. If the enemy battleships or carriers are still afloat, a second torpedo raid is possible, depending on the response to the first two strikes - if it looks too dangerous, he will leave any damaged ships to his submarines. Somerville's job is to stop the Japanese with minimal loss (Malaya will stand or fall on the actions of the Army, he can only help them), and so the option of sending in his battleships to take out any damaged ships has been ruled out in the face of an uncertain amount of land-based air power. Initial reports from the RAF have described a worryingly competent Japanese air force. While some of the RAF officers have dismissed this in preference to their pre-war opinion that the Japanese can't fly, Somerville's air officers are rather more cautious until they have combat reports from their own pilots.

For their part, the Japanese are looking to a combination of a heavy land-based escorted strike, and (if the enemy gets close enough) a night torpedo strike by cruisers and destroyers. Admiral Kondo accepts that his two carriers, which only have some 50 planes between them, are too weak for a decisive strike and are better used to defend his ships while he closes to use the torpedoes on his cruisers and destroyers.

Chapter 3 - First Battle of the South China Sea 13th-14th Dec

Map 3 - The South China Sea

Force Z's best estimate of the position of the Japanese fleet was southeast of Cambodia point, which made sense if they were in fact covering the Japanese troop convoys. Somerville intended to close to about 150 miles - closer than needed for a strike, but it allowed time for the radar-equipped Spearfish to locate the enemy if needed. For their part, the Japanese were less sure of the position (and indeed the composition) of Force Z, but their last location was off the coast of Sarawak, heading northwest. Accordingly, reconnaissance planes were sent out from French Indo

China to get a fix, while the torpedo bombers and their fighter escorts were made ready for an attack. Force Z was in fact located by them at around 1400 on the 13th, some 400 miles from their own ships. This was thought fortunate, as that meant a surface torpedo attack would be possible, especially if their bombers could slow or sink some of the ships.

The Japanese plane was ordered to keep contact with the British fleet, something that it managed for half an hour before a pair of fighters was vectored onto it, despite its attempts to hide in scattered cloud. For his part, Somerville's main worry about being discovered was that the Japanese might pull back too far north for a safe engagement. The reconnaissance plane did report three carriers, which worried Kondo slightly, but his air staff assured him that meant their own air power would have the opportunity to inflict a crushing defeat on the Royal Navy. The Japanese had been very disappointed that the attack on Pearl Harbor had not found any carriers, and hoped to at least partially remedy that by sinking the three British carriers they had located.

Kondo wanted to, at the very least, damage Force Z so badly as to force the British to keep out of the northern part of the South China Sea, in order to allow his convoys to travel safely to Siam. He had planned a series of attacks - first a land based strike to cripple the carriers, then a torpedo strike to sink or damage the big ships. The following day would bring more air attacks from land and his own carriers, and if conditions allowed a final conclusion with his torpedoes and the big guns of his battleships.

Force Z was keeping a CAP of twelve planes in the air, with more spotted on deck; the range of the Japanese planes was uncertain, and Somerville wanted plenty of fighter cover just in case. This caution was justified when at 1530 a large formation of planes was reported approaching from the north at 90 miles. The carriers immediately turned to launch the ready fighters on deck, and additional planes were brought up to be fuelled and warmed up - this looked to be a substantial attack. All other planes were struck below, unarmed and empty, as the carriers prepared for an incoming attack. This was the strike from the land bases in French Indo China, and the Japanese knew the virtue of a single large attack as opposed to a series of small ones. The attack was actually made up of three kokutais (sections), and as a result (and the inexact position of Force Z), actually arrived in two parts. The first element consisted of 50 G3M Nells armed with torpedoes, and escorted by sixteen Zero fighters; the second element showed up on radar a few minutes later, heading to the west of Force Z; it consisted of 26 Nells with torpedoes, and a twelve Zero fighter escort. This was basically all the available naval aircraft in French Indo China.

As the fighters clawed their way up to altitude, the fleet formed into its AA defence formation with the ease of long practice - apart from HMAS Melbourne, pretty much all of the ships had done this before in the Mediterranean. By now, the CAP consisted of sixteen Goshawks and eight of the new Sea Eagle, and another sixteen fighters were being warmed up on deck. The carriers escort destroyers closed up to add their fire to that of the carriers, while the battleships moves to either side of them. The FAA pilots had been made aware of the initial reports of the RAF engagements with Japanese fighters - in any case, their job was to shoot down bombers rather than to get into a dogfight, and they had been reminded of that before takeoff. There was considerable speculation as to whether the incoming strike had fighter cover - the force seemed to be coming from land, and it would be at extreme range for a fighter to reach out this far. With two different types of fighter, the basic plan was for the Sea Eagle to engage the bombers - its speed would allow it to recover and make more attacks. The Goshawks would cover any fighters present, while also engaging the bombers. The plot showed the largest part of the formation losing height while a smaller part kept above it; to the experienced men on the carriers this meant fighters escorting a torpedo attack, and they informed their planes accordingly. The fighters already at altitude would try and keep the enemy fighters away from their torpedo planes, while the ones just launching would stay low and go straight for the torpedo planes if they didn't have time to get sufficient height. The light cruiser Bonaventure would be the pivot ship, and if possible keep the carriers safe inside the other ships.

First contact was made around 15 miles out by the Sea Eagles diving down onto the Nells. The speed of their diving attack shocked the Zero pilots escorting them, and the Eagles managed to shoot down four of the bombers in their first attack run. They also got credit for a kill on a Zero - a number of the escorts had instinctively dived to follow the fighters swooping on their charges, and one of them had flown out of its wings. The Eagles used their speed to climb for altitude again, turning to make another run at the bombers. The Goshawks were somewhat slower, and seeing the formation of Zeros breaking up, all but four went for it as planned. The result was a very confusing fight - the Zeros trying to draw the Goshawks into a turning dogfight, while the defenders were trying to make slashing attacks on the Japanese fighters then turn and come back again. The net outcome was inconclusive - the Japanese force lost six Zeros, the defenders seven Goshawks. That left twelve fighters to harry the slower torpedo planes, which they did with enthusiasm. A pair of the escorts broke off from the fight above to try and protect them, and had a shock when the Sea Eagle they were heading for simply flew away from their diving attack in level flight. They did draw the attention of some of the fighters, however, managing to shoot down a Sea Eagle who lingered too long in front of them before both were shot down.

In the meantime, the remaining fighters were swooping onto the Nells, another nine being destroyed before the rest of the fighters arrived. They made a head-on attack, having been unable to gain sufficient height for the usual diving attack from the rear, and another five Nells burst into flames and fell into the sea - this was becoming the usual fate of these bombers, and would lead to the FAA crews derisively terming them 'Ronsons' (from the US lighter companies famous advert, 'light first time'). The planes, despite their losses, were heading steadily for the fleet, and their speed meant that some were going to get through. By the time they reached the AA zone, the fighters had dispatched all but eighteen of them, although two injudicious Goshawks had been hit by their defensive fire, one fatally, the other managing to bail out, to be picked up later by a destroyer.

The Nell pilots then had an unpleasant introduction to the amount of AA fire the Royal Navy considered appropriate for a carrier group. Even the destroyers mounted twelve 40mm, plus a number of 20mm AA guns, and the fleet carriers and battleships close to 80 40mm each. The remaining torpedo planes drove into a storm of light AA tracer and 4.5" shellbursts as they headed for their targets, the battleship Prince of Wales and the fleet carrier Illustrious. Only twelve of them managed to launch - four had already been shot down, and two more damaged so they were unable to get a clear launch. Somerville, standing on the bridge of HMS King George V, was impressed with the skill and determination with which the attack was made - this was easily as good as anything the Luftwaffe had managed, and he would have to plan his future tactics accordingly. The first group of planes launched six torpedoes in two groups against the Prince of Wales, who turned into them to comb the tracks. She almost managed to get away with it, but not quite - one of the torpedoes hit her forward on the starboard side as she attempted to jink between the tracks. The huge ship shuddered, slowing as the Captain tried to minimize the damage caused by the ships own speed. The ship got some revenge, as its 40mm guns shot down another of the bombers as it tried to make its escape.

The second group were still heading for the Illustrious, and although two of them were hit by the carrier and her escort's fire, they managed to launch. The Captain of the Illustrious again turned towards the torpedoes, the men on the flight deck clinging on as the big carrier heeled over as it did its imitation of a 25,000-ton destroyer. Thanks to this, and the weight of fire having its effect on the planes attack, he managed to avoid all the torpedoes. The ship, however, did not get away from the attack unscathed. One of the Nells, already streaming fire from one engine, made what was afterwards described as a 'deliberate' suicidal crash onto the ships flight deck. Illustrious was still a lucky ship; the plane struck at quite a shallow angle, and almost bounced off her thick flight deck, before exploding and sending burning aviation fuel over the forward part of the deck. Sadly, this caught a number of the deck crews, as well as two Goshawks being prepared on deck, which also started to burn. A thick pall of smoke started to climb into the air above the carrier.

While the first attack was dissipating, the radar plot had seen the second raid turning in their direction, presumably alerted to their position by the first raid. Although this looked smaller, it was still a substantial force. The fighters were brought back and started to gain height although two of the Sea Eagles and a Goshawk had to be landed on the Implacable as they were out of ammunition. There was concern that some of the other fighters were also low on ammunition, but there wasn't enough time to rearm them. Implacable did manage to catapult off two more Sea Eagles, but Illustrious's flight deck would be unusable for some time.

As with the first raid, this too seemed to consist of escorted torpedo planes. With the planes in the air, the controller managed to get all of them up to altitude and vectored onto the raid as it closed. With the burning fuel on the Illustrious visible for a considerable distance, it was clear that there was no chance of evading them. This time, with a height and position advantage, the Goshawks dived down on the bombers first, while the Sea Eagles turned in to attack their escort. This raid only consisted of 26 bombers, and the sixteen Goshawks managed to shoot down 18 of them as they bore in. They had hoped to claim them all, but a number of the fighters ran out of ammunition during their attacks. Meanwhile the battle between the Eagles and the Zeros had held off the escort from defending the bombers, only three of them managing to get in a position to attack the Goshawks. They managed to shoot down three of the Goshawks (another one was lost to the bombers), for the loss of two of their number. The Sea Eagles were proving to be more than a match for the Zero, able to attack and then use its considerable speed advantage to disengage and make another attack. The Eagle pilots tended to be experienced - there had been considerable competition for a place in the new squadrons - and although the Japanese pilots fought with both skill and determination, they lost seven Zeroes for five of the defenders.

The last eight Nells entered the AA zone, and again flew into a storm of fire. Three of them were destroyed before they could launch their torpedoes, and the remaining five turned with the aim of attacking the one carrier they could make an approach on, HMAS Melbourne. The light carrier turned into the torpedo tracks to try and comb them, but had less time and was less agile than one of the fleet carriers. The ship shuddered and slowed to almost a halt as two of the Japanese torpedoes hit her port side and right forward, causing her to list over to port. With the fighters out of ammunition, the remaining five planes fled north away from the fleet.

As the last Nell fled the fleet, followed by the fleets vengeful AA fire, the main concern of Somerville was his damaged ships, foremost among them HMAS Melbourne. The ship had stopped and was listing, but after a short time, she reported that while she had considerable underwater damage forward, she was in no danger of sinking, and expected to be able to proceed in an hour, once she had made immediate repairs and counter-flooded. However, her engineer expected her speed to be cut to under 20 knots due to the damage (in fact she proved unable to exceed 18 knots without starting to damage her emergency repairs). Once she was stable, she would even be able, albeit with some difficulty, to operate aircraft. This was pleasing, as the initial strike had left Somerville worrying that she would sink, or be so badly damaged that he would have had to sink her himself

The fleet's fighters had suffered at the hands of the Zeros, and the main priority was getting them down on Implacable and getting a new CAP up for protection. While there was nothing on radar, it was still possible another strike would come in before it got dark. Indefatigable flew off her remaining six Sea Eagles, then proceeded to land on the fighters - her own to be struck below deck, the temporary orphans from Melbourne to be kept on deck until they could be returned.

Damage to the Illustrious was fortunately slight, although it had looked spectacular from a distance. The worst loss had been to the flight deck crews, many of whom had been killed or burnt in the fuel explosion and fire. The firefighting team had extinguished the flames, and the red-hot wreckage of the bomber had been pushed over the side. The only damage to the armour plate of her flight deck was a deep gouge caused by the unexpected arrival of the Nell, and her shipwright assured her captain that with some quick-setting cement she would be 'almost as good as new' in a couple of hours.

The Prince of Wales's damage was again fortunately not serious. The TDS had absorbed most of the blast, and although she had lost some fuel and had taken in a few hundred tons of water, she was in no danger, slowed slightly but still able to keep up with the fleet.

The return of the bombers was greeted with great concern by the Japanese. While they knew attacking a fleet was dangerous, the level of losses was staggering. However the reports of the pilots indicated they had achieved good results. One carrier was torpedoed and obviously sinking, a second was heavily on fire, and if not sinking would at the very least be unable to fly off aircraft. A battleship had been hit and had been seen to slew out of line, so would probably be unable to keep up with the rest of the force and be an easy target. The fighter escort reported shooting down at least 40 enemy fighters, maybe more, which meant that the fleet's air defences were probably now minimal, and Admiral Kondo's carriers could make the planned morning strike. While the Nell force was now too weak to be of much use, the Navy still had a force of 27 G4M Betty bombers available for tomorrow. The worry was the lack of fighter cover. Even working all night, the ground crews could only get six Zeros operational. It was assumed that by the morning Admiral Kondo would have sunk or incapacitated the remaining British carrier, so these should be sufficient. Unfortunately, the available torpedoes were all used in the last raid, so the Bettys will have to carry bombs.

As darkness fell, Somerville's next decision was whether or not to make the planned night attack. He was still worried about Melbourne, who despite her captain's protestations was obvious seriously damaged, yet he wanted to do the maximum damage to the Japanese fleet. The final decision was to close to 200 miles of the Japanese force, and strike using every available torpedo plane (while the FAA had used dive bombers at night in attacks on ports, it was simply felt too difficult and dangerous against a mobile target). To maximize the torpedo planes, Cormorants would be used to drop the flares needed for the night attack. Melbourne would fly off her attack planes, after which she would retire at her best speed; the rest of the fleet would catch her up by dawn. In addition, he had signalled Singapore to request additional fighter cover. It had been arranged that if needed a squadron of Goshawks from Singapore would fly to Sinkawang in Borneo to give additional cover. Fuel had been arranged, although lack of their normal ground crews meant they would be operationally limited. As naval planes, he could always recover them directly to his carriers if needed.

The chance of a dawn strike, while still seen as possible, would now only be used in an emergency; the presence of the damaged Melbourne reduced his offensive opportunities, and he wanted her at least to be in range of air cover from the land by the morning. The strike would launch at around midnight, preceded by eight ASV-equipped SeaLance who would locate the Japanese for the strike. The strike itself would consist of eighteen of the new Spearfish (carrying the new, heavier MkXV torpedo), 45 SeaLance and twelve Cormorant dive bombers carrying flares to illuminate the targets. The SeaLance would go in first, the priority targets being the Japanese carriers. If they succeeded, the Spearfish would use their heavier torpedoes against the Japanese battleships. All the planes would recover to the Implacable and the Illustrious, the Melbourne by that point on her way southwest.

For their part, Kondo and his staff were working on their best solution for a surface/torpedo attack on the British fleet. While his two battlecruisers were fast, they were old (originally built in 1915-16, although extensively modernized before the war), and could not be expected to meet the Allied battleships head-on. The solution was of course to go in first with a torpedo attack with his cruisers and destroyers, sacrificing them if necessary to cripple the battleships and open a path for his battlecruisers to exploit. He had six heavy cruisers available (the seventh, the Mikuma, was having her torpedo damage patched up in Saigon harbour ready to return to Japan for proper repairs), as well as fourteen destroyers. He would keep six of his destroyers back to protect his capital ships against possible submarine attack (both British and Dutch submarines were known to be operating in the South China Sea), and the rest would go in with the cruisers to attack with torpedoes. It was his intention to steer southwest during the night; even if, as he thought possible, the British retired west that would put him into a reasonable position to attack. He would send off a strike from his carriers (as well as one from land) as soon as the British had been located, and that should finish off their remaining carrier, allowing him to track them without opposition and arrange his attack to his advantage. While the casualties to the afternoon raid had been high, he had been informed that additional G4M Bettys were available, which with the planes from his two carriers should be ample - with two carriers out of action, the number of defending fighters would be severely limited. In order to maximize the chance of locating Force Z, he would also use the cover of night to advance his cruisers and spread them out in a search line ahead of his main group.

Somerville on the other hand had no intention of reversing course yet - his intention was to so damage the Japanese force that they would be too weak to protect the convoys bringing troops and supplies into Siam, and ideally sink the entire force. He was still closing, and at 2200 was some 220 miles away as he launched his radar planes in a search pattern to locate the Japanese ships. At 2315, one of the SeaLance reported multiple contacts of large ships, the pattern and speed indicating it was Kondo's force. Orders were given to launch the strike already armed and spotted on the flight decks of the three carriers.

Battle of the South China Sea (the night strike)

At midnight, a full strike was launched into the tropical night by Force Z's three carriers. They had made a number of course changes under cover of darkness, in order to try and evade the Japanese - Somerville was worried that they might have informed submarines in the area where they were (they had, but in fact there were none close enough to intercept a fleet advancing at 18 knots). As soon as her planes had been flown off, HMAS Melbourne turned to head southwest, accompanied by the cruiser HMAS Hobart and two destroyers. The rest of the force would meet up with her at daylight.

Further reports of the contact had been coming in while the strike launched, and in addition to the main body already discovered, another plane had reported a single contact some distance in front of it. The best analysis suggested this was one of (probably a number) of cruisers or destroyers out in front of the main body as a screen. Assuming a normal layout for such a screen, although Kondo's main force was some 180 miles away, it was possible a cruiser could be no more than 50 miles away. Accordingly the remaining search aircraft were ordered to search the area any closer ships would be in, and the force reorganized itself to put the battleships and some of the cruisers on the side of the most likely surface threat, just in case of unwelcome surprises.

While these precautionary measures were being put in place the air strike was approaching Kondo's main body. In addition to the two carriers and two battlecruisers, he had retained the heavy cruisers Mogami and Suzuya as well as eight destroyers as antisubmarine escorts to allow him a secondary striking force in case the unexpected happened. They were also ready to move to support one of the screening cruisers if they discovered enemy ships. No one on the ships was expecting a night attack by aircraft - such a thing was unheard of at sea, and Kondo himself was asleep, getting some rest before what he expected would be an early start and a long day's action in the morning.

The first alarm was given by a lookout on the Kongo, who heard the sound of an aircraft engine in the night. The bridge staff assumed that this was either a plane that had merely strayed over the fleet, or perhaps a reconnaissance aircraft, although it would have had to be a very lucky pilot to find them in the darkness. Maybe someone in the fleet had inadvertently broken the blackout. Since the fleet was currently operating under radio silence in order to remain concealed, the other ships were signalled by lamp, a slow procedure but one that was reasonably secure. Before all the ships could be alerted flares were seen, floating down on their parachutes along one side of the ships and casting long shadows on the sea. At this point the Admiral was woken, while the bridge crew commentated on the fact that the pilot obviously didn't know what he was doing, the flares weren't close enough to properly illuminate their ships. Even as they were agreeing that no Japanese naval pilot would make such a mistake (although an army pilot probably would), the first wave of SeaLance torpedo planes hurtled out of the darkness, aiming straight for the two carriers outlined by the slowly-falling parachute flares from the Cormorants circling high above. The flares not only outlined the carriers, they helped destroy the night vision of the crew, who couldn't help but look at them as they tried to work out what they were for. Indeed, the lookouts were assiduously searching the sea in case this was in fact the warning that they had been discovered by the British fleet, but as a result weren't looking high enough to see the approaching planes, even if they were at the moment well concealed in the dark.

As it was expected (or at least hoped) that the initial attack would have the advantage of surprise, the aircrew had adopted a somewhat different first approach. Instead of the classic torpedo 'hammer and anvil' attack, which would have required full illumination of the ships rather that outlining them against the flares, they had gone for a single heavy strike from one direction, counting on surprise to allow them to overwhelm the carriers. Indeed the first aircraft had almost reached their dropping point before they were finally spotted by a lookout, who had difficulty getting the bridge to realize what was happening. Everyone knew a night strike by planes wasn't possible...

Indeed, it was not only possible but something the FAA had been practicing assiduously for a number of years - the addition of ASV radar being the final piece which made it so effective a tactic. The usual tactic in a daytime strike was for the torpedo planes to attack in groups of three, which made some allowance for the ship attempting to dodge the initial torpedoes. In this case, they had committed eighteen planes to each of the carriers, flying in two groups of three flights each, to get the maximum spread of torpedoes while they still had the element of surprise. The first carrier to be hit was the Zuhio. Even surprised, she had managed to start to turn to comb the torpedo tracks, but with nine torpedoes in the water already, and another nine launched only a minute later, the effort was futile. Three of the first nine fish drove into the side of the carrier, dooming the small ship even before another two from the following planes sent plumes of water over the already heavily listing ship. Zuhio never recovered from that initial roll, most of one side shattered underwater. The carrier simply rolled over, only a handful of men escaping from her into the pitch black waters.

The fleet was by now firing off every AA weapon it had, some of which were even going in the direction of the attacking aircraft. The second wave of SeaLances was already levelling out from their run in as Zuiho was hit for the first time, the target the second carrier Hosho. This ship was even smaller than Zuiho, and with the need to cram as many aircraft as possible into her, even more lightly built. She handled quite adroitly, the small extra amount of warning at least letting her turn in the direction of her attackers, and only one of the first wave of torpedoes hit her, almost on the bow, blowing it off and making her lurch as she slowed quickly. However the second wave had already seen her turning - it was, after all, what they were expecting, and another three torpedoes hit her, two almost amidships, the final one turning her rudder and propellers into useless twisted masses of metal. At least she managed to survive the initial hammer blows for a short time, although it was immediately obvious that she could not handle such damage. The captain ordered an officer to take the Emperor's portrait off, then commanded the crew to abandon ship.

Admiral Kondo looked at the scene from the bridge of the Kongo in horror. It what only felt like moments, both his carriers were shattered and sinking, brought down by planes that had been barely visible in the night. By now, the cruisers were shooting starshells to illuminate the area. In the light of them, and the flares still falling slowly around his ships, he could see more planes coming straight for him. These were the Spearfish flights; equipped with ASV radar, they had led the other planes into their attack, and then curved off and around to regroup and see if they would be needed to give the carriers the coup de grace. As this was obviously now unnecessary, they instead lined up for the secondary target, the battlecruisers. With the constant dropping of flares, the scene was now illuminated from all directions, and the planes used this to commit to a hammer and anvil on Kongo, silhouetted as she was against flares from a number of directions. The old battlecruiser was still agile enough to handle well, but with nine planes coming at her from two different directions, there was little she could do. Kondo looked on with almost fatalistic calmness, admiring how fast the large planes were as they dropped their lethal loads at his ship. She managed to dodge all but one torpedo from the attack to port, but the one that hit struck her near the bow, wrecking her forward and causing the pressure of water on the unbalanced, ruined steel to slew her sideways, ironically further into the second attack. This time three of the torpedoes hit her on the starboard side. These were the new MkXV fish, only carried by the Spearfish so far - armed with a Torpex warhead and heavier than the older models, the aerial torpedo did almost as much damage as a pre-war 21" submarine-launched weapon. No old battlecruiser, even rebuilt, could handle four strikes of that magnitude. The shock alone had caused the ship to lose power, and she was slowly starting to lean over to starboard as water rushed in, too fast and too much to contain. Much more stoutly built than the small carriers, she settled slowly, and a destroyer moved in to take off first the Lieutenant clutching the Emperor's portrait, then as many of the crew as it could. Kondo was not among them - according to the surviving bridge crew, he ordered them to abandon ship, staying there himself. The only consolation to the crew was that one of the Spearfish had been seen to hit the water just after it had dropped its lethal load, cartwheeling across the surface in a shower of spray before sinking short of the ship.

The action was not yet quite finished. The SeaLance force still had nine planes which had not yet dropped their torpedoes, and there was still a battlecruiser sitting there as a tempting target. The three flights broke up to attack the Haruna from three different directions. This time the AA fire was more accurate, and two of the torpedo planes were hit on the way in. Despite this, the other seven launched at close range. One torpedo hit the ship amidships, causing serious, but not critical, damage. The second torpedo however hit her close to the bow, and the pressure of water on the tangled metal, forced against her by the ships 30 knots of speed, almost ripped the bow of the ship away, forcing her to a shuddering stop, dead in the water.

That was the final blow of the FAA planes. Job done, they climbed into the darkness above the remaining, sputtering flares, as they reformed to head back to their carriers. The only planes remaining were two of the Cormorants, busy taking pictures of the destruction before heading back themselves. For the loss of three aircraft, the Japanese covering force's heavy ships had been ruined in barely half an hour.

Chapter 4 - First Battle of the South China Sea, the surface attack

The British pilots were exuberant as they headed back to their carriers. While the exact damage they had caused would have to wait for the photographs now being taken to be analyzed, they had already seen two small carriers going down. Back at Force Z, however, the return and recovery of the strike was starting to become complicated due to things happening on the surface. Kondo had not been certain that his cruisers would in fact encounter any British ships that night - indeed the main aim of them was to make sure Force Z did not somehow slip in close so it could use its battleships against him. However if the British were encountered, a single cruiser could do damage, especially if it achieved surprise, and would locate the force for him. He had spread the four heavy cruisers out in a search line, interspersed with the destroyers he had sent with them, to cover the maximum amount of sea.

At 0200, while the strike planes were on their way back, a blip was spotted on the radar of the battleship HMS Prince of Wales. The British were suspicious there were Japanese ships in the area (indeed the patrolling ASV SeaLances had already reported some contacts during their search for the main body), so the cruisers and heavy ships were between the carriers and where it was thought that any enemy ships, if they were present, would appear. The battleship signalled her sighting to her escorts, and kept it under observation. Her captain was pleased to be informed that no radar signals were being detected from the ship, however he was reluctant to just open fire on it for two reasons. First, it would give their position away - gunfire being rather noticeable at night, secondly that it was possible that there were still Dutch or neutral merchant ships in the area - it would be embarrassing to put a salvo of 15" shells into a small merchant ship. Accordingly, the ship and its consorts came to readiness while keeping a close eye on the contact. It was obvious after a short time that this was highly unlikely to be a merchant ship - small, old vessels of the sort found in these waters were not known for making 24 knots. The problem still remained as to when would be the best time to give away their position.

The heavy cruiser Kumana, for her part, had not detected the British ships - perhaps not surprisingly, as the distance was still some 17,000 yards. The bearing indicated that she would come to within 10,000 yards if she did not change her course, and the captain of the Prince of Wales decided this was too fine a margin - if the ship zigzagged to avoid a potential submarine threat it was quite possible it would run right into them. The captain also preferred to engage before the moon rose at around 0230 and reduced the advantage of radar he currently enjoyed, even if it was only four days from new. As the range closed to 15,000 yards, the order was given to open fire.

Although the contact was on radar, the first shells to be fired were starshells from the battleships secondary armament - there was still a need to definitely identify the ship. The falling flare illuminated what was clearly a large cruiser of Japanese design, and the next order was to shoot for effect. The escorting cruiser, HMS Ceres, also opened fire at this point. The Kumana was taken by surprise by the sudden illumination of the starshells, but her well-trained crew reacted swiftly, turning to fire off her own illuminating rounds. The identity of the enemy hiding in the dark was made very clear as the first salvo of five 15" shells plunged into the water close to the hapless cruiser, sending monstrous pillars of water into the air.

The cruiser was not surprised to see that it was illuminating what was obviously a battleship, already at close range for the calibre of guns she mounted. Rather than try to escape, which was probably futile, the captain ordered a general sighting report to be made out to Admiral Kondo and the rest of the cruiser force. He did not know that Kondo was already dead by this time. Although only a few ranging salvoes had been fired, the battleship's huge shells were already far too close for comfort, the Japanese captain being impressed by how fast the British had found the range at night. It was already looking like his ship would not escape, so instead he turned to bring his torpedoes to bear. The Kumana had twelve torpedo tubes for the Long Lance torpedo, six on each side. At the same time, her 8" guns were firing back at the British ships - two now, as she saw the gun-flashes from a second, smaller ship in company with the battleship.

The cruiser fired her first salvo of six torpedoes from her port tubes, and then, still firing, started to turn in order to bring her starboard tubes to bear. She never completed the turn, as at that point a 15" shell crashed into her side and exploded. The whole ship shuddered. The Kumana had been built lightly in order to cram in the maximum firepower, and even if that hadn't been the case, no cruiser was designed to take that sort of punishment. As she kept on turning, she was hit again, this time on the bridge. The explosion killed the entire bridge crew, leaving no one in charge of the cruiser at a critical moment. Ironically, the absence of helm orders actually helped her for a few minutes, as the battleship's fire control had assumed she would keep dodging, but once these had passed the ship was hit heavily by a number of 15" rounds as well as shells from the Prince of Wales's secondary armament and the escorting cruiser. It took very little time to turn the Japanese ship into a floating target, and although the crew brought her under control again, it was too late. A shell (it was never known from which ship) finally exploded close enough to the torpedoes to send white-hot splinters into some of the oxygen tanks, and the aft of the ship exploded in a huge fireball. When the observer's on the battleships dazzled vision cleared, the cruiser was already broken in two and sinking.

The Long lance torpedoes were fast, but even so it took time for them to cross the eight miles between the ships. With only six torpedoes in the salvo, the chances of a decisive hit were small, but this time the Japanese had luck on their side. Although five of the torpedoes missed, the final one hit the cruiser HMS Ceres aft. Ceres was small for a cruiser, at only 4,300 tons well under half the displacement of the more modern ships in the fleet, and had been modified into an anti-aircraft ship before the war. The hit by the large warhead of the Japanese torpedo was too much for the old ship to absorb, and it was obvious to her crew within a few minutes that she was doomed. One of the escorting destroyers, who had already closed when they saw the action in progress, moved up alongside her to take her crew off as the ship slowly sank under the inrush of water.

The men on the bridge of the Prince of Wales were puzzled by the sudden explosion of what was surely a torpedo. The cruiser seemed to have been far too far away for a torpedo attack, and no other ships had been spotted on the radar. The explosion was also very large, indicating a big warhead, and there was some discussion that maybe the Ceres had in fact struck a mine, or maybe been torpedoed by a submarine. The timing though was suspicious; it fitted in with torpedoes launched shortly after the enemy ship had been engaged.

While the action of the Prince of Wales had been spectacular, the main activity of the carriers was landing back the strike on the two fleet carriers. Indeed, the only problem was that aircraft had to be held in the deck park, the air commanders having assumed somewhat pessimistically that more planes would have been lost. In fact all but three planes made it back to the carriers, although a couple were rather badly shot up. At 0315 Illustrious signalled to Somerville that all aircraft were safely back and that the planned move back towards base could commence.

Somerville was growing increasingly anxious about just what Japanese ships were out there in the night. Having achieved what looked like a satisfactory victory for a low cost, he did not want to be ambushed in the dark while his fleet was busy conducting air operations. It was a justified fear. The report of the Kumana had indeed been picked up by some of the other Japanese cruisers, and one had been close enough to see the flashes of the guns over the horizon. The heavy cruisers Takao and Atago, accompanied by two destroyers, were stealthily closing on his force under the cover of darkness.

The ASV planes had also been recovered after the strike; Somerville wanted to get four airborne to cover any night surface threat, but first they had to be refuelled - the maximum strike against Kondo's force had used the planes usually held back for such operations. The Japanese target was the Prince of Wales. She had been hit by two 8" shells during the confusion of the night action, and while they hadn't done any serious damage they were still putting the fire caused by one of the hits out, and the cruisers had been tempted by the faint, distant flicker of flames in their binoculars. Unfortunately for the ship her radar was also temporarily out of action - the firing of a battleship's main guns often had a negative effect on her radar sets - and with the Ceres sunk, the radar coverage of Force Z was reduced in that area of the screen.

The approaching ships were only spotted when they were 12,000 yards from the battleship by the cruiser HMS Exeter, who immediately signalled the Prince of Wales as she loaded her guns with starshell. After the earlier attack it had been assumed that these were more Japanese cruisers (it was in fact two cruisers and two destroyers, but Exeter initially reported this as four cruisers). Immediately after informing her consorts of the danger, she fired, illuminating the Japanese force with her starshells. The gunnery radar of the Prince of Wales was still operational, allowing her to start to range on the enemy once they could be seen. The Japanese for their part had expected to be found at some point, although getting rather closer for a surprise attack would have been advantageous, and it was only moments after the Exeter's shells burst high above them that their own illumination rounds were on their way.

The Prince of Wales had two destroyers close to hand, HMS Electra and HMS Jupiter, who had recently finished rescuing the survivors from the Ceres. They immediately started to work up to full speed and put themselves closer to the attackers. They could see at least one Japanese destroyer (the Fubuki) closing at speed. Visibility was better now than it had been for the earlier action; not only were both sides firing off illumination rounds with gay abandon, but there was a certain amount of light from the moon over the area. The bow wave of the attacking destroyer was clearly visible, and they headed for her to stop her executing a torpedo attack on the battleship.

The second destroyer (the Hatsuyuki), again moving around to try and engage the battleship with her torpedoes, was engaged by HMS Exeter. Destroyers made a poor target, especially at night, but the Exeter was renowned for her gunnery. As the destroyer was still moving into position to launch on Prince of Wales, the Exeter hit her with two 8" shells from her third salvo. While a destroyer could often take a surprising amount of damage, the splinters from one of the shells found her weak spot - her engine spaces. Superheated steam filling two of her engine rooms from shattered pipes, the destroyer slowed dramatically, leaving her a sitting target for the cruiser, who proceeded to pummel her into a blazing wreck.

The battle between the Fubuki and the Electra and Jupiter was more even, but the odds favoured the British destroyers. While the Fubuki had 6 5" guns, only two of these could bear forward, and as she was currently heading at the British ships, they were outgunning her by 6 guns to 2. The sea around the speeding ship was very soon filled with waterspouts as all three ships fired as fast as possible - in a destroyer action, it was often the first serious hit that counted, and in any case, very accurate fire from a destroyer was normally impossible. The disparity in guns soon showed, as fires started to burn on the Fubuki. Realizing he was unlikely to get past the two British ships to attack the battleship, her captain turned, firing off his nine torpedoes at the destroyers instead. In the confusion of the night battle, both the ships missed seeing the torpedo tracks (in any case, the use of oxygen in the Long Lance made its trail very difficult to see), and it was only when one of them impacted close to the bow of the Electra, that they realized what had happened. The Electra was a small destroyer, and the half-ton warhead of the type 93 torpedo blew her bows off almost to the bridge. Her own speed then killed her - although the pressure of water against her now very blunt forepart stopped her quickly, it also forced open more of her watertight bulkheads. It required no order to abandon ship, it was obvious immediately she was sinking, and in minutes, she had slid under the surface, taking over half her crew with her. It was too late for the Fubuki, though. Even while the torpedo had been making its deadly way towards the Electra, the fire of the two British destroyers had been turning her into a shambles. The final stroke was a hit on the oxygen equipment used to recharge her torpedoes, which cleared much of her upper deck and left her slowly sinking.

Meanwhile the battle between the Prince of Wales and the two heavy cruisers was continuing. The battleship was slowly getting her salvoes closer and closer to the Takao, as the cruisers manoeuvred to be able to launch torpedoes. Indeed, they had no real difficulty with their first salvo, as the Prince of Wales was hardly expecting a torpedo attack from over 10,000 yards away. Unfortunately while the Type 93 had ample range to hit the battleship from that range, its accuracy over that distance was not good, and none of the twelve torpedoes fired by the two ships hit anything. Indeed, the British force was not even aware a torpedo attack had been made. The cruisers then turned about to make an attack with their port batteries, although by that time the Takao had received two hits from the Prince of Wales, fortunately not disabling ones, although two of her turrets were now out of action. While the torpedoes sped towards the battleship, she finally managed to land a salvo almost on top of the cruiser. When the spray from the misses cleared, the Japanese ship was seen to be on fire and sinking forward.

The Atago meanwhile was trying to reload her torpedoes. While this was a standard operation for Japanese ships, doing it at night in the middle of a gunfight with a battleship was most definitely not, and as a result, the operation was going very slowly indeed. While she was doing so, plumes of water from a new source of heavy guns lifted up around her - the Richelieu, the next ship behind the Prince of Wales, had managed to get a clear arc of fire. Feeling somewhat put out at the way the Royal Navy had been hogging all the fun tonight, the French battleship was firing both accurately and with enthusiasm. A single battleship was more than enough to handle even a heavy cruiser; two was enough to pound the Takao into scrap before she could even come close to reloading her torpedoes.

This time the torpedo salvo from the doomed cruisers was more accurate. Although by now both Japanese ships were on fire and obviously in deep trouble, first one then a second huge plumes of water lofted up above the masts of the Prince of Wales as the huge ship shuddered under the massive explosions. The shock was enough to cut off power to the ship, and it was fortunate that the Richelieu had already engaged, otherwise the Takao at least might have gotten away or reloaded her tubes to do even more damage. As it was neither cruiser was able to do more than land a few shell hits on the French ship, only one of which did any really serious damage - the ships wine storage room was wrecked!

The Prince of Wales was seriously damaged by the two hits. The ships TDS was not designed to handle this weight of warhead, and the ship was suffering heavy flooding along one side and into her forward engine and boiler rooms. Even with counter-flooding of the TDS on the other side of the ship, she was listing at 8 degrees and having real problems getting back under control. It wasn't until 10 minutes after the hit that her engineers managed to reset the shock-damaged circuit breakers and restore some power, but by then the ship had already taken in thousands of tons of water. Fortunately, that was the last Japanese attack of the night, but even so Admiral Somerville spent an anxious half an hour before the ship signalled that she had the damage at least temporarily under control and was able to make way, even if only at 10 knots.

As dawn broke over the South China Sea, Force Z was heading slowly southwest at 12 knots. The Prince of Wale's engineers, pushed on by the knowledge that they were still well in range of the Japanese land-based planes, had managed to get her up that fast, but the ship was handling poorly with the amount of water inside her. The quarterdeck was only inches from the water, and indeed waves were breaking over it frequently. Nevertheless, the ship pushed on as fast as she could. The Melbourne had now rejoined the fleet, and in view of the serious damage to two of his capital ships, Somerville had decided against any further air strikes against the Japanese unless a ship was directly threatening them. Instead, he had eight fighters up as a CAP and four ASV-equipped TBR's sweeping the sea around his force. He had signalled Singapore with the results of the night's action, and a squadron of Goshawks was on its way to Sinkawang airfield in Borneo where they would be able to help cover his force by the following day, landing on his carriers if necessary.

It was just as well that the fleet had reformed its air defences, as the IJN planes would indeed be in action again today. Not as early as expected - the situation after the night action was somewhat confused at headquarters, and it was not until nearly 1000 that someone got around to sending off the first reconnaissance planes. From the reports of the cruisers they had a reasonable idea of where to find them, and even though their job wasn't helped by the increasing cloud covering the area they found the retreating ships by noon, radioing their sighting back to base. Of course, it would have been a much more powerful strike if more aircraft had been available, and especially if they had been armed with torpedoes. However no one seemed to have informed higher command as yet of their problems and asked for more planes to be deployed to them. In any case, this would have taken time, as all the suitable and available naval planes were heavily involved in the attack on the Philippines, and asking the army for help was going to be a very hard decision to make.

Somerville and his staff were busy analyzing the night's actions, and working out what to do next. It was clear from the action photographs and the surface action that the Japanese covering force had been shattered and was effectively unable to interfere in the area until reinforced. The new Sea Eagle had proven itself in combat, and the carriers themselves had taken less aircrew losses than had been originally feared. On the other hand, he had lost a cruiser and a destroyer and had a carrier and a battleship severely damaged, which reduced his own options until he could regroup. In any case, his remit had never been to destroy the Japanese Navy in the area, but merely make it unable to support the invasion of the British possessions. Of course, destroying it was one way of accomplishing that. It also was looking increasingly as if the IJN had a fast, very powerful torpedo that no-one had known about. While the initial strike on the Ceres could have been a submarine, the later hits on the Prince of Wales and the timings made this unlikely, as any submarine would have had to be right between the ships even though they were moving at high speed. Judging from the power of the explosions, it would be a big beast, which probably explained the range as well - it looked like it could go at least 10,000 yards. This would be a problem in future surface actions if the Japanese could mass their ships to ensure a decent number of hits.

The staff deliberations were interrupted by the news that the fleet had been spotted by a Japanese scout plane - fighters were trying to shoot down the shadower, but the cloud cover meant that for once the Japanese plane got away - base had not ordered it to keep close contact no matter what, so the pilot managed to evade the fighters who seemed to have a surprisingly good idea of where he was. Somerville estimated he had no real choice but to fight off today's attacks, unless he wanted to abandon the Melbourne and the Prince of Wales. He had no wish to do this unless the situation got far worse, and by tomorrow he would have additional land-based cover, and two more days should see him in Singapore. He decided to fight it out. The question now was how much had the Japanese managed to reinforce their land-based strike force since yesterday?

The problem the IJN faced was a lack of fighter cover. Only six Zeros were available to cover the 27 G4M Betty bombers, but they took heart from the reports of the damage done already to the British force. A carrier sunk, and another carrier severely damaged yesterday, as well as a battleship damaged. And it seemed that their cruisers had had successes overnight, while the reports were fragmentary, it seemed that before they had died bravely they had sunk another battleship as well as some more cruisers and destroyers. While it was possible the British had two carriers left (judging by the night attack), they knew that their own planes had shot down large numbers of their fighters in exchange yesterday - they couldn't have many left now. Their targets were the remaining carriers – removing them would leave the British fleet naked to the power of the Japanese air force.

Force Z had been waiting for an attack ever since the spotter had been detected, and they finally saw it approaching at 1430. The fleet still had 30 operational fighters, and 24 of them either were already in the air or would be sent up to meet the raid. This was a gamble by the controllers - it left them more vulnerable if there was a second attack soon after, but with two slowed and badly damaged ships that would have difficulty evading and indeed surviving more torpedoes they wanted to have the best chance of driving the raid off rather than just surviving it. The fleet had also adopted a different pattern - the damaged Melbourne and Prince of Wales were between the two fleet carriers, this group surrounded by the other three battleships and the remaining AA cruiser.

The confidence of the Japanese airmen was rather discommoded some 25 miles from the fleet when two groups of fighters drove in on them, and they realized that a third was already engaging their top cover of Zeros. The twelve Sea Eagles had used their speed and power to climb above and then dive onto the Zeros at a speed approaching 500mph. While the experienced Zero pilots in fact spotted them as the dove in, they were simply unable to cope with the sheer speed with which the Eagles arrived, and the heavy cannon armament of the British fighters sent four of them spiralling down to the sea before any of them could get a shot off. The FAA had learned from the last few days, and instead of staying to fight the Zeros they just pulled hard out of their dives to come around for another straight-on attack.

While the Zeros were being engaged, the Goshawks had gone for the Bettys in two groups of six. To the delight of the fighter pilots the Betty proved as delicate and as combustible as the Nell. Without any interference from the remaining Zeros, who were busy fighting for their lives against the Sea Eagles, the Bettys were doomed. Still 20 miles from the fleet they had hoped to bomb, the Goshawks kept driving in towards them, determined that they would not reach the ships they were protecting. They didn't, although no one could fault the skill and bravery of the Japanese pilots in trying. In the end, some 20 of the Bettys were lost before the remainder, some damaged, dropped their bomb-loads to turn and escape. None of the six Zeros survived. The victory was not without cost to the defending fighters; despite the advantage of their initial surprise, one of the Sea Eagles was lost to a Zero, and three of the Goshawks were shot down or damaged so badly the pilots had to bail out due to the Betty's defensive fire. Two of the pilots were picked up by one of the escorting destroyers.

It was the last air attack of the day; just as well, as the carriers were now down to only 19 operational fighters between them (although a few more would be fixed by morning). It was also the end of the IJN air attacks for the time being. This wasn't realized at the time, and the 15 Goshawks that had flown to Borneo the previous day were flown onto the two fleet carriers the next morning to improve the Fleet's defence. Force Z carried on its slow withdrawal, covering the damaged ships and praying that the weather would stay favourable - a bad storm could easily have finished the Prince of Wales. As it was, the battleship barely made it into Singapore on the 17th, her stern so low she had to crawl into the dock at high tide. The Melbourne was not in quite such a critical state, her buoyancy reserve not having been so badly damaged. While Singapore was a fully equipped dockyard, it was also in range of Japanese air attacks, and it was decided that Melbourne would be patched up quickly and then sent to Ceylon for proper repairs. The Prince of Wales would need more work, due to the considerable amount of water she had taken in, but as soon as enough had been done to make her seaworthy she would go to Durban for what was expected to be another 4-6 months of work to make her operational again. The Richelieu, although hit by three 8" shells, had no major damage, and was expected to be fully repaired in a few weeks.

While Force Z had been making its withdrawal, covering its damaged ships, the Covering Force had been doing the same. The main damage to the Haran was to her bow, and this was so bad that she couldn't move forward - the resistance of her damaged bow, and the pressure of the water on her repairs, was simply too great. So after a discussion, the cruisers Miami and Suzy took her under tow. Backwards.

Which view was of considerable interest and in fact a certain amount of amusement to the Captain of HMS Triumph as he looked at them through his periscope that morning. He'd already been lurking in the general area, hoping that the Japanese force would come in range, but last night's sighting report from the FAA planes had been all he needed for an estimate of how to intercept the force. He was quite surprised to see so few ships; he assumed that the rest of the force was elsewhere, leaving him this nice fat damaged battleship all for his very own.

The Triumph was one of the earlier T-class boats, having four external bow tubes as well as the more usual six internal ones. While the external tubes were a nuisance and impacted her performance, they gave her a very heavy initial salvo indeed. The sight of the Japanese battleships was simply too tempting not to go for all ten torpedoes at once. The Triumph had no problems lining up her shot - being towed backwards by two cruisers wasn't exactly the fastest form of propulsion - and the captain allowed the boats turn to ripple fire the torpedoes across the battleship. Normally he would then have dived to start his evasion on the assumption that the enemy would be looking for him as soon as they saw the torpedo tracks, but he had only seen one destroyer, which was a good distance away, and he just HAD to watch what was going to happen.

Being towed as she was, the Haruna could do nothing to escape, and the shout from a lookout of "torpedoes!" was greeted with despair on the bridge. In quick succession three huge plumes of water burst over the ship as the torpedoes detonated against her side. With the damage already done, that was more than enough to overcome the old ship. Reconstruction could do only so much, and as with all old rebuilt ships, she suffered from weak underwater protection by modern standards. The cruisers had no option but to slip their tows before the increasing weight of the Haruna broke the cables, and could do little more than circle back to her, watching as she slowly, even gracefully, heeled over on her final trip to the bottom.

The destroyer accompanying the ships made for where she supposed the enemy submarine was, but by the time she got around to her estimated position the Triumph had slipped away, slow and silent, and the depth charges did little more than rattle her slightly and kill a considerable quantity of fish. The boat did, after the depth charges died away, take another look - there was, after all, always the chance that a ship might have hung around, and her internal bow tubes were reloaded, but after taking off the crew the cruisers had decided that there was no point in them hanging around and had headed for port at well over 20 knots, followed by the destroyer (who was already claiming a kill on the submarine) The final act of the Battle of the China Sea was over.

The reports by both sides on the results of their actions were interesting, and it was a shame that an impartial observer was not able to correlate the two, as they made quite different reading.

From the British point of view, the action had been successful. Force Z had lost an AA cruiser and a destroyer, and had a light carrier and a battleship put of out action for a considerable time. However they had sunk two light carriers, (granted, old, small ones), two battlecruisers, three heavy cruisers and two destroyers, a quite satisfactory ratio. They had also destroyed the IJN land-based air force until it could be rebuilt. On the tactical side, the performance of their fighters had been adequate, and the new planes in particular had performed well, although it had been noted that the Japanese pilots were brave, determined and the fighter pilots in particular were highly skilled. The Japanese strikes had been as good as anything the Luftwaffe had done in the Mediterranean, and future missions would have to be undertaken with this in mind. The Staff analysis was that, for the time being, the Japanese surface force in the area was so severely weakened as to probably be unable to act. Somerville intended to keep reasonable pressure on the Japanese, especially with his submarines, but did not intend to pursue aggressive actions unless necessary to protect British possessions - the amount of airpower the Japanese had deployed was still uncertain, and his force was not powerful enough to wage a full-scale air battle on its own. However for the time being it looked like the east coast of Malay was safe and life was looking difficult for the Japanese convoys, which he intended to harry as much as feasible. Somerville intended to replace his losses from the ships finishing working up at Ceylon, although he wanted more ships if possible - he was in particular short of carriers and destroyers, and he needed replacement aircraft urgently. He also wanted a small commando force - he thought around 1,500 men would do, plus sufficient landing craft to lift about twice this. He had in mind using the current naval dominance of the area to consider the possibility of landings behind the Japanese front line, as had proved so successful in General O'Conner's North African battles.

While the night attack had been a major success, he warned there were still issues. The attack had concentrated too much on the carriers; a more careful approach might have sunk the entire Japanese force. Also, although radar helped, there was still no true counter to a night attack by air, and the Japanese airmen had proved skilled enough to learn how to do this. He wanted immediate action to determine how best he could defend against this type of attack, and what needed to be developed to help this defence.

The Japanese report was surprisingly optimistic - at this stage in the war, their command seemed rather uncritical of the combat claims of its men. While it was accepted that the covering force had suffered heavy losses, this was only to be expected in action with the Royal Navy, especially as they had been outnumbered. Despite this, they had inflicted serious losses on Force Z, and pointed out that the British ships had withdrawn as a sign that they too realised how much damage the Imperial Navy had inflicted on them. A battleship had been nearly sunk, and would not be in action for a very long time, and a second battleship had been hit by the aircraft; it too would no doubt be out of action for some time. A carrier had been sunk by the aircraft torpedo attack, and another one left in flames; since there was no sign of it in Singapore dockyard it had probably sunk from that damage. At least two cruisers and a number of destroyers had been sunk. While it was admitted that they had suffered heavy losses to their land-based air force, the British carrier airgroups had also been savaged. The British had obviously had four carriers with them (as shown by the strength of the night attack), now they only had two, and would need to rebuild their air groups. At least one British submarine had been sunk.

While the Japanese command admitted that their own losses meant it would be difficult to take much offensive action at sea until they had received reinforcement, the same applied to the Royal Navy, and they were much further away from their home bases. This meant that there was no overriding reason why the next phase of landings could not go ahead broadly on schedule, although they would need more planes before this would be entirely safe. Regarding the longer-term plans, they pointed out that if the Royal Navy was reinforced again, with the current forces they expected to have it might be difficult to keep pressure on Malaya at sea. They therefore suggested two possible courses of action; first, to send significant reinforcements, this would mean battleships from home waters as well as at least part of the carrier striking force. If this proved impossible, a modification of the plan could be made. Instead of moving on the DEI by means of two pincers from the PI and Malaya, as the actions in the Philippines seemed so far to be going satisfactorily they could keep the pressure on the British in Malaya with the army, then roll up the DEI from the east against the anvil of their advance into Malaya. This would allow them to keep the planned attack into Burma as soon as the Army had moved sufficiently far into Malaya.

All in all, although they had received a setback at the hands of the Royal Navy they had damaged their opponent equally severely and the overall plan was still going well, although small modification might have to be made to keep abreast of the changing situation.

Chapter 5 - Holding Actions

Dec 14th

In Europe, Germany blames the failure of the attack on Moscow on the bitter Russian winter, and vows that as soon as it finishes German troops will march through the ruins of the Kremlin over the bodies of Josef Stalin and his commissars.

In the north of Malaya the Japanese army keeps pressure on the defenders of Jitra, although at the moment the Australians defences are holding firm, thanks to the delaying tactics that gave them extra time to prepare. After being forced to withdraw down the eastern coast due to the pressure of Japanese attacks, Imperial troops have formed new defensive lines and positions. This has been helped by the use of some Australian troops and tanks to form blocking positions to allow the retreating force to recover and re-establish their lines. Reports from the Australians report that the Indian troops appeared badly shaken after their retreat, but steadied once they realized reinforcements were to hand to cover them and allow them to reorganise.

The government of Siam signs a treaty formally legitimizing the Japanese invasion as 'necessary to prevent a British invasion of our country'. This was a disappointment to the British, as they had been hoping their battle against the Japanese invasion would at least make the Siamese government wait until the outcome was more certain. It was not realised until after the war that the men in charge of the government had already made an arrangement with the Japanese.

In the Mediterranean, the cruiser HMS Galatea is sunk by a U-boat. Cunningham, while no longer having much to worry about from surface ships, and currently having the air situation under control (especially with the bulk of the Luftwaffe currently frozen to the ground in Russia), is having problems with the U-boats sent to harass him and the convoys. A study is underway as to the best way to neutralize this threat, as the situation in the Far East will be much easier to supply if the route through the Mediterranean remains reasonably loss-free.

The results of the Bomber Command raid on Hamburg have been analyzed, and are impressive - even Dowding considers it a success. The raid involved some 500 Lancaster and Halifax bombers, and had resulted in the estimated destruction of 70% of the cities shipyards, a major producer of U-boats, mainly due to the large fires caused by the incendiary loads. Bomber Command has a number of other raids planned, on differing targets, to evaluate the new techniques before starting a major campaign. 23 bombers were lost during the raid, which is considered acceptable. Work is also continuing to find a way to destroy the huge U-boat pens the Germans have been constructing.

Dec 15th

Northwest of Moscow, the Soviet Army retakes Klin and Kalinin. Russian radio announces that the advance of the Red Army against the frozen and pitifully unprepared German army will continue until they are forced from Russian soil.

The Japanese force investing Hong Kong attempts its first landings on the island itself, but these are repelled, albeit with difficulty. It is clearly only a matter of time before the colony falls.

The RAF in Malaya resumes offensive operations against the Japanese airfields in Siam from the more southerly bases. These bases are in no danger from the Japanese army at present, and are inside the southern Malaya radar net, allowing the defenders more warning of attacks.

The day sees a number of confused raids from both sides, each trying to catch the other on the ground as well as damage the airbases they are using. The RAF loses six Blenheim bombers, eight Beaufighters and nine Sparrowhawks. The Japanese lose seven Sally bombers and eleven Nate fighters. The use of a radar system and ground control is starting to give the defenders an advantage over the Japanese tactics of small, constant raids, but it is clear that the operators require considerably more experience before the threat can be completely contained.

In the USA, there has been much controversy over the construction of the Alaska-class battlecruisers. Many feel they are unnecessary, and even though a war has begun, there is no sign of the Japanese battlecruisers they were intended to fight. There is pressure by the 'air faction' in the navy to cancel them, and build three additional Essex-class carriers in place of them, especially since the Royal Navy is steadily showing that a surface ship is as the mercy of a carrier which comes within range. The first ship of the class is about to be laid down; as a result of the discussions, this is postponed for two weeks until a final decision can be made.

Dec 16th

The U .S. War Department gives Brigadier General John Magruder, head of the American Military Mission to China (AMMISCA), permission to divert Chinese lend-lease supplies to the British, provided the Chinese agree. The operations in Malaya have been of sufficient intensity to worry the British regarding their logistics. It isn't realised yet just how inadequate the Japanese logistics system is compared to that of the Allies.

The Secretary of the Navy approves an expansion of the pilot training program from the existing schedule of assigning 800 students per month to one calling for 2,500 per month, leading to a production of 20,000 pilots annually by mid-1943.

The Japanese army postpones the planned invasion of Borneo for a short time. This is to allow the Royal Navy force to retreat to Singapore, out of easy range of interfering. While the Navy is convinced that Force Z is retreating beaten, the Army is less trusting, especially when getting reports sourced by the Navy.

Admiral Fletcher's Task Force 11 is deployed in support of Admiral Brown's TF 14. This consists of the fleet carrier Saratoga, the fleet oiler Neches, seaplane tender Tangier (loaded with supplies), the heavy cruisers Astoria, Minneapolis, and San Francisco, and ten destroyers. The convoy carries the 4th Marine Defence Battalion, a fighter squadron equipped with Grumman Wildcat fighters, along with 9,000 5 in (130 mm) rounds, 12,000 3 in (76 mm) rounds, and 3,000,000 .50 in (12.7 mm) rounds, as well as a large amount of ammunition for mortars and other battalion small arms. TF 14 - consisting of the fleet carrier Lexington, three heavy cruisers, eight destroyers, and an oiler - is to undertake a raid on the Marshall Islands to divert Japanese attention.

After the recent events in theatre and in SE Asia, Fletcher was instructed to relieve Wake 'with all speed'. Unofficially the commanders have it pointed out to them that the Navy's honour requires them to be seen to act in support of US interests and territories, especially in view of the comments some Congressmen are making. There is some concern at the way the fleet is being used in small elements, inviting defeat in detail, after the way it has been shown in the war so far that better results are obtained from concentrated force. With the present available forces, and the sheer size of the Pacific Theatre, such dispersion is seen as inevitable.

Dec 17th

In the Crimea, German attacks by 54th Corps of the German Army Group South begin against the city of Sevastopol despite continuing Soviet offensives in other areas.

A plan is drawn up for using Australia as an Allied supply base under command of Major General George H. Brett, USA. Meanwhile B-17 Flying Fortresses, evacuating the Philippine Islands, begin arriving at Batchelor Field near Darwin, Northern Territory. It is not yet certain if the planes will be based here, but as it is likely the DEI are the eventual target of the Japanese attack they will stay here to be used to attack the expected incursion.

The Australian "Gull Force" (1,100 men from the Australian 8th Division) lands on Ambon Island, DEI to reinforce the Dutch garrison. The Dutch are poorly equipped, and the Australians urgently recommend supply of items such as radios and other basic military supplies.

Dec 18th

MacArthur is promoted to full General. There are a certain amount of barbed comments (carefully not in the presence of senior officers) as to what rank he would have been promoted to if he had been successful at defending the Philippines.

In northern Malaya the Japanese assault on the Jitra defences continues, with fresh troops from the 18th division aided by tanks. The Australian defence is starting to weaken as the continuing assault allows them little rest, and the infantry infiltration and assaults, although often costly to the Japanese, are steadily eroding their positions. With the local airfields now evacuated and destroyed, planning is made to withdraw the defenders to the defence line further south, which they have bought time to have prepared and manned. The Australians will blow bridges and cause as much delay as possible while defence lines are strengthened. While it might have been possible to hold Jitra by committing his reserves, Blamey is concerned at being outflanked by a push from Kroh, the Japanese having now overcome the earlier delaying tactics. Fortunately for the defenders the Japanese have had to pause in their attacks on a number of occasions to wait for more supplies. Apparently the planned convoys are having some difficulties. Indeed, Yamashita has already ordered that the maximum amount of supplies be brought overland, requisitioning whatever his logistics troops can get from the locals. So far the Australian and Indian troops have lost some 3,000 men, about 1/3 of them killed. The Japanese have lost over twice this (including troops lost on the transports), mostly killed, and the 5th Division is running very short on men.

The issues with the transports are only going to get worse. Dutch submarines operating out of Singapore have sunk four transports and an oiler (although with the loss of three submarines to attacks and mines), the US submarine Swordfish has sunk a freighter off Hainan, and the British submarines have sunk two more tankers. For the time being, there is little surface shipping available to supply 25th Army

The attack has been costly in terms of aircraft to both sides. The RAF and RAAF have lost another eight Sparrowhawks, nine Beaufighters and five Blenhiems as they struggle to attack the Japanese ground troops and the air bases. The Japanese have been defending their bases and helping their troops on the ground with air strikes and strafing attacks, losing eleven Oscars and fifteen Ki-51 Sonjas. Both sides are now asking their command for more planes and pilots. It's not only the number of planes lost in combat; both sides are suffering from depleted squadrons due to non-combat damage. This is hitting the Japanese worse as the airfields they are using are not surfaced, and planes are being put out of action due to poor landings. While the planes are normally repairable, the strain is telling on the ground crews.

As the Royal Navy returns to Singapore, the Japanese mount a heavy night raid against the city. It had originally been planned for this to be made by navy G3M Nell and G4M Betty bombers, but after the Battle of the South China Sea, these are 'not available'. A heavy raid is therefore undertaken by 40 Ki-21 Sally bombers. There is some concern that the lack of a moon will make navigation difficult, but the position of Singapore Island makes it easier to spot.

The new moon also gives the bomber pilots confidence that they will be difficult to intercept. This confidence proves misplaced when twelve Reaper night-fighters are vectored onto the bomber groups by the island's radar net. While the Japanese bombers have good performance, their target is obvious, and as a result, fifteen of them are shot down, many before they even reach Singapore. The only loss to the night-fighters is one which crashes on landing. The bombers which do manage to attack find that with some of the fleet in, the AA fire from the docks is heavy, and by now, the authorities have worked out how to fix the blackout. One more plane is lost to AA, and while bombs are scattered across the base, causing a fair amount of damage, nothing critical and no ships are hit.

The northeastern part of the South China Sea had been kept under observation since the battle by Dutch Do34 flying boats. On the 17th a formation of ten transports and a tanker were spotted some 300 miles north-west of Lutang. Although there were now Dutch fighters on some of the Borneo airbases, the Dutch were not equipped adequately for anti-shipping strikes, and a squadron of Beaufighters is arranged to leave tomorrow, stopping at Kuching airfield to refuel.

Planes were not the only forces the Allies had in the area, however. Although she had been unlucky in not managing to find any of the Japanese warships in the earlier action, the submarine HMS Unbroken had been looking for trade off the Borneo coast. She was close enough to intercept the convoy on receiving the sighting report from the Dutch aircraft. The small submarine found the convoy without any proper naval escort - it was surmised that the Japanese had assumed the naval actions had drawn all the Allied warships away from this area, and only one destroyer was seen accompanying the transports. In two attacks, she sank the tanker and two of the transports before the convoy escaped. While the Unbroken was depth charged (and claimed sunk by the Japanese destroyer), she suffered only minor damage.

Dec 19th

General Brauchitsch is formally removed as Commander-in-Chief. Hitler assumes the duties personally. The German attacks on Sevastopol continues with the Soviets managing to bring in 14,000 reinforcements via sea between today and the 25th. The Red Army is still pressing the Germans back in the north, as the German Army suffers from the extreme cold.

The USN's Task Force 8 (Vice Admiral Halsey), formed around the aircraft carrier USS Enterprise (CV-6), heavy cruisers, and destroyers, sails from Pearl Harbor. It is tasked to join with TF 11 and support the reinforcement of Wake Island. Since Admiral Fletcher's force is expected to pause to refuel (so his lighter units are able to fully use their speed in case of attack), he expects to join up with him just before he reaches Wake. Current intelligence is mixed; the Japanese obviously got a bloody nose on their first attack, and are preparing for a second attempt. There are unsubstantiated reports that a carrier is being sent to the area, and also battleships, though this is seen as less likely with the sinking by the Royal Navy of two of the IJN's 11 battleships in the South China Sea.

The battleships HMS Valiant and HMS Malaya, moored at Alexandria, are badly damaged by explosions under their keels planted by human torpedo's operated by Italian frogmen of the Decima Flottiglia MAS. The damage is so great that these two ships are deemed unseaworthy. However as both of them are in the shallow harbour, reconnaissance photographs taken by the Italians indicate the attack was a failure and the ships are still operational. Both are in fact sitting upright on the bottom.

In northern Malaya the planned withdrawal from Jitra goes ahead, covered by the artillery firing off all its remaining stocks (a shortage of shells due to the Japanese attacks and the consequent difficulty of resupply was one reason behind the withdrawal). The infantry head south, covered by the remaining Matilda tanks. Only eight remain operational; 22 have been lost, although only seven in combat, usually to a suicidal attack by Japanese infantry with satchel charges, the Matilda being immune to any conventional weapons possessed by the Japanese. The others have been lost to the Matilda's perennial problem, mechanical breakdown. While a withdrawal under fire is always a difficult operation, the experienced troops carry it off with efficiency, aided by the heavy Japanese losses - this has made the commanders at the front rather wary of the Australians, and by the time they realise this is a withdrawal rather than a trap the Australians are on their way south.

The Japanese convoy which attracted the attentions of HMS Unbroken yesterday has continued on to Borneo, where it lands elements of the 16th Division at Miri, Seria and Lutong. Although the loss of some of his force en route made the commander consider only landing in two places, he has decided to take all three, confident his troops can defeat any local opposition, as Lutong is in any case close to Miri.

Dutch reconnaissance aircraft from Singkawang, Borneo, continue to make reconnaissance flights over the Japanese invasion fleet. Despite a lack of torpedoes, a Dutch Dornier Do-24 bombs and sinks Japanese destroyer HIJMS Shinonome off Miri, Borneo. Meanwhile RAF Beaufighters are preparing to make a strike on the ships; they left from Singapore before dawn, and refuelled at Kuching airfield. They then flew north, to be joined by a squadron of Dutch Buffaloes, to make a strike on the ships. The first group of ships was sighted off Miri, and the first twelve Beaufighters were happy to find them not only anchored and busy unloading, but with no fighter cover. Opposed only by the AA from the ships, they placed their torpedoes carefully, leaving three of the five ships sinking, and two more damaged. They then carried on to Seria, where they found the remaining three transport ships. Although they only had four torpedoes left, they sank one of the three and damaged a second, They and the fighters then strafed the remaining ship, leaving it on fire (although the crew managed to put this out and save the ship). Apparently the Japanese had not expected any opposition to the landings apart from on land, and after the heavy losses in aircraft they had sustained recently had decided that this force did not need air cover. One Beaufighter had been damaged by AA, and made a forced landing at Kutching; a second was lost when it landed badly.

The Japanese landings had gone quite successfully until the arrival of the Beaufighters, and they had landed their troops, although supplies would now be a problem. After the events in Malaya and Thailand, the commanders had decided that no matter what reassurances they got from the IJN they would get their troops at least off the ships and onto land as fast as possible.

While the warning given to the local defenders allowed them to resist the landings, they were heavily outnumbered (even with the losses the Japanese had suffered to the submarine attack), and by noon the Japanese were in possession of the town of Miri.

There had been considerable discussion on whether there was any serious chance of holding Borneo if the Japanese invade. It would be helpful to deny them a base so close to Singapore and the oil in the area, but it might mean writing off any troops sent. The Dutch are reluctant to commit more men as they expect to be fighting for the DEI once the Japanese have finished in the Philippines. After secret talks with the Australians, it was decided to send about 1,500 men from the reserve 8th Division and about the same number of Ghurkhas from Malaya. For political reasons an Australian commander is named. The force from Malaya sailed today, having been prepared once the Japanese invasion fleet was detected, and the Australians will hopefully leave today or tomorrow. It is still being decided where the best place to land them will be.

Air support is a problem; the heavy air fighting in Malaya has depleted the RAF and RAAF force, and replacement planes have not yet arrived. On the positive side, the RN has butchered the long-range bomber force, and the Dutch promise fighter support to both defend the force and aid with ground attacks. Admiral Somerville is unsure just what Japanese naval support will be give, but a light striking force of three cruisers and four destroyers is held at Singapore for the time being. Any operations will be close to the Borneo coast, so he expects land-based fighter support to be acceptable.

Dec 20th

In a major reorganisation at the top of the USN, Admiral Ernest J. King is appointed as Commander in Chief of the US Fleet.

The Japanese increase their strength in the Philippines by landing at Davao an invasion force of fourteen transports covered by a cruiser squadron and the light carrier Ryujo. In order to prevent interference a heavy force of bombers attacks Del Monte airfield, while other airfields are strafed by their fighters.

A British convoy arrives at Singapore carrying supplies, more aircraft to replace those lost, and the 18th British division. It is intended to add this division to the 8th and 11th Indian divisions, but as the defence line in the north is currently holding well, Alexander instructs that the troops will undergo a rush course in fighting in the jungle while they acclimatise, bearing in mind they may need to go into combat at any time.

Force Z arrives in Ceylon to fly on replacement aircraft and to load more supplies (torpedoes in particular). The carrier Bulwark will replace Illustrious while her deck is properly fixed, then Illustrious will rejoin to equip Somerville's force with three fleet carriers. He also intends to strengthen his cruiser force, although he still suffers from a shortage of destroyers. He has suggested that ships that have had to retire from the Philippines are sent to Singapore where they can add to his escort force, but this has to clear political objections in the USA.

A large convoy leaves the UK headed for the Far East. It is intended to take it straight through the Mediterranean to save time, and plans are made to give the maximum possible protection. The convoy carries supplies for Burma as well as Malaya, as the Chiefs of Staff expect it only to be a matter of time before the Japanese launch an attack to gain the Burmese oil fields and push the British back to make supporting Malaya more difficult. Part of the convoy escort will remain in the Far East to increase Somerville's force. The Chiefs of Staff are also looking at sending squadrons from the Mediterranean and Middle East areas out to the Far East and replacing them directly from the UK.

The RAF has been following up its raid on Hamburg with raids on Bremen and Wilhelmshaven. As before, the main target has been the docks and heavy engineering to reduce the production of U-boats. It is intended to carry on these raids for another month before evaluating the effect on U-boat production. It is also practice for a much larger bombing campaign planned for when the high-altitude Coventry bomber is available in suitable numbers.

Discussions have been taking place with the French regarding support in the Far East. The Admiralty has already expressed its satisfaction with the French naval support, and while the bulk of French forces will stay in the Med for operations closer to France, it is agreed that a token force of some squadrons of aircraft and a Brigade of the Foreign Legion will be sent east to show the mutual support the Allies are giving to each other's fights. It is as a result of this, and the increasing French army force in North Africa, that French representatives will be going to the Arcadia conference in Washington. While it is accepted that the USA and Britain are the big players, France will also go to speak for themselves as well as the other occupied nation forces, as the UK will for the Empire. There is a certain amount of self-interest by Britain here, as they consider the French rather more understanding of the realities of the war than the Americans are at present, and indeed at the moment the French are supplying considerably more divisions than the USA to the conflict.

Dec 22nd

A reinforced Japanese landing force known as the Wake Occupation Force leaves Kwajalein bound for Wake Island. It is under the command of Rear Admiral Kajioka Sadamichi. Air attacks are continued by the Japanese carriers Soryu and Hiryu. The attacks by 'carrier-type planes' have been reported by the island, and are seen as likely intelligence that at least one Japanese fleet carrier is in the area. There is some pressure on the USN to abandon Wake rather than risk a carrier engagement which could result in the loss of a carrier. Although this is seen a risk not normally worth taking, it is pointed out that refusing battle because an IJN carrier is around, especially after the recent South China Sea action by the Royal Navy, would have severe effects on the morale of the Pacific fleet. The relief of Wake is authorised to go ahead, although 'with caution if a Japanese carrier is encountered', which leads at least one US Admiral to mutter about "making sure we carry the blame whatever happens".

The Japanese land the 38th Division at Lingayen Gulf on Luzon. The Japanese soon establish a strong beachhead and finish unloading their troops by the 23rd.

The Arcadia Conference between the Allied governments in Washington DC begins with talks between the two main countries, the USA and the UK. They confirm the policy from Placentia Bay in August of 'Germany first'. They also establish the Combined Chiefs of Staff for the entire Allied military effort. Since this will be in the main a US-UK effort, in order to keep the organisation to a manageable size the representatives will be from the UK and USA. Other countries such as France, Canada and Australia will have representatives, but they will not sit on the Combined Chiefs of Staff. A general strategic program is approved of a US build-up in Britain, particularly in air power, to continue the bombing offensive. The concept of further losses in the Pacific is accepted with the understanding that a stiff defence will hold these to a minimum. This conference will last through to the 7th of January.

The Japanese force which landed at Miri has a problem. The plan had been to move down the coast by ship to take the airfield at Kuching. However, the transports necessary for this plan are either sunk or disabled, and only 3,000 of the planned 4,500 men were landed. They are told to remain where they are while the IJN sends more transportation for them, however the commander does send some reconnaissance forces down the coast. They are a constant worry to the British petroleum engineers at the oil fields; the fields have been comprehensively prepared for demolitions, but they have been told to wait, if possible, until they see the Japanese moving in their direction. The Allied forces in the area around the invasion are little more than armed police and militia, and have no real chance of stopping the Japanese if they decide to advance.

Discussions are ongoing between the Chinese, British and Americans about the idea of Chinese divisions being sent to Burma to help defend it. The Chinese are of course worried about the road links over which most of their supplies come. The British are concerned about seeing Chinese troops in what is, after all, a British possession. A compromise is finally reached; the Chinese will send a number of 'observers', to keep an eye on the situation and be ready to advise Chinese troops if they are deployed. The Chinese will keep the equivalent of two western divisions available, but they will not enter Burma unless the Japanese invade. It is not a perfect solution, but at least it is acceptable to all sides.

The USS Wasp, the USS Ticonderoga and their escorts sail from the West Coast, destination Pearl Harbor. The availability of light and escort carriers in the Atlantic has allowed the USN to allocate all its fleet carriers to the Pacific theatre. They are also acting as escorts carrying more Wildcats for the fleet and a load of the new Corsair fighter (which is not yet carrier-qualified)

In reward for the results of the Battle of the South China Sea (and also to give him more leverage in dealing with Allied forces), Somerville is promoted to full Admiral.

Chapter 6 - Second Battle of Wake Island

Dec 23rd

On the afternoon of Dec 23rd, the USN had managed to concentrate two carrier-centred Task Forces only some 400 miles from Wake; the fleet was currently refuelling (Halsey's high-speed run to catch up meant he needed to refuel as well). There had been talk about sending the supply ships on ahead with some cruisers, but the intelligence reports of at least one Japanese carrier in the area seemed quite definite, and the risk was simply too great - if the supply ships were lost so was Wake. Halsey and Fletcher had also had it pointed out to them that while relieving Wake was important, it was not worth a carrier.

The US carriers had sent off reconnaissance planes, searching for any Japanese carriers in the area, as much for their own protection as to locate the enemy for a strike, but nothing had been located. The intention was to close the island during the night and land the supplies the following afternoon, also taking off unneeded civilians. The fleet was still closing Wake when the Japanese started the second attempt to invade the island. The Wildcats had been in combat over the last few days, first with bombers then with Zeros which the defenders were certain had come off a carrier. Although they had shot down some six Zeros, as well as over twenty land-based bombers, there were now no Wildcats left to defend the island.

The second Japanese attack went in before dawn on the 24th, two old destroyers running aground to allow the troops they were carrying to unload. Although the gun defences set one on fire, the Japanese considered them expendable and by dawn over 1,000 men had been disembarked, quickly occupying the southern wing of the island. The news was quickly passed to the task forces, which caused consternation and not a little anger - just a few more hours and they would have been in a position to stop the attack. While it was already looking too late for Wake, it was not too late to make the Japanese navy pay a high price for their action.

The Saratoga and Enterprise launched their search planes at first light. Unlike the Japanese and British carriers, who when operating in pairs kept fairly close together, the two US forces were over 10 miles apart. Since the commanders knew that there would be Japanese warships in the area, anti-shipping strikes had been readied. It was still felt that there could be a small chance of saving Wake if an invasion fleet could be hit (it was not appreciated at this point that the force transported in the two sacrificial destroyers had already doomed the island).

The search planes set out to cover a wide arc across Wake Island, with some additional planes tasked to cover the area around the island. These were the first to report in, informing Halsey that they had spotted two cruisers and some other vessels off the island. It was decided to strike these immediately, using half the carriers' attack force, while getting ready for a second strike if the other search planes spotted a suitable target. Halsey also proposed to send off two heavy cruisers and a destroyer escort at full speed to aid the island defenders with their heavy guns, and if necessary sink any other Japanese ships in the area. Even before the strike had formed up, the cruisers Astoria and Minneapolis and four destroyers were heading for Wake Island at high speed.

The Americans were not the only people sending out search planes that morning, although the Japanese were using floatplanes, preferring to hold their TBR planes back for a possible anti-shipping strike. While they did not know if any US ships were in the area, there was always the possibility a force had been sent to reinforce Wake, and if so, they wanted to be ready to sink it. In fact the first indication that they had that US carriers were in the area was an urgent call from the cruiser Yubari, who had been detached to aid the landings at Wake, that she and her two destroyers were 'under attack by carrier aircraft'.

At least one of the search planes altered course to see what was happening, as 30 Dauntless dive bombers, escorted by five Wildcats, turned into their near-vertical dives over the unfortunate Yubari. The dive bombers were carrying 1,000lb bombs, which meant certain death for a cruiser if they were to hit home. While the captain manoeuvred his ship with great skill, the attack of that many bombers, untroubled by any defending fighters, meant it was hopeless. Five hits later, the Yubari was rolling over, the waters closing over her as she sank in a matter of minutes. The dive bombers also hit one of the two destroyers with her, causing her stern to break off, although the final destroyers evaded the remaining few dive bombers, only to suffer the indignity of having over 20 of her crew injured or killed by the strafing of the Wildcats.

The two search planes had watched the sinking of their ships while slipping in and out of cloud cover. The US planes were concentrating on the ships, and did not notice them slip behind them as they turned and formed up for their run home back to their carriers.

Meanwhile the US search aircraft had finally found something. Aided by earlier information from the island's defenders, they had made an educated guess as to the likely location of a Japanese carrier force which was in fact reasonably accurate. At 1100, they radioed a report of 'two carriers and escorts sighted, 120 miles west of Wake Island'. Halsey immediately ordered the remaining dive bombers and torpedo planes to be readied for a strike on the Japanese carriers. The strike would launch as soon as the inbound planes from Wake, now almost back, had landed and been struck below. While this was going on the carriers would head northwest to close the distance (they were now some 150 miles south-east of the island, outside of comfortable strike range)

While the US carriers were fitted with radar, they as yet had nothing like the capability of the RN carriers to process and handle the data and the airborne planes. Such a capability had been proposed by the 'Canadian' observers on the Royal Navy Fleet Carriers, but peacetime procedures had held such improvements up. It didn't help that while well trained, the operators were somewhat distracted by the recovery of the first successful US carrier strike of the war. As a result the two Japanese search planes were able to get a good look at the force and radio its position without being discovered in all the excitement. Indeed, it wasn't until the planes started to be launched and form up for the strike against the Japanese carriers that an operator realised that there were a couple of echoes on his screen that didn't seem to correspond with any of their own planes. A pair of Wildcats was sent to investigate, and a short time after they reported shooting down a Japanese floatplane which had failed to dodge into cloud cover fast enough.

While the American force had been closing the Japanese carriers and readying a strike, the Japanese had been doing exactly the same thing. Before it had to head home to refuel, the final US plane had spotted activity on the flight decks, but the need to keep hiding in clouds to avoid the prowling Zeros had made anything else too dangerous. As he headed home, the Japanese carriers were turning into the wind to launch their strike. With only two carriers available, and only 32 TBR and 32 dive bombers available, they had decided to launch a full-strength attack against the American carriers spotted. For their part, the US carriers were sending off some 32 dive bombers and 16 TBR with a small fighter escort (at this stage of the war, despite warnings from the Royal Navy, the US carriers were still operating with small fighter groups - as they expected to be fighting in mid-ocean rather than in range of land based strikes, more offensive power was seen as more useful than a better defence).

Although the US carriers had actually started to launch first (having had the planes pre-prepared for a strike), the Japanese were much more efficient at launching a daytime strike from two carriers, and their planes were heading for the US ships while the American planes were still forming up. In fact, the two US carriers never succeeded in joining up their planes into one large strike, and it would arrive at the Japanese ships in two separate groups.

The two strikes actually passed each other on their separate ways, although neither side spotted the other. By reason of their higher efficiency, it was the Japanese strike that was first detected inbound on the radar plot of the Enterprise. The two carriers immediately started preparations to receive an attack, fortunately the recovered strike from the cruiser was safely below decks and the fighters had by now been refuelled and rearmed. This was just as well, as the two carriers only had 25 Wildcats between them, and ten had been sent off with the strike at escort. One of the planes from Wake was unserviceable due to AA damage, but by the time the Japanese planes were within 40 miles the remaining fourteen were up to protect the ships.

The Japanese were in fact heading directly for the Saratoga; later reports indicated they had initially missed the Enterprise, not realising how far apart US carriers tended to operate at this stage in the war, and having seen one very large carrier had headed straight for it. The strike consisted of 32 Val dive bombers and 32 Kate torpedo bombers, escorted by twelve Zeros. The Wildcats intercepted the strike some 15 miles out from the carrier, going for the torpedo bombers (seen as the more dangerous of the attacking planes). The Zeros had been waiting for this, and moved in to protect their charges. Although information from the British on the results and suggested tactics against the Zero had been passed on to Pearl, the carrier force had already left and so was still using the pre-war doctrine. This was a mistake. While the Wildcats did succeed in shooting down three of the torpedo planes, and four of the Zeros, far too many allowed themselves to be drawn into low speed turning fights, and only five of them finally managed to get away from the Japanese, two of them damaged.

The attack by the Wildcats had succeeded in one thing - it had decoupled the dive bombers from the torpedo planes. The result was that the dive bombers would be the first planes to attack the Saratoga. The Japanese aircrew were still searching for the second carrier they believed to be in the area, and so the first attack was by sixteen Vals, which dove down towards the huge US carrier in nearly vertical dives. The AA fire from the ship and the two close-by cruisers, while heavy, was not nearly enough to deflect the attack. In quick succession, three 250kg bombs struck the flight deck of the carrier, despite her best efforts at dodging (sadly, the Saratoga was not the most agile of carriers). One sliced in forward of the hangar, destroying the catapult and the first 50 feet of the deck. The other two did more serious damage, penetrating the thin wooden flight deck, one bursting in the hangar, the other going even deeper, splinters shutting down the forward engine room in a burst of escaping high-pressure steam. The planes in the hangar were not fuelled, but the bursting HE bomb did considerable damage and started a large fire which quickly plumed into the air above the ship.

While the Saratoga was still reeling from the impact of the bombs, her lookouts spotted the Japanese torpedo planes boring in. With no fighter opposition left, they had split into two formations, allowing a classic hammer and anvil attack. The Saratoga, still manoeuvring despite her heavy damage, managed to slip past the first wave of torpedoes, but two of those launched on her other side hit; the one that struck amidships did minor damage, the big ship absorbing the hit, but the second hit further aft, starting to flood her engineering spaces, the shock damage cutting her power and causing her to start to slow to a stop. Ironically the sudden loss of speed actually helped her to avoid some of the second strike, the torpedoes passing her forward, but the Japanese naval pilots were highly skilled and she was hit by three more torpedoes, causing the now almost stationary carrier to start to list steadily to port.

The dive bombers, busy during this attack in searching for the second US carrier, had finally found her. The Enterprise, however, was a more difficult target than the lumbering Saratoga. Despite the best efforts of the Val pilots, she twisted and turned, evading all the bombs except the last one. That hit her just forward of her island, right in the centre of the flight deck, exploding in the hangar below. Again, there were no fuelled planes below, but it would take some time to bring the fire under control. Indeed, the smoke billowing up through the hole in her deck was so thick the Japanese pilots were already convinced that she was sinking. In fact she was in no real danger, and her damage control teams had the fire out in 40 minutes, the crews already repairing the deck with the urgency of men who knew their planes were about to return, and had nowhere else to land.

While unknown to them the skilled Japanese pilots had been eviscerating their carriers, the strike from the Saratoga had finally sighted the enemy. Sixteen Dauntless dive bombers and twelve Devastator torpedo planes drove steadily into the attack, covered by four Wildcat fighters. The Japanese carriers had kept back eighteen Zeros to defend themselves, but while the pilots were skilled the methods of controlling them onto the attackers was primitive. The first group of four Zeros didn't actually spot the approaching Devastators; they were alerted by one of the cruisers firing her main armament in the direction of the attackers to warn them. The first four were in turn attacked by the Wildcats, but again these suffered from poor tactics, not being aware of the Zero's agility. All four of the Wildcats were shot down for the loss of one Zero destroyed and one damaged. Meanwhile the torpedo planes had been closing to their launch point.

Thanks to the lack of radar on the Japanese ships, and the poor methods of controlling the CAP, the twelve planes found nothing but AA between them and the first carrier, which was the Hiryu. Although one of the Devastators was shot down by the carriers AA, the other eleven made a textbook launch. It was a shame that the US torpedoes weren't up to the job. The maximum speed of the type 13 torpedo was 33 knots. The maximum speed of the Hiryu was 34 knots. The carrier simply turned away at full power and ran away from the torpedo attack.

While she was doing this, more of the CAP was engaging the dive bombers, which were peeling off into their dives above the speeding carrier. They had been spotted by another four Zeros, and with no fighter protection had to make their own way through the defences. This was not easy, and six of them were shot down as they got into position, although not before their rear gunners had shot down two Zeros. The ten dive bombers hurtled down onto the Hiryu, who started to make radical course changes more suitable to a destroyer than a carrier. This sort of radical manoeuvring was a part of the Japanese doctrine for evading air attacks, and her captain managed to avoid all but one of the 500lb bombs. That one struck her well forward on the flight deck, exploding in the front part of her hanger deck and starting a serious fire.

The planes from the Enterprise had been looking for the Japanese carriers - they had not been as accurate as the Saratoga's flight leader, but the radio messages from the attackers, plus the thick plume of black smoke coming from the Hiryu was all the help they needed. Sixteen Dauntless and eighteen Devastators headed for the burning carrier, whose fighters were mainly engaged in chasing away the last of the Saratoga's planes. Not all of them as some of them were still covering the carriers, and the dive bombers found ten Zeros turning to engage them. The six Wildcats with them dove into an attack, but the Zeros, expertly piloted, split, four engaging the fighters while the other six went for the torpedo bombers (still seen by the Japanese as the main threat to their ships, being unaware of the poor performance of their torpedoes). Despite a constant stream of attacks the Devastators clung together, losing eight of their number for only one Zero. Despite their losses, ten of them got close enough to drop their torpedoes, only for the fish to suffer the same humiliating results as had those from the Saratoga. However one of the torpedoes exploded in the carrier's wake, making the retreating torpedo planes think that they had indeed scored a hit.

The concentration of the Japanese fighters on the low-level torpedo planes had left the Enterprise's dive bombers unnoticed, and indeed, they were only finally spotted by an observer on the Hiryu as they angled down into their attack dives. The ship responded with sharp and violent course alterations at full speed - so violent that a number of flight deck crew vanished overboard - but the Dauntless crews were determined to finish off the Japanese carrier. Despite all her AA could do, she was hit by three 500lb bombs, which were hardly slowed by the carriers 1" of deck armour. Two of the bombs exploded in her hanger, starting new fires and also killing or incapacitating many of the men fighting her existing fire; the third bomb sliced lower, exploding in one of her engine rooms. The carrier slewed to a halt, huge clouds of smoke billowing from the gaping holes in her flight deck.

The surviving American pilots turned away for home, convinced that the carrier, if not already sunk, was sinking and would soon go down, the thick smoke almost hiding her from their sight as they evaded the last of the angry Zeros on their way to safety.

They were in fact quite correct. Although due to the range the US dive bombers had only been carrying 500lb bombs rather than their preferred 1,000lb ones, the thin flight deck of the Hiryu was insufficient to stop a bomb of any significant size, and her hanger deck was now a mass of flames, her fire-fighting hampered by the temporary loss of power due to the hit in her machinery and the fact that many of her damage control men lay dead or incapacitated in the burning hangar. While the crew did their best, it was not possible to contain the fire, and soon an explosion rocked the huge ship as fire reached one of her avgas tanks, causing the volatile fuel to explode with even more force than the American bombs. The ship was obviously doomed, and the Captain had no alternative but to order his men off to the waiting cruisers and destroyers, although there was still a faint hope the ship might survive - if burnt out above her hangar deck - and be recoverable.

Back at the Enterprise the sight of the listing and sinking Saratoga was at least offset by the news from the strike that one of the Japanese carriers was burning 'like a Fourth of July fireworks display' and sinking. Now the task was to get the flight deck ready to take on the returning planes, it was already obvious that Saratoga would never land another plane. There was also the issue of fighter defence. The TF had carried few fighters, and many of these had been lost. However, the Enterprise was carrying some additional Wildcats. These had been intended to be flown off to Wake, which was obviously pointless now. The original plan had been to carry them all on Saratoga, but she was already filled with aircraft, and when the plane was expanded to include the Enterprise, the squadron had been spilt. This gave Enterprise six additional fighters. They hadn't been used earlier due to caution - while taking off from a carrier to land on Wake was one thing, flying operationally off a carrier with non-qualified pilots had been thought too risky, a crash on a crowded deck was the last thing that was needed. But now circumstances had changed, and the marine pilots were informed they were about to become very rapidly carrier-qualified.

At first the news coming in to Halsey was good; one Japanese carrier burning from multiple hits, and a second hit by a torpedo. As more information came in, things didn't look so promising. One of the flight leaders had radioed that in fact the second carrier hadn't been hit, although the one burning was definitely in serious trouble and already starting to list. The nastiest shock came when one of the groups of returning planes reported yet another Japanese carrier some distance from the others. It wasn't realised for some time after the action that this was in fact the Japanese seaplane carrier Chitose, which had a partial flight deck and resembled a carrier at first glance. This put Halsey in a dilemma. One Japanese carrier remaining meant a second attack would have a reasonable chance of success; he still had some 23 dive bombers on board, plus the survivors of the first strike which could be turned around. His main problem was his lack of fighters; providing a second strike with a useful fighter escort would strip his task force of defenders. Two Japanese carriers meant that even if he sunk one the other would likely retaliate and in view of what had happened to Saratoga it was quite likely that with only a few fighters to defend her Enterprise could be seriously damaged or lost.

The original mission to reinforce Wake Island was obviously now in ruins. It had been intended to reinforce the island base before it was attacked again, the US force was simply not equipped or trained to make a combat landing against opposition, and the current reports indicated that the runway was untenable (it would shortly fall to the Japanese). He decided with more than a little reluctance that under the circumstances his orders from Nimitz meant that the survival of his remaining carrier was worth more than at attack at 2:1 odds - the Japanese pilots had shown earlier that day that the pre-war estimates had been woefully incorrect. The small cruiser force (ironically almost at Wake now) was recalled, and preparations made to withdraw once the strike aircraft had been recovered. Due to the losses in the raid and the defence of the task force, all the remaining aircraft could be fitted on the Enterprise.

The Saratoga, although now evacuated, was showing her reluctance to sink. It was obvious that she could not be saved, especially so close to an enemy force, indeed the smoke still towering into the sky above her was endangering the entire force. There was no alternative but to order the cruisers to sink her with torpedoes. That afternoon the first US carrier to be lost in the war finally slipped under the waters of the Pacific ocean, as the task force headed east back to Pearl Harbour. It had now become obvious that the war against the IJN was not going to be nearly as easy as some of the pre-war analysts had suggested. The situation was not all black; realistically it would have been very difficult to hold Wake Island in the long run, and at least they had come out even in the fight against the Japanese carriers

For their part, the Japanese were far happier about the outcome of the battle, although this did show a considerable amount of false optimism on their part. They had captured their objective, Wake Island (a rather important point after their original humiliation at the hands of the defenders), and their pilots had reported the sinking of both American carriers, which meant that the planes that had survived attacking them would be lost as well. Of course the Hiryu was in serious trouble, but there was always the possibility that she could be recovered. A search was conducted of the area off Wake where the US carriers had been, but nothing was found, confirming that they had indeed caused the Americans to flee with the loss of two carriers. Apart from the ships intended to take and hold Wake, the rest of the force was headed back to Japan. There was annoyance at the loss of aircraft; the losses to the attack planes had been satisfactorily small, but losses to the fighters had been heavier (the force only had sixteen Zeros left), and they had been forced to ditch any damaged planes over the side in order to make room - indeed some undamaged planes had to be lost, although the pilots were safe. At least Soryu would have some 3/4 of her air group available when she returned.

By the following morning the Hiryu had finally stopped burning. That was mainly because there was not much left of her to burn, and she was little more than a skeleton above her engineering spaces. Nevertheless, an attempt was made by the cruisers Kato and Kinusaga to tow her, but the seas were not kind to the ruined carrier and although some progress was made that day, the following afternoon the tows had to be severed as worsening weather proved too much for the burned-out hulk and she joined the Saratoga on the seabed. The IJN had lost the first of its fleet carriers.

Chapter 7 - Borneo

Dec 24th

The Japanese force in Borneo comes into contact with the local forces covering the oilfields. While this is in fact only by a couple of patrols, the defenders panic and orders are given for the engineers to destroy the equipment. They do so with impressive thoroughness, and the civilians then split into a number of groups to get away from the Japanese landings - it is hoped to evacuate them later if the Japanese can be contained.

The Imperial troops sent to Borneo are meanwhile organising themselves in the south. The local transport system is poor, and it is intended to start moving north towards the Japanese on the following day. They are also impressing small craft to allow at least some of the force a faster passage along the coast.

The troops in Malaya are now all behind the defence line that has been built up over the last two weeks. The Japanese were expected to attack this immediately with the ferocity they had already shown in the initial battles, but instead have paused somewhat short of the prepared positions, although they have been aggressively patrolling. It is not clear if this is just a momentary pause to reorganise, or a more significant delay caused by problems with their logistical support. Reconnaissance shows the Japanese air force moving into the abandoned air bases in the north, although they are not yet properly operational - the British had time to properly demolish the runways and infrastructure, and it looks like the Japanese will be operating off non-hard strips, which is expected to prove difficult in bad weather.

The British have a number of men reporting from behind enemy lines (the jungle makes it quite easy to hide a small group of men, especially with support from the local population. They are starting to radio back reports, some worrying - the Japanese are treating the locals very badly, and the reconnaissance troops are trying to discover just what is going on, as they are having difficulty believing the actions that are being reported to them. There are also odd reports of the Japanese seeking out and impounding bicycles which Intelligence cannot work out. Reports that the enemy is also impounding coastal craft are more understandable - although any large vessels that could move were used to evacuate troops and civilians, many of the local fishermen refused to give up their boats, and though the bulk were hidden (for obvious reasons), the Japanese are steadily finding them.

In Europe, the RAF suspends bombing raids, officially for 3 days over the Christmas period, but actually for a week to take stock of the new pattern of raids it is employing. Results have been good; while the average raid has only been 400-500 aircraft, the increased accuracy of the new methods have made the bombing much more effective than in the previous year.

Dec 25th

The Soviet winter offensive continues to gain ground. The Germans have lost significant strength and are now at approximately 75 percent of their June strength, and Guderian has less than 40 panzers available.

Russian amphibious forces land on the Kerch Peninsula. Count von Sponeck's XLII Armeekorps is charged with guarding it and initially do well against the Soviets.

This evening the British forces in Hong Kong finally surrender. It has always been known that the colony could not hold out against any serious assault, and the defence has only been prolonged as a point of honour. The Canadian Brigade which was to have reinforced the colony has been diverted to Australia, as it was obvious it would not be possible to get it to Hong Kong in time due to the earlier shipping problems.

Admiral Chester W. Nimitz arrives at Pearl Harbor to assume command of the US Pacific Fleet.

Dec 26th

British intelligence calculate that the combination of RN and Dutch submarines, plus the activity of the Beaufighters, are sinking some 30% of the supplies that the Japanese are attempting to ship into Siam by sea. It has been noted that a significant increase in land-based traffic is ongoing, which is significant in view of how difficult this is with the relatively poor Siamese transport network.

General Yamashita orders the Imperial Guard division to move forward into Thailand; after the losses he has suffered he intends to use them to allow one of the original divisions time to recover. He has two more divisions available to him in Japan, and one will be moved to French Indo China as soon as shipping allows. Given the resistance put up so far, and his logistical issues in supplying more front-line troops, he is expecting it to take another 3-4 weeks to drive the British out and south from the current lines, especially with the problems his air support seem to be having. While he was given additional troops once the British build-up was noticed in the summer, the supply difficulties limit how many he can deploy at once.

The British land 260 commandos on Moskenesoy in the Lofoten Islands. Their mission is to destroy a fish-oil factory. This is Operation Anklet, targeted at the islands of Reine, Sund and Soervaagen and designed as a diversion for Operation Archery.

On hearing of the battle off Wake, Somerville gets permission from London to send a higher-ranking officer as liaison to the US Pacific fleet in Pearl Harbor. He also suggests a similar officer should be sent by the USN to Singapore or Columbo so the two navies can coordinate their intelligence and tactic more efficiently. While the loss of the Saratoga is of course sad, the reports that the US task force took out a Japanese fleet carrier make her loss worthwhile. Halsey's report has been honest about the problems that became evident, and Somerville is hoping to help the Americans in their early days of combat without raising too many hackles.

Somerville is also looking at his options for the use of the Far Eastern fleet. He has already ordered a small force of cruisers and destroyers east of Singapore to be ready to attack Japanese convoys to Borneo if possible, and make sure the Japanese surface fleet doesn't interfere with the Allied reinforcements in the south. He is still short of destroyers, and suggests that Admiral Hart and his ships could be based at Singapore to carry on fighting, backed by the heavy units of Force Z. He is trying to get intelligence as to when the Japanese carrier fleet that attacked Pearl Harbor could sortie south; such a powerful force would be difficult for him to stop with his present carrier force, especially if the Japanese replenish their land-based aviation. He hopes that actions by elements of Force Z and the USN can keep the Japanese off balance until he receives his promised reinforcements of ships and planes.

Dec 27th

The British land 600 commandos on Vaagso and Maaloy in the Lofoten Islands. These landings are on the heels of the landing yesterday, on Moskenesoy. Their targets today will be a fish-oil factory and a radio station. These are dummy targets to mask the real intention: an Enigma machine and weather codes at the weather station, on the "Vorstenboote", a 200-ton trawler. The boat was machine-gunned to cut down the crew but not to sink it.

MacArthur declares Manila an open city. US forces have fallen back to their 3rd defence line which runs east and west from Paniqui. This is upsetting to Churchill, who thinks that the Japanese should be made to pay for every inch of ground, and that it is unconscionable to allow them to take the capital of the islands at little cost. Alexander accordingly makes it known to the press that the Imperial forces will defend every inch and every town and city as hard and as long as possible. Alexander agrees on the condition that he has full operational control to NOT do this if he feels it necessary.

The RAF is getting further aircraft from Australia and the Middle East, although the versatile Beaufighters are still in high demand. Now that the Japanese are established in the north Malaya airfields, they are conducting small harassing and strafing raids over the British airfields and troops. The RAF and RAAF are responding in kind, and the better airfields, radar and the general toughness of the British forces mean that despite the undoubted skill of the Japanese pilots they are slowly losing the battle of attrition. In addition to the replacement planes, Park has been promised additional squadrons, including two of Wellingtons once they can be prised free of the Mediterranean Theatre. He has also asked for more of the long-range Whirlwind reconnaissance version to keep an eye on the Japanese ships in the South China Sea, and intends to use the Wellingtons for gardening operations against the Japanese ports. The problem he has is simply the size of the theatre; no one seemed to have realised before the war that a very long range would be needed, and so it is difficult for the British to cover anything much past the French Indo China southern coast. As a result Somerville is having to keep more of his T-class submarines on picket duty than he would like in order to try and make sure a heavy Japanese naval force doesn't take him by surprise.

The Japanese attempt to reinforce their bridgehead in Borneo with a convoy of four small merchant ships escorted by two destroyers. The convoy manages to evade the Allied air patrols in poor weather, but lose one of the transports (and have a second one damaged) to an attack by a Dutch submarine. Despite this setback, they manage to land another 600 troops plus supplies. The British have sent another 1,000 men from the recently arrived 18th division to Borneo, as the Dutch move forces further north. It is hoped that if they can contain any build-up the Allies will be able to defeat the attempt at invasion. The Dutch are also preparing for air strikes against the Japanese force, although they are reluctant to move too many of their available force from the Dutch East Indies, which they see as a target as soon as the Philippine Islands fall, which only seems like a matter of time.

Dec 28th

Alexander is considering ways of making the Japanese supply situation even more difficult - the worse this is, the more time the British have to reinforce and strengthen their defences. As the navy is making life difficult at sea, the planners are looking at ways to strike the coastal railway down the east coast of Thailand which is now the Japanese main supply artery. This is already being supplemented by forced labour - 'voluntary' in Thailand, not even that in Malaya, but cutting the rail line will make it far more difficult to move heavy equipment and supplies. A possible strike from carriers to the west has been considered (the east coast is considered too dangerous), possibly as part of a campaign to strike the airfields in the northwest. While Somerville has no objections to the idea, he points out that until he receives more aircraft he cannot reduce the full-strength squadrons he is maintaining due to the dangers of a heavy Japanese naval attack. It has been three weeks since the attack on Pearl Harbor, and he expects that the main Japanese carrier force will be available for a new deployment very soon. Until it commits itself, its strength means he has to be cautious about keeping his fighting power concentrated. The current preferred options are attacks by Special Forces and/or commandos, either infiltrated across the border or put ashore and recovered by submarine.

Preparations are started in the Middle East to move the newly formed Australian armoured division and a Brigade of the French Foreign Legion to the Far East. A shortage of troopships mean they can't be transported immediately - instead, the plan is to bring them out as soon as the troopships currently with the convoy heading east can return. While this is happening the ships carrying their equipment will be assembled in North Africa.

As well as Malaya, reinforcements are still arriving in Burma, which is seen as the next target for the Japanese. It is expected to shortly have four divisions plus an armoured brigade in place (although 1 Burma division is not considered sufficiently trained), plus the possible addition of up to two Chinese divisions to protect the

Burma Road. The main aim of Burma command is to hold the Japanese at bay until the monsoon season makes any major attack impossible; with the additional time this will bring, it is expected that Burma will be sufficiently supported to make a Japanese invasion impossible over the poor overland supply routes, so long as the Bay of Bengal remains impassable to Japanese troop convoys. Possession of the sea route will allow the British to move and reinforce troops, and in particular supplies, much more easily than the tracks which pass for roads in most of rural Burma.

Elements of the Japanese 33rd division have made a number of small incursions into southern Burma, presumably in advance of major operations planned soon. Since any forces attacking the country will have to share the same supply network as the army in Malaya, the interdiction of the coastal railway is moved up in priority.

Dec 29th

The Imperial forces landed at Kuching in Borneo contact the Japanese in the northern part of the country. Both sides suffer casualties as aggressive patrols run into each other. The Imperial troops have been having more success at 'borrowing' small craft to move up the coast. The Japanese policy of brutality is steadily spreading through the native population, and the mood of the natives towards their oriental 'liberators' is turning nasty.

Major General Lewis H Brereton, Commanding General Far East Air Force, arrives at his new headquarters at Darwin, Northern Territory.

The submarine HMS Triumph fails to return from patrol, thought to be the victim of a mine. The RN has been steadily clearing mines laid by the Japanese at the start of the war, but apparently their submarines are re-laying some of them.

Dec 30th

In Borneo, the Imperial formations make an attack on the Japanese. This is a confused affair of infantry actions in the jungle, and the Japanese, more experienced in jungle fighting, finally come out best, pushing the Allies back and inflicting 700 casualties for the loss of 500 men. While the Imperial forces reform, the Dutch expect to be able to make their own attack the following day, keeping up pressure on the Japanese. Both the RAF and the Dutch air force are flying patrol missions along the coast, and so far this seems to be deterring the Japanese from further reinforcing their position.

The US forces on Luzon fall back from positions at Tarlac. These are their last prepared positions before Bataan. They need to hold this line because the forces to the south must pass through Manila to get to Bataan - if they fail to hold here, they will be lost.

The air echelons of two USAAF Far East Air Force B-17 Flying Fortress squadrons arrive at Sinosari, Java, Netherlands East Indies, from Batchelor Field near Darwin, Northern Territory, Australia.

Admiral King is appointed CINCUS (Commander in Chief) - US Fleet. To avoid use of what he considers the pejorative acronym CINCUS, he introduces COMINCH

General Alexander and Admiral Somerville hold discussions with the Dutch as to where best to deploy to protect Borneo and the western part of the DEI. Borneo is a large country with poor communications, and realistically a successful defence will require control of the sea. However if it can be held it will force the Japanese into a single line of attack through the DEI, unless they in turn can control the sea area. After considerable discussions the Dutch agree to place their naval forces under British overall command, as the Far Eastern Fleet is obviously the heavy naval force in the area. As a start, aggressive patrols by light forces of cruisers and destroyers will continue, with the capital ships being held ready to contest any attempt by Japan to move into the area with heavy ships.

As a result of these decisions, London is informed of the need for more aircraft as soon as possible to control the eastern part of the sea area. While a considerable number of aircraft are on the convoy heading east, the longer-range planes can make it their on their own through the established air routes. The USAAF is also asked if it can provide planes to help, pointing out that the further forward the Japanese can be held the easier it will be to retake the Philippines. Discussions are ongoing to move Admiral Hart's remaining ships to bases in the DEI and Singapore. As a result of the telegrams to London, that evening HMS Ark Royal, HMS Renown and a destroyer escort enter the Suez Canal.

Dec 31st

Two of the RN's T-class submarines are recalled from patrol to take part in Operation Stiletto. A force of SOE-trained men and Australian volunteers is already training for their part in the operation.

General Yamashita is pushing the Imperial Guard forward as fast as possible; he needs these troops for his planned new offensive in Malaya. There has been considerable discussion in the army about which coast is the best for an advance; in the end the west has been chosen due to the far superior transport network (the Japanese supply officers in Thailand and French Indo China are starting to get nervous tics when pushed on the issues of supply shortages), and the eastern coast is only viable if the Japanese navy controls the sea, which they don't. A number of diversions will be conducted on the east coast, using coastal craft if possible. He hopes to have all the men in place in a few days.

The Japanese attempt another night raid against Singapore. This is again roughly handled by the radar-equipped night fighters, and thirteen bombers are lost out of 50 for the cost of light damage to an airfield and the city. As a result Somerville thinks it will be possible to station heavier forces in Singapore, although he does point out that if the Japanese start to conduct effective air raids he will be obliged to pull them back again.

Chapter 8 - A New Year

Jan 1st 1942

The Chinese request lend-lease aid for construction of a road across northern Burma to link with the Burma Road. The projected road would extend from Ledo, India, to Fort Hertz and Myitkyina, Burma, and Lung-ling, China.

The RAF conducts a heavy raid against Italian oil storage facilities near Rome, leaving half the storage tanks aflame, the planes flying on to North Africa to refuel. On their return trip, they make another raid, this time on armament works.

Dutch troops attack the Japanese in Borneo, aided by air strikes from the Dutch air force, including heavy strafing operations by the Dutch Buffalo squadrons. This time the situation is less confused than the initial attacks by the Allies, and although the Dutch do not push the Japanese back, both sides lose about 500 men killed and wounded. The Allied force to the south has reformed after its initial defeat, and will strike north tomorrow to put further pressure on the Japanese.

Jan 2nd

Japanese troops occupy the remains of Cavite naval base as well as the capital of Manila as US forces withdraw to the Bataan peninsula. This is good news to the Japanese army, who immediately start looking at options to redeploy some of the troops, and in particular, the transports they have been using, to other areas which are not progressing as well.

President Roosevelt announces the beginning of the Liberty Ship program, the construction of 200 merchant ships of a standardized design. This is welcomed by the British, as while the opening of the Mediterranean and the use of North African supplies has eased their shipping situation, the new requirements in the Far East are threatening to overwhelm existing capacity. This is not helped by the need to move large numbers of troops and the lack of a US sealift capability.

Lieutenant General Hugh A. Drum, Commanding General First Army, tentatively selected for a field command in China, arrives in Washington, D.C. where he confers with various military leaders, finding widely divergent opinions as to role of U.S. in China.

The Imperial Borneo force strikes the Japanese positions while they are still recovering from the Dutch attack - a rather fortuitous timing. This time the force keeps pressing the Japanese, who finally start to pull back after suffering over 600 casualties to the Imperial losses of some 400.

Jan 3rd

During the night of 3/4 January, RAF Bomber Command dispatches ten planes on a mine-laying mission in the Frisian Islands; one aircraft is lost.

In Washington President Roosevelt and British Prime Minister Churchill announce the creation of a unified command in the Southwest Pacific, with British General Alexander as supreme commander of American-British-Dutch-Australian (ABDA) forces in that area. General Alexander is directed

(1) To hold the Malay Barrier (the line Malay Peninsula-Sumatra-Java-Northern Australia) and operate as far beyond the barrier as possible in order to check the Japanese advance

(2) Hold Malaya, Burma and Australia

(3) Restore communications with the Philippine Islands through the Netherlands East Indies

(4) Maintain communications within the theatre

Above all, Alexander's forces, mostly Australians and British, are to hold Australia and Burma. In another move, Chinese Generalissimo Chiang Kai-shek is named Commander in Chief of Allied Forces in China. The Arcadia Conference makes Chiang Kai-shek, a Chinese leader, the leader of Allied troops stationed in and around China. In order to relieve Alexander of direct responsibility for Malaya, General Blamey is appointed head of ground forces in Malaya, a promotion which is popular in Australia.

Military planners come to the realization that it will be impossible to reinforce the Philippine Islands and the troops in those islands are doomed. When told of this, Secretary of War Henry L. Stimson notes, "There are times when men must die."

Jan 4th

Japanese Lieutenant General Homma, Commanding General 14th Army, meets with Manila Mayor Jorge Vargas. Homma imposes a Japanese Military Administration under Major General Hayashi. He imposes a curfew, blackout, martial law, firearms turn-in, a ban on radio transmissions and listening to non-Japanese statements. He also warns that any hostile act against the Japanese will result in ten Filipinos dying for every Japanese that is killed. All industries, factories, banks, schools, churches, and printing presses must come under Japanese control. The flying of the Filipino or U.S. flags or singing of the "Star-Spangled Banner" is forbidden.

The Japanese begin an air offensive against Rabaul on New Britain Island, the strategic base in the Bismarck Archipelago, garrisoned by 5,400 men (principally the Australian 2/22d Battalion, 8th Division; an RAAF detachment; 100 men of the New

Guinea Volunteer Reserve; and a few Royal Australian Navy officers). Located at Rabaul are a fighter strip at Lakunai and a bomber strip at Vunakanu.

The Imperial Guards division makes a series of probing attacks on the British defensive line in Malaya. These are beaten off (in some cases with difficulty). The Imperial Guards have a reputation as fearless troops, but they have no recent combat experience. The British have built up defensive positions supported by artillery and small armoured units, which while discommoded by attempts to attack by infiltration have no great difficulty in holding their positions and wiping out the Japanese units in the rear. After the first day Blamey informs Malaya command that the Japanese appear to have no new tactics or equipment, and his experienced Australian troops are confident that unless the circumstances change considerably in favour of the Japanese they can be held here. Unfortunately, it is likely that nothing but local counterattacks can be made until the reinforcement convoy arrives later in the month.

In the Mediterranean British and Greek commandos start what will be a series of raids against the Greek coast. As with the raids in Norway, the main purpose is to keep the Italians off balance and occupied while the Allies build up strength for a major amphibious operation.

Jan 5th

Carried away by recent small successes and against the advice of his chief of general staff, General Zhukov, Stalin orders his army to undertake a general offensive along the entire Eastern Front.

U.S. Forces in Australia (USFIA) is redesignated U.S. Army Forces in Australia (USAFIA), and Major General Brett assumes command. Headquarters is located in the MacRobertson Girls High School in Melbourne, Victoria.

The last of the reinforcements planned for Burma before the Japanese attacked, 17th Indian Division, start to arrive in theatre. Also arriving are Hurricanes diverted from the Russian shipments, which have been assembled and then flown in. In fact the current shortage is of pilots, and Middle East command is currently gathering transport planes; the convoy that left Britain last month has dropped off pilots and ground crew in North Africa, from whence they will be flown to Burma. While some spares and other operational equipment were part of the Russian supply, further equipment and stores will have to wait on the convoys.

The steady, if low-level, attacks against Italy in the Mediterranean are causing political problems in Italy. There is considerable pressure on the Italian Government to bring back some of the large Italian forces in Russia to defend Italy and allow them to respond to the Allied attacks. Mussolini refuses to withdraw Italian troops, pointing out it is necessary to support Germany as they had been supporting Italy; a compromise is reached, where Italy will suggest reducing the army in Russia. This actually has a certain amount of support from some German generals, who would rather have their limited logistics supporting German soldiers than what they see as poor-quality Italian ones.

The attack by the Imperial Guards division continues to press the Australian defence. Undeterred by what seem to the defenders to be heavy losses, they are managing to push back the line in a number of places. Blamey responds by bringing forward some of the Indian division held in reserve to help seal off the infiltration attacks the Japanese are using. While this works better in theory than practice - the idea being for the defenders to hold firm when attacked from the rear, while the fresh troops attack the Japanese in their own rear, in practice it tends to result in a number of confused actions with each side surprising each other - it succeeds in blunting the attack. By nightfall, the Japanese have been pushed back to their start lines with considerable losses, the inexperience of the Japanese formations showing.

The British forces in Borneo pause to regroup and bring up supplies (always a difficult task here), allowing the Japanese to reform their perimeter, although they have been pushed back a considerable distance. The Allies are maintaining as strong a reconnaissance as possible, as they think it likely the Japanese will try to reinforce by sea again.

Jan 6th

The Second Marine Brigade (Brigadier General Larsen, USMC) embarked in troop transports SS Lurline, SS Monterey and SS Matsonia, and cargo ship USS Jupiter and ammunition ship USS Lassen   sails from San Diego, California, for Pago Pago, American Samoa. The initial escort is provided by Task Force 17 (Rear Admiral Fletcher), formed around aircraft carrier USS Yorktown.

During the night the Japanese land an amphibious force at Brunei Bay, having managed to evade detection in poor weather (at present, the Allies have no radar-equipped search planes able to cover the area off northern Borneo). They land an additional 800 men and supplies for the original detachment, which has been running very short of ammunition after the encounters with the Allied forces.

The Japanese Imperial Guard Division makes a final effort to break through the Australian defence line. This is the first time Imperial troops have encountered what will come to be known as Banzai Charges, as the Imperial Guard manage to force a break in the defence line. Although the local troops are overwhelmed, the experienced Australians refuse to panic, and close up, allowing the Japanese to push through the gap. However there is a full division in reserve behind the line, and while some of it has been used to close off infiltration attacks, the Japanese find themselves facing a full brigade of infantry, with armour attached. The tanks and artillery support from the Australians still in place to either side of the breakthrough allow Blamey to pinch it off, and by the following morning, it is the Japanese who are surrounded, the defence line having reformed, albeit with considerable difficulty. The situation is often confused by the fact that the 'defence line' is in fact nothing of the sort, rather a line of mutually supporting positions.

In order to try and pinch off more landings by the Japanese in Borneo, the light carrier HMAS Brisbane with an escort of the cruisers HMAS Australia and HMAS Hobart, plus escort destroyers, arrives at Singapore. The force is commanded by Admiral Crace, who hopes to conduct sweeps up the Borneo coast to allow his planes to find and sink Japanese supply convoys in the north. The force will be supported by fighters operating from land bases in the south of the country. This is a calculated risk by Somerville, as the air threat in the area would indicate a force of two fleet carriers would be more suitable, but he is reluctant to commit such a high proportion of his air strength when the intentions of the main Japanese fleet are still unknown. It is also looking like more troops will need to be sent to Borneo, and ships are being readied in Singapore to travel under the protection of the RAN force. Four of the RN U-class boats as well as the Dutch submarines are ordered north and northeast of Borneo to target Japanese ships.

Somerville is also wondering what to do with the fairly large number of old US submarines soon to arrive in Singapore from the US Asiatic Fleet. While the base can do much of the maintenance, major equipment failures will be a problem, and a bigger issue is the lack of torpedoes. An urgent request has been made to the USN to deliver at least the torpedoes and ammunition for the deck guns. In the meantime, he is waiting on his suggestion to Admiral Hart to use some of the boats for the Stiletto operations, allowing them to unload most of their torpedoes to allow other boats to go on patrol with larger loadouts. Hart agrees this would be sensible, but has to wait on permission from Washington.

Jan 7th

The siege of Bataan begins as U .S. and Filipino forces complete their withdrawal from the Layac Line.

In Malaya the 8th Indian Division makes an attack on the pocket of the Japanese Imperial Guard trapped behind the Allies defensive lines. Even though the Japanese have little in the way of heavy weapons, it takes the Indians two days to finally snuff out the pocket. Of the 2,000 Japanese troops trapped, only around 100 are captured, all of them injured. The Indians take nearly a 1,000 casualties themselves, despite their advantages in artillery and armour.

Alexander and Blamey are concerned that more attacks of this ferocity could rupture the defence lines and force a withdrawal further south. It is decided to replace the Australian Brigade that has suffered the brunt of the attacks to the rear to regroup and recover, while a brigade of the 18th British division replaces them. The 8th Indian will remain as a reserve formation behind the line to attack and contain any Japanese units that infiltrate or break through the lines. Meanwhile the engineers will start work on a defence line further south, in case it is found necessary to withdraw.

In fact, the British are overestimating the Japanese capability to attack. So far Yamashita has had two divisions gutted and is short of some supplies, in particularly artillery ammunition. Due to the difficulty of moving safely by sea the troops are arriving overland from French Indo China, which takes longer, and he estimates it will take a week to reorder his formations for a new attack. The British are concerned at what they see as a lack of reserves - they have four divisions deployed forward, and a division's worth of forces held back further south, as well as two brigades of the 18th Division, but until the next convoys arrive they have no more available troops and Borneo (and further ahead the Dutch East Indies) is looking at taking an increasing number of men. They are also in need of replacement tanks; due to attrition and breakdowns, the 1st Armoured (which had not started at full strength) is down to about 120 operational tanks. While the tactics to repel the Japanese attacks have proven successful, the heavy drain they have made in the reserves of artillery shells and machine gun ammunition will need to be addressed before any serious attack can be made.

Intelligence puts the Japanese forces at five divisions in place with another on its way from French Indo China, and possibly more to follow - the estimate is quite accurate, but the British do not realise that currently two of the divisions are tasked to attack Burma, and that two are in no fit state to attack for a while. The Japanese practice of attempting complex interlocking operations with minimal troop strength and logistics has yet to be appreciated by the analysts. The situation in the air is seen as equally balanced. The air defences have made Singapore too hard a target (although if the Japanese can push further south, close enough to escort their daylight attacks with fighters, that will change), and currently the losses on both sides seem fairly even. The RAF feels it now has the measure of the Japanese planes except for the Zero, which continues to cause problems and catch unwary or inexperienced pilots. The need to base aircraft in Singapore and Borneo has stopped any serious attempt at an air offensive for the time being. Alexander orders that Operation Stiletto be advanced as much as possible - his pressing need is to delay the Japanese reinforcements until his supply convoys start to arrive.

Jan 8th

In Baghdad, a court sentences Rashid Ali, who led an anti-British coup last year, to death in absentia.
With more Japanese troops having arrived in Borneo, the British feel they have no alternative but to deploy more of the 18th Division. A further 2,000 men arrive today in a convoy escorted by the RAN task force. The Allies now have fighter cover over the southern part of Borneo, but a lack of suitable airfields (and the proximity of Japanese troops) means that the northern part of the island is uncontested. The Dutch promise to find another 500 men to reinforce their force in the north.

A new attack is made against the existing Japanese positions; this is intended to be a joint attack by Australian and Dutch units, but the lack of practice at joint operations mean that the attacks go in piecemeal. The Australians lose some 200 men, the Dutch around 150, for an estimated loss of some 250 Japanese troops.

Alexander is more doubtful of the possibility of holding Borneo in the long term - if the Dutch East Indies fall it will be easy for the Japanese to put in an overwhelming force. In order to prepare for the worst case, a small group of British and Australian officers is sent to Sumatra, their mission to determine the best way and the forces needed to defend it. This is vital to the defence of Singapore; no matter what happens in the north, if Sumatra falls, it will not be possible to get supply convoys through to Singapore. Alexander is also looking at the possibility of ordering a small spoiling attack from Burma to distract the Japanese from pushing further south into Malaya.

Jan 10th

General Zhukov has launched a powerful offensive against the German "winter line" that runs from Bryansk north through Vyazma to Rzhev. The Red Army, unlike the Germans, has no intention of stopping in place until the warm weather comes, and is forcing Germany into a retreat which, in places, is becoming a rout.

The Russians have taken Mosalsk, on the road to Smolensk, and are threatening to encircle the German base at Mozhaisk. They have also nearly surrounded 100,000 Germans at Demyansk. Field Marshal Ritter Von Leeb asks Hitler for permission to retreat. The Fuhrer refuses.

The USN Bureau of Ships orders that the Cleveland Class light cruiser Amsterdam (CL-59), which is under construction in Camden, New Jersey, be completed as an aircraft carrier (CV). She will be commissioned as USS Independence (CV-22) on 14 January 1943 and be reclassified as a small aircraft carrier (CVL-22) on 15 July 1943. This is the first of nine light cruisers that are completed as small aircraft carriers.

Chapter 9 - The Dutch East Indies

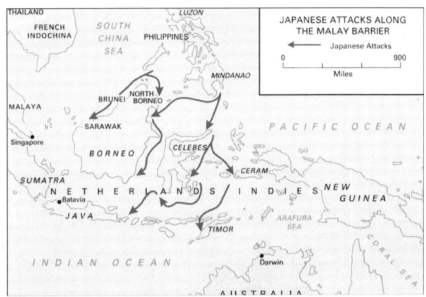

Map 4 - The Malay Barrier

Jan 11th

The invasion of the oil-rich Dutch East begins when the Japanese use paratroopers for the first time. They land on Menado, on Celebes, and take Langoan air base. The Dutch garrison fight hard against the Japanese, who also made an assault by sea from sixteen transports, but were forced to surrender after setting fire to their oilfields. Fighter cover from the Philippines meant that Dutch planes missed spotting the ships. The area is difficult to cover with fighters, as the available airfields are not that close and the Japanese now have ample air bases in the Philippines. The Allied command instead tasks a number of submarines into the area in an attempt to interdict follow-up convoys. Oil is critical to the Japanese, and the Dutch East Indies is the most accessible source of it.

The Japanese invade at two points. The central assault force, consisting of the 56th Regimental Group and the 2nd Kure Special Naval Landing Force (SNLF), with air support from Jolo Island in the Philippines, lands at oil rich Tarakan Island at midnight. The eastern assault force from Davao, Mindanao, consisting of the Sasebo Combined SNLF and the 1st Yokosuka SNLF, invades Celebes Island at Menado and Kema at approximately 0300 hours. A Japanese Naval paratroop force of 334 men is dropped on the airfield just south of Menado and suffers heavy casualties (30 dead and 90 injured). Dutch planes are unable to halt the Japanese, and the small Dutch garrisons are quickly overwhelmed. The Japanese soon put Tarakan and

Menado into use as air bases from which to support operations to the south. This landing in Borneo is another threat to be met by the small Allied force on the island.

The Dutch request air support from the Americans, both fighters to be based locally and heavy bomber support (probably from Australia). Currently however the USAAF does not have much in the area. Planning is advanced by Somerville's staff for possible ABDA operations in the DEI area, bearing in mind that unless more fighters are made available it is likely they will be working in a hostile air environment.

The Naval Station Pago Pago in Samoa is shelled by a Japanese submarine.

Operation Paukenschlag ("roll of the kettledrums") descends upon the eastern seaboard of the U.S. like a bolt from the blue. The first group of five German submarines takes up station off the east coast of the United States on this date. Over the next month, these will sink 26 Allied ships; the presence of the enemy off the eastern seaboard takes U.S. Navy antisubmarine forces by surprise. It is far less of a surprise to the Royal Navy, who felt it was only a matter of time before the dense East Coast traffic was attacked, and in fact had repeatedly told the USN this.

The Combined Chiefs of Staff (CCS) approve U.S. plans to garrison the islands along the proposed ferry route from Hawaii to Australia. Local defence forces are to be based at American Samoa, Bora Bora, Canton Island, Christmas Island, the Fiji Islands and Palmyra Island. The CCS also approves the deployment of a USAAF fighter squadron to New Caledonia Island in the New Hebrides Islands. There has been considerable controversy over this, which is seen by some as abandoning positions in the Malay barrier in order to carry out purely precautionary operations.

On Bataan, the Japanese exert strong pressure against the II Corps, particularly on the west, while taking up positions for a concerted assault. The 51st Division, is hard hit and gives ground, some of which is regained after reserves are committed. In the centre the Japanese push back the outpost line of the 41st Division.

Three USAAF B-17's arrive in Australia after flying a new southern ferry route from Hawaii. It is hoped that this can be built up quickly enough to be able to aid the defence of the DEI.

The Japanese submarine HIJMS I-121 mines Clarence Strait, the body of water connecting Van Diemen Gulf and the Timor Sea, off Australia's Northern Territory, at the approaches to Darwin, the Asiatic Fleet's main logistics base.

The wartime Office of Price Administration said standard frankfurters would be replaced by "victory sausages", consisting of a mixture of meat and soy meal. The true costs of the war are starting to be felt in America.

Jan 13th

Allied troops in Borneo are slowly closing in on the Japanese invasion force, slowed by the poor transport system (despite making all available use of small coastal boats), and the need to bring up artillery. The sweep by Admiral Crace's squadron has not detected any shipping on the west coast, and after the landings on the northeast part of the island it is expected that the Japanese will reinforce there under cover of their own fighters. Before withdrawing south the carrier uses its bombers to attack the Japanese supply dumps, still near the coast; while no significant damage is done the raid does make the defenders waste time moving their supplies under better cover.

The Dutch commander on Tarakan Island surrenders to the Japanese and they complete mopping up the island. The Japanese assault force boards ships the next day for the assault on Balikpapan, leaving a small force to defend the island. The assumption is that the Allies cannot attack the island, as they will be unwilling to risk shipping under the Japanese air umbrella. However a battalion of Dutch troops, originally tasked for the earlier invasion, is detached to head north in the hope that something can be done to take the Japanese by surprise.

The Soviet Army has driven deep a salient between the German 2nd Panzer and 4th Armies on the central front southwest of Kaluga; the salient deepens with the capture of Kirov.

The U-boats taking part in 'Drum Roll' are surprised to find peacetime conditions on the U.S. coast, with lighthouses and marker buoys still lit. In addition, there is no radio silence and positions of merchant ships are frequently given away in radio communications. These conditions and the inexperience of the USN escort vessels lead to a loss of 150,000 tons of shipping in the first month of the operation.

Jan 14th

Following their seizure of Kirov yesterday, Soviet forces recapture Medya, on the central front northwest of Kaluga, driving a wedge between two Panzer divisions.

The headquarters of the USAAF's Far East Air Force transfers from Darwin in Australia to Malang in Java. Three squadrons of the 7th Bombardment Group, equipped with B-17's, begin operations out of Singosari in Java. The USAAF hope that they will be able to slow the Japanese advance into the area by attacking their convoys. Although the RAF are somewhat dubious of the ability of the USAAF to engage ships at sea, there is hope that with sufficient reconnaissance the aircraft can do considerable damage if the convoys can be caught in harbour. The main problem the Allied air forces have is the distances involved; until the Japanese invaders at Labuan can be destroyed, it is not practical to base Beaufighters (the preferred aircraft for convoy interdiction) close enough to the Japanese convoy routes.

A Japanese naval force leaves Guam, destination Rabaul in New Britain.

The Japanese army sends 27 Sally bombers, escorted by 15 Oscar fighters, to raid Rangoon in Burma. With ground activity in Malaya temporarily halted to allow Yamashita's divisions to reorganise, the army is hoping that the heavy air defences shown in Malaya mean that Burma has only been left with light defences. To a certain extent, they are correct; Malaya is more heavily and more effectively defended in the air than is Burma. However since the build-up started in the Far East the Burmese air force has not been completely neglected, and while the radar coverage is not comprehensive as it is in southern Malaya there is at least coverage of the major targets such as Rangoon.

The RAF in Burma is rather surprised they have not been attacked earlier; this is thought to be due to the steady losses the Japanese air force has been suffering in Malaya. The fact of the raid is a worry to Alexander, as it implies that the Japanese air force has replaced its losses. The time given to the RAF has allowed the air defences of the country to be improved considerably since the beginning of December. Although no more Sparrowhawks or Beaufighters over the original squadron of each have been delivered (the need for these aircraft in Malaya has meant all fresh aircraft have been sent to Singapore), there is now support from the Flying Tigers (flying US P-40's), and four squadrons of Hurricanes (diverted from the supplies originally intended for Russia) are now operational.

The attack is spotted on radar, although the operators are still inexperienced and it takes longer than expected to get the defenders into the air. The result of the raid is that some damage is done to the dock area of Rangoon, only one bomber being shot down by the AA. In the air battle that takes place over the city, the Japanese lose four Oscar fighters and another six Sallys for the loss of four Hurricanes and two P-40's, with another four aircraft damaged.

Bomber command resumes their campaign against German industry with a heavy raid by 300 planes on Hamburg, causing considerable damage to the dockyards and the railway system.

Jan 15th

In Russia, Army Group Centre (Field Marshal von Kluge) evacuates the Kaluga sector and takes up winter positions 20 miles further west. While Hitler is still insisting on holding ground wherever possible, the realities of the Russian winter is forcing some backwards movement to more suitable positions onto the German Army.

Troops of the Japanese 55th Division advance into Burma north of Mergui. The aim is to reduce a possible attack by the British which would cause problems for the Japanese army attacking into Malaya. The British only have light forces this far into Burma, as the narrow strip of land abutting Thailand has always been seen as indefensible against serious attack. The attack is supported by the Japanese air force, and due to the distance from the British airfields it is difficult to mount any practical defence. The RAF in Burma responds to the previous day's attack, and this new invasion, with raids by Blenheim bombers on some of the Japanese airfields in Thailand. Four Blenhiems and three escorting Hurricanes are shot down for the loss of four Oscars in the air, but a number of Japanese aircraft are destroyed on the ground and disruption caused to their operations.

The British ground forces start a slow retreat up the narrow peninsula, destroying roads and bridges as they go to slow the Japanese attack. There is concern that they could be cut off by an attack further north; in this case it is hoped to evacuate the men by sea, and light coastal craft have been assembled at Rangoon with this in mind.

Jan 16th

Three USAAF LB-30 Liberators based at Singosari Airdrome on Java, staged through Kendari Airdrome on Celebes Island, attack Tarakan Airdrome on Tarakan Island. Two of the bombers are damaged by Japanese aircraft and both are further damaged when they crash land in remote places. These are the first missions of the Liberator, and the USAAF is disappointed to find that the heavy bomber is having such difficulty defending itself without fighter escort.

Japanese submarines continue mining the approaches to Darwin, as seventeen P-40's of the USAAF's Far East Air force use the port as a staging area to reach Java.

In northern Malaya Yamashita mounts a limited attack on the eastern part of the Imperial defence line, hoping it might not be as well defended as he has found the western part to be. Unfortunately for him it is, and after probing attacks against Australian and Indian troops he pulls back to his start lines having lost some 500 men.

In Borneo, the Allies mount a full-scale attack against the original Japanese invasion. Despite having to withdraw some of the men planned for use, they still outnumber the Japanese over 2:1, and have the advantage of air support. The Japanese are also very short of supplies, especially artillery shells, having been forced into far more extensive actions than had been originally planned. As a result the attack makes good progress, although the attackers suffer heavily from the fanatical defence and the Japanese lines are finally broken by a shore bombardment by Admiral Crace's heavy cruisers. By nightfall the attackers are confident that they will have eliminated the positions in a few days.

Jan 17th

Hitler has been busy removing some of the Generals he sees as having failed him by not achieving victory in Russia. He sacked Field Marshal Walter von Brauchitsch on the 19th of December and took the opportunity to make himself C-in-C of the army.

General Guderian was sacked on Christmas Eve for a withdrawal in defiance of Hitler's orders.

Field Marshal von Leeb, the commander of Army Group North, resigned yesterday after Hitler refused permission to retreat from Demyansk where 100,000 men are nearly surrounded. Another Field Marshal, von Bock of Army Group Centre, was relieved on 20 December at his own request because of stomach trouble brought on by his failure to take Moscow. Field Marshal von Rundstedt of Army Group South was sacked for telling Hitler it was madness not to retreat after the loss of Rostov. Today von Reichenau, who took over from von Rundstedt, died when his plane crashed while flying him to Leipzig for a staff meeting. Hitler is now in supreme command.

A heavy series of raids by French medium bombers out of Malta causes considerable damage to Italian installations and airfields in Sicily. This comes as a surprise to the Italians - the area around Malta has been relatively quiet of late, and as a consequence the defences in Sicily are rather caught by surprise. The raids target ports and airfields in particular, causing the Italian command to start to worry at the possibility that this is a prelude to further action or even an invasion.

On Bataan, the II Corps counterattacks to restore the western portion of the line, and makes limited progress. The U.S. 31st Infantry, moving north from the Abucay Hacienda area, reaches the Balantay River on the left but is unable to make much headway on the right. Reserves move forward to plug a gap between the assault battalions. The Japanese encircling column begins an unopposed march down the Abo-Abo River toward Orion. In the I Corps area, the defenders of Moron fall back under enemy pressure to a ridge south and southeast of Moron.

The Japanese Carrier Striking Force sails to participate in operations in the Bismarck Archipelago.

The Japanese air force continues to make raids into Burma, although General Yamashita protests that they should be concentrating on Malaya - he sees Burma as an unnecessary diversion at this point in the campaign. The raids do cause the RAF to lose a number of aircraft on the ground, and damage is caused to Rangoon again, with a steady trickle of losses in the air for both sides. So far the RAF in Burma is confident that they can cope with this level of attack, particularly as substantial reinforcements of Hurricanes are on their way via the Middle East.

Using the dark of the moon for concealment, Operation Stiletto kicked off last night, using two British and three US submarines. They slip up the east coast of Malaya, reaching the Thai border after dark. Using small boats the submarines put some 200 commandos and volunteers ashore in ten groups. The men head for the vital rail line that goes down the coast, along which the bulk of Yamashita's supplies are being transported. Their main aims are any parts of the railway that will be difficult to repair - bridges, cuttings, any part where an explosion can collapse rock onto the line, as well as the line itself.

While the Japanese have guards along the line, they view it as an easy post, mainly to deter the local population from doing anything. They are completely unprepared for the raiding parties that slip out of the dark and slit their throats before planting explosives on the track. The raiders fall back to their submarines that night, only losing nine men in total. The submarines head out from the coast and then submerge to prepare to sit out the day on the bottom. By the time the men are heading back to their boats, the handful of men left to detonate the charges see the rail line cut in at last 22 places, many of them in positions that will be difficult to repair, as well as taking down a number of bridges. The only disappointment to them is the lack of any trains running - they would have dearly loved to blow a bridge with a train on it. Yamashita's already tight logistical situation just got a lot worse.

Jan 18th

Burma's Prime Minister, U Maung Saw, was arrested in Haifa when his plane touched down while he was returning to Burma from talks with British representatives. He had been trying unsuccessfully to secure a British promise of Burmese independence in return for supporting the war effort. The nationalist U Maung Saw is unpopular with the British authorities, who see him of suspect loyalty. This suspicion is now justified, because he contacted Japan's legation in Lisbon on his return flight. He was unaware that Britain had broken Japanese codes and knew of these overtures.

The Allies continue to mop up the Japanese forces at Labuan, at the cost of considerable losses themselves; the Japanese infantry fight to the last, and the RAN cruisers have had to withdraw southward after an abortive attack from some ten Japanese bombers - although the cruisers escaped without damage, they were considered too valuable to risk on just a fire support mission.

A Japanese convoy anchors at Sandakan in northern Borneo. Due to bad weather (monsoon rains and wind), the convoy remains in the port during the day. As a result of the weather, the Japanese troops had not unloaded and so did not take the effectively undefended port, but the Allies are now aware of its presence. Admiral Crace asks permission from Somerville to engage in a night attack, which is given. His force moves north up the western coast that day, and by 2300 is in position to launch an attack on the ships. His light carrier holds twelve SeaLance and twelve Cormorants, and all are launched (with some difficulty in the poor weather).

Due to the limited preparation, not all the planes manage to find the port - six of the Cormorants never manage to locate it, and have to head back to the carrier. The remaining aircraft spot the anchored transports illuminated by their flares. They only spot two transport ships, and the dive bombers are found not to be needed as the torpedo planes sink both of them. Gunfire is noticed from a number of large fishing boats also in the harbour (these had been carrying many of the men), and the aircraft strafe these, setting some on fire before they withdraw. Crace sets sail southwards after recovering his aircraft, to get under cover of the fighters at Kuching before the Japanese air force has a chance to respond. While the strike has destroyed the invaders equipment and most of their supplies, it has only killed a few of the troops who were being carried on the fishing boats. With only their small arms now available the Japanese commander now has to decide whether to land or retreat the next morning.

Jan 19th

Reports from Sandakan indicate the Japanese only have a few hundred men ashore, and with the pockets around Labuan finally wiped out, 400 Ghurkhas, on any transport that can be found, set off for the port that afternoon in the hope of surprising the Japanese before they can be reinforced.

Nine USAAF Far East Air Force B-17's out of Singosari Airdrome on Java are dispatched to attack shipping at Jolo Island in the Philippine Islands. Three aircraft abort due to weather but the remaining six bomb the ships and then land at Del Monte Field on Mindanao Island in the Philippines, which is still under American control.

Intelligence reports (mainly traffic analysis) indicate that the Japanese carriers are at sea and heading somewhere. At the moment, there is no idea where they are, the force maintaining radio silence. However Somerville has to assume that they might be headed for Singapore, and in any case the increasing Japanese activity in the Dutch East Indies requires some sort of response (if only to make the Japanese more cautious and slow them down). It helps that the Pillar convoy is due to arrive off Ceylon tomorrow morning; he intends to use a substantial force to escort it to Singapore and then reinforce Crace.

Chapter 10 - The Bismark Archipelago

Jan 20th

Mozhaisk, about 60 miles west of Moscow, falls to the Russian army.

Major General Brett, Commanding General US Army Forces in Australia (USAFIA), halts ferrying of aircraft from India to the Netherlands East Indies. The USAAF has been sending heavy bombers to Java by way of Africa and India, but the Japanese are able to inflict prohibitive losses on the aircraft on the last stops of the route by interception from newly acquired airfields close to Java. Since Singapore is still considered safe, and with the Japanese air force currently occupied in the north and in Burma, the bombers will operate from the RAF bases in southern Malaya until it is possible to safely move them further forward. Park warns that the operations will be limited due to shortages of aviation fuel, although the keenly anticipated convoy does have a tanker carrying more.

A Dutch Dornier flying boat spots a small vessel off the coast of Samboaja, heading for Balikpapan, Borneo. The flying boat lands near the vessel, the motor boat Parsifal, and takes aboard a two Dutch officer captured on Tarakan Island and three Japanese soldier-interpreters, flying them to Balikpapan. They carry a message from the Japanese to the Balikpapan Garrison Commander, demanding that the oil refinery installations there be handed over to the Japanese Army without being damaged; this offer is refused by the Dutch commander and the three Japanese were returned to their units.

Ninety Japanese carrier-based aircraft from the aircraft carriers HIJMS Akagi, HIJMS Kaga, HIJMS Shokaku and HIJMS Zuikaku attack Rabaul on New Britain Island in the Bismark Archipelago, causing serious damage. No. 24 Squadron RAAF loses six aircraft (three shot down, one wrecked after take-off and two damaged in crash landings) leaving two Wirraways in commission. The squadron commander sends the following message to Northeast Area HQ: "Two Wirraways useless in defence. Will you now please send some fighters?" Kavieng on New Ireland Island is also attacked by air but by a smaller force.

The U.S. Second Marine Brigade (Brigadier General Larson) arrives at Pago Pago on Tutuila Island, America Samoa, in transports SS Lurline, SS Matsonia, and SS Monterey, along with cargo ship USS Jupiter and ammunition ship USS Lassen, to protect that portion of the important lifeline to Australia. Cover for the operation is provided by Task Force 8 (TF 8) formed around aircraft carrier USS Enterprise 6) (Vice Admiral Halsey) and TF 17 (Rear Admiral Fletcher) formed around aircraft carrier USS Yorktown. The two carrier task forces then set course for the Japanese-held Marshalls and Gilberts to carry out the initial raids on the enemy's defensive perimeter. There is growing political unrest at the scale of these essentially defensive actions far from the action taking place in the Philippines and the Dutch East Indies; while some defence of the islands is required, some see it as too heavy and taking away the men available to fight the Japanese before they overrun the Dutch East Indies as they already have the Philippines. At least one political opponent of Roosevelt has been heard to comment 'when we surrender to the Japanese we will at least have the best-defended rear areas in the world'.

General Yamashita receives his engineers' reports on the damage to the rail line, and it is very bad news for his campaign. Thailand is not overabundantly supplied with material to repair the railway (although it is pointed out that some existing rail lines could be cannibalised for track), but the biggest problem will be the repair of vital bridges and the clearing of a number of landslides that have swept away or covered the track. The commandos had proved quite exuberant with their use of explosive. The estimate is that most of the track can be repaired in two weeks if given full priority, but the bridges will take longer. While all available Thai resources are 'volunteered' to help, the net effect will be to cut supplies by this route to 10% for the first two weeks, then to 50% for another 2-3 weeks before the line is fully operational again. As the RN and RAF are still sinking over 30% of his shipping, this is depressing news, and means that it will not be possible to undertake any major offensive operations for at least two weeks, and quite possibly longer. He orders his engineers to start repairs immediately, conscripting any Thai people or materials they need; in the meantime, he orders his supply officers to source all the army's food from Thailand, in order to allow his limited logistical train to concentrate on ammunition and equipment. This will cause resentment and soon worse among the Thai population and the political opposition.

Jan 21st

The Chinese Government accepts the proposal that U.S. Major General Joseph W. Stilwell act as chief of the Generalissimo's Allied staff and agrees to give him executive authority over Allied Units. The Chinese 49th Division of the 6th Army is authorized by Auchinleck to move into Burma to help protect the Burma Road.

Japanese aircraft from the aircraft carriers HIJMS Akagi and HIJMS Kaga again bomb Rabaul on New Britain Island while aircraft from HIJMS Shokaku and HIJMS Zuikaku bomb Kavieng on New Ireland.

In response to the movement of the Japanese convoy sighted the previous day in Makassar Strait, a USN task force under Rear Admiral Glassford, consisting of the light cruisers USS Boise and USS Marblehead and four destroyers sails from Koepang, Timor, Netherlands East Indies to engage it. Turbine trouble limits USS Marblehead to only fifteen knots, so the admiral orders the destroyers and the Boise on ahead.

The Allies are having problems in attacking the Japanese off the east coast of Borneo due to the sheer size of the island. There is a deficiency of airstrips capable of handling the heavier anti-shipping Beaufighters in range of the Japanese convoys (some that are capable are considered too dangerous due to lack of protection from Japanese landings), and the longer-ranged heavy bombers of the USAAF, while they

93

have the range, are ineffective anti-shipping weapons. Accordingly, Somerville orders more of the Dutch and US submarines into the area, and four of the RN T-class are sent to the Java Sea. The need to keep attacking the Japanese convoys to Thailand limits how many of the RN submarines are available. Since there is a shortage (at the moment) of Japanese airpower in the area, he intends to move a striking force including fleet carriers into the Java sea to allow him to intercept future convoys - the almost non-existent road network in Borneo means the only practical way of transporting supplies, and often troops, is by sea.

Jan 22nd

Evacuation of nearly 500,000 citizens from Leningrad begins along the "ice road" across Lake Ladoga. (The Russians will manage to transport around 440,000 people out of Leningrad between 22 January and 15 April 1942.)

The USAAF Far East Air Force B-17's launch at least 15 missions out of Malang, Java, against shipping moving through Makassar Strait between Borneo and Celebes Island. Four missions abort due to bad weather, six end with negative results, and the remaining five suffer heavy losses but sink four ships. That evening the transports headed for Balikapang are intercepted by the USN cruiser and destroyer force. They find twelve transports, guarded by a light cruiser and seven destroyers.

Shortly before the USN force entered the bay, a Dutch submarine torpedoes a 7,000-ton transport, and the confusion allowed the American force to enter without being detected. The destroyers attacked the transport with torpedoes, while the Boise held off in order to use her main guns. It was not until the Boise actually started to hit one of the transports that the Japanese belatedly realised that the new attack was not another submarine. The escorts were hunting the Dutch submarine, and as a result, the destroyers were able to torpedo five transports, one more being set on fire by their guns, while the Boise left three more blazing and not under control, (two of these later had to be abandoned and scuttled).

When the Japanese escort finally turned back, the US destroyers, although they had expended their torpedoes, formed a line to protect the Boise, who was shelling the remaining transports, and had also torpedoed one. The Japanese force engaged the US destroyers, and managed to break through them to torpedo the Boise with one of the Long Lance torpedoes. At this point, the whole action was in confusion on both sides, and although heavily damaged the USN force was able to break off and retire under cover of the darkness, leaving eight transports sunk or sinking behind them.

It is now apparent that the Japanese operation in the Bismark Archipelago was much more than just the raid that intelligence had surmised, as aircraft from HIJMS Akagi and HIJMS Kaga attack Rabaul on New Britain Island for the third straight day, destroying the last of the fixed defences.

Japanese troops land on Mussau Island, largest island in the Saint Mathias group, located 113 miles northwest of Kavieng, New Ireland Island.

Off New Guinea aircraft from HIJMS Shokaku and HIJMS Zuikaku attack Lae, Salamaua and Bulolo.

These actions cause considerable worry to the Australian Government, as a Japanese landing in New Guinea would allow them to build up a major threat far too close to Australia, and far enough east to be difficult to protect from Singapore. After consultations with Alexander and Blamey at Singapore, it is agreed that the remaining two brigades of 8th Australian division be made available for movement to New Guinea if needed, and the Australians are also considering use of their conscript forces. Up until now, these have only been deployed on Australian territory, but there is a growing argument that it is better to fight offshore than on Australian soil. It is mandated though that all conscript forces will be under Australian command, not directly part of the Allied command structure.

A substantial part of the Far East fleet sails to support the Pillar convoy, allowing its light escorts to put into Ceylon to refuel without the convoy having to stop. The carrier Ark Royal also goes into port, as it was not intended for her to accompany the convoy to Singapore. While the attacks on Rabaul indicate that the Japanese carrier force is too far away to intercept it (assuming their intelligence realises it has reached Ceylon), Somerville takes no chances, two fleet carriers and two battleships as well as lighter ships reinforcing the convoy escort. If the Japanese break off the Rabaul attack, he expects these plus the land-based planes in the Singapore area to be sufficient cover, but he also orders Admiral Crace to make for Singapore to join him. Both he and General Alexander consider the supplies (and ships) of the convoy are vital to the continued defence of the Malay Peninsula.

Jan 23rd

The Japanese 55th Regimental Group, numbering about 5300 troops, lands at Rabaul on New Britain Island. At the same time the Maizuru Special Naval Landing Force lands at Kavieng on New Ireland Island. The small Australian garrison at Rabaul numbers 76 officers and 1314 other ranks. The garrison is unable to stop the landings, and after initial resistance retire back into the jungle in the hope a relief operation will be undertaken.

Elements of the Japanese Fourth Fleet invade Kieta on Bougainville (in the Solomon Islands) without opposition.

With the Philippines effectively under Japanese control it is almost impossible for Alexander to intervene effectively in the eastern DEI due to lack of air cover - the Dutch air force, though fighting bravely, is short of modern aircraft and he still needs to defend against the considerable Japanese air force presence in Thailand. The worry is that if the Japanese advance far enough into the DEI they will uncover Australia, meaning more forces will be needed to protect the north of the country. He asks the Dutch to prepare some airstrips so he can deploy torpedo-carrying Beaufighters further forward, although the RAF is worried about the lack of protection on the ground, which has so far been shown to be inadequate. He also expects to receive a number of Wellingtons suitable for long-range torpedo attacks (already on the way from the Middle East), but their ground support will arrive on Pillar. He also asks if the USAAF can deploy any more fighters to contest the Japanese.

Despite the losses to the USN night attack the remaining Japanese transports unload their troops at Balikpapan. However due to their heavy losses en route they go no further than the town itself while they wait for an additional convoy. A second convoy passes through the Moluccas passage in order to land troops on Kendari on the east coast of Celebes Island, capturing the airfield there.

TF 6814 departs New York for New Zealand and then to New Caledonia. This unit with other additions will become the famous Americal Division.

Two RAF Hurricane squadrons arrive in Sumatra. Conditions are described as 'primitive even by North African standards'.

In Manila Japan sets up a puppet government, in which three-quarters of the pre-war senate agree to serve.

Jan 24th

400 Ghurkhas, who have travelled around the coast of Borneo on a couple of rather ancient ships found in the harbour after the Japanese defeat at Labuan, finally make an arrival off Sandakan. Given the conditions of the voyage, and the fact that few Ghurkhas can swim, the troops insist on immediately offloading and seeking to attack the Japanese. Aided by information from some of the local police who had escaped the Japanese invasion, as soon as it is dark they infiltrate the town. Shortly afterwards the night is disturbed by gunshots, grenades and the Ghurkha's bloodcurdling battle cry. In a confused action that lasts some hours the Ghurkhas hunt down and kill the Japanese troops, many of whom were initially caught by surprise. The Ghurkhas themselves take over a 100 casualties, but by the morning report that the town is in Allied hands again.

The Japanese attack into Burma halts; the British defenders are not certain if this was just a probing attack, or if in fact the damage to the rail system has caused the Japanese to become more cautious. It had been intended to evacuate the British force by sea, but as the attack seems to have stopped for the moment this is postponed. Alexander expects any serious attack to come in further north (despite the appalling road system available to support it). There is also a small possibility that the force in the south of the 'handle' may be a route into Thailand if the Japanese can be pushed back from Malaya.

The Japanese Eastern Invasion Force lands at Kendari on Celebes Island. A USN seaplane tender, the destroyer USS Childs, is leaving Kendari harbour and spots the Japanese. A rainsquall obscures the seaplane tender for a while, allowing her to avoid two Japanese destroyers. She is attacked by six Japanese aircraft at 0800 hours, but managed to escape to the south. By the evening, Kendari is fully occupied by the Japanese. Most of the Dutch troops are captured by the Japanese; some fight a guerrilla war for a short period, while others try to escape to safer parts of the archipelago. Kendari Airdrome is considered the best in the Netherlands East Indies and is immediately put into operation by the Japanese 21st Air Flotilla. The loss is a blow to the Allies, who had been hoping to build the forces at the airfield up once ground troops could be found to make it secure, but the rapid fall of the Philippines has not allowed them time to find the required men.

USAAF B-17's based at Malang, Java, and Dutch Martin Model 139WHs and Brewster 339s (the export version of the Buffalo) bomb invasion shipping, sinking a number of transports.

On Bataan, II Corps begins disengaging and withdrawing combat troops. The Japanese maintain pressure on the Philippine Division and attack the covering force, but the bulk of the troops withdraw successfully. The situation in the I Corps area is deteriorating rapidly. The 1st Division, Philippine Army, exhausted by prolonged fighting along the main line of resistance and critically in need of supplies and ammunition, remains under pressure.

As a result of the capture of the first Australian territory by the Japanese (the islands of New Britain and New Ireland off Australian New Guinea, the Combined Chiefs of staff put the port of Darwin under the command of ABDA. Unless the Japanese carrier fleet can be eliminated or at least reduced in strength, the RN does not have the strength to defend Singapore/Ceylon and conduct operations off New Guinea, especially as the location of the Japanese fleet is often undetected until an attack - it is pointed out that there is a lot of the Pacific ocean to hide in. Only the British have radar-equipped planes, and not very many of them. There is also the problem of keeping a large force at sea in the area - Darwin, while useful, is hardly a major fleet base. The best suggestion at present is more air power, in particular reconnaissance planes. After pressure from London the RAF agree to release twelve ASV-equipped Stirlings from Coastal Command - with the current preoccupation of the U-boats off the US coast, these can be spared. It is hoped their range and radar will allow better coverage north of Australia, especially if the US can provide additional Catalinas.

There is some good news for the RAF when they ask about the possibility of more fighters. The Mk8 Spitfire is now in full production, and in addition to increased performance has a much longer range that the earlier models. While the Spitfires are needed in Europe to face the Me109's and Fw190's (and in any case isn't considered suitable for much of the Far East due to its relatively delicate undercarriage), this means that it will be replacing the fighter version of the Whirlwind (it is considerably cheaper to produce). Park has been talking with his old mentor Dowding, and the suggestion is to refurbish the Whirlwinds as the Spitfires replace them, and also modify some to the earlier reconnaissance version. This will give the RAF in Malaya a long-distance fighter, as well as a very fast reconnaissance aircraft. The planes have enough range to fly themselves out, but this is delayed for a few weeks so that the equipment needed to support them can be assembled and sent out.

Park is promised the first squadrons before the end of February, although it will take longer to get their support equipment and personnel in place. Park asks that the reconnaissance version is given priority, as he already has support available for that model, and they can be used to replace lost or damaged aircraft.

US Marines land on the island of Samoa to protect it from the Japanese. While it is agreed protection of the islands between Australia and the US is important, there is growing criticism of what is seen as an overly defensive mindset that is deploying the available troops far from any likely Japanese action, as well as tying up the carrier forces on convoy escort duties. The British positions in Malaya make the western route to Australia secure, and while losing an island or two to the Japanese would be inconvenient, the critics point out it would not be a disaster.

Jan 25th

The Thai government declares war on the United States and the United Kingdom. The governments of Great Britain, New Zealand and the Union of South Africa respond in kind. While Thailand has effectively been at war since the Japanese arrived, this action is seen as a response to growing internal criticism of the Thai government. It remains to be seen if the Thai army will be used in action against Imperial forces.

The Pillar convoy and escort are spotted by Japanese reconnaissance planes as it approaches the coast of Sumatra, heading for Singapore. This has been anticipated by Somerville, and the convoy is escorted by the fleet carriers Illustrious and Bulwark as well as the light carrier Colossus, who keep a heavy CAP over the ships at all times. The RAF in southern Malaya is also on the alert, and raids go in for the next few days onto the Japanese airfields in Thailand to disrupt any concerted action against the vital convoy. The only attack that day is by submarine; a torpedo passes astern of one of the escorting destroyers, and after a short action by the escorts a thick patch of oil and other debris indicates the demises of the Japanese submarine. The British are happy the Japanese don't attempt more in the way of air strikes; it is not known at the time that they are still waiting for more torpedoes (torpedoes are a very heavy item to ship, they require careful handling, and the fragile logistics structure in the area isn't really up to transporting them yet).

The RAF also use the presence of the convoy to stage a heavy raid against the repair work on the Thai railway line, using Beaufighters with 250lb bombs and AP and incendiary shells for their cannon, which prove to be most effective 'train-busters'. The raid is a success - the Japanese are concentrating on the convoy on the other side of the peninsula, and at least three engines and considerable engineering supplies are destroyed. This leads to an increasing number of ever more angry notes from General Yamashita to his air force counterparts. It will also tie up more fighters until the railway is repaired.

The Australian government orders full mobilization. The War Cabinet orders that "all able-bodied white male British subjects" between 18- and 45-years-old should be called up immediately for service. The central government also assumes control of all state budgets. There is some political opposition to this in Australia, but the unified government makes this easy to ignore.

The USAAF Far East Air Force's 20th Pursuit Squadron, which is preparing to depart Brisbane, Queensland for Port Moresby, New Guinea, is ordered to fly to Darwin, Northern Territory, as quickly as possible for duty in Java. It will be replaced in New Guinea by an RAAF Sparrowhawk squadron. After the events of the last few weeks the Australian aircraft industry has been breaking its records for production of the Sparrowhawk and Beaufighter aircraft, and these will equip new squadrons based in Northern Australia and New Guinea. The British government has also agreed to send 100 Cormorant dive bombers to Australia; these are not currently needed by the carriers as reserves for them are seen as satisfactory, and there is a lack of naval targets in the European theatre. While there were suggestions that they could be used to give the RAF a force of dive bombers, this idea was not looked on favourably in the Air Ministry.

Despite their losses, by dawn the Japanese Assault Unit that landed near Balikpapan has occupied the airfield. Their advance southwards slows as the bridges on the coastal road have been destroyed and the unit does not reach the northern outskirts of Balikpapan City until the night of the 25th. The Dutch garrison troops had been withdrawn and the unit entered the city without a fight. While the main body of the unit was advancing along the road to Balikpapan City, it ran into a Dutch military column attempting to escape from Balikpapan. After defeating this Dutch column, the Surprise Attack Unit proceeded to Balikpapan City. The city was completely occupied during the night of the 25th.

This leads to considerable anger in the Imperial command. They expect the Dutch to at least fight for their territories if they and the Americans are to expend their own people helping them, and the withdrawal in the face of an already badly hit Japanese unit is seen as defeatist. The plans to hold part of the Dutch East Indies to protect Singapore by defending Sumatra are given precedence over those to hold Java itself as a consequence.

Chapter 11 - Pillar arrives at Singapore

Jan 26th

An advance party from 8th Australian division arrives in Java. It is expected that the rest of the division will soon be committed either to Java or to Sumatra; however the planners are also looking at the possibility of using them further east if necessary to protect Australia.

On Bataan, the Philippine II and I Corps complete their withdrawal to the final defence line on Bataan in the morning, closely followed by the Japanese.

HMS Audacious is formally commissioned. The first of a new class of large fleet carriers, she has been rushed as fast as possible due to the needs in the East (her sister ship Courageous will not be ready until the late summer as a result). She immediately starts her sea trials; it is hoped to have her on her way east in a few weeks. Her air group has been training for some time in readiness, and in order to speed her workup an unusually high proportion of experienced crew from Glorious (currently being used to train crews as well as pilots) have been assigned to her.

Jan 27th

The long-awaited Pillar convoy reaches Singapore. This brings badly needed supplies and replacements, in particular over 100 tanks and replacement aircraft and spares, as well as men - a complete infantry division (the 51st), and two commandos from the Middle East along with their landing craft. It had originally been hoped that this force would allow an attack north to attempt to recover northern Malaya, but the deteriorating position in the DEI and Borneo mean this might not be possible. The convoy also strengthens the Far East Fleet; the fleet carrier Ark Royal is now at Ceylon, and some of the cruisers and destroyers which escorted the ships will remain to strengthen the fleet. The transports will head back as soon as they have been unloaded; they will also carry some non-essential personnel and civilians back to Ceylon as well as supplies of tin and rubber. The troopships will head back to Alexandria, where additional forces are readying to move east.

The Far East Fleet now has four fleet and two light carriers available, and this will allow Somerville to send an aggressive force into the DEI while still retaining enough air power to protect Singapore. While the light carrier Colossus has an experienced aircrew, up till now all their work has been on antisubmarine duties and her aircrew will receive a few weeks training in the local training and tactics before being assessed as fully operational. He also asks if the Australian air wing (currently enjoying Ceylon as their carrier is having her hull mended) could be made available for use from Darwin - this would give a useful defence and search capability over the local sea area until their carrier is fixed. He is also now prepared to release his reserve squadron of Cormorants to be used from land bases - he now has spare aircraft if needed to replenish his airgroups.

Jan 28th

It is decided to make the remaining two brigades of 18th Division available for use in the Dutch East Indies/Borneo area, as they have completed training in the local conditions. The 51st Division will undergo similar training while acting as Alexander's emergency reserve. Given the difficulty in moving around Borneo, mainly infantry will be used, but it is hoped to quickly build up the Imperial force on the island up to some 5,000 men. Given the small size of the Japanese landings it is hoped this will be sufficient, so long as sufficient coastal transport can be obtained. Alexander also allocates them half the landing craft that came with the commandos, to use as coastal transport - in order to supplement this, available coastal shipping and vessels are being commandeered in Borneo and acquired in southern Malaya. While the eastern side of the island is looking problematical, the western and southern areas are, so far, under Allied control.

In the north of Malaya, 7th Australian division, backed by tanks, attacks the Japanese positions in a limited attack. Given the damage to the Thai railroad clearly visible in photographs, Blamey intends to see just how bad the Japanese supply situation is. The attack manages to penetrate some five miles before increasingly intense counterattacks bring it to a halt. As there is now an armour reserve at Singapore, Blamey informs Alexander he intends to press the attack with Australian and Indian troops the next day as well, to see how fragile the Japanese defence is.

At Rastenburg, Hitler decorates the ace pilot Adolf Galland with the Diamonds to the Knight's Cross. Goering is appalled that the jewels are paste.

The Japanese land on Rossel Island, the easternmost island of the Louisade archipelago. The island is located about 490 miles east-southeast of Port Moresby, New Guinea, and 420 miles west-southwest of Guadalcanal, Solomon Islands, an ideal position to block shipping from either point. The Japanese immediately begin building an airfield.

Jan 29th

The British offensive in Malaya continues, backed by the RAF who attack both the Japanese airfields and the troops on the ground. The Japanese air force returns the compliment. Aided by fresh Indian troops and a further armoured attack, the Australians advance another three miles, causing a serious dent in the Japanese defensive line. One so severe in fact that overnight the Japanese retire to new positions, leaving a noticeable bulge in their defence line. The Australians also retire slightly in order to give them a better line to hold. While the attack has been successful, the fanatical defence the Japanese have put up is worrying to the staff, who see it as making the re-conquest of northern Malaya expensive - infantry casualties in particular have been high.

Based on the results, the most effective operations seem to be by the tanks, for which the Japanese have no real answer. The need to use the available armoured force to reinforce the defence lines means there is no substantial reserve (even allowing for the reinforcements on Pillar). The staff suggest that unless the Japanese get substantial reinforcements themselves, the best plan might be to wait for the Australian's armoured division, currently packing up in North Africa ready to move, arrives to be the centre of a new attack intended to break the Japanese defence and push them back into Thailand. Given that the need to use his forces to help protect the Dutch East Indies is looking more and more likely, Alexander and Blamey agree that planning will start on this option. This is a disappointment to them, but just pushing the Japanese back to the Thai border won't do much to change the situation in the north; unless the force is available to press on, they consider it best to stay in position and let the Japanese blunt their attacks on prepared defences and their supporting artillery. The continuing need to bolster the Dutch forces is a drain, and Alexander again asks when US ground forces will be available to help.

Imperial General Headquarters orders the Navy to secure Lae and Salamaua, New Guinea and then Tulagi, Solomon Islands. The Army and Navy are ordered to combine their efforts and seize Port Moresby, New Guinea. Both Navy and Army staff officers foresee problems.

The Japanese land at Badoeng Island and Mampawan on Celebes Island in the DEI.

The Combined Chiefs of Staff establish the ANZAC Area, covering ocean expanses between Australia, New Zealand, and the French territory of New Caledonia in the New Hebrides Islands. This area is to be under U.S. naval command

Five-inch (12.7 cm) projectiles containing radio-proximity fuses are test fired at the Naval Proving Ground, Dahlgren, Virginia, and 52 percent of the fuses functioned satisfactorily by proximity to water at the end of a 5-mile trajectory. This performance, obtained with samples selected to simulate a production lot, confirmed that the radio proximity fuse would greatly increase the effectiveness of anti-aircraft batteries and leads to immediate small-scale production

Jan 30th

The Japanese invade 314 square mile Ambon Island in the Dutch East Indies, which has the second largest naval base in the East Indies archipelago. The defenders include Dutch troops and the Australian 2/21 Battalion plus supporting troops. During the night of 30 January two Japanese landings are launched; the 1st Kure Special Landing Force lands at Hitu-Iama and the 228th Infantry lands on the southern coast of Laitimor. The defenders are at a disadvantage to contest the landings, only a few Dutch detachments were in the area. At Hitu-Iama on the north coast the defending infantry and machine-gun crews are quickly overwhelmed and bridges on the road leading to the town of Paso are left intact allowing the Japanese to speedily advance south across the Hitu Peninsula. Other landings occurred around

102

Hutumori; the Japanese split westward to the town and northward to Paso using captured Ambonese compelled to act as guides.

Jan 31st

Two small transport ships leave Singapore bound for Darwin with some of the supplies from the Pillar convoy. This includes additional AA guns and material to expand the capabilities of the air base there, such as torpedoes to allow Beaufighters to operate anti-shipping strikes. In addition, two transport planes fly out with spares for the radar at Darwin, which is down to its last electronic tubes for some equipment.

The U.S. Military Mission to USSR, which is to advise and assist Russians on lend-lease matters, arrives at Basra in Iraq; the group subsequently proceeds to Tehran, Iran, where they establish their headquarters.

New Zealand continues to dig in for war by introducing air-raid shelter regulations, and inviting women to join the Emergency Precaution Service as firewatchers. All men must register for the Emergency Defence Corps. So far, the sheep are not being called up.

On Ambon Island 2,000 Japanese troops attack Laha late in the afternoon; they are repulsed by an outnumbered platoon of Australians on the northeast of the airfield.

Task Force 11 (Vice Admiral Brown), formed around the aircraft carrier USS Lexington, departs Pearl Harbor to cover the retirement of TF 8 (Vice Admiral Halsey) and TF 17 (Rear Admiral Fletcher) from the Marshall and Gilbert Islands.

In preparation for a bombing raid on Japan, Captain Donald B. Duncan, USN, flies to Norfolk, Virginia to make arrangements with Captain Marc A. Mitscher, USN, captain of the USS Hornet, to have three B-25 Mitchell medium bombers hoisted aboard on the next day for trial takeoffs.

Major General Eaker is designated Commanding General, Bomber Command, U.S. Army Forces in British Isles (USAFBI) and ordered to proceed to the UK.

Feb 1st

The Soviet Army continues its offensive throughout February but with diminishing success as German resistance stiffens with the arrival of reinforcements. Further efforts to break through to Leningrad and Sevastopol are futile, but some success is achieved in other sectors. Soviet forces use the opportunity to reinforce the Crimea area.

On Ambon Island the Japanese capture ten Australian soldiers and bayonet them to death. The Japanese commander says the POWs would be "a drag" on his advance.

This is witnessed by two Australian soldiers hiding in the jungle; they will later escape and get back to Allied territory to report the atrocity. A growing number of similar incidents have been reported in various actions, but there is reluctance among the staff to believe that the Japanese are actually acting like this. However as more reports are confirmed, the belief is gaining ground, and the troops are already aware of the stories.

Task Force 8 (Halsey), formed around the aircraft carrier USS Enterprise, raids the Marshall Islands concentrating on Kwajalein and Wotje, with the heavy cruiser USS Chester bombarding Maleolap Atoll.

At Kwajalein, SBD Dauntlesses and TBD Devastators from USS Enterprise sink a transport and damage the light cruiser HIJMS Katori, submarine HIJMS I-23, a minelayer, an auxiliary netlayer, an auxiliary submarine chaser, a submarine depot ship, an oiler, a tanker, and an army cargo ship; in the bombing of shore installations, Rear Admiral Sukiyoshi (Commander Sixth Base Force) dies in combat when an SBD scores a direct hit on his headquarters.

Off Wotje, gunfire from heavy cruisers USS Northampton and USS Salt Lake City sink a gunboat while the destroyer USS Dunlap shells and sinks an auxiliary submarine chaser.

Japanese retaliatory air attacks by six Mitsubishi G3M Nells of the Chitose Kokutai on TF 8 results in damage to USS Enterprise (near-miss of a crashing land attack plane) and heavy cruiser USS Chester (by bomb dropped by a carrier fighter).

Three SBDs are shot down over Roi Island by Mitsuibishi A5M Claude fighters and one "Claude" is shot down by a SBD gunner

TF 17 (Fletcher), formed around aircraft carrier USS Yorktown, raids the Gilbert Islands targeting enemy installations on Jaluit, Makin, and Mili.

Aircraft from USS Yorktown cause less damage than the attacks on the Marshall Islands, due to a scarcity of targets at the objective; nevertheless SBD's bomb and strafe a gunboat at Makin and destroy two Kawanishi H6K at anchor, while SBD's bomb and strafe a cargo ship at Jaluit.

TF 11 (Brown), formed around aircraft carrier USS Lexington, supports the operations from the vicinity of Christmas Island in the Line Islands.

The carrier USS Ticonderoga arrives at Pearl Harbor to join the US carrier force in the Pacific. At the moment the USN is deploying three single-carrier task forces to cause the maximum disruption; Nimitz is considering adding the Ticonderoga to one TF in the hope the Japanese might respond as if against a single carrier (he does not have enough escorts to form a fourth independent task force in any case). In the next few months, it is hoped to have six fleet carriers in the Pacific, forming three Task Forces. He is also expecting more Wildcat fighters so the fighter complement of the airgroups can be increased, and the first Corsair squadrons are expected for land-based operations in a few weeks.

A serious setback to British intelligence in the Battle of the Atlantic has taken place. The U-boats in the Atlantic have adopted a new cipher, Triton, linking them directly to Admiral Dönitz's headquarters in Paris. Triton has an additional rotor to the three used in the normal Hydra cipher. Bletchley Park's Bombe, the deciphering machine developed by the mathematician Alan Turing for cracking the codes, only has three rotors and hence cannot tackle Triton. The change is not because the Germans know that the British are reading Enigma but is due to Dönitz's wish to exert tighter control over the operations of his wolf packs so that they will sink more ships. The ciphers used by the U-boats training in the Baltic (Tetis) and in coastal waters (Hydra) remain unchanged.

The Admiralty's submarine tracking room can still monitor each newly commissioned U-boat and those entering and leaving the Bay of Biscay and Norwegian waters. The inability to read Triton means that the Admiralty no longer knows the intentions of the U-boats operating in the Atlantic. It will be more difficult to route convoys to evade the packs. Fortunately, the supply of escort carriers and conversions means it is rare now for a major convoy to sail without air protection, but it is still anticipated that having to fight them through will mean greater losses.

The Japanese carrier striking force (Akagi, Kaga and Zuikaku) leave Truk to attempt to intercept the US carrier force raiding the Marshall Islands. The pursuit is abandoned the next day.

Chapter 12 - New Guinea

Feb 2nd

HQ of the USAAF's 49th Pursuit Group (Interceptor), with its three subordinate squadrons of P40 fighters, arrives at Melbourne, Victoria, from the U.S.A. The aircraft are in crates and must be assembled and the vast majority of the pilots do not have the skills to survive in combat and must undergo combat training. The first squadron will not fly their first mission until March.

The Japanese launch their first air raid on Port Moresby in New Guinea, in preparation for a planned amphibious assault.

The RAF in Malaya presents a report which points out the surprising weakness in Japanese air power since the early battles in December. While the RAF has been resupplied with aircraft, the Japanese air force seems to be growing steadily weaker. This is surprising, as with its sources of aircraft much closer, the staff had expected the opposite. What they do not know is the terribly low aircraft production in Japan. In the period December to March, they will only build some 700 fighters and bombers. To put this into perspective, Australia's normal production is 60 Sparrowhawk and 40 Beaufighters a month, and with the current scare has raised this (albeit temporarily) by 50%. In addition, the British were supplying Russia with some 120 Hurricanes a month which have been diverted. These two minor sources alone are over half again the Japanese production. The RAF are convinced that the shortage in Malaya is because they are building up somewhere else, their best guess being in the DEI, although there is also a possibility they are planning action in Burma or to the east. They simply cannot believe that the Japanese aircraft production is so low.

The Japanese begin a combined, concentrated attack against Australian troops at Laha Airdrome on Ambon Island using infantry, dive-bombers, fighter planes, warships and artillery; the Japanese capture the airfield by mid-morning. Later in the day the surviving Australians at Laha approached the Japanese with surrender negotiations.

Feb 3rd

Port T, a top-secret British naval base on Addu Atoll, becomes operational.

Two Japanese Zero fighters, recovered after force landings in Malaya (albeit in slightly bent condition) commence testing by the RAF and USAAF. The aircraft have been fully repaired (sufficient bits of Zeros were readily available), and the flight testing is being done with maximum priority to help design better tactics against the fighter once its true performance is known.

In the Philippine Islands, the submarine USS Trout unloads 3,500 rounds of ammunition, refuels, loads two torpedoes, and requests additional ballast. Since neither sandbags nor sacks of concrete are available, she is given 20 tons of gold bars and silver pesos to be evacuated from the Philippines before submerging shortly before daybreak to wait at the bottom in Manila Bay until the return of darkness. She gets underway that night using the gold as ballast on the return voyage to Pearl Harbor.

The Japanese begin pre-invasion air attacks on Java. Japanese Navy aircraft from Kendari on Celebes Island attack Soerabaja, Madionen, and Malang. While returning to base, the crew of a Japanese aircraft reports the presence of Allied ships off Madoera.

At Singosari Airdrome four fully loaded B-17's are destroyed, and a fifth is shot down. Three Royal Netherlands Navy Catalina flying boats are destroyed at Soerabaja and a FEAF B-18 Bolo bringing radar technicians from Australia to Java is shot down with the loss of everyone aboard the aircraft.

At the fighter base, Blimbing Airdrome, FEAF P-40s are unable to climb to altitude to intercept the bombers but they manage to shoot down two Japanese fighters and a bomber for the loss off one P-40.

The Japanese attack at Ambon is considered by Somerville's staff to be the precursor to an invasion of Timor. This would cause serious problems, as Timor is needed to stage fighter aircraft through from Australia to the DEI. As he now has another carrier, Somerville decides to move a strong task force forward south of Java, and base a light carrier with some cruisers and destroyers out of Darwin. He realises that this is not sufficient to take on the full strength of the Japanese carrier force, but only intends to contest lighter forces. Two of his T-class submarines are also ordered to patrol east of Timor. His hope is that the IJN may attempt to take Timor with inadequate escort, in which case he can attack them at favourable odds. If the IJN support is too heavy, he will attempt to trail his coat to it while concentrating his fleet carriers and submarines against it. To aid the fleet, a squadron of Sparrowhawk fighters is to move to Timor, as are additional ground troops. He also instructs that the cruiser/destroyer formations used are not to leave Allied fighter cover without good reason - he does not want to lose more ships chasing rumours. The current aim is to contain and nibble away at the IJN forces while denying them their objectives, rather than force a major concentration - Somerville is aware that the Japanese have more carriers that he has currently available, as well as land based support.

The merchant ships that made up the Pillar convoy set off for Alexandria escorted by the two fleet carriers at Singapore. The carriers will return as soon as the ships are safely clear of Sumatra, as Somerville wants to be able to concentrate his carrier force if need be. This will cause some problems in coordination; the usual RN practice is a group of two carriers, occasionally three, but five will mean operating in two groups - there has not been any time to practice the coordination of larger carrier forces. The home convoy will pick up additional troops and supplies at Alexandria.

Feb 4th

Japanese reconnaissance flying boats contact and shadow the Allied force (Rear Admiral Doorman, RNN) of four cruisers and accompanying destroyers, sighted yesterday by 1st Kokutai aircraft as they transited the Madoera Strait to attack the Japanese Borneo invasion fleet. The Allied fleet is now south of the Greater Sunda Islands, about 190 miles east of Surabaya, Java. On the strength of that intelligence, Japanese naval land attack planes of the Takao, Kanoya, and 1st Kokutais bomb Doorman's ships, damaging the heavy cruiser USS Houston and light cruiser USS Marblehead. The Dutch light cruisers HNMS De Ruyter and HNMS Tromp are slightly damaged by near misses. USS Marblehead's extensive damage (only by masterful seamanship and heroic effort does she reach Tjilatjap, Java, after the battle) results in her being sent back to the United States via Ceylon and South Africa; despite the loss of turret III (one-third of her main battery), USS Houston remains. The action is later to be criticised for entering an area under Japanese air dominance without fighter cover; Admiral Doormans actions to protect the DEI are seen as far too careless of the ships under his command.

The small Australian garrison on Ambon Island, largely the 2/21 Battalion, surrenders to the Japanese.

The US Asiatic Fleet (Admiral Hart) ceases to exist. Units of the Asiatic Fleet are organized into Naval Forces, Southwest Pacific Area under Vice Admiral Glassford. By previous arrangement, he will operate under Admiral Somerville, the Royal Navy now moving further forward into the DEI to provide the capital ships and carriers the current light forces lack. Somerville considers Malaya and Singapore safe for the time being, and also has a powerful carrier and battleship force in reserve to protect that area.

Two Dutch destroyers at Darwin take the first reinforcements to Timor. The island is currently in range of Japanese air cover, but not Allied planes, so these fast ships are considered the best way of getting the troops in. As soon as Allied air cover can be provided a more substantial effort will be made.

Feb 5th

Admiral King orders Nimitz to use the "maximum force available" of the Pacific Fleet, including battleships, to raid the western Pacific to divert Japanese strength from the Far East. It is hoped that between them the USN and RN can divide the attention of the IJN and prevent them properly supporting the invasion of the Dutch East Indies. The US code breakers are steadily getting a grip on the IJN codes, and the hope is that a breakthrough will allow a concentration against the IJN to the advantage of the Allied navies.

A brigade of the 18th British Division moves to Sumatra, to start preparing in case the Japanese advance through the DEI reaches this far. If Sumatra falls, Alexander's only option to keep Malaya supplied is to force the Japanese back past the Thai border in the west, which would at least make it possible to fight convoys through Japanese air cover. Losing Sumatra would also put Singapore far too close to Japanese air bases for cover, and would force him to commit more men to defend the area in case of a Japanese invasion. If necessary, he is prepared to give up Borneo and Java to preserve Sumatra, although he has not told the Dutch this.

General Yamashita is censured by the high command in Japan for his lack of aggression and progress in Malaya. He defends himself by pointing out that his actions are severely constrained by lack of supplies, caused by poor support from the Navy, and that the early stages (when he had full supply) were going satisfactorily. The main result is an escalating series of blame passing between the Army and the Navy, while Yamashita struggles to get his forward units properly supplied. The IJA is currently giving priority to the successful invasion of the Philippine Islands.

Feb 6th

In the I Corps area on Bataan, the Japanese receive reinforcements and attack late in the day to relieve pockets. While some elements increase pressure against the 1st and 11th Divisions, Philippine Army, others drive toward Big Pocket until stopped by the 11th Division 800 yards from their objective. A small salient in the corps main line of resistance is formed and called Upper Pocket. In the Manila Bay area, Japanese artillery that is emplaced along the south shore of the Bay in the vicinity of Ternate begins a daily bombardment of the fortified islands. Forts Drum and Frank receive the main weight of shells.

A joint British/French commando operation raids Sicily at night, spending an enjoyable few hours blowing up aircraft on one of the airfields before being recovered. The retaliation on Malta in the morning by the Italian Air Force is met with Allied fighter cover and takes heavy casualties. The raid had two purposes; to keep the Italians edgy, and to get a better idea of the state of the defences on Sicily. The British Chiefs of Staff also enquire if the US Army is in a position to supply a division to the Mediterranean for planned actions later in the year - if not, it will carry on as a joint Imperial-French operation. There are sufficient divisions now in the theatre for proposed operations - the bottleneck is amphibious shipping and landing craft - but the addition of an American division would be good politically as well as blooding the American troops.

Feb 7th

The Nazi armaments and munitions minister, Fritz Todt, returning to Berlin after talks with Hitler, is killed when his plane crashes on take-off. It is announced as an accident. Albert Speer is appointed as Minister of Munitions in his place.

Nine USAAF 5th Air Force B-17's based at Singosari Airdrome on Java attempt to bomb Japanese shipping at Balikpapan but are driven off by fighters.

The RAF agrees the final details of its spring offensive with the War Cabinet. This will involve two phases of operation. First, a number of attacks, as heavy as possible, on selected cities such as Hamburg, each planned to last a number of days in order to cause the maximum damage to the city and (where applicable) U-boat production. Once this has been accomplished and the tactics validated, Bomber Command will commence a sustained attack against the Ruhr, which is expected to last some months - how long will depend on the damage done verses the losses. Bomber Command accepts that such a sustained attack will also damage their bomber force, but the reduction in German war production is expected to be worth it. These campaigns will also see the first use of the high-altitude Coventry bomber, which at least at first is expected to be immune to the German defences. In addition to new bombers and tactics, Bomber Command will also be using a new radio-navigation device, Gee, which it is hoped will reduce the missing of the marked target by less experienced crews.

In addition to the heavy raids by the heavy and high-altitude bombers, it is also expected to conduct a parallel set of attacks using the new Mosquito bomber. While this aircraft cannot carry the heavy loads of the four-engined bombers, its speed allows it to make daylight attacks without the risk of unacceptable losses. The Mosquito force is still being built up, but the current plans are to hit small but valuable targets, and to stress the German defences by attacks both day and night.

The RAF is also hoping to conduct a campaign against the U-boat pens in France, but this needs to await new bombs which will be necessary to penetrate the immensely thick roof that covers the pens. The Coventry bomber is capable of carrying the proposed bombs at the altitude required, and the heavy bombs are currently being developed; it is hoped to have them available after the Ruhr campaign is finished.

There has been considerable controversy over the deliberate delay of the campaign in order to build up the bomber force so that the new tactics and weapons will have the greatest effect. In the end, the success of the Army and Naval operations in the Mediterranean and the Far East allowed the arguments for the delay to win out - it was seen as far less politically necessary to mount a bomber offensive to boost morale.

Feb 8th

Lieutenant General Homma, Commander of the Japanese 14th Army, orders a general withdrawal northward to more favourable positions, where troops can be rested and reorganized while awaiting reinforcements for the final assault on Bataan.

Feb 9th

Japan occupies Makassar in the Celebes. About 8,000 Japanese troops land near Makassar City and south of Makassar at Jeneponto on Celebes Island. They immediately head for Makassar City, where they capture a bridge and the Dutch troops who were guarding the bridge. A company of native soldiers opens fire on the Japanese causing casualties, and in reprisal the Japanese tie the Dutch soldiers in groups of three and throw them from the bridge into the water to drown.

Four destroyers from Rabaul land troops of the Japanese 144th Infantry at Gasmata, a coastal town on southern New Britain Island

Feb 10th

USAAF 5th Air Force LB-30 Liberators bomb and damage the Japanese seaplane carrier HIJMS Chitose in Makassar Strait south of Celebes Island. Unfortunately, due to the still-poor operational communication between the USAAF and the British, by the time this is realised the seaplane carrier has escaped out of easy attack range by FAA aircraft.

A small U.S. Army defence force arrives on Christmas Island. The force consists of 2,000 troops (one each infantry, coast artillery and antiaircraft artillery battalions) plus the 7th Air Force's 12th Pursuit Squadron with P-39's

HMAS Melbourne and her escorts arrive at Darwin to refuel. She will then cover a reinforcement convoy to Timor. In order to allow the light carrier to provide better air cover she has flown off her Cormorant dive bombers, landing on a squadron of modified Sparrowhawks. There are no Goshawks available in Darwin, but the Sparrowhawk, derived from the naval fighter, is easily modified to be carrier-capable (the Australian Sparrowhawks always retained the fixing for an arrester hook, and the radio equipment has been replaced with the naval variant from stores in Australia). This allows her to carry 28 fighters. The RAAF are already basing two squadrons of Cormorants at Darwin, and it is hoped to move one to Timor. Unless the IJN use battleships to escort their invasion fleets, it is felt the dive bombers will be more useful in anti-shipping attacks, backed up by a squadron of Beaufighters to be used as gunships against the lighter coastal craft.

While the Allies do have a need to keep intercepting the Japanese invasion forces, and if possible keep them off Timor, Somerville does have an ulterior motive; he has two fleet carriers and a light carrier ready to strike hard at any large concentration of Japanese shipping, and he hopes that if the Darwin and Timor based aircraft prove effective they can annoy the IJN into entering a trap. He is also hoping to use them as cover to allow Australian forces to counter-attack some of the smaller islands the Japanese have invaded. While the Japanese are invading a considerable number of targets, it has been noticed that the forces used are often small, leaving them vulnerable to counter-attack by modest forces. If the IJN increases the cover and amount of these attacks, this may leave them vulnerable to a counter-concentration by Somerville.

Feb 11th

The RN Anti-Submarine command insists on a meeting with Prime Minister Churchill concerning the success of Operation Drumbeat off the Eastern USA. They are accompanied (very unofficially) by their US liaison officers. They point out that although the USN has been fully informed of the tactics needed to successfully protect shipping, they have insisted (against the advice of the USN officers who have been observing RN operations in this field for years) on using outdated tactics and measures that have proved to be ineffective. Churchill cannot, for political reasons, force the USN to amend their methods (although he is sympathetic as the Battle of the Atlantic is still seen as critical). The only thing he is prepared to countenance is the approval of RN-escorted convoys of British owned and controlled shipping, although he promises to raise the matter personally with Roosevelt.

HMS Audacious finishes her sea trials and enters dock for a number of defects to be fixed. She will then sail for the Far East.

With the return convoy safely clear of Japanese air attacks, Somerville is busy concentrating his carrier force. Current plans are to have two fleet carriers and escorts south of Java, a second pair of fleet carriers at Singapore ready to either sail into the South China Sea or reinforce south of Java, and a light fleet carrier supporting the light forces off Borneo. His second light carrier will be based for the time being at Darwin. Depending on how many carriers the IJN moves into the area, he will either bleed them as he retreats under his land based air cover, or attack to sink (especially if a night attack can be carried out).

Feb 12th

The battleship USS Nevada is refloated in Pearl Harbor. Even though struck by a torpedo and possible up to three bombs, she got underway on 7 December 1941, the only battleship that managed to do so. While attempting to leave the harbour, she was hit again and fearing she might sink in the channel and block it, she was beached at Hospital Point. Nevada receives temporary repairs at Pearl Harbor and then sails for Puget Sound, Washington, for complete repairs.

As a result of the heavy losses being taken off the USA to U-boats, a British convoy is formed in the Caribbean to travel to Halifax. This as much as states the lack of confidence in the USN protection provided in this area, but the British are not prepared to keep losing their valuable ships when they could be saved. The measure is met with considerable enthusiasm by the merchant captains, and indeed a number of US-flagged vessels ask to join the convoy. This is in direct disobedience to their orders to travel on their own, an order to which the merchant seaman have turned a Nelsonian blind eye. Although the RN are not (officially) supposed to be convoying any ships not under British control, when asked they point out blandly that the US ships are not part of the convoy, they merely happen to be travelling at the same time and in the same direction.

Feb 13th

Operation Sealion is formally cancelled. This is the plan for the cross channel invasion of England. While postponed many times, this cancellation makes it final.

The governments of the USA and Canada approve the construction of a U.S. Military Highway through Canada to Alaska.

Japanese dive bombers raid the Bataan peninsula, killing some of their own men by mistake.

Chartered U.S. passenger ship SS President Taylor, transporting 900 Army troops to occupy Canton Island, runs aground on a reef off her destination and becomes stranded.
The superstitious Admiral Halsey refuses to take Task Force 13 out as scheduled; renumbered Task Force 16, it will sail tomorrow.

Japanese sub I-17 shells the oil depot at Goleta, California, to no effect except to cause consternation to the local American defences and raise queries in Washington as to how direct attacks on the continental US are possible. Considering the pinprick nature of such attacks, these enquiries are allowed to vanish into the USN system of paperwork.

Feb 14th

The Canadian Brigade originally intended for Hong Kong before transport problems (fortunately) delayed them, arrives at Singapore, having taken an indirect route to avoid the DEI. While the bulk of the Canadian army is currently concentrated in the UK under its own commanders, it has been decided that this brigade will join the Imperial forces defending SE Asia and Australia as a gesture of solidarity. Alexander has scheduled a month (if time allows) of jungle training and acclimatisation for the troops; they will then be used either in Malaya or in Sumatra.

Chapter 13 - Action off Timor

Feb 15th

U.S. Army transport USAT Meigs, U.S. freighters SS Mauna Loa and SS Portmar, and Australian coaster Tulagi, escorted by heavy cruiser USS Houston (CA-30), destroyer USS Peary (DD-226) and Australian corvettes HMAS Swan and HMAS Warrego sail from Darwin, Northern Territory, for Koepang, Timor, Netherlands East Indies. Air cover is provided by the light carrier HMAS Melbourne. The convoy is carrying the Australian 214 Pioneer Battalion and the U.S. 148th Field Artillery Regiment (75mm Guns, truck-Drawn, less the 2d Battalion), to reinforce Allied troops on Timor. The 148th is an Idaho National Guard unit inducted in September 1940. The units are to secure Penfoie airdrome, the only staging point on Timor for flights to Java. It is hoped that the USA can provide additional P-40 fighters to defend the airfield

The Japanese aircraft carriers Akagi and Soryu leave Palau escorted by Cruiser Division 8 to attack Darwin and Timor, as well as any Allied ships found in the area. The use by Somerville of only one light carrier to support Borneo and the reported losses in earlier battles has led the IJN to calculate he only has one, or at the most two, fleet carriers available. Intelligence from Singapore supports this with a report than these ships are in Singapore, too far to intervene in any case. The carrier Kaga was to be part of the force but has some slight underwater damage due to running onto a reef at Palau, which while not as severe as originally feared has reduced her maximum speed to 18 knots. As the strength of Allied forces in the area is uncertain, this speed would subject the carrier force to unacceptable risk if enemy ships were in fact present in any force

A second Japanese force is also at sea in the area, an invasion force for Timor escorted by the light cruiser Nagara (Rear Admiral Kubo) and seven destroyers. The aim is to destroy the Allied aircraft on Timor by a carrier strike, then land the men while the carriers and light forces hold off and destroy any Allied attempts to interfere. If Allied response is light or ineffective, the Japanese also intend a strike on Darwin to destroy the port facilities and any ships in harbour. In view of the absence of the Kaga this will only be attempted if aircraft losses during the taking of Timor are acceptable

The Allies have a number of forces in the area. First, a light surface force under the Dutch Admiral Doorman, consisting of three Dutch cruisers, ten destroyers, and the ships escorting the supply convoy to Timor. In addition there are two RN T-class boats southeast of Timor, and a RN carrier striking force southwest of Java, although this is currently too far away to support Timor.

Feb 16th

RAF Bomber command had hoped to start its Ruhr campaign today, taking advantage of the long winter nights, but this has had to be postponed for some weeks as a number of minor problems with the Coventry bombers have had to be rectified. Although only around 40 of the new bombers are expected to be available at the start of the campaign, they are an integral part of the bombing strategy and it is considered best to wait a short while for them to be available. In the meantime the force will be used to attack targets in Italy (particularly in the north) and on other Italian bases in the Mediterranean as part of the ongoing preparations for an amphibious assault.

The German Operation NEULAND begins with simultaneous attacks on Dutch and Venezuelan oil ports to disrupt production and flow of petroleum products vital to the Allied war effort.

The British 70th Div arrives in North Africa. It is not yet certain if this division will be sent on to the Far East - there is a limit to how many men the Empire can supply until the logistics have been improved. There is also a possibility it might replace the New Zealanders, although currently New Zealand is building a new division to fight in the Far East and it is preferred for political reasons to include New Zealand troops in the Mediterranean.

Feb 17th

A Dutch reconnaissance plane spots the Japanese invasion convoy heading for Timor. Due to the weather (scattered rain makes observation difficult), the main carrier force some distance behind them is not spotted. The supply convoy is instructed to offload as much as possible and to sail for Darwin at nightfall at latest, even if they have not fully unloaded. The covering force will concentrate south of Timor and be joined by Admiral Doorman's force. The RN carrier force off Java also alters course to the east, in case the Japanese have a covering force. Meanwhile a strike on the Japanese from Timor is being prepared. The airfield at Timor is home to an RAAF Beaufighter squadron as well as fighters, and it is hoped to hit the Japanese convoy late that afternoon or early evening before they close the island. HMAS Melbourne is mainly carrying fighters, and is to cover the surface force and to provide them with air reconnaissance

For their part the Japanese seaplanes have spotted the supply convoy (although not the additional surface forces or the carrier, as with the Allies the weather is not conductive for spotting ships and they have been concentrating on the island). Their intention is for the carriers to destroy Allied air power by a dawn strike (and also sink as many of the warships escorting the convoy as possible), followed by a landing to take the island. The Japanese do not realise that this is the second supply convoy, and that the defenders on Timor now outnumber their attack force. The carriers will cover the invasion force until nightfall just in case they have been spotted.

First Battle of Timor

The first action off Timor was the attack by the RAAF Beaufighters on the invasion fleet spotted earlier. The island had a limited supply of torpedoes, so it had been decided to use them on the first (and hopefully most effective) attack. There were a certain number of errors on both sides; the Japanese didn't realise that the island's airfield was hosting a full torpedo squadron, and not having spotted any Japanese carriers the Allies expected the fleet to have no air cover. As a result of these mistakes the Beaufighters were sent out without benefit of fighter cover. Meanwhile the 4,000 men defending the island were put on invasion alert, and the unloading of the supply convoy continued at breakneck speed.

The Japanese invasion fleet was approaching from the north, and it was correctly concluded that their destination was Dilli. The torpedo planes struck first, at 1700, 18 planes attacking in groups of three. Unknown to the pilots, the Japanese carriers were keeping a patrol of six Zeroes over the fleet, and the first the Beaufighters knew of these was when two of them were shot down into the sea. The highly experienced Japanese pilots continued to harry and attack the incoming planes, but with only six aircraft, they could not protect the fleet properly. Although many of the attackers were either shot down or driven away with their attack ruined, six planes managed to get in torpedo runs against the transport ships. The net result was one transport sunk, and a second damaged and unable to make more than a few knots. One escorting destroyer was also sunk - almost by accident; it had run into the path of a torpedo jettisoned by a Beaufighter evading one of the Zeroes. The attackers lost eight planes (six to the zeroes, one to AA and one which crash-landed on the island, unable to make the airfield at Dilli). Only one Zero was lost, having strayed in front of one of the Beaufighters - not a safe thing to do given the Beaufighter's heavy armament.

Both sides were rather shocked - to the Allies, it was now obvious that at least one Japanese carrier was lurking in the area, probably to the north of the island; to the Japanese, the island defences had been underrated. The Japanese prepared accordingly; a full-strength carrier strike was to be made on the airfield at dawn to neutralise it and allow the remaining transports a free run in. As yet the Dutch surface force had not been spotted, but it was hoping to make contact with the Japanese invasion force that night. HMAS Melbourne's force was, as per standing orders, edging southeast - unless the Japanese turned out to only have one light carrier, her orders were to stay clear of superior forces and support the surface force. However, she was carrying a dozen SeaLance, and her captain had decided to make a strike against the transports if at all possible. The intention of the Dutch to attempt a night surface action had complicated this, making his original intention of a night strike too dangerous to friendly ships, but there was always the next day.

The Dutch force made contact with the Japanese convoy later than planned. They had originally hoped to attack around 0100, allowing them to retire south under cover of darkness away from the likely position of the Japanese carriers. Contact was not made until 0330, and then only by part of the force. The Dutch ships were not equipped with radar, and had had to spread out to intercept the invasion force. While on paper the Dutch force was superior, its cruisers were very light ships and they were inexperienced at night combat, unlike the highly trained Japanese escorts. The Japanese detected the Dutch first, and the initial sign of contact was starshells bursting over Doorman's flagship.

The action did not go well for Doorman; after half an hour, the Dutch cruiser HNMS De Ruyter was on fire and sinking, HNMS Java was stationary after a long lance torpedo had blown off her stern, and two Dutch destroyers were out of action, although one would manage to limp away under cover of darkness. In return, one Japanese destroyer was disabled and slowly sinking. After this the rest of the Dutch ships make their escape before daylight, leaving the Japanese convoy able to reform and again head for Timor, although due to the night action they were now not expected to arrive until the afternoon.

Dawn brings more aerial action. After the news of the night surface action, the Japanese carriers allocate twelve dive bombers and an escort of six Zeros to go after and sink as much as possible of the Dutch force. The rest of their attack planes, some 36 level bombers and 30 dive bombers, escorted by 20 Zero fighters, attack the airfield on Timor shortly after dawn. While Timor does have a radar set, it has not been operational for long and the ground control is poorly trained; as a result less than ten minutes warning is given. Some of the planes had already left; although the torpedoes were used up yesterday, the remaining ten Beaufighters (some of them hurriedly patched up), escorted this time by eight Sparrowhawks are on their way to the invasion fleet. In their keenness to attack the island the carriers only have four Zeros over the transports and escorts, and this result in the Beaufighters being able to make their attacks while a melee ensues between the Sparrowhawks and the Zeros. Four Sparrowhawks are shot down for the loss of two Zeros, but another transport is left disabled and burning from the 500lb bombs of the Beaufighters, and a destroyer is in difficulty after being riddled with 20mm fire.

The strike force sent to find the retreating Dutch vessels finds the unfortunate ships an hour later, but the manoeuvrable destroyers are difficult targets, and only one more is lost even with the experience of the veteran Japanese pilots. The airfield has not been so lucky; although eight Sparrowhawks and four P-40's were in the air (a dawn strike had, after all, been expected if the Japanese were in range), they were not a match for the escorting fighters. Three of the P-40's and four of the Sparrowhawks were shot down for the loss of only two Zeros (although a third was unable to make it back due to damage, crashing on the edge of the islands as it tried to make it back to the carrier). The carrier planes did considerable damage to the airfield and its operational facilities, and destroyed some nine planes on the ground, although they only partially damaged the runway. As the last of the carrier planes headed back north, it was not clear how long it would be possible to keep the airfield operational.

The attack on the airfield had not been without loss to the attack planes. Two of the level bombers had been shot down by the defending fighters, and another by the ground defences, and two dive bombers had also been lost to AA fire. The runway was still operational for fighters, and the remaining CAP managed to get down with only one loss to the damaged surface. The repair crews started work immediately, and hoped to get the airfield operational again by that evening.

Meanwhile HMAS Melbourne had closed the island from the south in order to make a strike on the invasion force which, despite the losses to aircraft and the Dutch, was still closing on Dilli. Twelve SeaLance, escorted by eight Sparrowhawks, had taken off shortly after dawn. Led by an ASV-equipped SeaLance they spotted the invasion force some 50 miles offshore later that morning. As the carrier strike on the airfield had needed escort (and some Zeros needed to be retained for defence of the carriers themselves), the force only had four Zeros as cover. A CAP had been expected by the attackers, and the Sparrowhawks moved to cover the TBRs as they broke into their attack formations.

Despite outnumbering the Zeros eight to four, the expert Japanese pilots managed to shoot down five of the Sparrowhawks for the loss of two of their number (a third was damaged, and never made it back to the carrier). The combat did make it impossible for them to interfere successfully with the torpedo strikes, and three of the four triplets attacked without airborne opposition, although one plane was lost to AA fire. As the SeaLance made their withdrawal another two of the remaining transports were sinking into the tropical waters. After the various strikes, the invasion force was now only in a position to land about 1,000 men plus a limited amount of equipment. The Japanese army commander decided to land anyway, declaring that the Bushido spirit of his men would overcome the opposition even if they were outnumbered. The invasion force would be in a position to land at around 1430.

Given the strength of the carrier attack on the airfield, the Allied command was certain at least two fleet carriers were standing off Timor, possibly three or four. The Melbourne was ordered to pull back as soon as her planes had been recovered; her escorts would then move southwest to be in a position to meet up with the withdrawing Dutch force, and then join with the RN carrier force heading east. Unless a direct threat was made to Darwin, the Melbourne was not to engage the Japanese carriers.

Hope by the defenders that the runway would soon be operational was dashed at 1200 when a large raid was detected approaching from the north. Despite the precarious nature of the takeoff, four Sparrowhawks and two P-40's managed to get airborne. This proved to be a strike by Japanese army planes out of the Celebes. The reports from the carrier planes had stated that the airfield had been destroyed, so the fifty bombers were attacking without escort. This led to the defenders shooting down ten of them for the loss of only one P-40, the pilot parachuting safely. The remaining planes plastered the remaining airfield buildings and runways, causing considerable damage and effectively closing the airfield. The Sparrowhawks managed to get down on fields nearby, along with the remaining P-40, but two of the planes were damaged and non-operational after their landings. The airfield repair crews resumed their work, but estimated that even if no more attacks took place, at best a runway would be operational for fighters by the morning.

While the Japanese had been attacking Timor, their carrier force had been recovering their strike. Losses had been light, and it was expected to make new attacks in support of the landings once they had taken place, although as the attack had revealed the presence of a carrier, an anti-shipping strike would be held back as a precaution. The planes would however prove useless against the attack that took place late in the afternoon. One of the RN submarines that were patrolling the area had found the carriers. Although the speed of the carrier force made interception very difficult, the T-class boat managed to set up an attack run, firing six torpedoes at the Akagi. Due to the poor presentation of the target four of the torpedoes missed. One hit the carrier forward, causing her to slow to a stop as water poured into the gaping hole in her hull; the second torpedo suffered a rare failure, merely thudding against the hull outside one of the port boiler rooms. The submarine then went deep and quiet, to evade the inevitable counterattack. Although prosecuted with considerable effort, the submarine was never held and finally slipped away, ready to report once it was dark.

The Akagi was a large ship, and the torpedo had fortunately not caused severe internal damage, although she had taken on a considerable quantity of water. Her speed was however reduced to some 16 knots in order not to cause further damage, and it was thought that this would make her too vulnerable for further action. If an enemy surface force or carriers found them (and although the escorts claimed the submarine destroyed, no debris had been seen and the claim was regarded as uncertain), the ship would be in severe danger. As the invasion force was starting to make its attack, and so it was expected the island would soon fall to the Japanese, the decision was taken to withdraw the carriers. Air support would be from the Celebes, and it was expected that an airstrip would soon be available on Timor to allow Japanese fighters to base there.

The IJN did not know until the following morning that in fact the landings had been a disaster. Heavily weakened by the air and surface attacks, the Japanese landed around 1,000 men in the face of defensive artillery fire and troops which matched their numbers and had artillery support. By nightfall the Japanese only had a tenuous hold on their landing area, having lost half of their force dead or wounded. The defenders were still holding the high ground, and after intense efforts the airfield had been repaired enough to allow fighters to take off. That would bring a most unpleasant surprise to the Japanese that morning.

The IJN decision to withdraw the carriers to the north had put them out of immediate range of Allied attacks. The other submarines in the area were too far away to close, and the boat that had attacked had, by the time it had made the necessary report, been positioned badly even though she attempted to close that night on the surface. The Japanese, well aware Allied submarines were in the area, were conducting heavy A/S patrols from daybreak, not allowing the submarines to close with them.

The poor communication between the Japanese Navy and Army had caused a delay in the air force in the Celebes realising that they would have to support the landing on their own. The original plan had been for the carriers to make another dawn strike to suppress the airfield and also the landings, but in the event it was not until midday that they sent another raid over the island. By that time it was too late to save the landing. Attacked at dawn by artillery and then subjected to air attack, first from the fighters and then from six Beaufighters that had managed to get off the airstrip, and outnumbered by the defenders, the invasion had effectively failed by 1000. The Japanese started to withdraw their ships at this point, one destroyer already damaged by a pair of Beaufighters. This withdrawal would in fact manage to save the remains of the force - the defenders spent the morning attacking the landings themselves, and that afternoon had to fight off another attack on the airfield. This time the bombers were escorted, and three defenders were shot down for the loss of two Japanese fighters and three bombers. The airfield was again unserviceable until additional repairs were made.

While the decision to withdraw the Melbourne in the face of a strong Japanese carrier force was criticised, it was seen as the correct one, although it meant the carrier was not able to attack the withdrawing Japanese invasion force. The Japanese landings took an additional two days to suppress and defeat completely, although with the strength of defenders it was never in great doubt. The situation on the island remained delicate, with continual small attacks being made on the airfield from the Celebes, but these were not capable of stopping the Allies from bringing in additional reinforcements, although it did make using the airfield to stage fighters through to Java more difficult.

On investigation, the underwater damage to the Akagi was fortunately not severe, and her propulsion plant had not been affected apart from temporary shock damage. She would however be out of action for some six weeks while her hull was properly repaired.

Feb 19th

General Dwight D. Eisenhower is appointed as Chief of the War Plans Division for the US Army.

Feb 20th

Major General Ira Eaker, who is to command the 8th Air Force, arrives in the UK by air with six staff officers to select a headquarters site and prepare for the arrival of American troops.

Task Force 11, consisting of the USS Lexington, the USS Ticonderoga and their escorts, is located and attacked by Japanese Navy land-based aircraft as they approach Rabaul on New Britain. After losing the element of surprise, a decision is made to abandon the mission, and the task force commences to withdraw. The USN is uncertain as to the number of aircraft based at Rabaul, so the task force deliberately lingers in its withdrawal so as to temp the Japanese to attack at long range. The tactic is a success; over the next day, some 25 enemy planes are shot down for the loss of two fighters as the Japanese attempt to attack without fighter escort. The information is collated at Pearl Harbor, where the lack of escorts is considered to be significant after the British reports reporting a lack of an expected aircraft build-up in operational theatres.

President Quezon has been evacuated on board the submarine USS Swordfish. He is accompanied by his wife and two children. Vice-President Osmena and other Philippine government officials are also evacuated

Feb 21st

The U.S. War Department orders General Douglas MacArthur, Commanding General U.S. Army Forces, Far East (USAFFE), to move his headquarters to Mindanao Island and then go to Australia. The War department intends to have the General take command of Allied forces in the Southwest Pacific, although this plan has not yet been discussed with their Allies.

Feb 22nd

Five Allied ships leave Fremantle, Western Australia, with 69 USAAF P-40s, motor vehicles and U.S. Army troops destined for Tjilatjap, Java. The convoy includes the seaplane tender USS Langley carrying 32 assembled P-40s.

President Roosevelt orders General MacArthur, Commanding General U.S. Army Forces, Far East (USAFFE), to leave the Philippines.

As it seems likely that the Japanese will make another attempt to invade Timor (especially if Java can be held as hoped), four RAF Whirlwind planes are sent to Darwin to provide long-range reconnaissance cover around the island.

HMS Audacious leaves the dockyard on her way to collect her escorts, destination Singapore. While her air group has been training during the final fitting out, her crew are still relatively inexperienced. Further workup will be done on passage, but unless the need for her is critical, Somerville intends to allow time for a further training period at Trincomalee. The ship will sail via the Cape; this is both to allow for the training, and to hopefully make it easier to hide the ship's presence. Somerville is hoping this new class of carrier will be an unpleasant surprise for the Japanese.

Feb 23rd

Shells fall on the US mainland again. The Japanese submarine HIJMS I-17 fires 25 rounds of 5.5-inch shells from a range of 2,500 yards at the Bankline Oil Refinery at Ellwood, California, 12 miles west of Santa Barbara. Little damage is caused, but the shelling causes panic in the local defence forces.

Feb 24th

Six German divisions cut off at Demyansk in the northern sector of the Moscow front are resisting the Russian efforts to destroy them. The Demyansk pocket and other similarly defended localities are frustrating the Soviet offensive.

One unusual part of the Demyansk operation is that the 100,000 men in the pocket are completely cut off and are being supplied with food, fuel and ammunition by air. All types of aircraft are being used. Junkers Ju52 transports are the main workhorses, but bombers are also carrying in supplies, protected by every available Bf109.

Supplies are also being airlifted into another fiercely defended pocket around Kholm. It is even more dangerous here, for the airfield is in range of Russian artillery and the Germans are being forced to drop supplies by parachute or land them by glider. The effect of the pockets of resistance is to break up the cohesion of the Russian front. The Russians cannot maintain their offensive and the Germans cannot regroup effectively. Both sides are now showing signs of exhaustion. The Germans lose more men from frostbite than from gunshot, and the Russians are simply becoming exhausted.

Beginning at 0710 hours, TF 16 (Vice Admiral Halsey) raids Wake Island to destroy Japanese installations there. SBD Dauntlesses and TBD Devastators from the aircraft carrier USS Enterprise and SOC-1 Seagulls of Cruiser Scouting Squadron Five from heavy cruisers USS Northampton and USS Salt Lake City bomb installations in the atoll. The bombardment unit consisting of USS Northampton and USS Salt Lake City and destroyers USS Balch and USS Maury (Rear Admiral Spruance) shells the atoll. The combined efforts of the USS Enterprise's planes (bombing and strafing) and ships' gunfire sink two guardboats and two Kawanishi H6K4 Flying Boats on the water; F4F Wildcat pilots later shoot down a third H6K4 near Wake at about 0830 hours. One SBD of VS 6 is lost.

Feb 25th

The RAF commences a campaign against the Italian mainland and Italian possessions in the Mediterranean. Home-based squadrons will attack targets in Northern and Central Italy, as well as Sardinia and Corsica, while the Middle East Air Force (in conjunction with the French Air Force in North Africa) attacks Southern Italy, Sicily and the remaining Italian island possessions. The intent is both to damage Italian installations (particularly military ones) and to stretch the Italian defences over a large area.

The convoy of merchant ships that resupplied Singapore arrives at Alexandria. It is scheduled to load up with more supplies and troops - the Australian 1st Armoured Division and a Brigade of the French Foreign Legion. Alexander is waiting for these reinforcements before going on the offensive in Malaya (although he realises that it might be necessary to divert some of them to Java or Sumatra).

Chapter 14 - The Japanese reach for Java

Feb 26th

Following the reports of the raids by US carriers in the Pacific, the Japanese Navy discusses plans to destroy Allied naval power in the Pacific and SE Asia and to support the Army landings, in particular those aimed at the vital oil installations.
The next planned Army operation is the invasion of Java. This will be supported by land based planes (both Army and Navy), and by up to three light carriers. This is considered sufficient; the Royal Navy is thought to have one fleet and two light carriers operational (with another fleet carrier possibly under repair), however one of their light carriers is isolated in what is seen as a misguided defence of Northern Australia. If the RN carriers do interfere, the IJN considers it has sufficient assets available to sink them. Allied surface units are seen as less of a problem as they will be vulnerable to the Japanese air power, and indeed might be useful in drawing the Allied carriers into an unequal fight. If the need arises, two more fleet carriers should be available at short notice

The IJN's next task is to repair the Akagi and make the Carrier Striking Force operational again. This will give them five fleet carriers, enough to conduct heavy strikes on two targets or an overwhelming strike on one. Ideally, the first use will be to destroy the Allies' carriers. Whether the first strikes are made in the Pacific (against the USN) or in the DEI (against the RN) will depend on the situation at the time. The second strike will then proceed to destroy the Allied carriers in the other theatre. While it is realised that the size of the Pacific means it may not be possible to completely destroy the enemy carriers, it is expected to sink enough to stop any meaningful offensive action for a considerable time. This will allow the Army to consolidate its gains and secure the vital oil fields in Borneo and the Dutch East Indies.

The Navy's preferred strategy will be to lure the enemy into a decisive battle with its carriers and heavy surface units, aided by their submarines. In particular, the presence of battleships and torpedo-armed cruisers will mean any damaged enemy carriers will not escape.

Feb 27th

The USN code breakers find evidence of a Japanese build-up prior to an invasion of Java. As yet they have not completely cracked the Japanese codes, but what they have, plus traffic analysis, is enough to indicate that a major thrust to invade Java is imminent. Unlike some of the recent Japanese operations in Borneo and Timor this is expected to be a major operation. Accordingly Alexander authorises reconnaissance flights of likely anchorages and airfields, accepting that some of these will be defended. He also asks Somerville to start positioning his forces to counter such an operation.

In a daring raid on France tonight Parachute Regiment soldiers seize top-secret German RDF equipment. The paras had been specially trained for this operation, jumping from their Whitley transports at night into snow near the clifftop target at Bruneval, near Le Havre.

Major John Frost charged with four men through the front door of the enemy chateau overlooking the site, shooting as he went. Royal Engineers, guarded by paratroopers, tore out the aerial and other essential parts of the Würzburg tracking device with crowbars. Enemy bullets hit the equipment as they worked. For a time afterwards it seemed as if the escape route down a cliff to a beach rendezvous was blocked by a cliff top machine-gun post, whose bullets hit Sergeant-Major Strachan in the stomach. Then a team of paras which had landed off the drop zone joined the fight after a forced march. Hit by unexpected fire the German gunners fled.

On the beach, survivors of the raid waited for their RN pickup. The paras embarked with the secret equipment and, as instructed, brought with them a captured RDF operator. They lost three dead and six captured.

At the same time, taking advantage of the confusion of attacking two targets simultaneously, Royal Marine Commandos landed from a submarine, target one of the coastal airfields. The Commandos were escorting four RAF pilots, whose targets were some of the Fw190 fighters on the base. The guards were completely surprised by the night attack, and the Commandos held the base for an hour, despite the attempts by the Luftwaffe personnel to retake it. This allowed two of the pilots to escape in captured Fw190's. The Commandos then made a fighting retreat to the coast, where they were to be picked up by RN coastal forces. Sadly, only one-half of the unit made it - the second part found that local troops had blocked off their escape to the beach, and later surrendered at dawn. The two planes were flown to a British airfield as planned, where they would be flown and analysed.

The US carrier Langley is attacked en route to Tjilatjap in Java. Nine unescorted Japanese bombers attempt to attack the old carrier (which is serving as an aircraft transport), but the attack is broken up by Sparrowhawk fighters operating from a forward base in Java. The defenders shoot down three of the bombers. Although the Langley is hit by one bomb and damaged, she later successfully delivers her cargo of 32 P-40 aircraft. The US freighter Sea Witch delivers another 27 crated P-40's, and these are given priority as the command in Java are expecting more Japanese raids now their air force is established in the Celebes.

Feb 28th

The first RN-escorted convoy to travel up the US East Coast arrives at Halifax (via New York). As a contrast to the heavy losses being taken by independently sailing ships, only one ship from the convoy was lost (and that a straggler). This is considered a great improvement, however later that day Admiral King learns that, despite his orders to the contrary, US merchant ships have been part of the convoy. He issues orders that the merchant captains of those ships be arrested for disobeying orders. This causes problems. The ships are in Canadian-controlled Halifax harbour, and due to what is termed 'administrative problems' the MP's there seem unable to find the captains. He also demands to know why the Royal Navy is not fulfilling the agreements made (that US ships on the East coast would be under US control), and is informed that the ships involved were not part of the convoy, having merely been travelling in the same direction. He does not take this explanation well.

March 1st

The issues over the East Coast US convoy escalates when a direct order is sent from the US Navy that no US-flagged or controlled merchants ships are to go with RN convoys under any excuse, and that any captain found doing this will be court-martialled. This causes outrage among the US skippers already risking their lives to deliver cargoes, who feel that the protection provided by the US Navy is inadequate (many of those same captains have experience of cross-Atlantic convoys). They bluntly tell the USN officers giving them the new orders that until the situation is resolved, they will not sail. On being told that means court-martials, it is pointed out even more bluntly that that is better than drowning. Although all this is currently supposed to be secret, a number of reporters are already around some of the naval bases and ports concerned and showing an interest. This is slightly embarrassing to the Royal Navy, who had hoped the results of escort would be kept quiet and merely encourage the USN to take advantage of their hard-learnt expertise. However the RCN officers involved seem to be rather more generous with the information they give to reporters, although at present the information is restricted and they are unable to publish.

March 2nd

The rations of the US-Filipino army on Bataan are reduced again, this time to one-quarter of the normal daily food allowance. The trapped troops supplement their diet with horse and water buffalo meat and even lizards. Disease is taking a heavy toll on the 95,000 men on Bataan and Corregidor - especially malaria, malnutrition and diarrhoea.

The Australian government finally declares war on Siam.

March 4th

The Japanese Imperial General Staff decides that once the occupation of Java is complete, to expand its conquest to New Guinea, the Solomon Islands, the Fiji Islands and American Samoa. Taking the Fijis and Samoa would cut America's supply line to Australia.

General MacArthur, (Commanding General U.S. Army Forces, Far East), begins reorganizing his forces in the Philippines in preparation for his departure. The Composite Visayan-Mindanao Force is divided into two commands. Brigadier General William F. Sharp retains command of forces on Mindanao; the Visayan forces are placed under Brigadier General Bradford G. Chynoweth. MacArthur's plans envisage the formation of two more commands. Major General George F. Moore's harbour defence forces on Corregidor and other islands in Manila Bay will constitute one, the forces on Luzon the other.

General MacArthur informs Rear Admiral Rockwell, Commandant of the Sixteenth Naval District, that he has been instructed to leave Corregidor. The plan is for him and his party to board the submarine USS Permit which is scheduled to leave Corregidor on 14 March.

The issues over the convoying of US ships off the East Coast of America, and the refusal of merchant captains to sail unless they are convoyed, reaches Churchill and Roosevelt. Both are annoyed, for different reasons. Churchill bluntly informs Roosevelt that the heavy losses of tankers can no longer be tolerated, and they either go in convoy or stay in port. Even though the RN escort forces are stretched, they will provide escorts, but he points out that it would be better if the USN escorts them, and this will look better politically. He also notes that it is not going to be possible to sit on the US press much longer, and that if news of the current situation gets out, it will be damaging.

March 5th

Japanese Imperial General Headquarters issues Navy Directive No.62 ordering Commander-in-Chief, Combined Fleet, upon completion of the Java operation, to annihilate the remaining enemy force in Dutch New Guinea and to occupy strategic points of that territory. The objectives of the occupation are to survey the country for possible sites for air bases, anchorages and oilfields, as well as to secure a good communication and supply line with British New Guinea.

A Japanese convoy bound for Huon Gulf, New Guinea, sails from Rabaul, New Britain Island, during the night of the 5th/6th.

Roosevelt orders the USN to sort itself out over convoys. Merchant ships WILL be escorted, with no arguments. Admiral King is furious, but is bluntly informed that he can be replaced if he won't obey the command - while Roosevelt does not want to do this, an Admiral who doesn't follow his orders is useless to him. When it is pointed out that the USN doesn't actually have the escorts available, a compromise plan is reached for the short term; ships will be escorted during the day, and go into port at night.

March 6th

U.S. Lieutenant General Stilwell, Commanding General American Army Forces, China, Burma, and India, confers for the first time with Generalissimo Chiang Kai-shek in Chungking.

General Alexander gives provisional acceptance for a campaign to drive the Japanese out of northern Malaya. This operation as envisaged requires the 1st Australian armoured division, which will not be in place for some three weeks, but it is hoped that unless it has to be diverted to Java it will be possible to attack before the monsoon sets in. The idea is to first break the Japanese defensive line, then strike north-west to control the coast and to allow the army to join up with a force striking south from Burma. This will give them control of the west coast, and they will then wheel and strike behind the Japanese defensive line with an armoured thrust. The RAF will both support and attempt the maximum interdiction of the Japanese coastal supply route. Success will not only recover all of Malaya, but will allow Singapore to be supplied even if all the DEI and Sumatra fall. Alexander's main problem is that he does not know how much of his force will be needed to support the Dutch in Java, and Park is still concerned over the 'missing' Japanese aircraft.

March 7th

While returning from a reconnaissance mission over Gasmata and Rabaul in the Bismarck Archipelago, the crew of an RAAF Hudson based at Seven Mile Airstrip, Port Moresby, sights a convoy of eleven ships heading for Salamaua. These contain troops of the South Seas detachment. This catches the Allies by surprise; they have been readying their forces for the soon-expected invasion of Java, and the Royal Navy forces are to the west of the DEI. The Allies only have a light force in the area, but on sighting what seems to be an invasion force a brigade of the 8th Australian Division is ordered to be ready for operations. This reserve brigade has been held at Darwin for possible action in the DEI, and ships are available at Darwin to allow at least part of the Brigade to be shipped (although this will mean a temporary hold in fortifying Timor). The Canadian Brigade that recently landed at Sydney will be moved to Darwin in its place, allowing it more time to acclimatise.

The Allied air force can only easily reach the convoy with the long range B-17's, which are not effective A/S planes; however the USN informs the Australians that one of their Task Forces should be in a position to intercept the convoy in a few days.

March 8th

General MacArthur, Commanding General U.S. Army Forces, Far East, issues a communiqué saying that his opponent, General Homma, has committed suicide out of frustration. This story gets heavily embellished and just as heavily repeated. Homma reads the report with some amusement. He is less amused when inspecting officers from the Imperial General Staff in Tokyo arrive to find out why he hasn't taken the Philippines on time. However, the staff officers realize that Homma needs reinforcements, and ship in the 65th Brigade of 3,500 men and the 4th Infantry Division from Shanghai. Homma is not happy, as the 4th's 11,000 men are the worst equipped division in the whole Japanese army. However 240mm siege guns from China are welcome

A Japanese convoy arrives in Huon Gulf during the night of the 7th/8th, and under cover of a naval bombardment lands assault forces at Salamaua and Lae without opposition. The 2nd Maizuru Special Naval Landing Force and 400-men of a naval construction battalion land at Lae while a battalion group of the 144th Regiment lands at Salamaua. Members of the New Guinea Volunteer Rifles stationed in the two towns carry out demolition work and then withdraw westward. The Australian brigade at Darwin commences loading the available transports, destination New Guinea.

During the day the crew of an RAAF Hudson of No. 32 Squadron, based at Seven Mile Airstrip, Port Moresby, attacks the transports and scores a direct hit on an 8,000-ton ship which is later seen to be burning and listing. The RAAF hopes to scrape up a squadron of Beaufighters to operate from this airfield, but it will take some days to get there and they will only have the torpedoes they carry with them.

March 9th

American troops, Task Force 6814 consisting of the HQ of the 51st Infantry Brigade and the 132d and 182 Infantry under the command of Major General Patch, land at Noumea on New Caledonia Island.

President Roosevelt again radios MacArthur to leave the Philippines and MacArthur agrees he will leave Corregidor by 15th March. The original plan was for MacArthur and party to leave in the submarine USS Permit on 14th March. However, the radio press in the U.S. has begun broadcasting demands that MacArthur be placed in command of all Allied Forces in Australia and the Japanese, expecting him to flee, have increased the size and frequency of naval patrols in Subic Bay and off Corregidor. A destroyer division is sighted in the southern Philippines heading north at high speed. Tokyo Rose is broadcasting that MacArthur will be captured within a month, and U.S. Navy officers give MacArthur a one-in-five chance. It is decided not to wait for the submarine, but instead to leave by motor torpedo boat as soon as preparations can be completed. The PT boats will take him to Mindanao Island and the party will then board three B-17's at Del Monte Field for a flight to Australia.

March 10th

The Japanese make a landing at Finschhafen on the Huon Peninsula. The Japanese need to capture towns such as Finschhafen and Salamaua to protect their forward air base at Lae.

TF 11 (Vice Admiral Brown), which includes ships of TF 17 (Rear Admiral Fletcher), on the heels of initial nuisance raids by RAAF Hudsons, attacks the Japanese invasion fleet off Lae and Salamaua. 61 SBD Dauntless from the aircraft carriers USS Lexington and Yorktown fly over the 15,000-foot Owen Stanley Mountains on the tip of New Guinea to hit Japanese shipping. They sink an armed merchant cruiser, an auxiliary minelayer, and a transport; and damage light cruiser HIJMS Yubari, destroyers HIJMS Yunagi, Asanagi, Oite, Asakaze, and Yakaze, a minelayer, seaplane carrier, a transport, and a minesweeper. One SBD is lost to antiaircraft fire.

Japanese troops land on Buka Island, the 190 square mile island just north of Bougainville Island. The two islands are separated by Buka Passage.

A convoy sets out from Darwin carrying Australian troops to New Guinea. It is expected that the Japanese will have consolidated their position before they can arrive, so they will land on the southern part of New Guinea. The USN TF 11 is asked to remain in the area S/SE of the island for long enough to provide the troop convoy with air cover if needed.

March 11th

General MacArthur leaves Luzon with the statement "I shall return!" General MacArthur, Commanding General U.S. Army Forces, Far East, his family, Rear Admiral Rockwell, and their staffs embark from Corregidor and Bataan in four motor torpedo (PT) boats, PT-32, PT-34, PT-35 and PT-41, of Motor Torpedo Boat Squadron Three. The plan is that the boats will make for Tagauayan Island, in the Cuyo Group, and arrive by 0730 hours the next morning. Three USAAF B-17's take off from Australia to fly to Del Monte Field on Mindanao to pick up the MacArthur party. One turns back due to mechanical problems, the second crashes at sea off Mindanao and the third lands at Del Monte; it is unfortunately in poor mechanical condition. Meanwhile Major General Jonathan Wainwright assumes command of the 95,000 Americans and Filipinos on Bataan and Corregidor.

In Brazil, President Vargas confiscates up to 30% of the funds of German, Italian and Japanese citizens resident in Brazil, recalls all Brazilian ships to port and confines the Japanese ambassador and his staff to the embassy. These measures are in response to the torpedoing of a fourth Brazilian vessel by the Germans and the mistreatment of the Brazilian ambassador in Tokyo.

More RAF Wellington bombers arrive at Singapore. Park intends to use these in their anti-shipping role (the crews are experienced ones from the Mediterranean), against the Japanese shipping expected to be used against Java. The long range and the two torpedoes of the Wellington allow them to operate from more distant bases, although any daytime attacks will need fighter escorts.

The Combined Chiefs of Staff suggest that General MacArthur be made commander of the proposed SW Pacific theatre. Currently the commands envisaged are

Burma/Malaya/West DEI (Alexander), DEI/New Guinea/Australia/ SE Islands (MacArthur) and Pacific (Nimitz). The suggestion goes down poorly in both London and Australia. They agree that Alexander and Nimitz are sensible commanders for the theatres suggested, given the nature of the combat expected there, but despite the strident US press support for MacArthur they fail to see what qualifications he has for the command. 90% of the troops currently in the area are Imperial or Australian, and the Australians in particular see MacArthur's only contribution to the war so far as to lose the PI. "A clapped out First World War general" is one of the more printable Australian comments. The Australian government counter-proposes Blamey. They point out a number of advantages; he will be commanding mainly Australian troops, he has been working closely with Alexander for some time (useful as it is obvious that in practice the command boundaries between the two will be blurred by operational necessity), and he has fought successfully against the Italians and Japanese. The British, while being more polite about MacArthur, are quite happy to support Blamey. He is seen as being a good solid infantry commander, and given the expected nature of operations in the theatre, armoured thrusts and grandiose complex assaults are expected to be few and far between. Having an Australian commander will also make it easier to deploy Australian militia troops abroad if necessary.

March 12th

General Alexander authorises preliminary work on the planned attack on Yamashita's troops in Northern Malaya, in particular stocking sufficient artillery shells to allow a heavy bombardment of selected positions. He expects expenditure of artillery ammunition to be high, and the attack itself will wait on his next supply convoy from the Middle East, expected in a few weeks, which will bring both reinforcements and more ammunition. As part of the preparations the RAF starts to make photoreconnaissance flights over the Japanese positions and supply lines, disguised as much as possible as part of the continuing operation of small attacks on the Japanese. These are also intended to wear down the Japanese air cover, so that by the time the attack is launched the RAF will have air superiority.

Middle East Command informs the Combined Chiefs of Staff that due to the advanced preparations for troop landings in theatre they do not feel a US division can be ready in time. They suggest an early deployment of one brigade from the US 1st Infantry Division, followed by the rest of the division as soon as possible. It would be impractical to include the brigade in the first operations, but it should be achievable for the posited third landing, and the political benefits would be obvious. Delaying until then will also allow the troops to be trained in the techniques required (MEC left out the opinion of a couple of officers sent to the US to look into the possibilities that the US unit would require additional training to bring it up to Allied standards). It would also be possible (depending on timescales) to use the entire division, although only one brigade would likely be trained for an assault landing.

March 13th

The two PT boats carrying General MacArthur and party, PT-34 and PT-41, arrive at Cagayan on Mindanao Island in the early morning. Later in the day, a third boat, PT-35, arrives at Cagayan. The three boats had made the 560-mile voyage in heavy to moderate seas in two days. The next leg of MacArthur's journey to Australia is to be by B-17, but only one has reached Del Monte Field and it had wheezed in to a wobbly landing. MacArthur, furious, will allow no one to board the "dangerously decrepit" aircraft, and demands the "three best planes in the U.S. or Hawaii," manned by "completely adequate, experienced" airmen be flown to Del Monte. Unfortunately Major General Brett, Commanding General U.S. Army Forces in Australia, has neither. The party must now await the arrival of three additional B-17's from Australia.

The Japanese, having gained firm positions in the Lae-Salamaua area, replace infantry with naval forces.

A Japanese force from the 4th Fleet sails from Rabaul, New Britain Island, for Buka Island, Solomon Islands, which is eventually seized together with other positions in the northern Solomons.

RAF and USAAF reconnaissance planes are still showing a steady build-up of Japanese forces in the Celebes, as well as preparations in the southeast part of Borneo (the area under Japanese control). An invasion of Java is now expected within two weeks. The Japanese are expected to use around two divisions, and Somerville is making plans to deny them the option of landing anywhere except on the eastern part of the island (he expects Japanese air cover to be too strong for surface forces to intervene east of Java). USN and RN submarines are being redeployed to cover the expected invasion routes. For the time being the small Japanese operations in the SE Pacific are a lower priority, as Java is seen as the main target. If Java falls Singapore will be exposed to close range air attacks and possible invasion, and the defence lines for the island, preparations for which had been given a lower priority after the Japanese were held in the north, have again been speeded up.

March 14th

Hitler advances the planning for a summer offensive against Russia. The defences in front of Moscow are now formidable, so the main target will be in the south, aimed towards the Russian oil fields. In the north, a new attack will be made to finally take Leningrad.

Japanese aircraft bomb Horn Island. This island, located in the Torres Strait between Queensland and New Guinea, will become the main tactical base for Allied air operations in the Torres Strait

US forces finally begin to arrive in Australia in large numbers. A convoy (originally intended for the PI when Japan attacked Pearl Harbor) brings 30,000 American troops who are to serve in Australia and New Caledonia. After a brief stay in Australia, the New Caledonia Task Force of some 14,000 officers and men arrived in Noumea on 12 March. The rest of the men are being readied for deployment on Java, but if events make this impractical a diversion to Timor and New Guinea is possible. Two more US divisions are on their way

The Australian government debates the use of the new divisions being raised outside of Australia, and agrees with the provision that deployments must have Australian approval. This is intended to allow the forward defence of islands such as New Guinea. There is also an unofficial implied consideration that the troops are under Australian command. So far the forward defence of the Malay barrier is working (although under severe pressure), and the Australians would rather fight the Japanese on the islands than in Australia itself. There is considerable political division on this, but the opposition is beaten down with the agreement that Blamey be put forward for command of the Australian theatre (although this is not made public). In public they start to pressure for Blamey to be appointed, with the public reason it would be good to have command clarified in view of the continuing Japanese attacks and advances. The divisions are, however, having an effect on Prime Minister Menzies, who is seen to be looking tired and worn after the debate.

The troop convoy from Darwin arrives at Port Moresby; additional forces including RAAF and USAAF personnel will arrive shortly. It is intended to hold a defensive position in New Guinea until the situation at Java is resolved.

The situation on the East Coast of the USA is slowly improving. The new 'bucket brigade' system is working well, and losses have dropped steadily. The first of the old US 'four-pipers' that were in the reserve are being activated and assigned to this operation, as their limited range is not an issue for these operations. They are not good A/S ships, however, and for the moment are being supplemented by RN and RCN escorts. Meanwhile the 'mutiny' by US merchant captains has been quietly forgotten with the proviso that the people involved keep quiet about the politically embarrassing matter.

HMS Audacious and her escorts arrive at Ceylon. With all of his current carriers available for action off Java, Somerville insists that she spends time getting fully operational before she sees action. He also wants to keep the arrival of the new carrier secret for as long as possible.

March 15th

At a staff meeting in Berlin, Chancellor Adolf Hitler and his generals study the situation in the Soviet Union. Moscow has not fallen, and is now unlikely to fall to a direct attack. German casualties from Soviet firepower and frostbite have been immense, but the Soviet counterattacks at Moscow, Staraya Russa, and the Crimea are coming to a close as the Soviets run out of supplies. The initiative is going back to the Germans, and Hitler forecasts the annihilation of the Soviet Army in summer. That evening at the Sportspalast, Hitler announces that the Soviet Union will be "annihilatingly defeated" in the next summer offensive.

Japan launches an artillery attack on Manila Bay. In the Manila Bay area the Japanese, having emplaced additional artillery along the southern shore of Manila Bay southwest of Ternate, renew intensive bombardment of fortified islands in the bay. The shelling is conducted daily and in great force through 21 March, despite U.S. counter-battery fire. Forts Frank and Drum are particularly hard hit.

March 16th

The submarine USS Permit delivers ammunition to Corregidor Island, and evacuates the second increment of naval radio and communications intelligence people.

The Japanese stage an air attack on Darwin. Since their failure to take Timor the Japanese have been staging minor nuisance raids against the island, both sides taking light losses. The attack on Darwin comes as a surprise (as intended), and the response is slow. As a result of this, some twelve planes are lost on the ground at the airfield before the bombers can be intercepted. The Japanese lose four bombers and three Zeros for the loss (in the air) to the defenders of five P-40's. Fortunately for the RAAF the planes at Darwin have been heavily dispersed (the original field was not designed to hold the number of planes now operating out of Darwin), and so only one fighter field was bombed before the defenders could intercept. The RAAF is not happy at the slow and disorganised response, as Darwin is becoming steadily more important as a base, and a number of officers are posted away as part of a general shakeup of the defences.

March 17th

New B-17's arrive to take MacArthur and his party to Australia. The attempt is interrupted by a Japanese raid (it would seem that the days of delay have given the Japanese some information that some sort of operation is underway). Two of the B-17's are damaged, fortunately not severely, and a number of ground crew, and some in MacArthur's party, injured. It would seem that the General himself has received a wound, although no details are yet available. The ground crews are racing to repair the planes before the Japanese can attack again.

March 18th

The B-17's carrying General MacArthur and his party arrive at Darwin. They will later fly on to the metropolis of Alice Springs on their way south. No official clarification is given on MacArthur's wound, though apparently the General was unable to sit during the journey south.

March 19th

Seventeen US Kittyhawk fighters are flown off from Townsville, Queensland, on their way to Port Moresby, staging by way of Cookstown and Horn Island. The Allies are trying to reinforce their air power in the area, but the huge distances involved are consuming time and fuel.

Reports from eastern Borneo indicate to British Intelligence that the attack on Java is now 'imminent'. Travel in Borneo is extremely difficult due to the almost non-existent road network, but the British have been building up small forces in the jungle in anticipation; they will be used to cause the maximum disruption to the Japanese reinforcement convoys which are expected to use the Borneo ports. Good news for Somerville is that the light carrier HMAS Melbourne is finally out of dock after having been damaged underwater in the battle of the South China Sea. He intends to deploy two forces, one north and one south of Java, each having two fleet and one light carrier; his other light carrier, HMAS Brisbane, will remain working out of Darwin for the time being. The carriers will be aided by land-based planes where possible. He hopes to be able to hit at least part of the invasion force, and certainly follow-up forces. His submarines have been redeployed in the area as well. It is unclear what the IJN will provide in terms of a naval escort, but it is expected to be quite heavy. As a result Somerville has added a couple of fast battleships to each task force.
The RAF and the French Air force have been steadily attacking Italian targets over the last month. Targets have included the mainland, the island of Corsica and Sardinia, and especially the island of Sicily. The Italian high command has ordered additional troops to Sicily, which they consider a target for the Allies. Meanwhile planning and preparation for an amphibious assault has reached a high degree of readiness; some twelve Imperial and French divisions (including two armoured divisions) are available, although shipping will restrict the initial landing sizes.

Bomber command has fixed most of the issues with the new Coventry bomber, and is getting regular deliveries of the Lancaster and Mosquito bombers. While the main force attacks Italy (with an occasional diversion to a French target), the new units are training for the planned Ruhr offensive.

Chapter 15 - The Battle for Java

March 20th

Major General Wainwright learns that he has been promoted to the rank of Lieutenant General and that Washington has placed him in command of all U.S. Forces in the Philippines.

Australian Prime Minister Menzies suffers a breakdown in Parliament. Doctors report that it is due to the stress of his job during the war, and while it is expected he will eventually make a full recovery, he will not be able to undertake any duties for at least three months. The Deputy Prime Minister, Curtin, will take over the post of Prime Minister.

In Tokyo, Navy minister Admiral Shimada says that in view of the Allies' "retaliation and hatred", Japan will no longer follow the recognized rules of sea warfare.

March 21st

US forces start a retreat to the heavily fortified island of Corregidor in Manila Bay.

Lieutenant General George H. Brett, Commanding General of U.S. Army Forces in Australia, assumes command of all Allied air forces in Australia. This specifically excludes all FAA aircraft operating out of Australia, as well as RAF/RAAF aircraft under navy operational control.

During the late morning, the Japanese Eastern Invasion Force headed for Java from the Philippines was located northeast of Java by a Dutch Dornier flying boat, which shadowed them for several hours. The Dornier then carried out an attack on the destroyer HIJMS Amatsukaze, releasing only one bomb which fell about 500 yards ahead of its intended target. This attack was followed by two B-17's dropping their six bombs from 13.000 feet. Two of the bombs fell some 500 yards short of the destroyer HIJMS Hatsukaze.

The size of this convoy (carrying the Japanese 48th Division) convinces Allied command that this is a full-strength invasion fleet aimed at Java. The RAF and RAAF torpedo planes are readied for a strike as soon as fighter cover can be arranged and army units are put on alert. The Allies now have a considerable force on Java - about 25,000 Dutch and local troops, two brigades of the 8th Australian division with 30 tanks attached from 1st Armoured in Malaya, and the British 51st Division, as well as about 1,000 US ground troops and additional numbers running and defending the airbases. The Dutch troops are of variable quality; their training was poor, but insistence by Alexander that this had to be improved has led to some improvement. The Dutch also have a force of US Stuart tanks available.

Somerville's main carrier force is east of Singapore, consisting of the fleet carriers HMS Implacable and HMS Illustrious, the light carrier HMAS Melbourne and the Battleships King George V and Richelieu, plus escorts. He also has a cruiser force further east, with the light carrier HMS Colossus for cover (as well as fighter support from Java itself). There are also a number of submarines, mainly British and American, in the area the Japanese fleet will have to go through. He asks the RAF for as many reconnaissance flights as possible; he is sure there is a heavy IJN escort for the invasion force and wants to know where it is.

Alexander also puts the Imperial forces in Malaya on alert - he suspects the Japanese will attack in the north, hoping his command and particularly the RAF will be distracted at Java. He has also requested 40 tanks from Burma to replace the ones sent to Java. Currently, supplies to Burma from shipments originally intended for Russia has left the Armoured Brigade there both fully equipped and with a useful tank reserve. As it seems unlikely a major Japanese offensive will head into Burma in the immediate future, he thinks the tank reserve will be more useful in Malaya. He would have preferred the 1st Australian Armoured Division, but this will take some weeks to arrive and have the necessary modifications made for operations in jungle conditions.

The train carrying General MacArthur's party heads south from Alice Springs. Reporters at Darwin have finally got copy through to their papers concerning the nature and location of the General's wound. This causes considerable amusement in Australia.

March 22nd

In New Guinea, 75 Squadron RAAF, based at Port Moresby, makes its combat debut. Six Curtiss Kittyhawks (P-40Es) make a surprise attack at dawn on the Japanese forces at Lae. Two Zeros are shot down for the loss of two Kittyhawks, although one pilot is saved.

A single Mitsubishi Ki-15 reconnaissance plane takes off from Koepang, Timor, to reconnoitre the defences of Darwin, Northern Territory, in readiness for a larger strike force of Mitsubishi G4M Betty bombers. Coast watchers on Bathurst Island notify Darwin of the approaching reconnaissance aircraft at about 1200 hours and it is shot down by a P-40 of the 9th Pursuit Squadron, their first radar-guided interception. As anticipated, the Japanese bombers make a raid that same day but not on Darwin. They fly 200 miles further southeast and bomb Katherine, Northern Territory. They presumably were hoping to find Allied bombers at the Katherine Airfield but none were there and damage at the airfield is minimal. Officially described as: "An aborigine was killed, another wounded and some damage was done to the aerodrome".

It is officially announced in Australia that John Curtin will officially take over as Prime Minister 'until such time as Robert Menzies has recovered'. There has been considerable debate in the Labour Party overnight about how to handle this; one part of the party wanted to use this as a reason to call an election, which they are confident of winning, but in the end were outvoted by more cautious elements in the Party. They pointed out that calling an election due to the collapse of Menzies while Australia is under attack would look like blatant opportunism, whereas waiting, and showing that they can do an even better job (especially as it is felt that the tide is turning in favour of Australia) will allow them to gather the middle ground votes who will be swayed by the display of statesmanship and putting Australia first, thus giving them a much stronger majority if they go to the country next year. Curtin announces that no changes will be made in Australian policy as a result of Menzie's collapse, but in private he has used his new office to stress that unless an Australian is appointed as head of the Australian theatre the Labour party might have to withdraw from the coalition. This is part of the strategy to show that a Labour PM can lead Australia in the war successfully. The appointment of Blamey has already been supported by Britain, and the ridicule MacArthur has managed to attain in the Australian press has hardly helped his cause. MacArthur himself is still heading south by train, and is out of easy contact with his government.

In support of the Japanese attacks on Java, General Yamashita commences an offensive operation in northern Malaya. Led by the 56th Division, the attack is aimed at what Yamashita considers two weak spots in the Imperial defence line; aggressive patrolling and reconnaissance has been undertaken over the last month to find these with a view to exploitation. The initial attack goes well, although the defences are on alert (an operation to take advantage of the attack on Java was hardly unexpected), but by nightfall the Japanese infantry have managed to push forward between a number of the Allied units. Blamey informs Alexander that he is not as yet concerned, and that he believes the Japanese do not have the force required for a serious breakthrough. He intends to let them get a little more forward before, as he puts it, 'cutting them off at the knee'. There are intense air operations on both sides in support of the ground action, and despite the precautions and alert state the RAF loses some aircraft on the ground to the initial Japanese raids. However the Japanese are now outnumbered by the RAF and RAAF, and by the end of the day they are preventing any serious air attacks on the Imperial defence line.

Map 5 - Malay/Burma

Off Java, Allied reconnaissance planes indicate that the Japanese invasion convoy is most likely heading for East Java. This is in fact in error, as late in the day part of the convoy splits off and heads for Bali, which has a usable airfield the Japanese want to support their invasion of Java. Somerville is reluctant to commit his heavy forces until he finds where the Japanese have placed their support - he does not believe that they would try and invade Java without air support from carriers - however the cruiser force is ordered to engage the invasion fleet after dawn on the 23rd. Air support will be from the air bases on Java, and from the CVL Colossus which is held some distance back from the cruisers. It is planned to have Beaufighters make a torpedo strike at dawn, which it is hoped will leave the convoy in disarray before the surface force attacks.

The force heading for Bali runs into a USN submarine that night; an attack is made but only one hit is attained on a transport. More usefully, the submarine radios in the location and heading of the force, which allows the defenders of Bali to be put on alert. The Allies had not expected the Japanese to attack Bali at this point (assuming they would have concentrated on Java), and only have small forces on the island. They order the airfield commander to destroy the airstrip to deny it to the Japanese (any planes are to fly off for Java before this is done), then delay the Japanese as far as possible before withdrawing.

March 23rd

On Bataan in the PI US and Filipino troops dig in for the soon-expected Japanese attack. General Homma has been reinforced by more army bombers, although the Japanese too are having difficulties with food, and the best part of a division of troops is in hospital
Dawn sees considerable action around Java.

At first light a heavy Japanese air attack destroys some aircraft on the ground at Timor, at the cost of a number of bombers; the Japanese need to keep the island's airfields suppressed until they have airfields at Java. The Allies do not have any spare long-range bombers available to attack the Japanese airfields in return; these are being held back to support Java.

Shortly after dawn the Allies launch a torpedo strike by 24 RAAF Beaufighters escorted by 16 Sparrowhawks. The heavy escort is needed, as the convoy is covered by a dozen Zero fighters. The Zeros damage one Beaufighter and shoot down a second before the Sparrowhawks intercept; in the resulting battle five Sparrowhawks are lost for four Zeroes. This allows the remaining Beaufighters to make their torpedo attacks impeded only by AA fire from the escort and the transports. As the final Beaufighter leaves the scene, three transports are sinking and a Japanese light cruiser is heavily down by the head.

The RAF and Somerville are coordinating attacks from Java, but these are put temporarily on hold as a USAAF Catalina finally finds the Japanese heavy support group. Before the Catalina is forced to take cover in cloud (the plane already slightly damaged by a Zero), the pilot reports 'at least two carriers and two battleships plus supporting ships'. In fact, the battleships are cruisers - this misidentification was a consistent feature for both sides in air reconnaissance. The Japanese force is well back from the invasion fleet, but it is likely that it supplied the defensive cover that disrupted the Beaufighter raid. Somerville expects his main force to be in striking range by late afternoon, and in the meantime, attacks on the invasion fleet will have to be handled by the RAF. Somerville also has two U-class boats in the general area of the Japanese, and hopes that they will be in a position to finish off any Japanese ships he can cripple with his air strikes.

While both sides were keeping their main carrier forces back, the first surface engagement was between the cruiser and destroyer forces that had been sent out; the IJN force to cover the invasion convoy, the Allied force to intercept it. The weather was not good for spotting ships, with too much cloud cover; in addition, the Allied planes were either keeping an eye on the convoy or being held back for the invasion. So the first contact was at 1100 when a lookout on HMS Exeter spotted the masts of the Japanese cruiser Haguru. The forces were fairly even. The IJN force consisted of the heavy cruisers Haguru and Nachi, the light cruisers Naka and Jintsu and 14 destroyers. The Allied force consisted of the heavy cruisers HMS Exeter and USS Houston, the light cruisers HMAS Perth, HMAS Hobart, HMS Dragon and HMS Danae, with 9 destroyers. The Japanese cruisers had been constructed with scant regard for the treaty limits and in balance outweighed the Allied squadron. However the first act of the captain of HMS Exeter had been to make a sighting report, and as a result HMS Colossus, held some 50 miles to the rear of the advancing cruisers, was preparing her torpedo planes for a strike.

Additional information on Japanese forces came from US cryptographers at Pearl Harbor. They had informed Nimitz some days previously that they suspected a Japanese carrier force was heading for the area of New Guinea, and a task force built around the USS Lexington and the USS Enterprise had been sent to cover the area. The sighting of the invasion fleet heading for Java and the news of fresh attacks in Malaya made Nimitz suspect that the suspected Japanese force was either another diversion, or perhaps (given the Japanese proclivity for complicated multiple operations) covering a follow-on invasion of New Guinea. In fact the shortage of available troops and transports had forced the IJN to make the operation just another diversion, and the fleet carriers Shokaku and Zuikaku with the light carrier Ryuju, supported by a cruiser force, were northeast of the island. Both carrier forces sent out search planes throughout the day, but no contacts were made until late in the afternoon when a Japanese seaplane sighted the Lexington. Due to clouds, she missed the Enterprise, and only one carrier was reported to Nagumo.

Somerville now has two main tasks; to fix and destroy the Japanese carrier force reported behind the invasion convoy, and to sink as many of the transports as possible. He intends to use his carriers to search the area for the carriers, while he prepares an anti-shipping strike. The RAF is ordered to attack the transports again.

In Malaya the Japanese attacks are still making ground in the gaps between the Imperial defence lines, but are slowing down as the Australian troops counterattack their rear. The RAF has established superiority in the air, and in addition to keeping the Japanese planes away from the ground troops, they are attacking any supply dumps and artillery parks the Allies have been able to find - some by air, some found using small patrols of Special Forces and locals infiltrated past the Japanese lines. Alexander and Blamey suspect the Japanese supply situation is not all it could be, and are intending to use the Japanese tendency to advance as far as possible to cut off and destroy as many men as they can. The armoured force is being prepared to cut off the Japanese spearheads, although small numbers of tanks have been used to delay the Japanese attacks.

The cruiser forces off Java start firing at 1155. Both sides' gunnery is unimpressive in its accuracy, and the Japanese force starts to manoeuvre for a massed torpedo attack. This commences at 1225, and the force fires off some 90 Long Lance torpedoes at long range. The result is less than devastating and only one ship, HMAS Perth, is struck. The heavy torpedo wrecks her bows and her forward turrets, and the cruiser is forced to turn away and slow to a few knots to avoid further damage. The rest of the Allied force moves to cover her, and at last a number of hits are made. HMS Exeter is hit on her rear turret, rendering it inoperable, and HMS Danae receives two 6" hits which fortunately only do minor damage. In response, the Haguro is hit twice by 8" shells, knocking out one of her forward turrets.

At about 1250, the strike from HMS Colossus arrived. The light carrier only had eleven torpedo planes available and operational, covered by eight Sparrowhawks, but the Japanese cruiser force currently had no air cover at all (the Japanese fighters were at that moment over the invasion convoy which was closing the coast of Java). The AA fire from the warships was intense, and one Sea Lance was shot down and another forced to withdraw trailing smoke. The other nine targeted two of the Japanese cruisers, hitting the Haguro with one torpedo and the Jintsu with one. The other ships were strafed by the Sparrowhawks once they realised that there was no air cover, and the heavy cannon fire resulted in the loss of one of the destroyers, which blew up after being strafed, breaking in two and sinking fast (it was later ascertained that a cannon shell had set off one of her oxygen-powered torpedoes). With the damage caused to both sides, neither side was willing to carry on combat for the moment, and both the forces withdrew slightly. The Japanese intending to make a night attack once they had repaired their immediate damage, the Allies to allow their air force to continue to reduce the enemy strength. In any case, the original Allied task of finding and attacking the invasion fleet was now thought to be better served by air attack, using the cruiser force once sufficient damage had been done.

The invasion fleet itself had been the subject of two more heavy attacks during the day from RAF and RAAF Beaufighters and a squadron of Cormorant dive bombers operating from land bases. The convoy had been covered by Japanese fighters, and the Allies had lost seven Beaufighters and three Cormorants as well as five Sparrowhawk fighters to the fighters and the AA. The Japanese had lost twelve fighters, and the cruiser HIJMS Mogami was sinking, as were four transports, with another two transports burning. The Japanese commander pressed on despite these losses, and by the late afternoon was ready to make his landings on the island. The troops had now been reduced to some 9,000, and a considerable amount of equipment had been lost. The Japanese intention was to establish a foothold for additional troops to exploit; another division was available in the Celebes to reinforce the landings.

As night fell, the two cruiser forces were still manoeuvring for advantage. The Japanese were trying to get into a position for a night attack, while the Allied force was trying to slip along the coast to get at the invasion convoy. A strike was attempted on the Japanese at 1730 from HMS Colossus, but was unable to find the force; the ASV-equipped plane leading the strike had equipment failure, and the rest of the strike did not spot the Japanese beneath the cloud cover. With the Japanese force now lost, HMS Colossus was ordered to fall back on the main fleet. However, her earlier attacks on the Japanese cruiser force have given away her approximate position to the enemy. At 1715, (while her own strike was on the way to the estimated position of the Japanese cruisers) a large enemy raid was detected closing from the northeast. This is a surprise to the plotting crew, who had not been expecting a strike from that direction. It is in fact a strike from the three IJN light carriers comprising the cover force for the invasion fleet; this force had been detected by a USAAF aircraft yesterday, and Somerville is intending to attack it. At the moment, his priority is the destruction of the invasion force. Due to a mishap, the report of the force had been missed by Colossus and her destroyer escorts.

The incoming attack consisted of 24 torpedo planes and 20 dive bombers, escorted by 16 fighters. As the Colossus was also covering the Allied cruiser force, she only had 14 fighters available, although all of these were either airborne or launched before the enemy raid arrived. Ironically this raid had been spotted by a Catalina on its way west, but it had been assumed it was headed towards Somerville's main carrier force, currently preparing to launch a strike of their own against the covering force, having spent the day closing the range.

The FAA fighters tried to engage the raid, in particular the dive bombers (felt to pose the greatest risk to a light carrier), but the Japanese escort fighters closed to protect them. In the ensuing fight ten Sparrowhawks were shot down for the loss of four dive bombers and seven escorting fighters. Another dive bomber and three torpedo planes were shot down by the AA fire of the carrier and her escorts. Despite radical manoeuvring, the Colossus was hit by four torpedoes, one of which failed to explode. The damage caused by those that hit was enough to force her to a halt as her both her engine rooms started to flood. This abrupt stop actually helped her evade the first of the dive bombers, who were unable to compensate for the sudden loss of speed, and six huge plumes of water rose into the air in front of the listing carrier. Despite all her AA could so, the remaining ten dive bombers dove down to deliver their 500lb bombs. The ship was hit three times, all three bombs penetrating her hanger. Two burst in the hanger itself (fortunately empty of planes), the third went deeper into the forward engine room (the light carriers had no hanger deck armour), where it exploded, wrecking the equipment. Colossus was left heavily on fire and listing from the water flooding in through the torpedo holes.

Even as the Colossus was being attacked, the main British strike was on its way. The force was centred around the fleet carriers HMS Illustrious and HMS Implacable, and the light carrier HMAS Melbourne. Their strike consisted of 24 SeaLance torpedo planes and 24 Cormorant dive bombers, escorted by 20 Sparrowhawks.

Somerville intended to follow up this attack with a night strike, but this would not be prepared until after dark (he did not want armed and fuelled planes on deck or in the hanger with a possible inbound Japanese airstrike). The strike arrived at the Japanese carrier force just after sunset.

The Japanese force was centred on three light carriers (despite the reports, they were only escorted by heavy cruisers, not battleships). These were the carriers Takasaki and Tsurigisaki (converted into carriers as part of the response to the increased RN carrier program in the late 1930's), and the CLV Taiyo. Between them, they carried over 80 planes. The carriers were escorted by four cruisers and eight destroyers. The incoming strike was not spotted until it was ten miles away from the carriers, the fading light having made the raid commander decide to go straight in. Due to the fighters sent off to escort the raid on HMS Colossus, the force only had fourteen fighters available, and with the short warning time, only nine were in the air when the strike arrived. The defenders were immediately attacked by the Sparrowhawks, preventing them from closing with the attacking planes, and only one torpedo plane was lost to the defending fighters. All nine of the Japanese fighters were shot down for the loss of six Sparrowhawks.

The attacks were led by the torpedo planes. One was shot down on its attack run, and another forced to drop its torpedo and turn away by the AA fire, but 21 SeaLance remained. Without enemy fighters to worry about, the swept in on the first two carriers in a classic hammer and anvil attack, hitting the Takasaki with three torpedoes, and the Tsurigisaki with one. These were not the new Mk XV aerial torpedoes, but even so the hits crippled the two Japanese ships. Even as the torpedo planes swung away, the dive bombers were falling into their near-vertical dives. Most of the planes were attacking the two already-damaged carriers (the third carrier, Taiyo, was some distance away and had been missed in the hurry to get the attack in before dark). The Cormorants were carrying 500lb bombs due to the range (the strike had been launched at near to the maximum range, as the Japanese force was under observation by ASV-equipped RAF planes which had been able to guide it in), but these were more than adequate against the poorly-protected converted carriers. The Takasaki was already reeling and listing from the torpedo hits, and with no fighters to worry about the Cormorants could take their time. Three bombs hit the Takasaki, leaving her blazing in the falling night, and four exploded deep inside the Tsurigisaki. Ten minutes after the raid ended the Tsurigasaki exploded, sinking soon after. She would be joined in an hour by the Takasaki, her converted merchant hull unable to handle the structural damage from torpedoes and bombs.

The remaining six dive bombers headed for the Taiyo, which had been finally been spotted. The light was failing in the swift tropical twilight, and the dive bombers did not manage to get any hits, although they reported the carrier as 'damaged', having mistaken a couple of close misses as hits. The planes made it back to their carriers after dark without major incident as, despite the risk of submarine attack, the carriers used landing lights to help the planes land safely.

To the south, the invasion convoy had finally made landfall late in the afternoon. The Dutch commander of the defences had decided to let them land then counterattack, a decision later criticised by the Imperial commanders. As a result by sunset some 4,000 troops had got ashore (although with little equipment), only resisted by local light forces. The Dutch commander reported he would launch an attack on the beachhead at 0700 the following morning.

Unknown to the Japanese, Somerville had a second carrier force off Java - the two fleet carriers HMS Ark Royal and HMS Bulwark. This force was south of the island, and had been steaming east all day at 25 knots, putting it in range of the Japanese landing by 1800. The force had not been detected; the Japanese reconnaissance was concentrated north of Java, as they had indications of a carrier force there, and their intelligence led them to believe the RN only had the ships available to form one force. This would lead to one of the FAA's trademark night strikes. At 1900, the first strike set off, led by the ASV-equipped Spearfish, and followed an hour later by the rest of the planes. As the Japanese had no night fighter capability as far as the RN knew, the strikes were unescorted. The first that the Japanese knew was when their frantic unloading of their ships was suddenly illuminated by flares dropped by the raid leaders. The only defence of the ships was by wild and ineffective AA fire, as the torpedo planes bore in to attack the transport ships. The second strike, by the remaining torpedo planes and the dive bombers, was even easier - by now the Japanese defence was erratic and uncoordinated, the sea and the remaining ships lit by the burning hulks left by the first strike. Although the dive bombers were under orders to pull out higher than usual (to allow a safer attack at night), the sitting targets of unloading transports were hardly radically manoeuvring destroyers. By the time the last of the planes were recovered to the carriers only three transports were left, and the aircraft had also sunk two cruisers.

The Japanese now had only 6,000 men ashore on Java, with only limited equipment and ammunition.

March 23rd - 24th continued.

As night drew on the two cruiser forces were continuing to manoeuvre for position. The Japanese commander was trying to close on the Allied force for a night torpedo attack. The original orders to the Allies, to get behind the Japanese and shell the invasion convoy, had been rescinded when the Colossus was hit, and on the report that the southern air strike was in progress. So both forces were moving westward, the Allies trying to stay between any enemy force and the burning carrier.

The engineers' report on Colossus was not good; the combination of underwater damage, loss of power and the fires were overwhelming the light carrier, and now only damage control parties remained onboard. It was in this condition that the Japanese cruisers found her. As the enemy force closed, the Allied cruiser force moved to intercept. Not all the Allied cruisers were equipped with radar, or used to working together in night actions, and it had been hoped to draw the Japanese cruisers away so they would be vulnerable in the morning - Somerville had a surprise waiting for them come daybreak. However, the light from the fires burning in the carrier's hanger deck had been spotted, and to allow the remaining crew to be evacuated, the cruisers moved in to the attack.

The first hits were obtained by HMS Exeter at 0030 - her radar had allowed her to be targeting the Haguro for some time, and her third salvo scored on the heavy cruiser. Fires broke out on the Japanese ship, allowing the USS Houston to also target her. The Allied force was roughly equal in gun power, even without the Perth (ordered to Singapore with two destroyers as escort after the heavy torpedo damage she had taken), but the Allies were short of destroyers. Two had been ordered to help take off the Colossus's remaining crew, leaving only five destroyers to the Japanese thirteen. This allowed the Japanese destroyers to close in on the Allied cruiser line and make a torpedo attack (the Japanese ships carried reload torpedoes, allowing them to replace the ones used earlier). They also split off a force of five destroyers, which headed for the Colossus.

The night torpedo attack was from a closer range than the earlier daytime attack, and was more successful. One of the Japanese destroyers was sunk, intercepted by the defending ships, but the remainder managed a launch against the cruisers. The cruiser line was by now heavily engaged in a gun battle with the Japanese cruisers - the Haguro was burning heavily with three turrets out of action as a result of fire from HMS Exeter and USS Houston, and the light cruiser Naka was also in trouble, being targeted by HMS Danae, HMS Dragon and HMAS Hobart, although Danae had also taken a number of hits. HMS Exeter was hit by two of the Long Lance torpedoes, the cruiser hit aft and in her engine spaces. Without propulsion or power, she slowed to a stop, although the forward turrets were still firing manually. USS Houston was barely missed by another torpedo which passed forward of her by a matter of feet. But the small cruiser Danae, the fire from her shell hits making her an easier target, was hit by three of the large torpedoes. She rolled over and sank in less than two minutes, taking most of her crew with her.

While this had been happening, the other Japanese destroyers had closed the carrier. Her damage control parties had been taken off, and the British destroyers watched from a distance as huge plumes of water shot up into the night sky from the stricken carrier, blood red in the light from her fires. Hit by five torpedoes the ship's end was fast, and ten minutes later she had slipped under the waters of the Java Sea.

After the torpedo attack on the cruisers, the Japanese force had no reloads left. Not realising how much damage they had done, they collected their destroyers and headed east. However the night action had drawn them well west of their earlier position, and as they regrouped the captain of the Nachi (now the leader due to damage to the Haguro) was shocked to see four huge waterspouts erupt close to his ship, gleaming white in the moonlight. HMS Warspite had arrived.

The Warspite had used the cover of darkness and her radar to close, and even as the Nachi's commander ordered star shells to be fired, her second half-salvo arrived, straddling the cruiser. The third salvo from Warspite landed a hit from a 15" shell on the Nachi. The heavy shell was barely slowed by the cruiser's armour, smashing through it to wreck her forward engine room. More were to follow, as the Warspite showed just why she was considered one of the best gun ships in the Royal Navy. In less than 15 minutes, Nachi was a helpless burning wreck, already sinking into the Java Sea.

Meanwhile the Allied cruisers had been exchanging fire with the Haguro and the Naka, both of which were already damaged. With only star shell to help either side, fire was inaccurate although Houston took one 8" hit, which temporarily knocked out her A turret. Neither Japanese cruiser was able to retire, and once the Nachi was helpless, Warspite turned both her main and secondary batteries on them. Neither cruiser lasted long.

As a result of the earlier torpedo actions, the only Japanese ship left with torpedoes was one of the destroyers. She had three left, as a result of a failure which had stopped them being launched earlier. As the battleship and cruisers were ignoring the destroyers (they were incapable of doing much damage without torpedoes), she managed to get into position behind the burning Nachi and attempted to launch all three at the Warspite. One torpedo failed to launch again, but the other two were successful. The Warspite was busy engaging the cruisers, and did not see the approach. One of the heavy torpedoes missed her, combing the water ahead of the ship, but the other hit her alongside the bridge. And failed to explode.

With his cruiser force being sunk from under him, the Japanese commander ordered the remaining destroyers to withdraw while the cruisers tried to buy them time - even so the Warspite, firing under radar control, sank one of them as they made their escape.

Somerville's carrier force had been preparing to launch a new strike at the remaining Japanese light carrier. Just before midnight, the British fleet was sighted at long range by one of the Japanese patrol submarines. Although she was too far away to attempt an attack, she radioed a sighting report of 'two large carriers steaming east'. As a result of this, the Taiyo was ordered to turn back and head north - one light carrier, some planes already destroyed, was no match for two fleet carriers, and the reports from the landing site were already indicating there was no invasion fleet left to support.

March 24th

The Japanese begin an intense air and artillery bombardment of Bataan. Luzon-based Japanese Army and Navy aircraft begin a heavy bombardment of Corregidor in support of this, and night air attacks are conducted for the first time.

On Java, the Dutch forces, supported by Stuart tanks and with an Australian brigade in reserve behind them, attacked the Japanese landings. The Japanese fought fiercely but with little hope - they were outnumbered 4:1 and had little heavy equipment or supplies. The situation for them worsened that morning as the Warspite sailed close to the landing areas and started to drop salvoes of 15" shells on their positions. The shock caused by these was so great that many of the infantrymen under bombardment were stunned enough to surrender. The rest of the landing force fought almost to the last man, charging with bayonet and sword when they ran out of ammunition - a foolhardy waste, as the Dutch armour dealt with them easily. It did take two days to clear the landings, but after the morning of the 24th, the final result was never in doubt.

While the landings were being destroyed, the Royal Navy was trying to save its damaged ships. The Exeter had been badly hit by two torpedoes, and even with HMS Dragon aiding her to pump the water out, she was slowly sinking even as she headed for Java. Luckily for her the weather was calm, but she finally limped into Surabaya with her rear deck awash. Sadly, although she had managed to make land, the damage to the small cruiser was so severe that she was declared a total constructive loss. She was however kept manned for some time in case her 8" guns would be needed in defence or to support the army, but this proved unnecessary.

In Malaya, the Japanese advance was still moving south, although slowing fast. Alexander and Blamey were happy with this - the further the Japanese pushed their head into the noose being created for them, the more of them they could destroy. By now virtually the entire Imperial Guards division was through the Australian lines, and an Indian division as well as the 1st Armoured, heavily supported by artillery, was waiting to engage them. Blamey estimated he would close the trap the following day, and hoped that as well as destroying a considerable part of the Japanese force facing him would be in position to drive through the opening and take at least part of the Japanese lines from the rear.

The US and Japanese forces in the Solomon Sea had been searching for each other for some time, both carrier forces having sent out search planes throughout the day, but no contacts were made until late in the afternoon when a Japanese seaplane sights the Lexington. Due to broken clouds, she missed the Enterprise, and only one carrier was reported to Nagumo.

Chapter 16 - The Solomon Sea

March 24th

North East of New Guinea, the Battle of the Solomon Sea

The US cryptographers had not yet decoded enough of the Japanese signals to decide on the aims of the carrier force northeast of New Guinea. The most likely possibilities were either another attempt at an invasion (covered by carriers) while the Allies were occupied with the simultaneous invasion of Java, or a feint. Given the previous Japanese operations, the most likely option was considered to be invasion, and as a result considerable reconnaissance assets were used to try and locate a transport force. In fact, while such an invasion had indeed been the preferred Japanese plan, a shortage of transport ships had made this impossible. Their plan was to use their carriers to draw off forces that might have been used to attack their Java invasion. Ideally they would degrade them in the process, then after Java was secured, invade New Guinea again.

Although the Allies had more search planes available, the need to search for a supposed second force meant that the Japanese were the first to spot their enemy. A search seaplane from one of the cruisers accompanying the carrier force had spotted the USS Lexington on the afternoon of the 23rd. By the time this had been reported and plotted, it was considered too late (and too far) to make a successful strike that day. Admiral Nagumo therefore ordered any Japanese submarines close enough to intercept the US force to attack, while changing course and speed ready for a dawn attack on the US carriers. Additional search planes would be flown off before first light in order to spot them and lead in the carrier planes.

The US carriers had spotted the Japanese plane on their radar, but the seaplane had manoeuvred cleverly to take advantage of the cloud cover, and the US carriers were unable to vector fighters onto the plane by radar alone (at this stage of the war, US tactical control was still not well practised). The US tactic was to be to send out a wide-ranging patrol before dawn, and be ready to conduct a strike as soon as the Japanese force had been spotted. They were still not certain if the plane that had found them had come from a carrier force or a surface force - seaplanes were known to be carried on the Japanese cruisers, which could be accompanying anything.

Both sides sent off their search planes before dawn. The Japanese were concentrating their effort in the area they expected the US carrier (they still assumed only one carrier was present), while the US search had to cover a wider area (but involved more planes). Nagumo was reluctant to use potential strike planes to supplement the search, and so the Japanese did not find the US carriers again until 1000. In the meantime the US planes were conducting their own search, and spotted a single carrier (the Shokaku) at 1030. This was reported as a fleet carrier. The Japanese were operating the Ryuju some distance away from the main carrier group, and this ship was at the time hidden under some rainsqualls. The two fleet carriers were operating in open order, and as the spotting plane had to dodge into clouds to evade the Zeros protecting the force it is possible both fleet carriers were never seen at the same time. As a result of these successful searches both sides started to ready their strikes; in addition to the extra half hour of warning, the Japanese were again to prove much faster at getting their planes armed and into the air.

The Japanese strike formed up and headed for the US carriers at 1115. It would take them an hour to reach the US ships. Although the Lexington and Enterprise were operating notionally together, they would in fact conduct two separate strikes, as they had not had a chance to train together. Both strikes were on their way before noon, just as the US radar spotted the wave of Japanese aircraft heading towards them.

The Japanese strike consisted of 18 Zero fighters, 36 dive bombers, and 24 torpedo planes. The radar detection allowed the US carriers to clear their decks and hangar decks of explosive and as much inflammable material as possible, in preparation for the coming attack. Eighteen Wildcats had been retained for defence, and all of these were in the air by the time the Japanese closed the carriers. The weather was variable, rainsqualls making it difficult to keep track of both the incoming planes and the manoeuvring carriers, and the Japanese planes (following their earlier reports of only one US carrier being present), missed the Enterprise under one of these squalls. While this was good news for the Enterprise, this meant that the full force of the Japanese attack would fall on the Lexington. The highly experienced Japanese planes split up into their attack formations, allowing the US fighters to attack some of them before their protecting Zeroes could get into position. While this was happening the USN ships had formed their close defensive formation, allowing them to concentrate their fire on the incoming planes.

The defending fighters managed to shoot down five Zeros and eight of the torpedo planes (as well as disrupting the torpedo planes' attacks), however twelve of the Wildcats were lost in this and the following dogfights. As a result of these actions, and the heavy AA gunfire from the mutually supporting US warships, only one torpedo hit the Lexington. The large carrier absorbed the damage without too much obvious effect, the torpedo damage fortunately forward of her machinery spaces.

Unfortunately concentrating on the torpedo planes meant that the dive bombers had been able to make their attack opposed only by the US AA fire. While the AA suites of the USN ships had been increased from some years ago, it was still considered light by RN standards, and only three dive bombers were destroyed during the attack. The remaining planes launched their 250kg bombs from near-vertical dives onto the Lexington. While the carrier's size had helped her absorb the torpedo damage, her poor manoeuvrability made it more difficult to evade the bombs. The Lexington was hit by four of them, and took serious underwater damage from a number of near misses. The planes left the carrier burning fiercely and covered in a huge plume of black smoke.

The cautious Nagumu had been holding the Ryuju's small air group in reserve; his intention had been to use it to finish off any US carrier that had survived his first strike. However even as his orders to send the planes off to attack the US carrier force were being sent, the first of the US planes arrived.

The US carriers had sent out a total of 93 planes - 18 Wildcat fighters, 53 dive bombers and 22 torpedo bombers. Due to their inexperience at conducting multiple carrier strikes, the planes had become separated into three groups. This proved unfortunate for the Ryuju; if the planes had been on course, they would have missed her. But as it was, the light carrier was just readying her planes on deck for launch when an alert lookout spotted 18 dive bombers and 22 torpedo planes heading straight for her. The Ryuju only had six fighters airborne to stop them, and although the US planes had lost their fighter escort, sheer numbers of attackers had already doomed the carrier. Although her defenders shot down six of the torpedo planes and three dive bombers for the loss of two fighters, the rest of the attack force simply overwhelmed her. Unlike the newer fleet carriers, the Ryuju was not fast enough to steam away from the US aerial torpedoes, especially when they were delivered in a hammer and anvil attack. Hit by three of the underwater missiles, her machinery rooms already flooding, the carrier slowed to a dead stop as the dive bombers swept down onto her. Five minutes later, hit by three bombs in addition to the torpedoes, the ship was already on fire and listing heavily. She would sink some 30 minutes later.

Of the remaining two group of US planes - one consisting of nine Wildcats and seventeen dive bombers, the other of nine Wildcats and eighteen dive bombers - the second missed all of the Japanese carriers, having either misunderstood or misapplied the directions. The final group however found the Shokaku and Zuikaku - as well as eighteen Zero fighters. Seeing the heavy CAP, the planes decided to concentrate their attacks on the Shokaku. Outnumbered by the Zeros, this was a very difficult task, not aided by the radical manoeuvring of the ship. The result was that only two bombs hit the carrier. One did light damage to her stern, hitting well aft (indeed it almost missed). The other hit her dead centre on her flight deck, penetrating it and exploding on her hangar deck. Fortunately for the carrier nearly all her planes were airborne, as the explosion caused a serious fire and left her unable to operate aircraft. However this carrier class was the only one the Japanese had built with serious hanger deck armour (indeed in this respect they resembled the RN Formidable class), and while it took time to extinguish the fires, the carrier was never in serious danger.

With only one flight deck left to them, not all of the returning Japanese planes were able to fit onto the Zuikaku, and a number of the more seriously damaged planes had to be ditched over the side. Meanwhile Nagumu was trying to decide if there were any US carriers left. Only one had been seen, and that had been left burning and sinking fast, according to reports (this misapprehension was ironically aided by the missed US strike - the planes encountered could, just, have come from one carrier. He had lost a light carrier, and the Shokaku would need repairs before she could again operate aircraft. Also, a considerable number of planes and pilots had been lost. With the US carrier force presumably eliminated, there was no likelihood of any interference in the Java campaign from the east, and so he decided that he would withdraw north, escorting the damaged Shokaku.

The Americans likewise thought they had defeated their opponents. One carrier was certainly sunk, and a second had been reported as 'burning heavily from multiple bomb hits'. As a result, there seemed no chance that the Japanese could land forces on New Guinea, and there was a badly damaged carrier to get back to Pearl Harbor. The US force therefore split into two parts. The undamaged Enterprise, carrying the aircraft from both carriers, would head back to Pearl, keeping between the likely position of any Japanese force and the damaged Lexington. The Lexington, escorted by two cruisers and four destroyers, would hopefully be able to make it back. By late afternoon the worst of her fires were out, and she was able to make 8 knots, increased to 15 by the night.

Sadly for the Lexington, although her engineers had performed a miracle of damage control, she would not make it back home. The Japanese had deployed a line of submarines prior to the fleet actions. They had missed the US force on their way out, as their deployment had not been made fast enough, however they were now in position to intercept the Lexington as she withdrew. At 0200 on the 25th the carrier was hit by two torpedoes, which caused serious flooding and finally put her already damaged machinery out of action for the final time. With no power to fight the flooding, the giant carrier slowly took on an increasing list. It was obvious there was no chance now of getting her back to Pearl, and so her crew was taken off and she was torpedoed by one of her escorting destroyers.

24th March

In Malaya Blamey has decided that the Japanese pocket has been pushed far enough south. While allowing it to deepen will trap more troops, he is concerned that the Japanese might break out if his defence is stretched further. He informs Alexander that the planned envelopment and counterattack will begin tomorrow. Alexander agrees, and also issues instructions for the 17th Indian Division (currently under the command of General Slim in Burma) to attack across the Three Pagoda Pass and down the coast towards Malaya. This operation will expose the troops to counterattack, however Alexander thinks that the Japanese will be busy with other things tomorrow.

25th March

The Japanese submarine HIJMS I-9 launches a Yokosuka E14Y1 Reconnaissance Seaplane to reconnoitre Kiska and Amchitka Islands.

The Allied counterattack and envelopment starts in northern Malaya, aided by every available RAF and RAAF aircraft. The plan is simple; the Japanese have pushed south to form a pocket, but that pocket is contained by the 8th Indian Division, supported by part of the 1st Armoured. The 'neck' of the pocket is now attacked by the Australian 7th and 9th Divisions, again supplemented by tanks. The Japanese have no weapon capable of countering the British infantry tanks, and the counterattack is supported by all available artillery. Attempts by the Japanese to counter with fresh troops were frustrated by the Allied air support and artillery. By the evening, the Australians had nearly closed the neck of the pocket. Yamashita is in a quandary. His instinct is to pull as many as possible of his troops out of the trap, but his orders are to push south as hard as possible. Unable to manage these two conflicting ideas, he compromises - fatally, as it turns out. He orders the troops at the neck of the pocket to hold and counterattack while he tries to reinforce them, but the British armour keeps forcing them back with very heavy casualties. The main problem the British armour has is running out of machine gun ammunition, although a number of tanks are overrun when they break down. Meanwhile Slim is pushing a Brigade group south along the coast, hoping to catch the Japanese while they are preoccupied with the Australians, and Ghurkha units are moving east through Three Pagoda pass.

26th March

At a meeting with the Australian Advisory War Council, General MacArthur gives his views on the situation in Southeast Asia and the southwest Pacific. He doubts that the Japanese are able to undertake an invasion of Australia, and believes that it would be a great blunder on their part if they attempted it. He suggests that the main danger is from isolated raids and attempts to secure air bases in the country and therefore, the first step is to make Australia secure. The War Council listen politely, but after the reports they have received from Blamey, Alexander and Somerville think MacArthur's ideas of Japanese expansion have been coloured by his experiences in the Philippines.

General MacArthur receives the citation for his Medal of Honour at a formal dinner in Melbourne, Victoria. He tells the audience, "I have come as a soldier in a great crusade of personal liberty as opposed to perpetual slavery. My faith in our ultimate victory is invincible, and I bring you tonight the unbreakable spirit of the free man's military code in support of our joint cause." The Australians non-military men in the audience are impressed; the military and ex-military less so. MacArthur continues, that the medal is not "intended so much for me personally as it is a recognition of the indomitable courage of the gallant army which it was my honour to command".

That night three B-17's based at Townsville, Queensland, evacuate Philippine President Manual Quezon and his family to Australia. This extraction is seen as politically necessary by the USA.

Admiral King relieves Admiral Stark as Chief of Naval Operations and thus becomes Commander in Chief U.S. Fleet and Chief of Naval Operations; Vice Admiral Horne (Vice Chief of Naval Operations) and Vice Admiral Wilson (COMINCH Chief of Staff) are his principal assistants. There has been considerable controversy over King's appointment after the fiasco of the US coastal convoys and anti-submarine operations, and the administration intends to keep him on a short least for the moment.

Rear Admiral Wilcox commanding Task Force 39 with the battleship USS Washington (BB-56), the aircraft carrier USS Wasp, the heavy cruisers USS Wichita and Tuscaloosa and six destroyers, sails from Portland, Maine, for Gibraltar. It is intended to include them in the Allied naval force starting to build up to support amphibious operations. Originally they had been tasked for the Pacific, but Roosevelt wants to have ships in place as part of the Allied fleet. It is intended to replace the Washington with one of the older, slower battleships as soon as one can be sent to the Mediterranean.

27th March

General Sir Thomas Blamey is named Commander-in-Chief of Australian Military Forces, and given command of what is currently being called the central Malay barrier (including Australia). He will take command once he is satisfied as to the progress of his counterattack in Malaya. This is a blow to General MacArthur who had hoped that he would have been given the job.

In Malaya, the two Australian divisions finally make contact. The bag is not completely closed; the terrain and jungle make it possible for small groups of Japanese to escape north, however to the surprise of the Allies few attempt to do so. Casualties have been heavy for the Allies - some 6,000 men killed and wounded, but far heavier for the Japanese.

The U.S. Army's War Plans Division issues "Plan for Operations in Northwest Europe," in which a tentative timetable for an invasion of France is offered. The plan calls for (1) a limited cross-Channel attack in the autumn of 1942 (Operation SLEDGEHAMMER) as an emergency measure if Soviet forces show signs of collapsing or (2) the main Anglo-American invasion (Operation ROUNDUP) in the spring of 1943 if SLEDGEHAMMER is not required. The build-up of U.S. forces and supplies in the U.K. for the major cross-Channel attack is coded Operation BOLERO. The Imperial Chiefs of Staff view SLEDGEHAMMER in particular as a fantasy, the shipping and landing craft simply are not available, and even an attack in 1943 seems far beyond Allied capabilities, especially as hardly any US troops are yet in Europe.

The Imperial Staff in Tokyo commences an evaluation of the status of the war so far, in particular the need to modify some of the objectives and forces provided in view of some of the problems encountered, in particular the lack of oil fields captured. This debate will go on for some time.

28th March

The Japanese, moving into position for all-out offensive against Bataan, feint against I Corps and push in the outpost line of Sector D on the II Corps front. Increasingly heavy air and artillery bombardment of Bataan is lowering the efficiency of the defence force as well as destroying badly needed materiel. Efforts to run the blockade and supply the garrison with necessary items have failed, and the supply situation is growing steadily worse.

U. S. Navy code breakers at Pearl Harbor decipher a message that reveals the Japanese plan a major offensive north of Australia in early May. The conclusion is drawn that the IJN expects to have finished repairs to its damaged carriers by then.

German Foreign Minister von Ribbentrop asks the Japanese Ambassador to Germany, Count Oshima, to secure a Japanese attack on Russia simultaneously with Germany's "crushing blow." The Japanese would attack at Vladivostok and Lake Baikal. The Ambassador listens politely but without comment.

The Imperial General Staff publish their plans for containment and offensive operations against the Japanese. These are considered general aims at present, as some are dependent on others, and the Monsoon is due to start soon in Southeast Asia. The planned operations are as follows.

(1) Alexander is to push the Japanese out of Malaya, and establish a front far enough north to link up with Burma and to stop the Japanese attacking Burma from the south.

(2) Following on, the Japanese are to be driven out of Thailand; the status of Thailand will be determined afterwards. This will secure Burma and Malaya, as well as the overland supply routes to China.

(3) When practical the Japanese are to be pushed back north through French Indo-China, in cooperation with a Chinese offensive. This will allow easier Allied supply by sea, and make Singapore, Malaya and Burma secure.

(4) The Allied forces under Blamey will reduce the Japanese forces in the DEI. The priority will be the Dutch East Indies, Borneo and the Celebes (as well as New Guinea). It is hoped that the USA will provide some ground troops.

(5) Once the DEI and Celebes are secure, an invasion force to retake the PI will be built up. This is expected to consist of mainly US troops.

(6) The RN and associated Imperial naval forces will secure the Malay Peninsula and the DEI as far east as New Guinea. Operations will be coordinated with the USN, especially operations in the eastern part of the area. It is expected that the IJN will intervene, and the opportunity will be taken to weaken it further.

(7) In cooperation with the USAAF, the attacks in the DEI/Celebes will be uses to draw in and destroy the Japanese air force. It is considered that the Japanese cannot stand an attritional campaign, which the Allies huge industrial base makes possible.

The Australian troops, having closed the pocket, now give way to a second Indian division moved up from the south. The fresh troops allow the pressure on the pocket to continue, while the Australians and the armour reform to thrust north. The strike down the east coast of Thailand has made good progress - the troops initially tasked to defend this area have been pulled eastwards in an attempt to force a way through to the trapped troops. As the situation in the DEI looks to be contained (the only Japanese left are around 3,000 men on Bali, which he feels the Dutch can handle, and the IJN seems to be unable to form up a convoy and escorts) Alexander releases some of his reserve force to reinforce the attack. An additional Brigade from each of 18th British Division and 8th Australian Division will soon be heading north up the peninsula. Somerville has recalled all his U-class boats to blockade the coast of Thailand in case Yamashita attempts to reinforce or evacuate by sea.

29th March

In Britain, Bomber Command has been building up its aircraft for a major offensive against the Ruhr and the coastal industrial cities building U-boats. This offensive will include new aircraft - the first full use of the high-altitude Coventry bombers, as well as new navigation aids. The Mosquito-equipped Pathfinder crews are now fully trained in these. Bomber command expects the offensive to last at least three months, depending on the weather and the casualty rate. The intention is to cripple the industrial heart of the Ruhr and the main U-boat construction yards. There has been internal controversy about the use of the heavy bombers for this aim rather than in support of the Army, but in reply it has been pointed out that the force is not trained for Army cooperation, and something needs to be done about the steadily increasing war production coming out of the Ruhr.

30th March

Admiral Chester Nimitz is put forward by the USA as Commander in Chief, Pacific Ocean Area (CINCPOA). The Allies have no objections to this; the Royal Navy is already fully committed without any diversions into the Pacific. It is agreed that the local subordinate commanders will consult about operations on the Pacific/Malay Barrier area.

The Japanese pocket in northern Malaya is slowly being closed as the Imperial forces hammer it with artillery and airpower. The Japanese have little heavy equipment, and have started to resort to suicidal infantry charges. Some of these have succeeded (at great cost), allowing some Japanese to break free and head north, but in no condition to do more than annoy the Imperial forces. With two Indian divisions containing the Japanese, the Australian troops start their move north, led by a brigade of the 1st

Armoured. Alexander is preparing backup troops to be available, either for the pocket (in case the Japanese look like breaking out) or, more likely, to support the advance north.

In Burma, Slim's forces have now reached the lower part of the Kra peninsula and have started to meet opposition from the Japanese. Slim has requested armour support, which will be sent by sea to the closest port able to land the tanks. In the meantime he has established positions just inside Thailand, securing the passes into Burma. At present the Thai army is an unknown quantity. It has not yet intervened in the war, and it is believed there is considerable political argument in the Thai government about what to do. The hardliners who supported the Japanese wish to attack the Imperial forces; the other factions are pointing to the lack of success of the Japanese and the fact that they will be facing a thoroughly annoyed British Empire, quite possibly without any Japanese help at all. The hardliners have not been helped by the way the Japanese have acted while in Thailand; they have behaved more like an army of conquest than as Allies, and their treatment of the local inhabitants has caused considerable enmity. The general consensus seems to be to wait and see which of the forces gains an ascendency over the other, then hopefully join the winning side.

Chapter 17 - Bataan Falls

31st March

Long-range reconnaissance planes indicate that the Japanese have started to improve the airbases captured in the Celebes. The indications are that this will allow more air support both of convoys and of army operations in the area. The RAF and RAAF are mainly engaged in Malaya; the USAAF is asked if it can start building up a force in the DEI and Malay barrier to help counter the projected Japanese air force. The main problem is the time this will need - supply lines are immensely long, and it takes time to build up the necessary infrastructure and supply dumps.

General Yamashita sends a report to Tokyo requesting permission to pull back from western Thailand and the Kra peninsula to concentrate his forces in the east. The appearance of additional Imperial troops in Kra means that if the attack through his centre continues then the troops to the west will be cut off, rolled up and lost. He reports that help or intervention by the Thai army is unlikely, as the government appears to be in political and military paralysis.

1st April

The Japanese Army resumes a series of major attacks against the US and Filipino forces on Bataan. The 24,000 men there are on 1/4 rations and ill from food shortages and tropical diseases.

The aircraft carrier USS Hornet and her escorting vessels sail from San Francisco, California, with 16 USAAF B-25 Mitchell bombers of the Doolittle attack group on her deck; Hornet's aircraft are in the hanger deck. That afternoon, Captain Mitscher informs his men of their mission: a bombing raid on Japan.

Yamashita receives a response to his request to withdraw. It is denied. He is ordered to hold and defeat the Imperial troops. The 'or else' is strongly implied in the communiqué. The Japanese government will pressure the Thai government to do what is expected of them, and an additional infantry division will be sent from the Home Islands to strengthen him. The missive leaves Yamashita depressed.

In Malaya, the Australians are still engaged with the Japanese troops trying to hold their defensive lines. The fighting is reported as very intense. Alexander and Blamey have expected this, based on the way the Japanese have fought so far. The aim is to overextend them in counterattacks while punishing them with artillery and from the air. Once this is done, they expect an armoured attack to break through the Japanese lines and allow them to be rolled up (at least in the west).

2nd April

After long and increasingly acrimonious discussions between the army and navy, the Japanese have finally decided on an amendment to their strategy. It has been agreed that the most vital resource needed is oil. While there is some in the Celebes, the main sources available to them are in the DEI, Borneo and Burma. In order to capture and hold this vital resource, the following strategy has been decided upon.

(1) The air bases in the Celebes will be improved to allow land based aircraft to escort the invasion convoys and attack Allied warships. Aircraft will be flown to the bases as soon as they are complete. The imminent capture of the Philippines will aid in this.

(2) General Yamashita has shown a lack of the spirit of Bushido in allowing himself to be driven back by the British. He is to be relieved, and reinforcements made available to the army from the Home Islands and China to allow the attack into Malay to recommence - successfully this time. It is accepted this will be slowed by the monsoon, but it is expected this will hamper the enemy, and in particular his armour, even more. The air force will be reinforced to allow them to destroy the RAF in Malaya as part of the advance. Once the northern part of Malaya is secure, attacks into Burma will be made to capture the large oil fields there.

(3) In order to prevent the Royal Navy interfering with the invasion and supply convoys in the South China and Java Seas, it will have to be eliminated or driven off. This will be the task of the IJN, aided by aircraft based in the Celebes and later on Borneo and the Dutch East Indies. It is estimated that the British have two fleet and one or two light carriers available. In order to attain local superiority, the five fleet carriers, as well as a sizeable force of battleships with their own carrier escort will be committed. Since the USN cannot be ignored, once this force has destroyed the British Far Eastern Fleet it will be moved east to do the same to the USN. While the operations are underway against the Royal Navy, the IJN's submarine fleet will cordon off the area to stop any American involvement.

(4) As soon as the IJN has cleared the RN out of the area, fresh convoys will land troops on Timor, Java and Borneo to crush the local defenders in detail. The carriers and land-based air will eliminate the Allied air power in the DEI. Additional diversionary attacks will be made on Darwin to force the Australians to concentrate on reinforcement of their homeland defences.

(5) The Carrier and Battle group will replenish and then attack the US island of Midway. It has been calculated that this will force the Americans to engage them, where they can be defeated and forced back to Hawaii and the West Coast.

In Java, the defenders are getting ready to retake the island of Bali. The Japanese are estimated at fewer than 3,000 troops, and there are still Allied forces on the island (although not engaging the invaders at present). It is intended to use about 6,000 men - split between Australians, British Commandos and Dutch - with air and sea support. There are still Japanese aircraft in the area, and Somerville insists on fighter cover before committing a surface force in support. The attack will take place in a few days once suitable shipping has been assembled.

3rd April

The Japanese open an all-out offensive against the Bataan line, which is by now under strength, undernourished, poorly clothed and equipped, and battle weary. After air and artillery bombardment lasting from 1000 until 1500 hours, the Japanese move forward, making their main effort against Sector D, the west flank of the II Corps, where the 41st and 21st Divisions, Philippine Army, are thinly spread and dazed as result of the preliminary bombardment. The 41st, on the west of the line, gives way and is rendered virtually ineffective as a fighting force, although a regiment on the extreme west succeeds in withdrawing in an orderly fashion.

In the Mediterranean, final planning for an amphibious operation aimed at Sicily is taking place. Reports from the Far East are encouraging, and the monsoon will soon put a stop to major operations in Burma and Malaya. Once it starts, Operation Husky will take place on the next suitable date.

4th April

In the II Corps area on Bataan, the Japanese attack is again preceded by a demoralizing artillery bombardment in conjunction with air attacks. The main line of resistance of Sector D collapses as the 41st Division Philippine Army withdraws again and the 21st Division is forced from their main line of resistance to the reserve line in front of Mt Samat. After nightfall, the Japanese regroup for an assault on Mt Samat.

The first large raid using all the new equipment and the Coventry bomber is made by Bomber Command against Hanover. The main raid consists of 150 of the new high altitude Coventry, which follow in the Mosquito pathfinders. Their bombs, dropped from 35,000 feet, do severe damage to the supporting structures of buildings, as well as breaking gas lines and water mains. This damage makes it much more difficult to fight the damage and fires of the following waves of bombers - 400 Lancasters dropping the new 4,000 lb bombs and incendiaries, and a final wave of Halifax bombers carrying more incendiaries and light bombs to interfere with the fire-fighting efforts. The raid is finished off the next morning when 150 Coventry bombers raid above the ceiling of the German air defences, losing only one plane over the target. They drop another 1,500 tons of bombs on targets that were missed in the night raid.

The raid is considered a success - a considerable part of Hanover's industry has been burned out or wrecked, and the sight of RAF bombers attacking apparently at will during the day had a serious effect on morale, many people fleeing the city. This raid will be a pattern for the RAF Spring offensive against the Ruhr and selected coastal cities.

In Malaya, the Australians break the Japanese defensive line. With orders to hold, Yamashita is unable to stop them forming a 'shoulder' in the east, allowing them to commence rolling up the western units, which are almost unable to pull back as they are also facing a slow infantry advance from the west under General Slim.

5th April

Fuhrer Directive 41 is issued and the Wehrmacht has its orders for 1942. Leningrad is to be captured and contact is to be made with the Finns east of Lake Ladoga, however this is a secondary objective. The main attack will be in the South, which involves 2nd Army and 4th Panzer Army breaking through to Voronezh on the Don River. 6th Army will break out south of Kharkov and combine with the 4th Panzer Army to surround the enemy. After that, the 4th Panzer Army and 6th Army will drive east under the command of Army Group B and surround Stalingrad from the North, while Army Group A's 17th Army and 1st Panzer Army will do so from the South. Once Stalingrad is taken, the 6th Army will hold the flank defence line while Army Group A drives south into the Caucasus to seize the oilfields. After this it will be possible to advance south and attack the British positions in the Middle East, taking the oil fields and the Suez Canal and cutting the direct link between Britain and the Far East.

After air and artillery preparation the Japanese resume their offensive in the II Corps area on Bataan, taking Mt Samat. They concentrate on the 21st Division, leaving it virtually ineffective as a fighting force. The Corps prepares to counterattack tomorrow with all available forces.

A Japanese invasion force of 4,852 troops sails from Lingayen Gulf, Luzon, toward Cebu Island, in the Visayan Islands, east central Philippines.

6th April

The First Canadian Army is formed in the U.K. under the command of Lieutenant General McNaughton.

7th April

Soviet Army troops force a very narrow corridor to Leningrad, opening a tenuous rail link to the city. Trains run into the city with desperately needed supplies and come out with civilians and the wounded, all under heavy artillery fire from the Germans.

8th April

Bomber Command mounts a raid on Essen. It is somewhat lighter than that against Hanover, but is again effective. The combination of the pathfinders and the Coventry bomber is causing the German defenders terrible problems, as the loss rate is very low and they leave the target open, burning and damaged for the follow-on bombers, which as a result are attaining a much better number of aircraft on target.

Harry Hopkins, Special Assistant to President Roosevelt, and General Marshall, US Army Chief of Staff, arrive in London for talks with British service and supply chiefs concerning the integration of US and British manpower and war production for action in Europe. General Marshall urges an offensive in the west to relieve pressure upon the USSR and promises a constant flow of US troops, including many air units, to the UK. The British treat these suggestions politely, but in fact they have no intention of attacking into France. Instead their operations are aimed at Italy. Since the only US Army involvement so far is a brigade of the 1st Infantry Division (compared to some 14 Imperial and French Divisions), Marshall has no troops to back his arguments with.

On Bataan, II Corps disintegrates completely under sustained Japanese attacks from the ground and air. The Japanese soon discover gaps in the Alangan River line held by the U.S. 31st Infantry and 803d Engineer Battalion; the Philippine Scouts' 57th Infantry, 26th Cavalry and 14th Engineer Battalion; and Philippine Constabulary troops, and stream southward at will. In a final effort to stem the enemy advance, the Provisional Coast Artillery Brigade, serving as infantrymen, forms a weak line just north of Cabcaben, but other units ordered to extend this line are unable to do so. Major General King, Commanding General Luzon Force, decides to surrender his troops and orders equipment destroyed during the night of the 8th/9th. Of the 78,000 men of the Luzon Force, about 2,000 succeed in escaping to Corregidor Island in Manila Bay.

   The submarine USS Seadragon delivers food to Corregidor, and evacuates the final naval radio and communications intelligence personnel.

   The air echelons of the 3rd, 17th and 20th Pursuit Squadrons (Interceptor), 24th Pursuit Group (Interceptor), and the 21st and 34th Pursuit Squadrons (Interceptor), 35th Pursuit Group (Interceptor) based on Bataan begin operating from Del Monte Field on Mindanao with whatever aircraft are left.

Somerville informs Alexander and Blamey that he expects to be able to lift the required troops onto Bali in a few days. While he has the naval support he needs, a delay has been caused due to all light shipping and craft having been evacuated to the west out of the range of the failed Japanese landings.

At 1200 hours, the aircraft carrier USS Enterprise, with the heavy cruisers USS Salt Lake City and Northampton , four destroyers, and the oiler USS Sabine, sortie from Pearl Harbor to rendezvous with the aircraft carrier USS Hornet which is carrying B-25s to attack Japan. Since the Hornet is unable to maintain normal air operations due to her decks being full of B-25's, the Enterprise will be her escort until the raid is launched.

9th April

After four months' epic resistance the 76,000 emaciated and diseased US and Filipino troops and civilians defending Bataan have surrendered. Major-General King said that he was defying orders not to surrender from Major-General Wainwright, now on Corregidor, in order to avoid a "mass slaughter" by the 50,000 strong Japanese army. 2,000 men were evacuated to Corregidor, which is still holding out.

The prisoners of war pose a logistics problem to their captors who are now turning their attention to the island of Corregidor. The Japanese plan to move the prisoners to Camp O'Donnell, but with the nearest railhead 65 miles away they will have to force-march them there.

After the last two RAF raids, Hitler informs the Luftwaffe that they will find a method of defending against the high altitude bombers. Such a program has already commenced, and it is hoped to have some prototypes available for testing in two months.

The Australian attack drives over the Thai border. Thai army units are mysteriously absent, leaving any defence to the Japanese, as the internal struggle in the Thai government intensifies. The local population, both Malay and Thai, seem more than happy to see the Australians. The Japanese have been acting more as troops occupying a defeated enemy than Allies. The 9th Australian Division, with some armour support, forms a 'shoulder' to prevent the Japanese from the east interfering, while the rest of the Australian corps turns west to crush the Japanese between them and Slim's advancing infantry. Given the impending monsoon season, Blamey informs Alexander than he intends to stop at approximately the original pre-war lines of defence in Thailand in the east and centre, but will join up with Slim on the west coast to form a solid defence line across the peninsula. This line will be strengthened during the wet season, ready to be used as a base for a new advance to drive the Japanese back to French Indo China once conditions make this possible.

13th April

Vice Admiral Ghormley, USN, is assigned as Commander-in-Chief South Pacific (COMSOPAC). He is to command all Allied base and local defence forces (land, sea, and air) in the South Pacific Islands, with the exception of New Zealand land defences. His line of demarcation with Somerville is set somewhat tentatively as east of New Guinea.

The British and Australian governments officially approve the appointment of General Blamey as commander Dutch East Indies/Australia. He will take over formally once he is satisfied he can leave the Malaya offensive in the hands of his divisional commanders and General Alexander.

A mixed force of British, Australian and Dutch troops is landed on Bali. Around 6,000 men are involved, outnumbering the Japanese some 2:1. There are also Allied troops remaining hidden from before the invasion, who have been passing on information on the invaders. While the battleship Warspite and some cruisers are available for support of the landings, in fact they are unopposed by the Japanese. It is expected to take some weeks at least to clear the island, depending on what sort of defence the Japanese make. In the meantime, Somerville is busy withdrawing his heavy forces back to Malaya to replenish.

16th April

Japan invades the island of Panay with a 4,000-strong force. The Japanese Kawamura Detachment (41st Infantry Division) lands unopposed at Iloilo and Capiz on Panay Island.

April 17th

The RAF follows up its heavy nighttime attacks with a daylight raid on the MAN diesel factory at Augsberg. Some 80 bombers leave the factory in burning ruins in a precision attack. Despite the speed of the Mosquito ten bombers are lost to various causes, mostly to AA fire.

General MacArthur, currently residing in Australia, is ordered back to Washington to discuss his next appointment.

Chapter 18 - The Doolittle Raid and its consequences

April 18th

A totally unexpected air raid today by American bombers on large Japanese cities, including Tokyo, has shocked Japan. The raid by 16 B-25 bombers was launched from the deck of the American aircraft carrier USS Hornet some 650 miles from Tokyo. The Hornet was in company with the carrier USS Enterprise, as the bombers on Hornet prevented her from operating her normal aircraft complement.

After completing their bombing runs, all 16 aircraft cleared the Japanese home islands and continued westwards towards the coast of China. The raid was planned deliberately as a psychological shock to the Japanese and a much needed boost to sagging American morale which has suffered from a cataract of military disasters since the Pacific war began. The US Army Air Force crews volunteered and trained vigorously in secret for this unorthodox and dangerous mission. To take off from the deck of an aircraft carrier with the very heavy fuel load required as well as bombs was a problem never before encountered by army pilots.

The raiding B-25's were unopposed when they crossed the Japanese coast. The raid was led by General James Doolittle. His plane roared over Tokyo at a height of 1,200 feet just as an air-raid practice ended and the barrage balloons had been winched down. He dropped his incendiaries before the real alarm was sounded. Over China, it was night and the weather was bad. A few pilots force landed their planes and of 63 crewmen who parachuted, five died and eight were captured. The raid caused little material damage but has boosted American morale.

Although the bombers were launched early, as a suspicious Japanese craft had been seen, it appears this did not make a sighting report, as the Japanese appear to be unaware of the source of this raid. President Roosevelt refers to Shangri-La in a radio broadcast, which hardly enlightens the Japanese command.

General Blamey signals General Alexander (with a copy to London) that all Japanese troops that invaded Malaya have either been captured or driven out of the country. Churchill is delighted, and sends a congratulatory telegram. The success of the Australian units is apparently ameliorating his earlier dislike of them.

20th April

The Japanese conquest of the central Philippines is nearly complete as Cebu and Panay are conquered. Small U. S. and Filipino garrisons have fled into the hills of Leyte, Samar, Negros and Bohol, but organised resistance has ended.

21st April

USAAF Major General Brett assumes command of the Allied Air Force, which has units based in northern and eastern Australia, with advanced facilities in the Port Moresby, New Guinea area. He will report to General Blamey as overall commander. Admiral Crace has been placed in command of the naval forces in the area, although until Japanese intentions become clear Somerville retains his heavy ships close enough to intervene if necessary. Crace will deploy a mixed force of cruisers and destroyers with the two Australian light carriers to harass the Japanese (with the aid of the Royal Navy submarines), but is not to engage a heavy task force.

The Germans request the assistance of the Italian Navy to deal with the ramshackle Soviet flotilla on Lake Ladoga (estimated at 6 gunboats, 2 large and 5 small torpedo boats, 32 armed minesweepers, 9 armed transport ships, 17 armed tugboats and 1 submarine, plus another 25 other boats).

The Italian Navy promptly agreed and sent the four torpedo boats of 12th MAS Flotilla, commanded by Capitano di Corvetta (Lt-Com) Bianchini. The Italians have received assurances from the Germans that no Royal Navy carriers are present on the lake.

In Washington DC, the federal government decides to build the "Big Inch" oil pipeline from Texas to New York so Allied tankers won't have to run the German submarine gauntlet along the East Coast. This pipeline has a diameter of 24", the highest-capacity oil pipeline ever built.

22nd April

The raid on Tokyo by US B-25 bombers has caused immense consternation in the Japanese command, as well as much loss of face - the Emperor could have been injured or even killed. An emergency reappraisal of the impending IJN operations is ordered. The Americans cannot be allowed to get away with such an attack on the Japanese home islands, even if it means altering or postponing operations originally thought to be more militarily important.

One consequence of the attack is that Admiral Somerville has made arrangements for his heavy units, particularly his fleet carriers, to undergo boiler and bottom cleaning at Singapore as fast as possible. It is expected that the raid will sting the Japanese into some sort of retaliation, and he wants the fleet to be as prepared as possible. Similar activity takes place at Pearl Harbor, although the wide disposition of naval units makes this more difficult. Nimitz's actions are expected to hinge on how well his code-breakers can decrypt Japanese signals, something at which they are becoming increasingly adept. Daily summaries are being flown by hand of officer to Singapore to keep the breaking of the codes secret.

23rd April

In retaliation for the recent RAF raids, the Luftwaffe raids Exeter at night. Considerable damage was done, as this was the first major raid in a considerable time, however the RAF night fighters took a heavy toll of the bombers. The number of aircraft used by the Luftwaffe is far fewer than in the heavy night raids of early 1941, and it is believed that they no longer have the bombers to cause more than occasional disruption by this means. The increased performance of the RAF defence and the better radar now in use means that unless the Germans can invent some new method of penetrating the defences the raids will continue to suffer severe losses which will limit their effectiveness even more.

24th April

The Australian-led attack on the Japanese in Thailand reaches its 'stop line' and halts major offensive action in the east and central parts. This is basically the line of defence originally intended to be taken by Operation Matador. While it would be possible to continue further, there are two considerations; first, the start of the monsoon season is expected very soon, and stopping now allows supplies to be brought up under relatively benign conditions, and second Blamey and Alexander have been informed that secret negotiations are underway with an anti-Japanese faction of the Thai military/government. The attacks against the Japanese to the west will continue until they are destroyed; the Japanese infantry are still fighting hard, but have run out of artillery ammunition and are thought to be low on all other supplies.

An emergency meeting of the Japanese General Staff comes to the decision that 'a heavy and devastating response must be made to teach the foreign barbarians a lesson.' Accordingly the Navy is tasked with coming up with an immediate plan. The Navy's response is that they have three options. First, an attack on the Royal Navy in the South China Sea to drive it back past Singapore and allow new landings in Malaya and Borneo. Second is an attack into the Coral Sea area to take New Guinea and draw in elements of the US Navy, allowing them to be destroyed. Third is an attack on the island of Midway, close enough to Hawaii to force the US fleet to defend it. These operations would use the carrier force (it is expected that repairs currently underway will be finished shortly), backed by the battleships. The intention is to attack a vital target in such force as to destroy the offensive options of the enemy for a considerable period, probably for a year.

After initial consideration the High Command suggests that the Coral Sea and Midway options seem the most promising, as it is imperative to teach the Americans a lesson for bombing Japan and risking the life of the Emperor. The China Sea operation should be considered a follow-up to destroy the Royal Navy capability in the area.

25th April

A new RAF raid by some 300 bombers attacks the Heinkel works at Rostock. Thanks to the efforts of the Pathfinders later reconnaissance reports show considerable damage to the factory. However a considerable number of the bombers missed the target due to deception measures. Losses were again low, but intelligence is reporting urgent Luftwaffe efforts to modify fighters to allow them to intercept the Coventry bombers. While existing fighters can reach the 35,000 feet needed, performance is poor at this height. This has been anticipated by the RAF, one of the reasons for delaying the bombing campaign being to allow a useful number of the new heavy bomber to be deployed to make use of the period before German defences were improved.

Paris is exhilarated today by the news that General HenriGitaud, who has been a prisoner of war since he was captured in June 1940, has escaped to Switzerland. The 63-year-old general's escape has given a boost to French morale. He succeeded in freeing himself from the castle at Königstein, in Saxony, which had been turned into a maximum-security prison, jumped on board a moving train and reached the French border. He is expected to join the Free French army currently in North Africa.

28th April

The full horror of a forced march by American and Filipino prisoners - in which as many as 20,000 men are believed to have perished from disease, hunger and the savagery of their Japanese captors - is beginning to emerge. The prisoners, taken after the surrender of the Bataan peninsula earlier this month, died as they were marched 65 miles to a captured US barracks near Clark Field airbase.

Even before the march began, many of the prisoners were racked by malaria, dysentery, beriberi and other diseases. The Japanese forced the pace with clubs, bayonets and unspeakable cruelty. Dozens of men were bayoneted to death; more were beheaded, shot and beaten at the whim of their captors. Those who could not keep up were clubbed to death or buried alive.

Filipinos bore the brunt of the brutality and, it is believed, the casualties. On 11 April, as the march began, Japanese soldiers massacred some 400 Filipino officers and NCOs - hacking them to pieces with their swords. All the prisoners of war were looted of personal possessions. The precise number of prisoners who started - and finished - this "death march" is not known, but it is believed that as many as one in three may have died.

The Allies make no attempt to hide the horror of the Death March - instead they use it to reinforce the opinion that the Japanese are barbarians who must be defeated totally and completely.

Cuba granted de facto recognition to Free French control over French territories in the Pacific, Equatorial Africa, and the Cameroons.

Canada has voted on conscription in a record turnout and the country is divided on linguistic grounds. English speakers (the majority) are in favour of a draft for service overseas. The French-speaking minority is split; initially it had been expected to vote against it, but passionate appeals by some of the Free French senior officers (brought in from Washington to argue in the debate) have swung more of the French vote in favour. As a result conscription is expected to take place, though for the moment forces sent overseas will still be volunteers.

A large convoy arrives at Singapore, bringing supplies and reinforcements. Among them are a brigade of the French Foreign Legion and 1st Australian Armoured division. This will relieve the 1st Armoured, allowing them to be sent back to the Middle East for a rest and to be re-equipped with new tanks. The existing armour will be withdrawn to Singapore as a reserve; the Australians are equipped with the more recent 6-pdr Valentine tank. The convoy will also transport considerable quantities of rubber and other raw materials back to Europe.

29th April

The Luftwaffe bombers have added Norwich and York to the list of towns visited in revenge for the RAFs attacks on Essen and Rostock. They bombed and machine-gunned Norwich for over an hour two nights ago, and last night they struck York. In each case the bombers delivered about half their loads on target, and despite their small numbers caused considerable damage and killed 400 people. British experts are sure that the bomber's accuracy is due to a new electronic target beam and are working on a way of confusing the pilots so that they drop their bombs in open country.

The Germans are also suffering heavy casualties on these raids. Thirty bombers have been shot down out of 150 used, and many of the lost crews are instructors thrown into action to appease Hitler's rage over the RAF attacks. The raids are doing more harm to the German war effort than to the British in the long run.

In the Philippine Islands, the Japanese are now shelling Corregidor heavily.

1st May

After deep consideration, the Japanese navy presents their preferred plan to draw the US Fleet into a decisive battle in the Pacific. Since the main aim is to draw the US Navy based at Pearl Harbor into a decisive battle and to defeat it, the best option is seen as a direct attack on an American island. This will be Midway, as holding Midway allows it to be used as a forward base for an attack or invasion of Hawaii. It is felt that this will be unacceptable to America, and so their fleet will be forced to do battle to defend Midway.

In order to achieve a crushing victory the attack will consists of the five fleet carriers, operating as a group to destroy the remaining US carriers in the Pacific. The spotting of a US carrier in the Mediterranean by the Luftwaffe has puzzled the Japanese, as logic would require the carrier to be used to bolster their force in the Pacific. Japanese intelligence estimates the Americans have two operational carriers in the Pacific, possible three if the Ranger has been moved from the Atlantic. The Japanese carrier force can deal with these easily.

The main body will consist of the Japanese battleships, led by the Yamato and escorted by at least three light carriers. This is just in case of US air attacks before the Japanese can destroy the US carriers. Once the fleet battle is won, an invasion force will be escorted to Midway. The captured island will then be used as a base to allow first air attacks then an invasion of Hawaii.

After discussions about exactly how the fleet will act, and its composition, the plan is approved and will be issued to the fleet and Pacific commands. It is expected to take around three weeks to get all the forces into position (some of the carriers are just finishing repairs), and the attack is set provisionally for the 24th May.

3rd May

The US decoders based at Pearl warm Admiral Nimitz of a proposed action by the Japanese aimed at the mid-Pacific. They consider the most likely target to be Midway Island. The interception of the intelligence has been helped by the volume of traffic needed to inform the various commands. Nimitz orders immediate plans to be drawn up to counter the invasion on the assumption that it is indeed Midway. As he only has old, slow battleships available, he intends to base his fleet around two two-carrier task forces as soon as the carriers used in the Tokyo raid have returned to Pear Harbor. He is worried by the volume of traffic reported - it indicates a very heavy attack by the Japanese, and if they commit their carrier force his four carriers may be overwhelmed, especially if they also have to worry about a heavy Japanese surface fleet. He therefore passes the intelligence on to Admiral Somerville in the day's despatches, asking him if it will be possible for the Royal Navy either to help by organising distracting operations in the SE Asia area, or sending a force to help.

4th May

Admiral Nimitz arrives on the atoll of Midway, and orders the Marine commander to submit direct to CinCPac a detailed list of all supplies and equipment required for a decisive defence of Midway. These items will receive the highest priority.

During the night of 3 May, the submarine USS Spearfish slips into Manila Bay and picks up 27 Army and Navy officers, including nurses, from Corregidor Island. She will be the last American submarine to visit Corregidor before the island is surrendered. On the same night Japanese troops land on the north coast of Mindanao.

In a nationwide crackdown on the growing and anti-Nazi resistance movement in Holland, the Germans today executed 72 members of the Dutch underground by firing squad. Seven others were sentenced to life imprisonment. A German statement broadcast on Hilversum radio said that the men were found guilty of making contact with Germany's enemies and possessing arms and explosives. The executions are seen as evidence that the Nazis have given up hope of persuading the Dutch to support Nazi Germany.

The Japanese bombardment of Corregidor intensifies in preparation for a landing. In 24 hours the Japanese artillery fires 16,000 shells at US positions. They also sink the minesweeper USS Tananger.

In view of the preparations needed for the Midway operation, the proposed second invasion of Port Moresby is postponed. The transports are needed to lift additional troops to Midway, and Yamamoto does not want to risk carriers in support, as they will be needed to sink the US Pacific Fleet. His intention is to concentrate his forces for the decisive battle the Japanese Navy has been seeking in the Pacific.

Chapter 19 - Preparations for Midway

5th May

The RAF commences jamming of the new Luftwaffe navigation aids being used in the current raids. This causes the percentage of bombs on target to fall from 50% to 13%.

The Japanese land on Corrigedor Island in Manila Bay just before midnight. They sustain heavy losses in consolidating their landing.

Off Corregidor, the submarine rescue vessel USS Pigeon is bombed and sunk while the tug USS Genesee and harbour tug USS Vaga are scuttled.

US codebreakers inform Nimitz that it seems that southward operations (into the New Guinea and Solomons areas) have been postponed. This again leads to the conclusion that the Japanese fleet will be used further north.

An urgent meeting is held in Singapore between Somerville, Alexander, Blamey, Park, and the other available area commanders to discuss Nimitz's intelligence and proposed operations. Somerville wishes to send a task force to aid the Americans, provided it does not damage his main task which is to defend SE Asia. Consideration is given to the results if the Japanese attack somewhere other than Midway (the signal traffic has convinced Somerville that some sort of operation will take place even if it not at Midway)

The two possible areas that affect him are an advance into the Solomons, or an attack into the South China Sea. The Solomons/New Guinea area is vulnerable to a large Japanese offensive, but would only bring limited gains. They would also put the Japanese navy at the end of a long logistics line, and there is nothing immediately critical to the Allies in the area - an invasion of the Solomons or another attempt on New Guinea would have to be countered, but the tying down of the Japanese fleet in support would be to the advantage of the Allies who could concentrate on them from two directions.

The second possibility is an attack supported by the fleet on SE Asia. Possible targets would be Malaya, Borneo and the Dutch East Indies. The Dutch East Indies is thought to be the least likely as it would expose the Japanese fleet the most. Malaya is less difficult for the fleet, but is now so strongly held that Alexander and Blamey feel any likely invasion would be defeated. In particular the Japanese would need not just to invade but to supply a large enough force in the face of the RAF and the RN surface and submarine forces, a task which is felt to be beyond them. As Somerville points out, if they had the capability why was it not used while their army was still in Malaya? Alexander has just received reinforcements, and by the end of the month, they will be acclimatised. While not as secure as Malaya, the Dutch East Indies are now well defended, and again an invasion force would have to be large. Air power can quickly be reinforced from Malaya, and the Allied submarines would make any protracted campaign very costly. Blamey is confident that unless the Japanese attack is unrealistically heavy he can hold the area, and the forces in Australia are steadily building up.

Borneo is an easier target, and using a strong fleet to support a number of small landings is seen as feasible - the logistics of Borneo make it unsuitable for large formations. However losing the half of Borneo they control will not be critical, and indeed the damage the defence could inflict on the Japanese fleet would make the island an acceptable sacrificial goat.

Bearing this in mind, Somerville suggests the following. He has been preparing the fleet for a new engagement. A task force of three fleet carriers plus supporting ships can be sent in 24 hours; it will take some 18-20 days to reach Hawaii. In order to maintain a high speed the force will need to refuel; this will be done first in Australia, and will also allow the force to be halted if it proves necessary. Sending the ships this far is low risk, but is best done now while further discussions are made - it would be unwise to wait due to the transit time required. He will hold two fleet and two light carriers in Singapore. He suggests that the US task force currently exercising in the Red Sea be sent on to Singapore to reinforce him (there would not be sufficient time for them to get to Hawaii unless the Japanese operation is delayed). This gives him another fleet carrier and modern battleship, which should be adequate. Even if the entire Japanese fleet were to be used he can always do as he planned in December and fall back to Ceylon while he is reinforced from the Mediterranean, but he thinks this eventuality highly unlikely - the IJN would be putting their ships into a noose of his submarines and torpedo planes. In order to protect the China Sea area, all Allied submarines will be pulled back into defensive positions, and the RAF will use its long-range reconnaissance aircraft to give the maximum warning. Blamey suggests than in addition aircraft in Australia could be used to reinforce, as an attack heavy enough to require this means no attack would also be possible towards Australia.

As a result, units of the fleet are ordered to make final preparations and sail for northern Australia within 24 hours. This is preparatory to making a final decision as to its destination. While the sailing itself cannot be kept completely secret, it will be leaked that they are heading to Ceylon then home, being relieved by ships from the Mediterranean, to undergo refits. Arrangements are already being made to keep the necessary refuelling in Australian waters secret. While the proposed task force is still a risk, the possibility of a crushing defeat of the Japanese carrier force is felt to make this risk worthwhile.

6th May

Attacks on seven cities yesterday signalled the start of an offensive along a 400-mile front by Chinese forces led by General Chiang Kai-shek against the Japanese occupation forces. The Chinese armies have started to receive the increased supplies sent along the Burma Road since the attack by the Japanese on SE Asia.

Shanghai and Nanking were among the cities raided, with Japanese communications and munitions supplies among the principal targets. Nanking, captured by Japan more than four years ago, is the seat of Wang Chingwei's puppet government set up with Japanese support.

General Wainwright finally surrenders on Corrigedor with 15,000 American and Filipino troops. The island fortress' defences had been weakened by a 27-day artillery barrage and were breached last night by Japanese commandos.

Lt-Gen Jonathan Wainwright, the US commander, decided to surrender this morning after radioing President Roosevelt. He told him he feared that his whole garrison might be killed. Even as he spoke, several hundred Japanese were machine-gunning the eastern entrance of the Manilta Tunnel, Corregidor's underground gallery which was sheltering 6,000 administrative staff untrained for combat and 1,000 sick and wounded. The president told Wainwright: "You have given the world a shining example of patriotic fortitude and self-sacrifice."

The fall of Corregidor has been anticipated since Bataan surrendered 27 days ago. Since then the island, only two miles away, has had 300 air raids and been hit by 300 shells a day.

Force Z, consisting of the fleet carriers HMS Implacable, HMS Bulwark and the new carrier HMS Audacious, supported by the battleships MNS Richeleau, HMS Anson and HMS King George V, with supporting cruisers and destroyers, leaves Singapore heading east. Somerville has also ordered for a tanker to be sent to Fiji as a matter of urgency; this will allow the force to refuel and so keep up a higher passage speed.

Churchill and the CIGS approve the fleet operation to support the US in principle. Washington will be contacted immediately to discuss sending the US Task Force in the Mediterranean to Singapore as partial replacements.

8th May

The German offensive for 1942, Operation Bustard, opens in Russia in the Crimea led by von Manstein's 22nd Panzer Division. The aim is to recapture the Kerch peninsula.

10th May

Prime Minister Churchill warns Germany that the British will hit it hard if it introduces poison gas in the USSR.

The 1st Army Group (consisting of the British 8th Army and the 1st Free French Army) in the Mediterranean under General O'Connor is put on alert for the impending Operation Husky. This is now provisionally planned to go ahead at the beginning of June, as soon as the German Army is committed to its summer offensive in Russia.

The aircraft carrier USS Ranger launches 68 USAAF P-40E fighters off the coast of Africa. The aircraft land at Accra, Gold Coast and then proceed across Africa, India then to the Dutch East Indies.

Assuming that the US intelligence is correct, and that the main Japanese fleet will be involved in Midway, Somerville starts to consider operations in the China Sea area. The most likely opportunity seems to be to retake the parts of Borneo currently under Japanese control. While he is very short of proper landing craft, coastal shipping is available, and with control of the sea and air can be used to overwhelm the small Japanese forces holding parts of the coast. He asks Alexander and Blamey what they can provide in the way of light/commando forces for this type of operation, assuming a start date of late May/early June.

11th May

Force Z arrives off Darwin during the night to refuel. The force sails soon after dawn, heading east along the north coast of Australia.

12th May

A two-pronged Russian attack on Kharkov begins. Marshal Timoshenko is attempting to trap German forces against the Sea of Azov. Tonight the Soviet high command claims that the Red Army has broken the German line after one of the biggest tank battles of the war.

Torrential rain continues to hamper operations but the Russians are pressing westwards after the fleeing Germans. They have captured a great quantity of munitions assembled immediately behind the front in readiness for the German summer campaign.

Admiral Yamamoto gives the go-ahead for the Midway Operation, scheduled to commence on the 31st May. Despite the proposals, he has no intention of using its capture to be a possible base for an invasion of Hawaii - the sealift is not available, nor, more importantly, is the fuel. He expects the operation to shatter the US Pacific fleet as an offensive weapon for the rest of the year, and allow his submarines to further weaken it if attempts are made to retake Midway. This will allow him to swing west and support an operation to take the DEI and the vital oil there as soon as possible.

14th May

Obsessed with winning the Russian war, Hitler refuses Admiral Dönitz's plea for all-out war on Allied merchant shipping.

The air offensive against Germany's industrial heartland - the Battle of the Ruhr - has reached a new intensity in the past 48 hours. On 12-13 May, the inland port of Duisburg was hit for the fifth time in a raid led by ten target-marking "Oboe" Mosquitoes, which were followed by 400 heavy bombers. The total weight of explosive dropped on this one town is now the best part of 10,000 tons. On 13-14 May, much of Bochum, a coal-rich area near Dortmund, was also reduced to burning rubble. So dense was the coverage that one Halifax returned with three incendiary bombs embedded in its wings.

Additional raids have taken place to stretch the German air defence and pull its attention away from the Ruhr. Targets have included Berlin, Czechoslovakia and Belgium. American Flying Fortresses have attacked the General Motors plant at Antwerp, US-owned before the war. The total bomb tonnage delivered in this 48-hour period was 4,000 tons. Over 50 aircraft have been lost, but Bomber Command reluctantly accepts such losses as inevitable, and the production program is currently able to keep up with the losses.

The first Japanese coded radio messages are completely broken that indicate the upcoming Japanese operation is indeed targeted at Midway. Previously only partial decodes had been made, although traffic analysis and other methods of determining where Japanese units were had all pointed to Midway. The estimate is that the operation will begin in less than two weeks.

16th May

The change earlier in the year to convoys and tactics on the East Coast of the USA has made U-boat operations steadily more costly. Today the first of the new US converted escort carriers joins the escort forces, and the US forces involved are rapidly improving their efficiency. Doenitz is increasingly concerned at the rise in his losses and the steady fall in sinkings (even though these are in fact being heavily exaggerated by his crews). He is starting to plan a withdrawal back into the Atlantic where the shorter range means more U-boats can be concentrated in an attempt to overwhelm a convoy's defences.

Admiral Somerville completes preparation for Operation Machete, landings on the coast of Borneo to destroy the Japanese on the north and east of the island. The operation will commence as soon as the Japanese fleet (expected to sail soon) is located. While the US code breakers have proved reliable so far, he wishes to locate the main Japanese fleet before he gives the go-ahead.

18th May

The USAAF's 7th Air Force in Hawaii is placed on alert in anticipation of a possible attack on Midway Island. For the next ten days the old Martin B-18's will be used on sea searches to supplement the B-17's. The VII Bomber Command receives an influx of B-17's during this period, and one squadron is converted from B-18's to B-17's.

Meanwhile the Marine Corps is sending more Corsair fighters to Midway. Before the start of the war against Japan the fighter, although showing very high performance, was considered dangerous to operate and had been refused deck-landing clearance. Since hostilities commenced the peacetime rules have been relaxed, however the Marine squadrons flying the plane have been scattered and it is only with the expected invasion of Midway that they have been given priority to build up on the island itself. It is hoped to get at least one squadron onto the island in the next week.

Force Z arrives at Fiji, where a number of tankers have been sent to provide the force with fuel. The force pauses only to refuel and take on water, then heads north, destination Pearl Harbor.

19th May

A strong German counterattack at Kharkov in the Ukraine against the Russians begins.

General MacArthur is recalled to Washington to discuss possible operational commands - there have been rumours circulating in the War Department about a new Allied commander being needed in China.

21st May

Task Force 39 with the battleship USS Washington, the aircraft carrier USS Wasp, the heavy cruisers USS Wichita and Tuscaloosa and six destroyers, arrives at Singapore after a high speed transit from Alexandria. The Task Force is assigned temporarily to work under Admiral Somerville while Force Z is with the USN. The opportunity is also taken to carry on the work started in the Mediterranean to integrate common procedures between the RN and USN to facilitate future combined operation. The Japanese attack in the mid-Pacific is now considered too close for the Wasp to arrive in time to aid it.

22nd May

Mexico declares war on the Axis from 1 June.

The German and Russian armies are involved in mutual offensives south of Kharkov. The Germans are in danger of surrounding part of Timoshenko's force, but he has to convince Stalin that the best course is to pull them back.

US submarines sail to patrol positions from Hawaii to counter the Japanese Midway operation.

23rd May

The Japanese 1st Carrier Fleet, under Admiral Nagumo, leaves the Inland Sea to begin their part in the Midway operation. The following day the main Japanese Invasion Fleet sails from the Marianas toward Midway.

The Americal Division of the US Army is constituted. It is organised as a square division, from units assigned to Task Force 6814.

25th May

The Japanese army issues orders to the Second and Seventh divisions to begin preparing for an amphibious attack against Hawaii. Training for the assault is to be completed by September 1942.

The light cruiser USS St. Louis arrives at Midway and disembarks Companies "C" and "D," 2nd Marine Raider Battalion, and a 37 mm gun battery of the 3rd defence Battalion. The aircraft ferry USS Kitty Hawk brings Marine reinforcements including a detachment of a 3-inch (76.2 mm) antiaircraft group of the 3rd defence Battalion, a light tank platoon and additional personnel for Marine Air Group Twenty Two. The Japanese operation is now imminent, and these will be the last supplies to reach the island before the Japanese attack.

Task Force 16, centred around the carriers Enterprise and Hornet, returns to Pearl Harbor. They are under orders to replenish as quickly as possible and be ready to sail on the following day. This is disappointing to the crews, who had hoped for shore leave after their last mission. No indication of the Midway operation is given to the crews until the ships are back at sea, to maintain security.

The remainder of the Japanese forces sail to join the Midway operation. This includes a number of ships tasked with diversionary missions.

26th May

Vice Admiral Lyster, the commander of Force Z, lands at Pearl Harbor by carrier plane to discuss the operation with Admiral Nimitz and his staff. In view of the operation planned, command of the RN force has been given to him due to his experience in multi-carrier operations. Admiral Somerville had seriously considered commanding in person, but his responsibilities in SE Asia and the issue that he would be the senior officer afloat (causing a problem as the operations are under US overall control) has forced him to remain in Singapore. The size of the RN force has made discussions of who is to command somewhat delicate (the USN and RN forces are of a similar size), but Somerville has already decided with Nimitz that the American local knowledge and territory mean it is best for them to be in overall command. Nimitz has agreed that Lyster will have as free a hand as possible over the use of his ships, particularly if the RN carriers can get off a night strike, something outside of the USN capability.

Task Force 16, carriers Enterprise and Hornet under Admiral Spruance, and Task Force 17, carriers Yorktown and Ticonderoga under Admiral Fletcher, sail from Pearl Harbor for Midway. Once on their way, the crews are ordered to paint large US flags on the flight deck to allow easier identification. Tricolour striping is painted on the turrets of the other ships. Admiral Halsey, originally intended to be in overall command, is in hospital with a skin condition and reported to be furious.

27th May

Czech partisans ambush SS Obergruppenführer Reinhardt Heydrich, the deputy Reichprotector of Bohemia and Moravia.

B-17's on detached service at Midway Island begin search operations. U.S. Navy PBY Catalinas concentrate their searches to the northeast, from where the Japanese invasion fleet is expected to approach.

The Royal Navy Force Z arrives at Pearl Harbor under as much security as the base can manage. Overnight the fleet is refuelled and a stream of US navy communications personnel and their equipment is hurried on board. Preparations have been made during their voyage to Hawaii to add the US radio equipment to allow them to communicate with the US Task Forces and aircraft. A US light cruiser will also accompany the force to aid in this. Engineers are also onboard helping with the inevitable small problems that have cropped up during the high-speed run. Fortunately, only one of the destroyers is forced to remain behind due to serious problems. The carriers also take on a USN deck landing officer each in case any US aircraft need to be recovered (the landing procedures and signals are different in the two navies).

It had been hoped that Force Z would arrive in time to integrate it with the US carrier group now on its way to Midway, but there was not time before the Japanese sailed. Current intentions are for the Force to move southwest of Midway, to catch the Japanese force between the two groups. The worry is that if the Japanese have concentrated their carriers, they will be able to defeat either of the two Allied groups in detail. If this proves to be the case, the orders are to pull back and draw the Japanese onto the combined carrier forces. As with the USN ships, flags and markings are painted on the ships to reduce the chance of mis-identification.

28th May

Force Z sails from Pearl Harbor - due to the size of the ships, especially HMS Audacious, the sailing was delayed to high tide, just in case, as the bridge crews are unfamiliar with Pearl. For additional security the force leaves harbour flying the US ensign to help disguise their origin - although the size of the Audacious makes this problematical, she is nearly twice the displacement of the US carriers.

29th May

The Germans complete encirclement of the Russian forces west of the Donets. 250,000 Russian soldiers are killed or captured.

A RN T-class submarine operating south of Formosa spots a Japanese force of 'a couple of cruisers and destroyers' steaming south towards the South China Sea during the night. The submarine is unable to make an attack, but Somerville asks the RAF to conduct a reconnaissance of the area to try and find out what they are up to.

30th May

Three Russian destroyers joined up with convoy, PQ-16 today to help escort it through the last stage of what has been the most hazardous Arctic journey so far. The convoy - with 35 ships - set sail on 21 May for Murmansk and Archangel. For the last three days, it has been under attack from no fewer than 260 German aircraft.

The convoy was joined on 25 May by a force of four British cruisers, HMS Norfolk, HMS Nigeria, HMS Kent and HMS Liverpool, and two escort carriers Only one ship has been sunk by U-boat, but three have been sunk by air attack despite the efforts of the escort carriers, one of which was heavily damaged by Stuka dive bombers. The attacks proved costly to the Luftwaffe, a heavy toll being taken of the attackers by the defending Goshawks. Nevertheless, 93,000 tons of new war material has been delivered to the USSR, including 320 tanks, 125 aircraft and 2,500 military vehicles.

Task Force17 under Rear Admiral Frank Jack Fletcher and Task Force 16 under Rear Admiral Raymond A. Spruance, rendezvous about 350-miles (648 km) northeast of Midway Island. The joint force, under tactical command of Admiral Fletcher, is composed of four aircraft carriers, seven heavy cruisers, 16 destroyers and two oilers. Supporting are 25 submarines deployed around Midway. The two forces sailed separately in case they were spotted by Japanese patrols.

31st May

The heaviest attack yet by the RAF targets the city of Cologne. Some 600 bombers, including 150 Coventry high-altitude planes, led by Pathfinder Mosquitoes, drop over 3,000 tons of bombs, half of them incendiaries. The city is left in flames, and the chemical works 90% destroyed. So heavy were the fires that reconnaissance planes were unable to get photographs on the following day due to the thick clouds of smoke.

The fighting south of Kharkov which started so well for the Red Army has ended in disaster. The Germans, who launched their counter-thrust, Operation Fridericus, at the base of the Soviet breakthrough, have destroyed the five Russian armies caught in their pincer movement. Throughout the battle the Russians were poorly supported by their air force, and the Germans had complete supremacy over the battlefield. They now hold a line along the Donets and are preparing to launch further offensives against their badly mauled enemies.

A force of Japanese midget submarines (the Japanese submarines HIJMS I-22, HIJMS I-24 and HIJMS I-27) each launch a Type A midget submarine which penetrate the harbour defences of Sydney and attack shipping. They fire torpedoes that miss the heavy cruiser USS Chicago but sink the accommodation ship HMAS Kuttabul and damage the Dutch submarine HNMS K 9 beyond economical repair. All the attackers are killed in the attack.

The Japanese Invasion Group is spotted by land-based aircraft from Midway. This is a few days later than expected, but getting the ships into position has taken the Japanese a little longer than anticipated.

Appendix One

This describes some of the aircraft in use by the Royal Navy and other air forces during the period covered by this book (1932 - 1941). Only naval aircraft or aircraft encountered in actions in the book have been included.

Aircraft in use by the Royal Navy

Gloster Goshawk Mk III (fighter)

The Goshawk is a single-engine fighter powered by the improved version of the Bristol Hercules engine. Performance is similar to that of the historic Spitfire at low level, but inferior above 20,000 feet - as was the usual practice with carrier aircraft of the period, performance was optimised for under 20,000 feet (since bombing above this altitude was too inaccurate for success against ships). Armament had increased to 4x20mm cannon over earlier version of the fighter. As with most naval planes, the Goshawk had rather longer range than its land-based equivalents, at the cost of a heavier aircraft (compensated for by the more powerful Hercules engine)

Fairy Swordfish (TBR - Torpedo, Bomber, Reconnaissance)

Developed in the early 1930's as a private venture, the 'Stringbag' as it was known would be used throughout the war in many different roles. No longer the frontline torpedo/bomber (although it was still to be found used in this role in the more remote theatres), due to its versatility and its ability to operate off of very small carriers in all sorts of weather, it would carry on as the anti-submarine plane on escort carriers and conversions throughout the war.

Martin-Baker Cormorant Mk III(Divebomber)

Developed in the 1930's, the Hercules-powered Cormorant was the Royal Navies first dedicated dive bomber. Initial versions carried either a 500lb HE bomb (on longer missions) or a 1,000lb against larger targets. With a later-version Hercules (with more power), it could also carry the 1,600lb AP bomb designed for use against battleships and similarly armoured targets

Boulton-Paul SeaLance (TBR - Torpedo, Bomber, Reconnaissance)

The replacement for the Swordfish, the SeaLance was an interim deign using the Griffon engine. Faster than the Swordfish, it was much more survivable against defended targets. With its increased performance, the Royal Navy carried on development of its aerial torpedoes to allow them to be dropped at a higher speed and from a greater height, also giving the crews more chance of surviving the attack.

Fairy Spearfish (TBR - Torpedo, Bomber, Reconnaissance)

The replacement for the SeaLance (which had originally been seen as an interim design), this plane was operational in late 1941. Performance was much better, thanks to the powerful Centaurus engine, but the limited availability of the engine limited initial deployment. It was the first carrier-based plane to carry the new, heavy MkXV torpedo, and it could deliver this at over 250kt. It was the first strike aircraft deigned to have an ASV radar equipped as standard, but production issues meant that at first only some aircraft were so fitted.

Gloster Sea Eagle (fighter)

This fighter started to replace the Goshawk in the autumn of 1941. Powered by the Centaurus engine, it was then the fastest fighter in the world, carrying 4x20mm guns. It could also carry some 1,600lb of bombs, allowing it to act as a naval attack aircraft as well as a fighter. Production was initially limited by low production of the Centaurus, and the weight of the plane meant it only operated off the later or modernised fleet carriers.

Aircraft in use by the RAF

Lockheed Hudson (anti-submarine)

The Hudson was a twin-engine light bomber in use by RAF Coastal Command as a reconnaissance and anti-submarine plane. The aircraft was bought from the USA, where it had originally been designed as a civilian aircraft, modified by the RAF to carry bombs and armed with a quadruple 0.303 gun turret.

Hawker Hurricane (fighter)

The Hurricane was a single-engines fighter powered by the Rolls-Royce Merlin. The first modern monoplane fighter in service in the RAF, its performance was similar to the Goshawk. Initially armed with 8x0.303" guns, by 1940 production aircraft were being armed with 2x20mm cannon and 4x0.303" guns, giving them more destructive power against German bombers. The plane would be one of the two mainstays of fighter command in 1940, before being phased out. The design did not benefit from a more powerful engine, and it was replaced in 1941 by the de-navalised version of the Goshawk, the Sparrowhawk.

Supermarine Spitfire (fighter)

The Spitfire was one of the great fighter aircraft of WW2. Developed before the war, it only entered service shortly before the conflict started. By 1940, it was already equal in performance to the best German fighters, and by the Battle of Britain was steadily replacing the Hurricane as the RAF frontline fighter. The airframe was far more capable of increasing performance when fitted with more powerful engines, and its development would continue throughout the war. Like the Hurricane, it was initially armed with 8x0.303" guns, but it was also upgraded to cannon by the time the Battle of Britain started.

Short Sunderland (anti-submarine)

The Sunderland was a long range, heavily armed flying boat, used for anti-submarine patrols. The heavy defensive armament led to it being used in areas like the Bay of Biscay where enemy fighters were encountered, and it was also capable of rescue.

Bristol Beaufighter (fighter, bomber, torpedo, attack)

The Beaufighter was the first true 'multi-role' plane in service in Britain. A powerful and heavy plane powered by two Hercules engines, it was capable of defending itself against all but the latest enemy fighters. Heavily armed, it was also used as a naval strike plane against light targets, and when carrying a torpedo, against larger ships. Its long range meant it was also used as a reconnaissance aircraft.

Consolidated Catalina (maritime patrol)

An American designed and built flying boat, this was used as an additional maritime patrol aircraft in the Atlantic and pacific theatres to supplement the limited production of the Sunderland, its long range being very useful in these areas. (This aircraft was also in use by the USN).

Short Stirling (bomber)

The first four engined bomber designed for the RAF, it suffered from a number of performance issues, in particular its low ceiling of some 16,000 feet made it more vulnerable in operations. As the more capable Halifax was in production, and a long range aircraft was badly needed for convoy protection, many of the Stirlings were re-assigned to this job, some being fitted with ASV radar for an additional reconnaissance role.

Aircraft in use by the Japanese Air Force

Mitsubishi A5M Type 96 fighter (Claude)

A very light and agile fighter used by the Japanese Navy. By the end of 1941 it was being replaced by the Zero. Its main problems were its slow maximum speed (slower than attack aircraft like the Beaufighter), and poor armament (2x7.7mm machine guns) which made it difficult to do sufficient damage to the more strongly built Allied aircraft.

Mitsubishi A6M Zero-Sen Type Zero fighter (Zero)

Probably the best Japanese naval fighter of the war, the Zero had only been operation since July 1940. Again a light and very manoeuvrable design, it was much faster than the Claude, and with a considerably heavier armament (2x7.7mm and 2x20mm cannon), it was far more dangerous to Allied fighters.

Nakajima Ki-43 Hayabusa Type 1 fighter (Oscar)

A fighter used by the Japanese army, the plane was very agile, but again had a poor maximum speed and armament (2x0.5" guns).

Aichi D3A Type 99 dive bomber (Val)

Introduced to service in 1940, this was the dive bomber in use by the Japanese Navy when war with Japan started. Roughly comparable in performance with the Cormorant or Ju87, its main limitation was that it was designed to carry a 250kg bomb, which was of limited effectiveness against battleships or the Royal Navy's heavily protected fleet carriers.

Nakajima B5N Type 97 TBR (Kate)

The standard torpedo bomber in use by the Japanese Navy at the start of the war, this plane was one of the best torpedo planes in service. Broadly comparable with the SeaLance in capability.

Mitsubishi G3M bomber (Nell)

A land-based heavy bomber (medium bomber by allied standards), the Nell was mainly noted for its massive range, which allowed it to appear and attack targets that the Allies (initially at least) thought out of range. Its bomb load was limited (1,800 lb), although it could also carry a torpedo. One of the reasons for its range was the poor protection, a fault which was to prove a setback in combat.

Mitsubishi G4M bomber (Betty)

The replacement for the Nell, this aircraft had only come into service in 1941. While a somewhat improved aircraft, it was not dramatically better than the Nell (although it was rather tougher, it shared the propensity of catching fire when shot at). The range and performance was on a little better than its predecessors.

Nakajima Ki-27 fighter (Nate)

Used by the Japanese Air force, this fighter was underpowered, under-armed and obsolescent by 1942. While manoeuvrable, its 2x7.7mm mg made it difficult to shoot down the heavy Allied planes, and it was unable to stand up to their heavy armament.

All Japanese planes were lightly built by comparison with Western designs. The advantage of that was it allowed them a much longer range, a very important characteristic in the vast Pacific theatre. The drawback was that this made them relatively fragile, especially to the heavy armament some of the Allied fighters carried by 1941.

Aircraft in use by the USAAF and USN

Curtiss P-40 Warhawk fighter

While this plane was due to be replaced in US service, it was in wide use in the USAAF as well as Allied air forces. A reliable fighter-bomber, its performance was comparable to the Sparrowhawk III and better than the Hurricane.

BoeingB-17 Flying Fortress

This heavy bomber had originally been specified for naval work, and was to be used in thsi role in the Pacific. Its very long range with a reasonable bomb load made it a useful plane, unfortunately the inability to hit moving ships (a failure shared by all high level bombers) limited its usefulness, although its heavy armament and toughness made it a difficult target for the Japanese in the air.

Grumman F4F Wildcat fighter

The standard USN carrier fighter (and Marine Corps fighter) in 1941/2. A heavy and tough fighter capable of taking a lot of damage with a good range, but by 1941 underpowered and less manoeuvrable than the Goshawk III.

Brewster F2A Buffalo fighter

This plane had been superseded by the Wildcat as a front-line fighter in US service, but in 1942 was still in service in the Dutch air
force. As with the Wildcat, it was unable to match the Japanese Zero for manoeuvrability.

Vaught F4U Corsair fighter

This powerful aircraft had been in production for some time by 1941/2, but problems had let to it being refused carrier certification. Once war broke out, this certification was speeded up, but it was in service with the US Marine Corps as a land-based fighter. Its performance was almost as good as the Sea Eagle (and in later versions with a more powerful engine would be just as good), and its range was longer, but it was under-armed with only 6 0.5" mg instead of 4x20mm cannon.

Douglas SBD Dauntless dive bomber

A modern and tough dive bomber, this was comparable with the Japanese Val and the British Cormorant. It could carry a heavy bomb load (up to 2,000lb), although in practice this was normally limited for carrier use to 1,000lb. The mainstay of the USN dive bomber force in 1941/2, it was a very accurate and damaging weapon in skilled hands.

Douglas TBD Devastator

The mainstay of the USN torpedo/bomber arm in 1941, the plane had been in service since 1939 and its performance had not kept up with comparable aircraft. Compared to the Kate and SeaLance it was slow and underpowered, and would soon be replaced by the Grumman Avenger. Its performance was not helped by the poor performance of the torpedo it carried in its anti-shipping role.

Appendix Two

Aircraft Carriers in service

Royal Navy

HMS Eagle
26,000t displacement, speed 22.5 kt ; 5x4" guns, approx 10x20mm. Normal aircraft complement 21

HMS Hermes
13,000t displacement, 25kt ; 4x4" guns, approx 10x20mm. Normal aircraft complement 20

HMS Argus
14,500t displacement, 20kt ; 6x4" guns, approx 12 20mm. Normal aircraft complement 20

HMS Furious
23,000t displacement, 31kt ; 12x20mm. Normal aircraft complement 36

HMS Courageous (sunk Oct 1940), HMS Glorious
27,500t displacement, 30kt ; 8x40mm, approx 8x20mm. Normal aircraft complement 48

HMS Ark Royal, HMS Illustrious
24,000t displacement, speed 31.5kt ; 16x4.5" guns, 64x40mm, approx 20x20mm. Normal aircraft complement 65

HMS Formidable, HMS Victorious, HMS Indefatigable, HMS Implacable
24,500t displacement, speed 32kt ; 16x4.5" guns, 64x40mm, approx 20x20mm. Normal aircraft complement 68

HMS Colossus, HMS Mars, HMS Vengeance, HMS Venerable (sunk April 1940), HMS Glory, HMS Ocean, HMS Edgar, HMS Theseus (renamed HMAS Brisbane), HMAS Melbourne, HMS Unicorn (repair carrier)
13,000t displacement, speed 27kt ; 16x40mm guns, approx 16x20mm. Normal aircraft complement 24 (40 maximum with deck park)

HMS Audacious
32,000t displacement, speed 32kt; 16x4.5" guns, 80x40mm, approx 24 20mm. Normal aircraft complement 100.

United States Navy

USS Saratoga, USS Lexington
39,000t displacement, 34kt; 12x5" guns. Normal aircraft complement (pre-war) 90

USS Ranger
17,500t, speed 29kt ; 8x5" guns, 40x0.5" mg. Normal aircraft complement (pre-war) 75 planes

USS Yorktown, USS Enterprise USS Hornet, USS Ticonderoga
22,000t displacement, 32.5kt ; 8x5" guns, 16x1.1"mg, 24 0.5"mg. Normal aircraft complement (pre-war) 90

USS Wasp
16,000t displacement, 29kt ; 8x5" guns, 16 1.1"mg, 24x0.5"mg. Normal aircraft complement (pre-war) 80

Imperial Japanese Navy

HMIJS Akagi
41,300t displacement, 31kt ; 6x8" guns, 12x4.7" guns, 28x25mm. Normal aircraft complement 72

HMIJS Kaga
42,500t displacement, 28kt ; 10x8" guns, 10x5" guns, 22x25mm. Normal aircraft complement 81

HMIJS Soryu
19,800t displacement, 34kt ; 12x5" guns, 28x25mm. Normal aircraft complement 63

HMIJS Hiryu
21,900t displacement, 34kt ; 12x5" guns, 31x25mm. Normal aircraft complement 64

HMIJS Shokaku, HMIJS Zuikaku
32,000t displacement, 34kt ; 16x5" guns, 42x25mm. Normal aircraft complement 72

HMIJS Ryuju
10,150t displacement, 29kt ; 12x5" guns, 24mg. Normal aircraft complement 37

HMIJS Chitose, HMIJS Chiyoda
15,300t displacement, 29kt ; 8x5" guns, 30x25mm. Normal aircraft complement 30

HMIJS Zuiho, HMIJS Shoho, HMIJS Taiyo
14,200t displacement, 28kt ; 8x5" guns, 8x25mm. Normal aircraft complement 30

HMIJS Hosho
12,500t displacement, 29kt; 4x5" guns, 8x25mm. Normal aircraft complement 24.

HMIJS Takasaki, HMIJS Tsurigisaki
16,000t displacement, 26kt; 8x5" guns, 8x25mm. Normal aircraft complement 28

Notes :

(1) The displacement is given as a 'normal' displacement. The displacement of a ship varies as it uses fuel and stores, and even the 'normal' displacement is somewhat variable, especially when reported to keep inside treaty limits

(2) The aircraft capacity of a carrier can be quite variable. In addition to the 'complete' aircraft carried, most fleet carriers would also carry a number of replacements, broken down into parts in the hangar which could be used to cover normal operational losses. The US carriers carried the most planes as they used a full deck park - aircraft were held on deck. The RN carriers and the Japanese carriers normally kept all their planes in the hangar, although they could increase the number available by using a deck park if they wished. However there were also practical limitations due to the need to carry the extra flight deck and maintenance crews for a larger aircraft complement.

Irrespective of the number of planes actually carried, carriers were also limited to how many planes they could launch in a single 'strike' due to deck space. During this period in time it was about 30-35 planes, after which planes would have to be brought on deck, armed, fuelled and placed ready for a second strike, a process which usually took around an hour or so (depending on the skill of the carrier crews).

(3) Armament, especially of the light 20mm cannon which tended to be fitted on wherever they could fit, also varied through the War. The numbers given are those deigned in; where major changes were made these are listed with date

(4) Speed. This assumes the ship is in good mechanical condition and with a clean bottom. During wartime service the actual speed was often lower due to the inability to refit the machinery and dock the ship for bottom-cleaning.

Glossary

AA - Anti Aircraft (guns).

AI - Airborne Intercept (radar). A small light radar set capable of being carried on a plane to allow it to intercept another aircraft at night.

ASDIC - what later became known as SONAR, a high-frequency sound system designed to detect a submerged submarine. At this time, rarely usable above 1,500 - 2000 metres.

A/S - Antisubmarine.

ASV - Air to Surface radar, a small airborne set designed to spot ships and, later, smaller objects such as submarines.

Avgas - Aviation Gasoline (fuel), very volatile and very dangerous.

Boom and Zoom - A fighter tactic that consisted of a high speed attack dive (from a superior altitude), - the boom - a slashing attack pass then continuing to dive past, usually pulling up once clear of the target - the zoom. Popular if you wish to avoid a dogfight with the enemy.

CAP - Combat Air Patrol, the act of keeping a number of fighters in the air above the carrier or fleet ready to intercept enemy aircraft.

DB - Dive Bomber, an aircraft designed to deliver a single bomb in a very steep (normally over 70°) dive.

DEI - The Dutch East Indies, now Indonesia.

FAA - Fleet Air Arm, the aeroplanes flown and controlled by the Royal Navy.

FIC - French Indo China, roughly modern Veitnam.

HA - also known as HA(AA), the guns capable of attacking a high-altitude enemy plane. Normally used against high altitude level bombing. While not terribly accurate at this time, the aim was to disrupt the formation of the attackers, making them miss, rather than to shoot them down. Level bombers depended on the 'shotgun' principle of bombing during this period.

Hammer-and-Anvil attack - a type of attack by torpedo planes. Two groups of planes will attack 90° apart, one the 'hammer', the other the 'anvil'. Dodging the torpedoes of one group will put the ship broadside on to the other group. The ideal torpedo attack against a moving ship.

HMS - His Majesties Ship (British); also HMAS - His Majesties Australian Ship.

HMCS - His Majesties Canadian Ship, HMNZS - His Majesties New Zealand Ship.

HIMJS - His Imperial Japanese Majesties Ship (Japan).

Kriegsmarine - the German Navy.

LA - Low angle guns, normally those unable to elevate above about 40 degrees, so unable to fire on a plane over the ship. In fact, these guns can be used as anti-aircraft guns, but only on aircraft some distance away (the angle of the aircraft increases as it closes the ship). Usually even less accurate than HA fire, as this type of gun was not usually matched with the control system designed to engage aircraft.

Luftwaffe - the German Air Force.

MN - Marine Nationale, the French navy.

PBY - the designation of the Consolidated Catalina patrol plane in US service.

Pom-pom - the name given in the RN to a fast-firing light AA weapon. Originally firing a 2-pdr shell, then the 40mm shell, given its name due to the sound the multi-barrel version made.

RA - Regia Aeronautica, the Italian Air Force (Italy did not have a separate naval air force).

RAF - the British Air force.

RDF - Radio Direction Finding, an early (British) name for Radar (so named to try and mislead what it actually did).

RN - Royal Navy, the British naval forces. Also the RAN (Australian), RCN (Canadian), and RNZN (New Zealand).

Round down - the aft part of a carrier's flight deck. This was 'rounded down' in a downward curve, which improved the airflow and made it easier for a plane to land. It also reduced the available deck parking area, and so was reduced on British carriers as larger strikes became more common.
SAP - Semi Armour Piercing.

Shadow factory - A set of factories built in the mid-30's in Britain ready to be used as aircraft factories in war. In fact the need for aircraft due to the expansion of the Luftwaffe meant they were brought into use before the war, and more built. The term 'shadow program' came to be used for anything built in advance of wartime needs, such as the Japanese programme of 'Shadow Carriers', merchant ships built ready for easy conversion into light carriers.
TBR - Torpedo, Bomber, Reconnaissance. A class of plane used by most navies in these three roles. Bombing was normally level bombing with light bombs, although some aircraft like the Swordfish could dive bomb at shallow dive angles.

Twins - or the twins, the two German Battlecruisers Scharnhorst and Gneisenau.

USS - United States Ship (USA).

###

Information on the next book in this series may be found at

http://www.AstroDragon.co.uk/Books/TheWhaleHasWings.htm

Book 4, Midway - The decisive Battle is due for publication in early 2014. This will cover the 'decisive battle' the Japanese Navy has been hoping for, as the carrier fleets of Japan, the USA and the UK battle over the Pacific island of Midway

Printed in Great Britain
by Amazon.co.uk, Ltd.,
Marston Gate.